Impietas

D J G Berkeley

Also available by D J G Berkeley:

Sacramentum

Impietas

Impietas

Copyright: Dr Daniel Berkeley

Published: 18th February 2014

The right of Dr Daniel James Gordon Berkeley to be identified as author of this Work has been asserted by him in accordance with sections 77 and 78 of the Copyright, Designs and Patents Act 1988.

All rights reserved. No part of this publication may be reproduced, stored in retrieval system, copied in any form or by any means, electronic, mechanical, photocopying, recording or otherwise transmitted without written permission from the publisher. You must not circulate this book in any format.

For Alfred, Lyra and Carys
And made possible by The Blistering Gas

And with thanks, as ever, to my Elite Proof Reading Team

A Note on Naming

Most Romans have three names:

The Praenomen - e.g. Titus - this is a name used only by close friends and family
The Nomen - e.g. Labienus - this is the family name
The Cognomen - e.g. Albus - used by the Nobility, often preferred by them to a **nomen**

A Note on Dates

Romans record their dates with reference to the year that Rome itself was founded:

Ab Urbe Condita (from the founding of the City).

Traditionally, this was believed to have occurred in 753BC.

Rome

2741AUC

She cowered and covered her face with her hands, but their horrified eyes would not leave her. She began to back away. The crowd watched cautiously, shocked at the sight of a thirteen year old girl drenched in blood.

Her stomach cramped up again and she fought back the vomit; he had hurt her so much. She started to run, expecting the crowd to give chase. She almost hoped they would, and that they would catch her. Then beat her, and her shame, to death on the ancient cobbled stones of the Imum. Like the Gracchi—beaten to death by their fellow senators two thousand years ago, but the Gracchi's crime had been to try to reform Rome to fairness, and her crime was minor in comparison.

As she stumbled along, another wave of agony swept her. She looked down at her torn clothes. The spreading pink stain through her skirt terrified her. She thought about her master's son, the way that he had been looking at her for weeks. How could she have been so stupid? She should never have let him get her on her own. She reached up and touched her cheek across her signum, where he had touched her. He had whispered that he loved her.

But a Roman and a Slave could never love one another.

She had tried to leave, but he was stronger than she was.

A shout rang out behind her—she had been spotted. She started to run again, every step an agony. The boy would have no punishment, except that of his own shame. She hoped it would last him the rest of his life. She, however, would be put to death. That she had had no choice in what he had done to her was irrelevant. She could never return home, never see her parents again, for they could not protect her. She had one hope: leave Rome. She had to escape, but to what? She would be alone forever in the world. Death would be preferable.

She darted down the nearest alleyway. She could hear the sounds of her pursuers as they charged up and down by the canal looking for her. Her eyes darted from side to side. She started trying the doors, desperately. All were locked. The sounds of pursuit were nearer. She began to sob, hammering hard on a large oak door. She sank down on her knees. Perhaps death would be quick. If only she was not so utterly alone.

The door opened.

She stared up into the eyes of a Slave boy about her age, and whom, to her surprise, she vaguely recognised. The sound of her pursuers grew louder, but she was not alone anymore. He took her by the hand.

'Don't worry,' he said, with a voice that seemed much older than his years. 'I will not let them harm you.' He put his arms around her shoulders and helped her into the hallway. She looked up at him and realised that she did recognise him. She had seen him by the canal before, always on the edge of his group of friends. He had often watched her, but she had been too scared to speak to him.

They crouched together behind the closed door, and waited. Footsteps came closer. A shadow passed the door. A wave of pain heavier than the last wracked her, but she did not cry out. The footsteps receded into the distance. She looked up again into the boy's face. His eyes looked kind, and sad, as if he was too wise to enjoy this world.

She kissed him.

Aether

2765 AUC

'No man can ever change who he is,' Jupiter stated. 'For what you are born, that you shall stay. Some to serve, others to rule, some to cower, others to rise.'

    'You speak nonsense brother-husband!' Spoke Juno, in her commanding, high voice. 'What we have created, man can shape, through the strength of will created within. Some to serve and to cower, one day to rise. One day to rule.'

The Book of Varro, Part 1. 1653AUC

I

'Antonius!' Titus barked.

'Boss?' The huge man turned his head slowly to look at Titus; he looked puzzled.

'Stop pissing in the fountain,' Titus ordered, exasperated.

A small girl, from the crowd filing past, pointed and laughed as Antonius shook off the last drops and jumped back down onto the Via Appia.

'We're not in Lugavalium,' Titus warned jokingly, wagging his finger at Antonius, 'Rome is a place of beauty, honour, and restraint.'

A laugh, much louder than the girl's, boomed out from just behind Titus. The owner of the laugh, an itinerant builder, clapped him on the shoulder as he walked past. 'You've not seen it for a few years mate!' he said, striding on towards the Eternal City.

Three of the others travelling with Titus moved up, and joined them at the fountain; three of his oldest friends who had fought alongside him in the Transmaritanus campaigns: Marcus, who had been his deputy all those years ago, wise Gnaeus, and the musician Tiberius. Titus looked behind to see what had become of the other two he was travelling with. His eyes fell on the couple, two hundred yards behind; a smartly dressed man and a willowy woman, walking quickly to catch up, but clearly still having the argument which had delayed them. Titus sighed. He wished he had not brought Quintus with him, but Quintus had been desperate to return to his birth city.

'Fucking half-breed!' Quintus cursed, striding away from the woman, who stuck out her tongue at him as she walked over to Titus.

'You do have some awful friends, husband!' Ceinwyn said, smiling up at him, her curly copper coloured hair, blowing gently in the warm Italian breeze, framing her pale face. A face paler even than usual because of the make-up that concealed her signum—the dark facial tattoo which would mark her out as a Slave. Titus kissed her, something he could never have done in public otherwise, lest he bring death on them both. The crowd walking past barely stared. A quiet wolf whistle tried to ring out, but was drowned by the noise of footsteps as yet another party of travellers marched on towards the Eternal City. Ceinwyn was beautiful, and at twenty four, seven years younger than Titus.

'Are we all that bad?' Gnaeus said, amused by her comment about Quintus.

Ceinwyn smiled at him, 'you and Marcus are like the opposite of Quintus. And Tiberius...' she said, looking over her shoulder at him, and diverting his attention from a group of girls on small volacurri, 'is such a good singer that I couldn't hold a grudge for long.'

'You don't know Quintus, Ceinwyn,' Tiberius replied. 'He's alright really; he just takes life extremely seriously.' Tiberius' focus was drawn away as the girls flew past again, their minimal clothing billowing in the wake of their slipstream.

Titus beckoned the group on and Ceinwyn jogged up so that she could walk alongside him. Her warm hand slipped into his.

'Sorry this isn't the honeymoon I promised you,' he said as they neared the crest of the hill. 'We will still have it, soon I hope.'

'It's alright,' she replied. 'You can't exactly refuse a summons from a Consul of Rome.'

'It was an invitation,' Titus corrected her.

'Summons,' she said flatly.

They had received the letter the day after they had been married, six months after he had overthrown her old master, the governor of Northern Britannia, Gaius Strabo. Titus had not seen the Consul Marcus Albus for over a decade, and he had once thought of him as a friend; Titus had fought for him in the Transmaritanus. A familiar sick feeling rose up inside him as he remembered the things that he had been made to do, and a little girl's face blinked up at him once more. Habit helped him forget, but it was never easy. Even harder now that he knew Ceinwyn, and the truth about her race, Slaves: thought of by most as dumb animals, but in fact as intelligent as Romans. Marcus Albus' letter had thanked Titus profusely for his overthrowing of the corrupt governor, and had invited him to Rome for a celebration, in his honour. Ever since the army had been disbanded he had been homeless and adrift, now his old friend had given him a way back, but that wasn't how Ceinwyn had seen it.

'I still don't understand why you want a party in your honour thrown by the most evil man in the entire world,' Ceinwyn said as they reached the top of the hill and stared down into the plain below them. 'But I do understand why you wanted to see Rome again,' she added with awe at the sight that spread out before them.

The City rose up in front of them. From the four corners of the Roman world, four gigantic roads rose up into bridges to pour into the city, at what Titus had remembered as the higher level, the Aether. Numerous smaller roads and paths twisted over the plain in front of them to reach the City, which itself was tiny, having never expanded beyond the ceremonial border, the Pomerium. This was meant to be the line Romulus had ploughed at the founding of Rome, but most people knew that the Consul Aurelius, nearly two thousand years ago, had completed the walls far beyond that ancient boundary. Despite this extension, Rome was no more than two miles across; the smallest city in the whole of Italia, possibly the world, but by far the most important.

To the North, beyond the City, stood a giant pinnacle, the Void Levator. At the bottom, the wide base held the great volacurrus port, and the air around it was thronged with volacurri from around the world, swarming down on the Eternal City. Above, there was a black spire, straight and narrow, stretching as far as could be seen, deep into the void above. A black container was inching upwards, and when finally it reached the top its payload would be re-arranged, reassembled, and placed into orbit. The need for launches and the casualties they caused had been eliminated by this, the pinnacle of Rome's engineering. Titus glowed with pride.

He looked back at the City itself and immediately his eye was drawn to the highest point. Last time he had been in Rome, a decade ago, Rome had been on just two levels: the Aether, where the Nobles and those who had worked hard and made themselves rich lived, and the Imum—the lower level. The Imum was where the poor lived, alongside masterless Slaves, amongst the ancient crumbling ruins of the old City. Occasionally a shaft, dropped down from above, shut off certain important ruins from the rest of the Imum. This allowed the rich to descend down to perform their ceremonial duties safely. No one of Noble birth would enter into the open Imum unless they absolutely had to. Indeed Titus himself had never been there.

But there was a new upper level now, its ivory tendrils clambering up over the Aether. The end nearest him was still being constructed, so all he could see was a mass of cranes and scaffolding, but at the far end of the city there were towers, spires, and domes. It amazed him.

Ceinwyn leaned in towards him and whispered with amusement: 'And they said: *'go to, let us build us a city and a tower, whose top may reach unto heaven; and let us make us a name, lest we be scattered abroad upon the face of the whole earth.'*'

Titus snorted under his breath. 'That ridiculous book Gnaeus gave you?' He found his wife's faith in one God as amusing as he found his friend Gnaeus'.

'Yes.' Ceinwyn said quietly, pretending to be hurt.

Titus sighed, 'and I'm sure you want to tell me what happened to the people who built the city with the tower that reached into the heavens don't you.'

'Why don't you read it yourself and find out,' Ceinwyn teased.

'And lose the benefit of your insight into it?' Titus replied sarcastically.

Ceinwyn laughed, 'our God blew the tower down, and the city crumbled away.'

'He'll have to fight off the one thousand or so gods that we have protecting it first then,' Titus said, and the pair walked down the gentle slope towards the Aurelian gate, with their friends following along behind. A cloud drifted across the sun and Ceinwyn shivered. Titus put an arm around her.

'The City of my ancestors,' he said in awe as they reached the towering gate, and began to queue half way up the foot ramp leading to the Aether.

'You said your ancestors were all drunken fools.'

'I could change that,' Titus replied, 'Marcus Albus wants to honour me.'

'Why do you need his honour?' Ceinwyn asked.

Titus didn't understand the question.

'All I need is my mountains; a house; you. I don't care if you are a Noble.'

'Think of what our children could do, brought up here!' Titus replied grandly. 'One day, one of them could become Consul.' It was as if Titus had not heard her.

'And have no mother?' Ceinwyn asked, exasperated now. 'Titus, how could I live in Rome for more than a few weeks without being found out?'

Her words jolted him out of his dream. Ceinwyn had a Slave father and a Roman mother who had died in childbirth. Marcus Albus would refer to her as a 'half-breed' and he had ordered any similar abominations cast out of the city six years ago; an act of serendipity, which had led to him meeting Ceinwyn. Make-up could protect her for a bit—she essentially looked like a pale Roman. However, a strikingly beautiful Roman looking woman with a Signum on her face, too tall and too pretty to be a Slave. . . ? He shuddered at the thought of losing her.

'It's only for a few days Ceinwyn,' he said, 'you're right. After the ceremony we will have a proper honeymoon and return to Northern Britannia. I'll ask Albus if he'll let me keep the governorship of Luguvalium; we'll have children, a goat and mountains.' It suddenly sounded very appealing.

Ceinwyn giggled and kissed him on the cheek. Titus took her by the hand and marched forwards, under the Pomerium beam that scanned them for weapons, and together they emerged onto the thronged streets of the Aether.

'My father will make us welcome,' Ceinwyn said, tugging at Titus' hand, and pointing down a narrow road which led towards the Aventine.

'He couldn't,' Titus replied, 'not without his master knowing.'

'His master is so old he wouldn't know what to wear or eat without my father,' Ceinwyn said, laughing. 'We can stay there.'

Titus turned and started to walk with her, but suddenly a young man wearing a toga dashed from the crowd and, out of breath, stopped the pair.

'Consul Marcus Albus welcomes you to Rome, Commander.' He paused, staring at Ceinwyn, 'and your lovely wife.' Titus' men who had just entered the city too, wandered up behind. Antonius flicked a bronze coin to a street merchant who passed him a bottle of beer, which he downed in one, burping loudly.

'Your men,' the toga-clad man continued. 'Have been temporarily stationed at the barracks.'

Tiberius opened his mouth to complain: the standard of accommodation in the barracks was deeply spartan.

'On full pay of course.'

Tiberius closed his mouth.

'Done, as long as it's the second cohort one,' Antonius said.

The toga-clad messenger looked at him quizzically.

'Best whores there,' Antonius said, looking at the others as if they were mad for not knowing this. 'Even Quintus might get his end away!'

Even Gnaeus laughed now, as Quintus haughtily stepped away a couple of paces with his head in the air. 'I will be staying with my *wife*, on the Caelian,' he said, striding away purposely.

'His wife must be very rich,' the messenger said, trying to break the awkward silence which had formed. The Caelian was home to Rome's most important Nobles.

Titus nodded. 'We have friends in Rome, so no need for the barracks for us. Please tell Albus that I will meet him tomorrow, and look forward to reminiscing about old times.' He felt the warmth of the beach on his feet, and the eyes of the girl boring into his. He closed his eyes and opened them again. The image was gone.

'The Consul, Marcus Albus, insists you stay at the new palace.'

'On this new floating platform of yours?' Titus joked.

'Oh no sir, it doesn't float; it's connected to the Aether by a complex system of struts, and even ropes and pulleys. . .'

'Spare me the details,' Titus laughed. 'As long as we can rest today, I don't mind.'

The messenger blushed. 'Sir, the Consul, Marcus Albus, requests your company at a display of the Praetorian guard *this afternoon*. Perhaps you can rest later?'

The way he looked at Ceinwyn as he spoke, made Titus suspect that he thought rest was the last thing on Titus' mind. Honestly, he just wanted to sleep. The sun reflecting off the scorched marble stung his skin; after nearly a decade in Northern Europe he wasn't used to Rome. He shrugged. 'We are his guests.'

'It's settled then,' the messenger exclaimed happily, holding out his hand towards a passing mercenacurrus. 'To the Summus! Take them to the palace. Guests of the Consul.'

The driver looked Titus' travel-weary clothes up and down. 'Get in,' he said, with a barely concealed sneer. The messenger tossed some sestertii into the hand of the driver, who nodded, and with a push of a button the currus burst into life.

They tore through the bustling streets of the Aether, past rows of boutique shops and cosy townhouses whose beautifully tended window box plants crept down their many storeys. The dimension rules, instigated half a millennia ago, had never been revoked, and no one, not even the richest businessman, could build a house wider than two rooms across in the Aether, but there were no rules to prevent them building upwards; apart from those of gravity itself. Titus gazed up at the new top level of Rome, the Summus, as it came into clearer view. Arcs of wire and gleaming silver planks of steel extended towards them, suspended fifty feet above the tallest buildings. Titus wondered what the view would be like from up there; surely you could see the sea?

The mercenacurrus passed beneath the outermost part of the Summus as Titus looked up, and saw a multitude of machines and people swarming around underneath at the edge of it. As Titus watched, pulleys lifted metal sheets into place. It looked like half of Rome had been employed to build the new level. Titus thought about the ruined town of Luguvalium that was now the seat of his province, Northern Brittania. He had been told there was no money to rebuild that after what the Reivers had done to it.

The currus was suddenly cast into gloom as the sun was blocked off by the leading edge of the Summus. They drove on. To the left, Titus caught a glimpse of a Praetorian, half way up a ladder, tearing down some sort of banner from a house. The occupants of the house looked on from a higher window, concerned. It was noticeably colder in this part of the Aether with no sun to warm it, and Titus shuffled across his seat towards Ceinwyn, putting an arm around her. Up ahead they were approaching the turning that would allow them to access the Summus. Beyond that turning lay a spiral of road, twisting upwards, towards the new roof of the Aether; upwards towards the sun above. On their right was what had once been a park. There were some children playing amongst the brown reedy stems that had once been luscious green bushes, and the Harpasta field was simply a dusty bowl, its sagging goalposts forgotten.

Surely, Albus must have thought of this problem before he installed another layer on Rome, and blocked out the sun?

Just then, Titus' thoughts were interrupted by a concerning change in their route. They had just driven past the turning for the Summus he had expected the driver to take. He leant forwards, 'you missed the turning.'

The driver turned around for a moment, smiled, and continued. Perhaps he knew another way? But looking up, Titus could see no other road spiralling towards the new roof hundreds of feet above them.

Ceinwyn nudged Titus. 'You're right, it's definitely up there,' she said, pointing back.

Titus tapped the driver on the shoulder who looked around angrily. 'Stop the currus.'

The driver let his foot off the accelerator slowly and the currus coasted to a stop behind a row of abandoned houses—clearly those that had the money had already moved to the Summus, or to a part of the Aether where the Summus remained unfinished.

'It really is that way,' Titus said, pointing back the way they had come. 'We are trying to get to the Summus.'

'Aren't we all,' the driver said, laughing. 'Get out.'

They sat still for a second, thinking.

'Are you fucking deaf? Out.'

Titus opened the door and walked around to the front of the currus where the driver met him.

'There is a tax on passengers for the Summus, an extra hundred sestertii, each.' The driver smiled menacingly, and Titus noticed how big he actually was.

'That's a lot of money,' Titus said slowly as he looked around at Ceinwyn, taking his chance to glance back down the road for avenues of escape. The road was narrow, and there were plenty of alleyways, however his thoughts of flight were cut off as three more men wandered out of the nearest of the alleys and approached.

'Hesychius,' the nearest one shouted. 'What have you found?'

'Look in the car,' the driver replied, nodding in the direction of Ceinwyn. 'She's worth two hundred sestertii, at least.'

Titus scowled.

'Well...' the man said thoughtfully, 'probably fifty a go. But then there are four of us, so... well... we'll be even once we've all finished.'

Titus reached into the folds of his travel toga for his purse, and realised two things. Firstly, the purse was with Marcus, who was probably in the barracks by now, over a mile away, and secondly that the driver was still staring intently at Ceinwyn.

He put all his weight behind the strike.

It caught Hesychius under the jaw which Titus felt crack under the blow. The man was lifted off his feet and crashed down, motionless, into the dust in front of his currus. Titus turned to face the other three. They rushed him at the same time, hoping to push him back against the currus. Titus dashed forwards instead and lunged at the fastest of the men, driving him down onto the ground. He rolled quickly and got back onto his feet, only to be tackled by another assailant. The pair rolled on the ground, exchanging blows. Titus was stronger and managed to wrestle the man onto his back. As he sat on the man's chest, fist raised ready to strike, a smile crept onto his face—it had been a long time since he had had a good fight.

Then he felt an explosion of pain in the back of his neck and was catapulted forwards onto the ground. Turning over, dazed, he groaned and looked up at the two other assailants, now wielding clubs. The biggest one, wearing a black vest, gestured back towards the currus. His companion ran across to it and started to drag Ceinwyn out. Hesychius, the driver, still lay motionless by the currus door.

Ceinwyn stared defiantly up at her captor and did not scream. Titus resolved that he would find a way to save her—he could not watch her being raped.

'Break his knees,' the man in the vest barked, striding back to the currus and Ceinwyn. The third man strode over to Titus in the half gloom, whirling his club slowly by its wrist strap. Titus braced his arms against the ground, ready to leap to his feet, but he was interrupted by a panicked shout from the group's leader.

'Praetorians!'

Titus sat up and watched as a pair of Praetorians, in full body armour, charged into the street. The three attackers began to flee but were cut off by a second pair of Praetorians emerging from a side street. The three men grouped together, facing outwards with their wooden clubs. They remained defiant until the Praetorians closed in. Then they dropped the weapons, put their hands in the air, and began to beg for mercy. Titus ran over to Ceinwyn.

'It's okay, I'm fine,' she said. 'I was ready to break his neck,' she continued, gesturing at the man who had been holding her. Titus laughed, knowing that she meant every word. He had been teaching her, not that she had needed that much teaching; she had already known how to use a sonifex before he had met her. They walked over towards the group of men to give their evidence to the Praetorians. Their statement would be needed in a few days when the case came to court. The men could look forward to several days in the Carcer before the trial, and perhaps years in it afterwards for their crime. If this had been a hundred years ago, they would certainly have been put to death—punishments were a lot more lenient now the world was civilised. Titus was surprised to see the men arguing with the Praetorians.

'You bastards build over us. You take our jobs! You work for a dictator,' the man in the vest shouted at the four Praetorians.

Titus was sure the Praetorians were glaring, but he couldn't see their eyes, hidden so deep behind the slit in the helmet; their whole body encased in the shiny black carapace of their amour.

'Silence,' hissed the lead Praetorian, drawing his fasces, the only weapon that could be carried in the city of Rome; a weapon which could only be carried by a Praetorian. The end of the fasces sparked and the induction coil at the base glowed faintly. Titus had been stunned by one once before, and he could remember its sting. The Praetorian leant it against the chest of the insolent man who fell backwards instantly and lay there groaning.

'They are from Filii Aquilae,' one of the Praetorians said, but Titus was not sure what this meant. The other Praetorians nodded and advanced on the men who began to shout and protest their innocence. Panicking, the man who had been stunned turned over and tried to crawl away.

'We are just thieves!' the man with the black vest implored, his hands outstretched, as a Praetorian reached him. The Praetorian swung his fasces up into the man's groin, bringing him down onto the ground. Laughing, he twisted a dial at the base of the fasces to bring the device up to full power. The thief screamed, and the Praetorian rammed the fasces down into his open mouth. Titus heard the crack as his teeth shattered. The man's body twisted and writhed as electrical current coursed through it. The other two men fought to escape, but were held easily by the three remaining Praetorians. The man in the vest was still jerking, the fasces still in his mouth. Vomit coursed up, out of his throat, splattering over the fasces and sizzling as it coated the hot electrode. The man's back arched high in the air and crashed back to earth hard. Titus heard a snap and the man's legs twitched less, a dark stain spreading onto the ground around him as he lost control of his bowels. One final spasm racked the man, and then he finally lay still. The Praetorian pulled the smoking end of the fasces out of his mouth and removed some of the seared flesh that had adhered to it with the fingers of his black plastic glove.

Titus felt sick. He approached the lead Praetorian who was now standing, watching his colleagues beat the other men to death with their fasces, using them as simple clubs to smash open the skulls of the thieves.

'You realise that I'm on my way to meet with Marcus Albus. I'll inform him that you have just executed three men without trial,' Titus said angrily.

The Praetorian removed his helmet, revealing a face younger than Titus had been expecting; the man looked no more than twenty. His head was completely shaved, but he sported a huge bushy beard, which seemed to have never been trimmed. 'No trial for traitors,' he said cheerfully. 'Marcus Albus will be extremely pleased: four Filii Aquilae are dead thanks to me.' He proffered his hand, still flecked with vomit and burnt tongue. 'I'm Verres, you must be Aquilinus?' His voice was loud and deep, and Titus could tell that he had had to learn to speak with an accent befitting a Praetorian.

Titus nodded, and accepted his hand. Verres had used his cognomen, knowing that he was a Noble.

'I thought you'd be older,' Verres continued. 'You're quite famous, you know. I'd expected a grey-haired warlord!'

Titus laughed; his short hair had once been dark brown, but was definitely flecked with grey now, whatever this young Praetorian officer said. He looked down at the men who would probably have killed him and raped Ceinwyn if it wasn't for Verres' intervention. He was barely over thirty, but perhaps he was getting too old.

You should be thanking me really rather than threatening,' Verres continued, 'but. . .' he pointed at the unconscious body of Hesychius by the mercenacurrus. 'You are clearly a fighter too, so perhaps you can understand why we kill these people?'

'They are just thieves! You killed three thieves,' Titus said, still angry with the overzealous young Praetorian.

'Four,' Verres said, hearing the crack as one of his colleagues broke Hesychius' unconscious neck. 'And they would have raped your woman too if it makes you feel any better. However, most importantly, if we had done as you suggested and put them on trial, they would escape justice.'

'How can that be? I witnessed the crime.'

'Filii Aquilae are rich; we have picked up dozens of their terrorists and seen them walk free. They bribe judges; they appoint the best lawyers. I would rather kill their men than see them walk free to kill one of mine.'

Titus nodded. Would he behave that differently in the same position? 'Who are Filii Aquilae?'

The Praetorian laughed. 'You've been away a long time General! They want to set up a dictatorship in Rome, depose Marcus Albus and Decimus Catula from their rightful position as Consuls. They are thick pigshit bastards from the Imum. But don't worry; the Praetorian guard are here to protect and serve you and Rome.' Verres glowed with pride and pointed at the dead vest-wearing thief. Flies had already landed and were busily buzzing in and out of his ruined mouth. 'Welcome to Rome, Aquilinus,' Verres said thoughtfully, taking Ceinwyn gently by the arm and walking the pair to his currus. Titus glanced back at the dead thieves once, before joining him.

II

As the armoured Praetorian currus ascended the final turn of the spiral road, Titus was bathed in sunlight once again. His eyes were dazzled by the brilliance. In front of him was laid out a city the likes of which he had never seen—the likes of which the world had never seen. The Summus.

Marble rose in arches, domes and jagged patterns that he had no name for. The ground was immaculate; marble in pure white to offset the rose marble used liberally on the surrounding buildings. Most of the structures were in the latter stages of construction but ahead he could see an area of perfection. A huge domed building with four massive wings stretched out before him. To its front, two marble staircases cascaded down, wide enough for fifty people to march up side by side, and in between them cascaded water, foaming white on the pale stone. As they approached it, some pigeons, which had been sleeping beneath one of the four domed turrets at the corners, rose up and flew soporifically up into the air. Their gentle cooing was the only noise Titus could hear in this silent, empty, perfect city.

'Welcome back,' Verres said, gazing round in awe, despite seeing the sight daily.

Titus stared up at the palace before him; so much greater than his palace in Luguvalium. He could never call that a palace again, having seen what Albus had built.

'Of course Marcus Albus is going to be making it a lot livelier,' Verres added excitedly. 'The entertainment quarter has not been built yet, there will be pubs there, and they are dismantling the Colloseum, brick by brick, and bringing it—'

'Dismantling the Colloseum?' Titus asked, amazed.

'Of course,' Verres replied. 'It's ridiculous that it's been left in the Imum so long, all of us having to descend down into the depths of Tartarus to watch shows. The amount of theft we have to deal with because of that! Every day of the games the criminal gangs of the Imum feast on the women and wallets of the hard working men of the Aether.' He thumped his chest with pride. 'I am a man of the Aether, and I'll protect men of the Aether from these Imum bastards.'

'What of this Summus?' Titus asked, gesturing around at the new palatial level growing around them towards the sky.

'The Summus is something for us all to aspire to,' he said quietly, and led them up to the foot of the marble stairs.

'I don't like this,' Ceinwyn said quietly, ensuring she would not be overheard by Verres.

'Why not; it's beautiful?'

'I'm not sure,' Ceinwyn replied, 'it feels... it's not real; there are no people. It doesn't feel like a city. More like a grave,' she added shivering, even though the sun was directly above them and the marble was warm beneath her feet. 'I want to go home Titus,' she said finally.

'We need to see Albus, and then we can go home.'

Ceinwyn sighed. 'I can't imagine you just accepting Albus' thanks for destroying Strabo and saving Luguvalium, and then just saying: 'thanks, but we're leaving'.'

'Why not?' Titus asked, slightly hurt.

'Because you like it here.'

'I don't!' Titus protested.

'You can tell yourself that as many times as you like, but it won't make it any more true. I know you, and I've seen the way you look at things here. You feel like you've come home.'

'Don't you?'

'It's not my home!' Ceinwyn said, laughing. 'Rome threw me out. They don't want 'half-breeds' here anymore. I couldn't even be standing next to you without this make-up.'

Titus looked up at Verres, now at the top of the steps. 'Rules change, perhaps one day they will welcome you. Perhaps I can re-write the rules?'

Ceinwyn shook her head angrily. 'Fool. You think you can change Rome? You forget that you yourself were thrown out. When did your family last have any weight in Rome? Rome abandoned you Titus, but *I* won't, I promise I won't. Do what you have to do here quickly, then come home with me and forget about this horrible place where people climb on top of each other to reach the sky.'

Titus thought about the dying Harpasta field, cut off from the sun it needed. He stopped, took Ceinwyn in her arms and kissed her. At first she muttered protest; Verres was watching, but then her mouth opened and their tongues touched. 'I'm going to take you home Ceinwyn,' he said solemnly. 'But first I need to do some things. I need to see what Albus wants from me, I need to see my father, and we need to see yours. Then we will go home.'

'I love you, but that's a long promise,' she said, smiling.

'You'll have to trust me.' They took each other by the hand and walked to the top of the stairway. From up here they could hear the faint noise of marching in the distance.

Verres gestured towards the entrance of the palace, shook Titus by the hand, and began to descend the steps back to his currus. 'He'll be in the Solarium,' he said over his shoulder, 'he likes it there—good view of the field of Mars.'

Titus and Ceinwyn walked hand in hand through the first courtyard. In front of them, a gigantic fountain sprayed water thirty feet into the air. Titus noticed that the centrepiece of the fountain was a depiction of the ruin of Carthage, and around it were frescoes from the life of Aeneas. Hidden away in a corner of the scene was a statuette of Dido, on her knees, with an overpowering Aeneas standing over her, one hand in her hair, whilst a strong fountain of water sprayed from his penis into her mouth. Albus had always taken a strong interest in Roman history. Titus quickly suppressed a laugh as Ceinwyn shook her head at the statue angrily.

They passed from this courtyard into a series of colonnades, each one filled with completely contrasting plants. As they walked, Titus realised that each was designed around a different Roman province. He marvelled how Rome now controlled every single square inch of the Earth. Well—if you counted the rebelling province of Asia Minor that was.

As they passed through the garden of the Transmaritanus, the smells reminded Titus of his youth. He remembered the fighting, his friends, and the pain. He held Ceinwyn's hand a little tighter—it was a long time ago.

'Titus.'

The voice was not loud, yet it filled the room. Titus felt the hairs on the back of his neck rise. In his head five words rang out—'kill these animals for me.' He turned around slowly, refusing to be transported back to that beach on the other side of the world; the beach he saw every night in his dreams. Above him, on a balcony, stood a man with long golden flowing hair down to his shoulders. He was wearing a traditional toga but cut the modern way. He was a few inches taller than Titus, lean but powerful, like a lion in his arena.

'Albus.'

The man nodded. Strangely, he looked younger than Titus did, which was odd as actually he was closing in on forty. 'You should come up Titus; you've come on a good day,' he spoke softly.

'Thank you sir,' Titus replied, feeling Ceinwyn cringe next to him. The pair climbed a silver spiral staircase that led to the next balcony; walking around the side of the upper colonnade, they came to Albus' balcony. His warm smile greeted them.

'Welcome to Rome,' he beamed, and stepped forwards to embrace Titus. Titus patted him on the back tentatively. 'And this must be your wife,' he said, sounding pleased. He looked at Ceinwyn and their eyes met.

She did not glare, but she did not look down at the ground as perhaps might be expected of a girl who had never met a Consul of Rome before. She stared into his deep green eyes, and as he stared into the equally deep, green, depths of hers, a strange look came across his face: as if he had just remembered a nightmare from his childhood, and realised it still had the power to quicken his pulse; but he recovered his poise immediately. He took her by the hand and gestured around the room with his other.

'Welcome to my palace. Come out onto the Solarium, and see what Rome has chosen to build to honour me.'

They walked across the room and out into the blinding sun. The balcony was twenty feet across. Albus marched forwards quickly, with Ceinwyn's hand, in his as Titus hurried after them. They reached the edge and Albus spread his arms wide.

'Everything you see is ours. Rome, the pinnacle of Man; the Senate, the pinnacle of men; and the Senate voted to build all of this, to show what the pinnacle of Man's men could do given infinite resources.' He raised his arms up and gestured around at the splendour. 'Marble from every corner of the world, the best food, water imported from the Blue Nile. Peace on Earth.'

'Not much left though now Albus; we better steady on a bit.'

Where Albus' voice was refined, quiet, yet filled the room, Catula's voice was in every way the opposite. He was reclined on the edge of the Solarium, simply in shorts, with his great belly, distended and crisscrossed with purple stretch marks, hanging down over the hem. He took a large draft from his tankard of wine. Titus wondered whether this image would be adorning the next cover of *'Ave!'* magazine. This fat pig was meant to be the other Consul of Rome. He understood why everyone mentioned Albus' name when the leadership was discussed; Catula might be equal on paper, but this creature had nothing except physical presence.

'Catula,' Albus said gracefully, 'it's good to see you out enjoying the sun.'

Catula shifted slightly in his seat, farted loudly and took another gulp of wine.

As the group stared out of the beauty of the Summus, far below, a troop of soldiers approached—real soldiers, not Praetorians.

'Titus. As I say, you have come on a good day. These are the Primiles; you remember the Transmaritanus?'

Titus nodded.

'Of course you do.' Albus said, sharing a look with Titus that clearly showed that the things they had seen and done would always be part of them, for better or worse. 'Well, men like these would have won us that war in half the time.'

A serving girl, naked from the waist up approached and poured a glass of rich red wine for Titus and Ceinwyn. Albus refused the drink, and the girl turned around and walked back into the palace. Titus noticed that she had no signum—she was a Roman, not a Slave.

'Well done on killing that fat idiot Gaius Strabo,' Albus said, casting a glance at the equally large Catula.

'He was extorting the population, and killing Slaves; he was not a good advert for Rome,' Titus replied proudly.

Albus laughed, 'can't have one of our boys extorting from local barbarians these days sadly, but killing Slaves?' he added quizzically. 'Surely no issue there?' Titus felt Ceinwyn bristle next to him.

'He was harvesting their organs.'

Albus sniggered again, 'sounds like a genius. Titus stop! I'm beginning to wish you'd let this bastard live!'

'Harvested,' Titus continued gravely. 'To have them implanted in ill Romans.'

Albus' laugh froze on his face, and he turned slightly pale. 'You mean,' he said, turning green. 'That there are people who would pay to have a Slave organ in their body?' His expression suggested that he barely believed Titus' words. 'That, my old friend, is the most disgusting thing I have ever heard.'

'Glad I spared you having to put up with him in Rome.'

Albus suddenly started smiling again, all trace of his response to Titus' words erased in a moment. 'Strabo, in Rome? Never. I sent him to the provinces for good reason.'

'Couldn't stand the smell,' Catula shouted from his recliner.

'He was planning to come back,' Titus said. 'The head of the Praetorian guard in Luguvalium mentioned something about him trying to become a senator.'

Albus laughed, 'but that would be impossible Titus. He'd have had no popularity here.'

'He thought it possible.'

'It was not,' Albus replied lightly.

The Primiles moved nearer, and swiftly formed a perfect line fifty feet below the Solarium balcony. A group of three high-ranking military officers filed in behind Albus who greeted them warmly.

Titus moved closer to Ceinwyn and took her hand. Together they leaned over the balcony, staring out over the white marble landscape and the intense activity at its far edge where the building work was in full swing. In the far distance, vertical scaffolding extended hundreds of feet into the air. Beneath it, the first circle of what would one day become the new Colloseum was being laid. Titus jumped at the sound of raised voices behind him.

'Four!' Albus exclaimed angrily.

'Do not concern yourself Consul; they are all dead,' the officer replied.

Albus cursed. 'Next time you catch one of these cunts, I want you to restrain your hothead Praetorians and bring him to the Mamertine. Forty eight hours with a Carnifex and we will know who the Aquila is.'

Albus hissed through his teeth, shook his head and walked back to Titus. 'Public order is slowly being restored. You should have told me what happened on your way here,' he continued, looking concerned for Titus' safety.

'Nothing I couldn't handle,' Titus said.

The pair laughed, remembering the days when Titus had fought as Albus' most trusted general in the Transmaritanus; when Titus had not even been twenty years old. 'We could do with another Transmaritanus, Titus,' Albus said, honestly.

Titus almost jumped with surprise. Here was Marcus Albus, the Consul who had been elected in place of his father, on the basis of bringing peace, and he was suggesting more war? 'There's nothing to conquer anymore,' Titus said, noncommittally.

'It's a shame. I do wonder then what we will do with these Primiles apart from enjoy watching them.' He extended his hands over the troop of special forces, and then let them fall slowly. The men drew their gladii.

What followed astounded Titus, who considered himself to be one the greatest swordsmen in the Roman world. He had studied the *Tripudium Mortis*, the dance of positions which you used if fighting singly, from the time that he had been old enough to hold a small wooden dagger. He could throw himself between the nine stances as quickly as anyone, apart from these Primiles. Pairing off, they spun through a series of *Tripudium Mortis* drills, their gladii hissing as they cut through the air millimetres from each other's bodies. Every single step was choreographed, beautiful and potentially deadly.

Albus stared down intently at his men. 'Times have changed since we were young. These men can use the gladius like a scythe, and we have completely new designs of sonifi, and new weapons you can barely imagine. Woe betide anyone who attacks Rome.'

Titus looked at Ceinwyn who rolled her eyes. Titus smiled at her and shrugged his shoulders. She smiled back, tossing her hair. As she did this, her top slid forwards slightly and Titus caught site of the curve of her breast. He touched her hand, and looked around to check no one was looking. All eyes were fixed on the display below, except, to Titus' surprise, that of one of the three generals. He was staring at Albus' back, and to Titus' horror, at that moment began to reach for a concealed gladius. Titus began to turn towards the man, ready to defend his Consul. The General drew the blade silently and lunged forwards at the Consul's unsuspecting back.

'Albus!' Titus shouted as he leapt forwards, knowing there was no way he could reach the pair in time, and that even if he did, he had no weapon with which to defend the Consul.

But Albus had heard Titus' shout, and he spun around.

He clearly had worked out that he had no time to draw his gladius, for he instead ducked down, at the last moment, beneath the officer's thrust and used his forearm to block the strike. The attacker danced back two paces, and realising that this was his last chance before somebody in the room felled him, darted forwards at Albus again. The Consul leapt to the side and brought a crashing elbow into the attacker's face, bringing him to the ground with a crash.

Albus stood over the would-be assassin, panting slightly, his muscles still flexed. Titus realised how strong and fast he was for someone who had no need, himself, to fight. His face was still held in a scowl, and for a second Titus wondered if he might take the assassin's blade and use it on him, but slowly his panting stopped, and his face returned to calm. He reached up, and with a couple of quick motions set his blonde hair back into its position of ordered disorder. He nodded to the other two officers, who rushed forwards and grabbed the assassin. 'Filii Aquilae?' he asked the man, as he was hauled roughly to his feet.

The assassin spat at Albus.

'Save it for the Carnifex,' Albus said calmly, turning around as the man was dragged away. He returned to watching the Primiles, who were just coming to the end of their dance, oblivious to what had just taken place on the Solarium above them.

Titus and Albus stood side by side watching the display as it ended. Titus clapped his hands twice, realised no one else was applauding, and sheepishly stopped. Albus broke the silence.

'As I was saying Titus, well done for killing Strabo. Thank you for taking on the governorship in Northern Britannia; there are few who would,' he added with a hint of sarcasm. 'But Britannia is just one province in this huge Empire Titus, and I do remember all of the service you have done for me: back in the Transmaritanus; in Britannia; and just now, saving my life. How would you like something bigger than Northern Britannia? Hispania for instance? I have one thing to ask of you, a simple thing, and that province could be yours.'

Titus nearly choked on his wine. The whole of Hispania? A rich province, warm, and beautiful. He glanced at Ceinwyn who saw the look in his eyes. He watched as the life seemed to drain out of her, and his heart thudded hard in his chest. He felt like he had slapped her, but he hadn't even spoken yet. He took a deep breath, knowing he had no choice in his answer.

'Thank you Albus, but you are too kind. I am content with my lot. I wish to stay as governor of Northern Britannia and if you will permit me, to keep it indefinitely.'

Albus' look became almost severe. 'The length of time is not an issue, if you must have Northern Brittania than I will happily grant you that barren wasteland until the end of your days,' he said, laughing. 'But Titus, I am offering you the chance to be rich, you and all your friends. I will grant you Hispania for life. You can live in great splendour, and end your days in peace, with as much food, wine and as many women as you like.'

Titus took Ceinwyn's hand, and stared back at Albus. 'I understand,' he said with a calmness and clarity he didn't feel, 'and I thank you for your kindness, but I choose Northern Britannia.'

Albus forced a smile back onto his face and shrugged. 'The choice is yours. Know that you can have Northern Britannia for as long as you live, yet I have no idea why you would want it.'

'But,' he added quickly, 'Titus, I wonder if you would stay awhile in Rome.'

'How long?'

'As long as it takes, General.'

'I'm not a general anymore.'

Albus shrugged his shoulders. 'You are if I say you are. And I need you to be a General; I need you to protect me from scum like that,' he gestured in the direction the Filii Aquilae assassin had been dragged in. 'I need your help to make this city safe again.'

'You want me to act as bodyguard?'

'No, I have already earmarked a promising man from the Praetorian guard for that. No Titus, I have a much higher role for you. I want you to find the leader of Filii Aquilae and destroy their terrorist organisation forever.'

'What if I choose to just go home?'

Albus laughed. 'Why would you? You are home at last, and your home needs you.'

Titus' heart leapt and he took a pace forwards to shake his old friend's hand. His grip was firm, warm and nostalgic.

Ceinwyn turned away and looked forlornly over the balcony. The Primiles were still standing there, in a perfect line, waiting to be dismissed.

III

'Don't you think it's a bit convenient?' Marcus said.
'What is?' Titus replied, as he brought the currus to a halt outside the banner-festooned house. They were deep in the Aether's Equiline district.

'That Albus suggests our first line of investigation should be his only serious rival for the Consulship,' Marcus replied sarcastically.

Titus laughed, 'you see a conspiracy in everything Marcus. Look,' he pointed up at the banners. 'This man looks like a trouble maker.'

He switched off the engine and the two of them, followed by Gnaeus, got out and approached the house. As they approached the door, they passed under two huge banners.

'Descende de Turris Eburnea!'—'*Come out of your High Tower!*' Rang out the largest, along with: 'Ubi Sunt, Non Vos Unde Sitis.'—'*Where You Are Going, Not Where You Are From.*'

Titus knocked on the door, and it was answered by a young girl of no more than twenty. She was short, very slim, and almost entirely dressed in black, but with some flashes of purple. She was pretty in a slightly unusual way.

'We've come to see your father,' Titus said.

'Are you the secret police?' the girl asked, smiling and showing off a large tongue piercing to go with the one in the side of her nose, and the one in her lip.

'No, just asking questions for the Consul.'

'The secret police then,' the girl said with a surprising calm. 'My father's been expecting you. Come on through.'

She led them through the house briskly with her short black hair bobbing as she did.

'Are you Tarpeius' daughter,' Gnaeus asked as they walked.

'Yes. Why do you ask?'

'Oh,' Gnaeus said. 'I'm not sure, just wondering really.' Titus watched as he blushed.

The girl walked on in silence.

They were brought right through to the back of the house, where the girl's father waited. Titus was surprised to see how elderly Tarpeius looked. The bald man stood up from his desk and stared at them with his grey eyebrows raised; he looked almost amused at their presence.

'So, Albus has finally sent the Praetorians to take me away! I should have guessed he wouldn't actually deign to face me on the election field.' He held his hands out, clearly expecting to be cuffed and led away.

Titus shook his head. 'No, don't worry, we're not here to arrest you. I need to ask you some questions.'

Tarpeius snorted, 'I have no doubts that if your leader has his way I'll be answering questions to a Carnifex before long.'

'Why?' Titus asked directly, 'are you a member of Filii Aquilae?' He watched the man carefully, expecting to have caught him off guard.

To his surprise, Tarpeius bellowed with laughter. 'Albus thinks I'm a member of Filii Aquilae? Quick,' he gestured to his daughter, 'write this down; it seems our leader is stupider than he looks. Filii Aquilae!' he laughed to himself again. 'Does your leader really think that I would stoop to the level of Imum tactics? I oppose Albus yes, but to try to kill him? I just want to show Rome what he really is.'

'And what's that?' asked Titus tetchily.

'A bully. A bully who thinks he is entitled to tell anyone on this planet what to do. A bully who taught us, from the moment we were born, that if we strived and worked hard, even broke ourselves, then one day there would be reward.' His hoarse voice gained some depth, and Titus began to visualise what presence Tarpeius must have had in his prime. 'I'm sure that you do not care, but I'm going to waste some of my time telling you, and showing you, who your master is.'

He led them out into the garden. Titus was astounded by the intricacy of it. A maze of small paths wound between perfectly manicured borders, and at the back was a tiny summerhouse. Every single plant was dead.

'This is awful,' Gnaeus said, outraged, looking up at the Summus above them blotting out the sun.

'I was born in the Imum,' Tarpeius said. 'My parents were poor, but I was clever. I excelled at school. The other pupils hated me. I didn't care, because I knew that I was going to make something of myself, and that they wouldn't.

'One day my parents took me on a trip to the sea. It is odd because memories of youth are usually so faint, but I still remember that day as if it was yesterday. I so rarely saw the sun, and there it was, directly above me, warming my skin as I played in the small waves. From that day, my dream was to escape the Imum and live in the Aether where I could see the sun.

'I couldn't wait to leave school, and the moment I did I started the climb. I went to medical school and I became a medicus.' He laughed again, bitterly this time, 'you have to remember that in those days we all thought that we could become anything we wanted to be. I wanted to escape the wasters at school, and elevate myself to the same level as the Nobles. The Senate encouraged it, they told us all through school that if we worked hard we could earn our way to the Aether—we could make whatever we wanted of ourselves. I accepted the bullying, I endured it, because one day I knew I could look back down on the bullies who had made nothing of themselves.'

Titus saw that Tarpeius' daughter was staring at Gnaeus. Their eyes met for a moment, and she looked away quickly.

'I remember the day I bought this house,' Tarpeius continued, 'up here where the air was clean and the sky so big. I had been a medicus for three years and I was loving it, but then things began to change. First of all, it was the conditions. Then they started to take our pay; it was gradual. That is the trick, Titus: change things gradually and people won't notice.

'But I noticed. Slowly over time, everything I had worked for was gone. I was in exactly the same position as the wasters I had so despised. They had encouraged me to work myself to death, but I was no better off, and the Nobles were living a life of luxury at my expense. They had taken me in—there never was any real chance of bettering myself. They just sold me that lie so that I would work harder for them.' He sighed, took a deep breath, and smiled.

'But even then I didn't let it get to me, because at least I still had my garden, my sun, and my sky. The dreams I had had before the other, newer dreams had arrived with the promise of wealth and power. Now,' he pointed up at the Summus above him, 'they have taken that too. The lights are too dim, and the 'rainwater' that is channelled down to us is polluted with sewage.'

Titus looked down, took a deep breath and decided to ignore the dark thoughts in his mind. He had been given a task, to help his City. He had wasted too much time already. 'I need to find Filii Aquilae. If you are not involved, where do you think I should look?'

'Why should I help you?' Tarpeius asked coldly.

'If one day you lead this city, then you need it cleaned of terrorists.'

Tarpeius laughed and wagged a finger at Titus carefully. 'Terrorist is a very clever term Praetorian, for in one word it robs your opponent of their legitimacy.'

'I'm not a Praetorian, I'm...' Titus paused, *what was he?* 'I'm a friend of Albus.'

Tarpeius smiled wryly, 'someone else climbing towards the sun? Trust me. It's always just out of reach.'

Titus felt himself flushing, angry and ashamed; what was so wrong with wanting to help the Consul of Rome? Moreover, Albus had said he would reward him.

Tarpeius' smile became warmer. 'Don't worry, 'friend of Albus', perhaps your dream will come true, even though mine has not, but keep an eye on those dreams; are they different to the ones you had in your youth? And if so, which are your real dreams?'

He gazed at the dead stems of his fruit plants. 'You need to explore the Imum if you wish to find Filii Aquilae, I would suspect. There are plenty of places for a 'terrorist' to hide in the Imum.'

'I'll get an up to date map from the Praetorians,' Marcus said.

Titus nodded and they turned to go.

As they crossed the threshold from the ruined garden to the house, Gnaeus turned around and walked back to Tarpeius. 'Do you have a campaign leader,' he asked quietly. Titus could tell that beneath his calm he was seething with anger.

'Albus doesn't allow much in the way of donations to rival parties. I'm pretty much a one man show. Well, me and my daughter,' Tarpeius replied.

Gnaeus looked across at the girl, who smiled at him. 'You have another assistant now,' said Gnaeus, reaching out his hand.

Titus raised his eyebrows. 'Defecting, Gnaeus?' he said, amused.

'No, just changing parties. Don't worry, I'll still help against Filii Aquilae, but I'm going to try to help get Tarpeius elected. It's been decades since there hasn't been an Albus as Consul.'

Tarpeius stared at Titus. 'Your path looks easier than that of your friend, but I worry for you. What is the point in being happy if no one else is? Be careful... 'friend of Albus'.'

The engine roared into life; they had given him the most powerful make of currus that the Praetorians used. It was the best vehicle Titus had ever driven. He put his foot to the floor and used its full power. He couldn't leave the dark side of the Aether fast enough. As he drove back out into the sun, he thought of Albus and Tarpeius. Albus was his friend, they had fought together, and now finally after ten years he was being rewarded for his service. He was sad that Gnaeus had been taken in by the old Tarpeius' rhetoric.

'I'm scared,' Marcus said. 'What are we doing?'

'Fighting for Rome, our City.'

'I don't want to work for a Senate that treats people like Tarpeius was treated.'

'There must be some oversight,' Titus said. 'I know Albus; he's a good man and he loves Rome. The lights under the Summus must be malfunctioning or something.'

'He's good enough to take people who have worked hard all their lives to earn their way on to the Aether, and then put them back underground so he can have a palace?'

'It's not just his palace Marcus, lots of people will live on the Summus, the best people. We could too if we work hard for Rome. Think of that. You will have no problems finding a wife when you—'

'No Titus,' Marcus interrupted angrily. 'I couldn't live there when people like Tarpeius are buried beneath me. Not like Quintus...'

'Quintus is moving to the Summus?'

'His wife's family are', he said. 'They are all moving, and he is too.'

'See,' Titus said happily. 'If Quintus is staying here then perhaps you should consider it too?'

'Titus,' Marcus said imploringly. 'Listen to Ceinwyn; she really does love you. We should return to Britannia. What reason do we have to be involved in this?'

'It's our city, it's Rome, the Eternal City. One day you will be able to tell your grandchildren about when you saved—'

'Your pride is going to get you killed Titus!' Marcus said, interrupting him, shaking his head in irritation.

'We are working for the Consul of Rome! You should be proud,' Titus said with exasperation.

Marcus laughed. 'Dress it up how you like. I think we are working for a Tyrant.'

Titus nearly jumped out of his seat. 'Marcus,' he said, shocked, 'you have to be careful. You can't say things like that!'

'The fact that you are worried about what might happen to me for saying that, confirms what I am saying,' Marcus said.

'Rome hasn't had a King for two thousand five hundred years,' Titus said proudly.

'It's like Tarpeius says, lots of little changes, people don't notice.'

'No. Albus is our friend and he has given us the chance to help Rome. I won't believe it Marcus.'

'I hope you're right.'

The pair stared ahead at the road shooting past them as they weaved through the streets. Titus tried not to feel worried. He was so proud that Albus had entrusted him with the task of protecting Rome from Filii Aquilae, but what he had seen at Tarpeius' house was not right. He wondered what Ceinwyn would make of it, but he already knew.

'Got the map,' Marcus said sullenly, breaking the silence and pointing to the large square reader interface mounted to the dashboard of the Currus. He lifted the interface off its holder and held it in front of him. 'But where do we start? We can't search the whole Imum.'

'We need to start at the Mamertine,' Titus said, remembering the brooding Praetorian headquarters sitting at the edge of the City, now also a prison for the most dangerous offenders. 'By now the Carnifex is sure to have extracted some information from the assassin.'

Marcus paled, and Titus shivered even though the air conditioning was broken and the currus was unpleasantly warm. Titus remembered the feeling of cold steel against his helpless body. He retched.

IV

Ceinwyn couldn't believe that she was actually in the same room as her father again. Five years ago, she had been driven from the city by the Praetorians, and she was lucky not to have suffered worse than exile.

When she had been a baby, all half-breeds born from Slave women had been taken away and murdered. Apparently, if your mother was a Slave and your father a Roman, your 'degeneracy' was even greater. She thought of Albus again. Albus' own father, at that time himself the Consul, had ordered those murders of her kin. Old and young alike had been taken from their homes, dragged to the Parthian rock, and forced over the edge in nets to be dashed to pieces on the rocks below.

'It's scary how much you actually look like a Roman,' her father said thoughtfully, his dark curly hair hanging gracelessly down over his pale face. His signum had been placed too near his mouth and it made his smile lop-sided. 'I'll need to get the ingredients for that make-up from you; we could use it.'

Ceinwyn's father was the leader of the Slaves in Rome. Ostensibly, he appeared to appeal for Slaves to work quietly and keep their heads down—going about their work carefully kept them safe. However, both Ceinwyn and her father knew that for their kind to truly be safe, one day they would need to be free of the Romans.

'What are you planning father?' she asked excitedly.

He shook his head. 'Nothing for you to worry about Ceinwyn. We are always 'planning', but do not worry, very little happens.' His voice had the same lilt as Ceinwyn's. He was originally from Britannia; perhaps that was why she had so happily adopted it as her new home, in place of the Rome which had carelessly discarded her.

'Maybe I could help?' Ceinwyn said eagerly.

'Not with that Roman you married,' came a voice from the corner of the room. The words belonged to her stepmother, Thana, and the years had not just strained her voice; her face was creased with worry, and Ceinwyn could think of no good reason why her father had chosen to marry her, especially as her real mother had been so beautiful.

'What do you mean, *'that Roman'*, Thana?' Ceinwyn asked angrily.

'Ceinwyn,' her father chided kindly, 'be kind to Thana, you've not seen her for five years.'

Ceinwyn rose, walked over to the window where she sat, and put her arms around her dutifully. Five years wasn't long enough. She hugged her once, quickly and tried to retreat, but Thana held her for too long so Ceinwyn broke away.

'I love *'that Roman'* Thana. He's a good man, and he wants to help us.'

Thana laughed. 'That will all change now that he is back in Rome. How he felt in the middle of Northern Britannia doesn't necessary translate to the streets of his birth city. I know Romans better than you.' Her voice was caustic, and she couldn't say the word 'Roman' without seeming to spit it.

'Not as well as my real mother did,' Ceinwyn said bitterly. Ceinwyn's real mother had been a Roman lady whom her father had been Slave to. He had apparently always admired her, but with him being a Slave, and her being a Roman, there was no chance to interact. But then, one day, when her parents had been out, Ceinwyn's mother had fallen on the veranda and cut her knee. Her father had gone to her and helped her, and she had realised that he was more than he seemed.

They had fallen in love and she, Ceinwyn, had been the fruit of their love. They ran away together before her pregnancy showed, and lived outside Rome with Ceinwyn's father desperately foraging for food. Barely older than children, they had grown thin and weak, and her mother had not survived childbirth.

But Ceinwyn knew it was not malnutrition ultimately that had killed her mother; it was Rome. For, if her mother and father had been allowed to love one another, then they would never have had to hide, and her mother would have been cared for.

She would have been born in an Aesculapium, not a cave.

'What's the palace like?' her father asked, to change the subject.

'Terrifying,' Ceinwyn replied. 'I've never seen such a waste of money.' She reached forwards and ate some more of the special bread her father had baked. It was an old Britannic recipe, full of dried fruit and delicious dark sugar.

A rocking chair creaked in the corner opposite Thana. 'Devin, bring me some of that what-do-you-call-it, you know?'

'Brith?' her father replied, and took across a slice for the old Roman who sat there. Sentius was her father's master, but age had taken his mind, and the role was reversed. Her father was extremely kind to him though, as if he bore no grudge. Ceinwyn wished that she possessed that kind of mercy. She thought back to Strabo's compound and the men she had killed; she had no regret, and she would happily kill more.

'Why do you think he built it?' her father asked as he returned to the table.

'What, the palace?'

'Of course the palace. In one month, he has to face the people on the Field of Mars and ask them to re-elect him. But rather than spending money on a campaign, he spends it on a roof over their heads, blocking out the sun.'

'Perhaps he doesn't care what the people think?'

Her father nodded. 'Certainly. Albus doesn't care what anyone thinks. But the rest of the Senate almost unanimously agreed to it being built, and many of them stand to lose their seats next month because of it.'

'Fools.' Ceinwyn laughed at the stupidity of the fat politicians, giving up popular support in order to build a fine castle in the sky.

'I want to make you a bet my little girl,' her father said, sweeping his hair off his forehead and smiling; his signum twisted, making it more of a scowl. 'I bet that only the senators that refused to support

Albus in his building of that monstrosity lose their seats in the election next month.'

Ceinwyn held out her hand for the money and smiled.

'You may scoff, but seriously. Wait and see.' He lent forwards so that old Sentius would not hear, although it would have mattered little if he had.

'Five years ago we started to find these,' he turned his portable scire around so that she could see. The screen was covered in lines of programming code that she could not understand.

'It's a scire virus, a very clever one; it can be used to control communications sent between the scire it infects and the omniajunctus.'

'To steal data?'

'Yes,' her father said, impressed. 'And to *manipulate* data.'

Ceinwyn realised what her father was suggesting. 'The vote.'

Her father nodded. 'We have evidence that infected scires have been used to secretly generate a vote for Marcus Albus regardless of who the user actually chose to vote for.'

Ceinwyn thought about it for a moment and realised a flaw in the conspiracy. 'But the people of Rome vote in person on the Field of Mars.'

'Yes,' her father said. 'But those in the provinces, voting remotely, far outnumber them.'

'So this virus has infected scires all over the world?' Ceinwyn said, amazed.

Her father shook his head. 'No longer, thanks to us,' he said smiling. 'We created our own benign virus last year. It uninstalls Albus' virus and protects the scire from its effects again, so the infection rate is now less than ten percent globally, but Albus still won last year's elections.'

He dropped his voice even lower and leant forwards to whisper in her ear.

'Would you like to find out how?'

'Devin,' Thana hissed from over the room.

'She's twenty four, Thana, she's grown up.'

'Please!' Thana implored, her thin voice breaking.

'I want to help you.' Ceinwyn said to her father, her voice serious.

Thana wailed and ran off upstairs.

Ceinwyn shook her head at her cowardly stepmother, and turned to face her father who looked pained by the scene.

'Where should I start?' she said, pleased to be trusted with a mission against Rome.

'That's the problem,' her father laughed. 'I've no idea either.'

V

Titus cursed the Carcer for his incompetence: the assassin had died under torture just after midday. Unfortunately, this event had taken place before much useful information had been obtained from what was left of his mind. All that was known was that Filii Aquilae had planned a bomb attack if direct assassination failed, but despite the Carnifex's skills, the location, timing and the names of any other members remained completely mysterious. Titus tried not to think of what the Carnifex had done to the assassin in the deep basements beneath the Mamertine. He knew, more than most, the feeling of complete helplessness that comes with being at the mercy of an interrogator. However, this situation was different: this man had dared to try to kill the rightful ruler of Rome, and Titus' job was to try to stop his associates from trying it again. That was why Titus was in the Imum.

He and Marcus had spent the last hour sitting in the corner of an alley, begging cups extended out in front of themselves. The rags they wore were a rushed attempt at disguise, but their tanned skin would easily betray them as Sursumas—Imum slang for those who dwelled in the sunlight.

The Praetorians had a network of spies throughout Rome, and the advice they had been given by them was to search the Aether; advice which seemed odd to Titus as he remembered Verres' words about Filii Aquilae: *'they are thick pigshit bastards from the Imum.'* Therefore, they had ignored the spies' advice and, instead, used the same spy network to spread the word that they were in the market to make coin through killing. So far, they had received a proposition to, accidentally, kill a man's unfaithful wife, and to destroy some independent coffee shops on the Aether to make way for a much larger competitor. Neither had they accepted, although Marcus had been fairly interested in the coffee shop mission, until it had become apparent there would be no opportunity to ransack the shops for cake.

A great crash alerted them to yet another heavy load of curri approaching. The street, which they were on, was a section of the ancient Appian Way, although its state of repair was so poor that it was highly unlikely that any of the ragged stones were originals from the old days of the Republic. A shaft from the Aether, two hundred feet above, shed a dim light down upon the scene. Titus wondered whether, when the Aether was entirely covered by the Summus, any light would filter down to the Imum at all.

People milled about around them, going about their work. Most of them were poor Romans, and most of them were surprisingly fat. Over a century ago, the death rate in the Imum had grown so high that the Senate had decreed that some limited help should be given to the poor there. The people of the Imum were now given rations if they were too poor to afford food. Titus had seen one of these packs once at school, and he and his friends had picked it apart, laughing at the contents. Titus wondered whether anyone in the Imum had ever tasted fruit.

The convoy rounded the corner. Each heavy currus was emblazoned with the name of the same company, *Coniunctus*. Yet again, it was carrying what appeared to be massive dark glass solar panels. The joins at the edges of each gigantic plate suggested to Titus that they could be joined to each other. He could think of no use for such a large amount of solar panelling—most of the world's power was generated in what was left of Dacia. The conditions there, he had heard, were even worse than down here in the Imum. Being sent to Dacia was the second worst punishment the Senate could meet upon you for breaking its laws. Titus wondered if perhaps that life of servitude was in fact worse than execution.

A bell rang out, and the door of the school next to the alley they were crouched in burst open. Several dozen schoolchildren charged out and ran out onto the street. A Slave who was walking past was knocked over and quickly scurried away, barely noticed by the children. The convoy of heavy curri screeched to a halt as the children inadvertently blocked its path. A tattoo-covered driver leant out and cursed at the children, making it clear that, if the laws were different and he was carrying a sonifex, none of them would be having dinner at the family table that evening; even the lowest men of the Aether despised anyone who had to live in the dark reaches of the Imum.

A man, who seemed to be the teacher of the children, stepped out onto the street and brought his hood up around his face. He marched out into the centre of the street and pointed his finger accusingly at the driver.

'You despise him because he has nothing?' he said, his voice echoing off the walls, deep and powerful. 'Because you and him are so different? Because you have been told your life is better than his?'

The driver stared at him, confused at the questions.

'But, you both hurry needlessly to get back to your equally terrible existences. Perhaps you are no happier than he is?'

The driver cursed at the teacher, struck the horn and sped off. The noise reverberated off the Imum roof, deafening Titus. The children ran on, almost oblivious, and their shouts were lost in the general bustle of the Imum.

The voice that had come from the man made Titus choke with surprise and jump to his feet. He stared at the man, now walking towards them, his eyes wide with astonishment.

It was his father.

But his father changed direction as he neared them, veering back towards the school he had come from.

'Father.' Titus' voice wavered.

His father turned and looked at him, lifting up the thick-rimmed spectacles he always wore. Titus swore they were the same ones that he had worn when he had last seen him. Then his father smiled and dropped his hood down, revealing a bald head.

'Titus, it's... amazing to see you. It's been years.' He looked down at the ground awkwardly.

'A decade.'

'That long?' His father scratched at his arm nervously. He looked back up at Titus and smiled again. 'I hear you went to Britannia?'

'Yes,' Titus said opening his mouth to say more, but not quite sure what to say.

'Lucius Aquilinus, it's so good to see you again!' Marcus broke the silence, and strode forwards to shake Titus' father by the hand, but Marcus was naturally one of the most awkward people Titus had ever met, and after the handshake, he too had no idea what to do.

'Do you teach here?' Titus asked, pointing at the school.

'Do I teach?' he said slowly, his mind seemingly completely elsewhere. 'Oh, you mean... no... well... sort of. I want to try to pass some of what I have learned on to the young. I spend most of my time writing, Titus, like I always did.'

Titus remembered his youth. His father had never once watched him play Harpasta. When he came back from the game, bloodied and bruised, his father would always be sitting there at his desk, music blaring, his stylus dipping and swaying over the paper in front of him. 'I always wondered what you wrote.'

Titus' father went slightly red. 'Oh, did I never show you. Perhaps I didn't think you were old enough?'

'I was old enough to fight for my country.' Titus didn't know why his voice sounded sarcastic, he didn't mean it to, but his father didn't seem to notice. 'I heard you are ill?' Titus said, remembering Strabo's words, which had cut him deeply—his father had not written to tell him.

'Oh no, not really, I am fine,' he said, shaking his head. 'Come on Titus, let's go home. He gestured to his currus, a beaten up grey thing that looked worse than the curri that Marcus had bought from a farmer near Luguvalium last year.

Titus shook his head. 'We are on a mission.'

'Well, whatever it is, I'm sure it can wait while you see your father?' His voice was almost imploring.

Titus shook his head again. 'It's a mission for Marcus Albus.' He felt so proud as he said the words. He, the boy whose family's name was in the gutter, who had had to join the army rather than join politics to make a name for himself, had returned from the far reaches of the Empire to work for the Consul himself. He was on the verge of the Roman dream.

His father laughed. 'Titus, in which case, it is doubly important you come with me.' His father gestured to the currus again, more firmly, suddenly all trace of awkwardness had gone. 'Come with me. We need to talk.'

The currus smelt of his childhood.

'So how long have you been back in Rome?' his father asked, as they drove along.

'Just a day.' The noise of the traffic in the Imum was deafening, and he could barely see anything in the cramped interior of the currus. There were meant to be lights in the ceiling of the Imum, but when he peered up, they were barely lit. It was the middle of day, yet his father had to have the headlights on full.

Then they swooped up onto the surface of the Aether. They were close to the Palatine, and the Summus hadn't reached here yet. The sun poured down into the currus and Titus felt warm again.

'You came back to work for Albus?'

'No, I came for my honeymoon,' Titus replied with amusement.

His father laughed. 'You always were romantic, Titus. Whoever she is, take her to Capri or something. Don't let Albus anywhere near her anyway; he loves pretty young things. I imagine she is pretty? They always were if I remember rightly?'

'Of course father,' Titus said smiling. 'She's also half Slave.'

There was silence in the car.

They passed a shrine to the goddess Pax, her sceptre outstretched with an overflowing cornucopia in her other hand. No one was knelt before her, and there were no flowers. Scrawled in graffiti were the words, 'Pax enim Informor'—'*Peace is for the Weak.*' Titus could not have imagined such words there a decade ago. Ten years of once longed-for peace had changed Rome.

'Perhaps you were not too young to read my books,' his father said after a long time.

'I was sixteen when I left home father,' Titus said resentfully.

'There are many people older than you are now, who are not ready to read my books.'

They pulled up outside Titus' old house. It was just as he remembered: decrepit, like their family name. Being descended from the Destroyer of Tyrants meant little if your ancestors were all alcoholics, suicidal, or traitorous.

They walked inside and his father pulled up three chairs for them on the veranda, and poured tea. The view was amazing. Even if their family name was nothing, they still had the house, for now.

'Why are you working for Albus?' his father asked quietly.

Titus was astonished at why such a question would need asking. 'He's the Consul, he can restore our family name, he *is* Rome. Fighting for him is like fighting for Rome again.'

'He's a fool, and so are you, if you believe what you just said. What does your half-Slave wife think of him?'

'She thinks he is evil, but then, she thinks pretty much all Romans are evil.'

'And she has a right to: we are really. What gives us the right to rule the whole world, and to subjugate Slaves?'

'But that's the way things work, you can't change it.'

'Why not try?'

'Like your books?' Titus asked bitterly. 'It didn't change much did it father?'

'Perhaps not,' his father conceded, and stared into the distance. 'Can I give you one bit of advice though?'

'And what is that?'

'Don't get too far into whatever it is you are helping Albus with. You know I don't trust him, and I know you think I am foolish for that, but whatever you think of me, be careful, don't change.'

'I won't,' Titus said earnestly.

'And leave Rome soon.'

'What?' Titus said, surprised that his father wanted to send him away.

'Take the girl away, enjoy your life. Rome will change you I think, no matter what.'

'I disagree.'

'Have you read the Chronicle of Varro?'

'What?' Titus asked, surprised.

'The Chronicle of Varro. It's old, but you can learn a lot from the classical tale. I'll lend it to you. It's about whether people can truly change or not, and it's about being careful that when you change outwardly, you don't change inwardly as well.'

'Sounds interesting,' Titus said, convinced of the opposite.

His father smiled. 'Read some of it. It's better than anything I have ever written anyway.' He jogged inside to get the book.

'Titus,' Marcus asked, 'how did you and your father end up so different?'

'You should have met my mother!' Titus said, thinking of his mother and her wild fierce eyes, and the stories she had told him as a child. She had always been at the edge of the Harpasta field, cheering him on as he got turnovers and scored terraffligos, and she had supported him joining the army.

'My father was always the thinker, but he never did anything, and he does the same now. He could be standing up supporting Albus, or he could be with that Tarpeius, working against him, but instead he just writes ideas down no-one will read.'

His father came back out, and Titus stopped talking suddenly, slightly ashamed of his words. Sitting down, his father handed him a well-thumbed tome. 'Start at the beginning, it's a good story. No skipping.'

'I've got plenty to worry about already father.'

'You dwell on the past too much,' his father said, as if he had read his thoughts. 'There's no point dwelling on the past, the mistakes our family made. It's not up to you to change it. Just be aware of what has happened before, so you don't make the same mistakes. The past only exists in the here and now.'

'Is that in your books?' Titus said wryly, raising his eyebrows at Marcus.

'Yes, and many other equally boring things,' his father replied with amusement. 'You'd far rather be sorting out this mission for Albus wouldn't you, so you can be off with this girl?'

Titus opened his mouth to agree and then shook his head. 'Sort of, but really I could not have come to Rome without seeing my father.'

His father nodded in gratitude. 'I'd like to meet your wife, bring her to see me some time.'

Ceinwyn would think his father was amazing.

'Is there any way I can help with the mission Albus sent you on?' his father asked.

Marcus spluttered the last of his tea. 'But you hate Albus!'

'I just want all of you to be out of this city as quickly as possible.'

'How can you help us?' Titus asked seriously.

'What are you doing for Albus? Actually,' he paused, 'let me guess. I'd imagine that you are doing intelligence work for him?'

Titus nodded.

'Good. Okay. You are trying to find his heir?'

Titus was completely taken aback, and then laughed incredulously. 'You're cold there! Albus doesn't have a child.' The gossip papers always hinted that Albus was desperate for a child to carry on the long and illustrious family name.

'Oh, he does,' his father said, suddenly sad. 'But he wishes he didn't. You know how Albus hates Slaves?'

Titus nodded.

'He hasn't always. When he was fourteen we believe he raped a Slave girl.'

'Who is this 'we'?'

'Oh. Just me, and some other interested academics; others who don't believe Albus' narcissistic propaganda.'

'Well, I think that's insane, and that's not my mission. I am meant to be finding the leader of Filii Aquilae.'

His father put his cup of tea down slowly, leant back in the chair, and stared up at the sun. 'Albus thinks that they are a threat to him?' He smiled at Titus. 'I can help you against them. They are just idiotic terrorists who live in the Imum.'

Titus grinned, pleased that his theory had been proved correct.

'A good friend of mine, a merchant in the Imum whose son goes to that school you saw me leaving earlier, had several tonnes of nitrogen fertiliser stolen from his van last week. He's a brave man, and he managed to trace the thieves himself, but strangely, the Praetorian guard have shown no interest in retrieving what was taken from him. They told him he was a 'victim of theft', but I wonder what a common thief would want with nitrogen fertiliser?'

'Thank you father,' Titus said rising to his feet and gesturing to Marcus.

'Just remember your end of this bargain. Get out as soon as you can. This place isn't really real, but your friends are real; that wife of yours is real. This foul Eternal City, and the money, power, glory? None of it really exists; it's just a fruitless voyage to achieve security. But,' he looked down at a selection of marks on the back of his hand that Titus couldn't place. 'What foolishness to chase that which we cannot attain.'

VI

'Oh Great Neptune, pour out your favour on Rome! Fill the Tiber, and water your people for eternity.'

Titus waited, with Marcus, outside the great temple of Neptune on the edge of the Circus Flaminius. The day was stiflingly hot still, but the breeze cooled him. Inside the temple, he could hear Albus declaring the start of the Neptunalia festival. It was Midsummer Day. Construction on the Aether roof had not reached here yet, but looking up he could see work continuing quickly; it would not be long before the Summus covered every inch of the Aether.

He thought of Ceinwyn, and how she had laughed at him this morning for heading to the Imum to work for Albus. She had said he should visit his father, as she was visiting hers. She had got her way in the end, by some strange work of chance.

'How long do we wait?' Marcus gasped, looking hungry and thirsty. Thirsty, Titus could understand, neither of them was used to the climate, but Marcus was always hungry and every year he got a little bigger. A man walked past with a tray of freshly cooked Lucanian sausage for sale, and Titus watched Marcus' eyes follow the platter hungrily.

Titus got up and started to walk towards the temple: Albus would want to know about their lead right away, and besides it was too hot to stand outside all day.

The interior of the temple of Neptune was dark and wonderfully cool. Titus could hear the sound of water gently lapping somewhere beyond him, and the sound soothed him. There was no incantation to Neptune currently; the ceremony seemed to have paused, and there was a gentle hum of conversation as he rounded the last of the pillars.

About fifty spectators, made up of what appeared to be senators and an assortment of important executives, sat on silk-coated chairs before the waist-deep Neptune pool. Beyond the pool, on a dais, stood Albus wearing his Pontifex Maximus head shawl, which marked him out as the High Priest to the gods. He was the first Consul to be allowed to hold the two most powerful roles in Rome simultaneously. A bull, restrained by ten men with thick ropes, gently struggled in the corner, all fight already extinguished.

The audience seemed restless. Albus was deep in conversation with somebody, and it was clear that the onlookers felt that he should be completing the ceremony instead, yet no one was brave enough to say so. Titus walked lightly to the side of the congregation and paused. The only path to Albus was the thin bridge that ran across the pool, directly in front of the audience. He shrugged; Albus had asked him to find Filii Aquilae and these people could wait.

As he started to cross the bridge the crowd muttered to themselves, but he ignored them. Ahead he could now make out whom Albus was speaking to in the gloom, and to his surprise, it was the Praetorian, Verres. Titus remembered how Albus had remarked that he had plans for a new bodyguard. Could he have appointed Verres? Titus hoped he had. Verres reminded Titus of how he had felt about Rome when he was young.

'Consul, I must insist we need to bolster the ranks—'

'No.' Albus' voice was calm, but firm.

'Public order is a major issue,' Verres continued brashly. 'Four of my men were beaten to death last night and dumped in the Tiber—'

Albus cut him off again. 'Then you need to train them to fight like men rather than girls.'

Verres laughed politely. 'With respect Consul, it's not their training that's the problem. There just aren't enough to protect against a riot. We haven't time to train enough, I see no other option but to—'

'Slaves will never stand shoulder to shoulder with Romans. I won't even have those animals in my household, let alone in my Guard.'

Albus said angrily. 'Do not worry yourself about public order Praetorian Verres, it is my primary concern, but it is also a temporary concern, and very soon it will be remedied.'

Verres turned to go, unable to argue further, and Titus took his chance to approach. Albus turned around to address the audience. 'Apologies for the interruption.'

'Oh, Titus. Good to see you,' he said half-heartedly, as he caught sight of him.

The crowd groaned.

Titus began to tell him of the lead they had about Filii Aquilae as Albus nodded. To Titus' growing frustration, he didn't really seem to be listening. Then he mentioned about the fertiliser that had gone missing and the fact that he was aware of its location.

'I don't see where this is going Titus,' Albus said quickly. 'Maybe tell me later. I need to start this ceremony properly before the bull bores itself to death.' Titus glanced over to the bull—it, just like the senators and executives, was glaring at him.

'They are going to make a bomb!' Titus hissed, irritated at himself for not managing to convey the urgency to Albus; surely Albus could see this was a serious threat? 'We need to move in, capture anyone there, prevent them making a bomb, and then hopefully learn from the people we capture where the leader is. Easy.'

It actually sounded easy. Then he could go home to Lugavalium; both he and Ceinwyn would be happy.

Albus seemed deep in thought, but then suddenly a smile crossed his face. 'Well done my friend!'

Titus beamed. The Consul of Rome, the man he had looked up to throughout his entire military career, was impressed. 'I'll investigate tonight, just me and my men.'

Albus shook his head firmly. 'No Titus, no. Leave this to me. I'll talk to Verres. He is heading up a new elite wing of the Praetorian Guard.'

'But Albus...'

'It's alright Titus, you can help them, but I want to give Verres a test. What do you make of him?'

Titus wondered what he was meant to say. He wasn't sure, so he just spoke from the heart. 'Verres is a true Roman.'

Albus suppressed a trace of a grimace. 'Perhaps', he muttered. 'But you, General, you are a true Roman. Let Verres blood himself, prove himself worthy. You—you spend a few more days in Rome.' He clapped him on the shoulder, laughed, and turned back to his irritated audience. Titus was dismissed.

The sun outside was dazzling compared to the dark interior of the temple of Neptune. Marcus was leaning against a pillar, tucking into a huge plate of sausage. He looked up at Titus guiltily, and Titus noticed him trying to suck his stomach in and push his chest out.

'Have you been working out?' he joked, walking up to Marcus and squeezing a saggy bicep.

'Not seen you lifting for a while, Titus,' Marcus said nonchalantly.

'Me? No, I was born this way...'

Marcus started to laugh, and Titus joined in.

'Rome,' Titus said as the pair sat down together on the warm stone outside the temple. 'I can't believe I've wasted so many years away from this place.'

'But it's horrible,' Marcus replied, to Titus' irritation, so like Ceinwyn. Perhaps Marcus would have been better suited to her after all?

'It's our City,' Titus replied. 'It's my family's city. Do you think Marcus, if I work for Albus enough, one day I might be able to stand up in the Senate and the name Labienus not be mocked?'

'Why do you care?'

'It's my name! And my father's. I could actually restore it!' He drew the battered golden circle of Valour from his pocket, won so many years ago, and carried everywhere still.

Marcus laughed again. 'Your father doesn't care about his name. Why should you?'

'But he should care,' Titus said bitterly. 'He spent his whole time writing, and not actually doing anything.'

'He seems happier than you do,' Marcus said shrugging and finishing off the last of the sausage.

Titus stared down at the stones. Infuriatingly Marcus was right, as he often was, but he could not let him see. How could you will yourself to be happy? He thought of Hispania. Hispania would make him happy, and Ceinwyn as well, when she came around to his way of thinking; when she saw the beaches and the food.

A bellow from inside the temple diverted their attention. They listened, as more bellows, and the sound of water frantically churning echoed from within. The bull was certainly not dying of boredom. Neptune would be most pleased.

VII

Ceinwyn giggled as Titus poured her another glass of wine. It was the most disgusting wine she had ever tasted, apparently it wasn't even made from grapes. It certainly didn't taste like it was, more like potatoes, or nettles even. She was feeling quite drunk, despite only drinking two glasses. At least she'd only partially inherited the genetic Slave defect that made it impossible for Slaves to drink alcohol.

'Wouldn't your old friend Albus provide you with some finer wine if you asked?'

'And waste this... delicious beverage, pilfered by Marcus, from the army barracks?' Titus joked. 'This palace life seems to be rubbing off on you.'

They were sitting out on their small balcony at a tiny wooden table, the thin silk curtains billowing like ghosts in the moonlight. The sun had set over three hours ago, and most of Rome was asleep, a whole level below them. The white marble of the growing Summus rose up around them, the domes and arches shining brightly. It was the best view in Rome, perhaps the best in the world. And it was theirs.

A Praetorian guard plodded slowly past, fifty feet below them, at the foot of the palace. Ceinwyn tipped the remnants of her wine glass over the edge of the balcony, giggling as some of them splashed off the Praetorian's black body armour. 'Sorry,' she laughed.

He looked up.

'She's a bit drunk,' Titus called casually.

The guard grunted and trudged on.

'Remember on our honeymoon when...' Titus began to reminisce about a night in the mountains, nearly a year ago now.

'This *is* our honeymoon,' Ceinwyn said. 'It's lovely,' she added sarcastically.

'Well, it's not *really*, is it? We were going to go to Capri. Perhaps when I've finished finding the Aquila...'

"Perhaps when I've finished finding the Aquila", she said in a mock version of his voice. "Marcus Albus and me go back a long way", she added grovellingly. 'Trust me,' she fixed Titus with her eyes and leant forwards so he could see her breasts swell against her thin top. 'I don't care if you find the Aquila—I want you just how you are.' She thought back to their first kiss, in that battered house Strabo had lent to him in Luguvalium, back when he was just a mercenary.

'I really will take you to Capri,' he said seriously.

'Will we have as much fun as that night in the mountains?'

'You mean when we...'

'Yes.'

They both laughed at the same time and hugged. Titus took a step back towards their room where their huge bed lay, waiting.

Ceinwyn pointed at the battered book that Titus had been reading before their meal and asked him what it was.

'Boring,' he said. 'My father lent me it, some sort of ancient political propaganda I think. Just over a thousand years old.'

'What's it about?' she replied, interested. She could hardly believe that people had been able to write a thousand years ago, let alone create a story.

'I'm not sure yet, I'm just at the beginning. So far, it's about a man called Varro who plots to overthrow his master because he isn't running their communal farm properly. They work hard for him, but get nothing in return. At the moment he's trying to get the other farmers to work with him.'

'Why do you think your father wants you to read it?'

'I've no idea. He's always wanted to overthrow Albus, maybe he sees himself as Varro!' Titus bellowed loudly at the idea, and Ceinwyn suddenly felt deeply sad. She loved her father, but Titus seemed to have no respect for his. She stared up at the stars. 'Is that your ancestral star?' she asked, pointing at what she thought was the constellation he had shown her a few months ago, when they still lived in Luguvalium.

Titus nodded, clearly pleased that she had paid attention. 'It's not just mine though, apparently everyone's ancestors go there.'

'Apparently?'

'No, not apparently. It's just bollocks.' He finished his glass of disgusting wine and poured another.

'Perhaps my mother is there?' Ceinwyn asked, curious.

'Perhaps,' he said half-heartedly.

Ceinwyn sighed. 'What do you believe Titus?'

'Nothing,' he sipped at his wine again and stared out at the building site at the far end of the Imum again. Ceinwyn followed his gaze, even at this late hour they were still working on the new Colloseum. 'Do you want to go to bed?' he asked hopefully.

'What about your gods?' she continued as if she had not heard him.

'It's stupid isn't it,' Titus replied. 'We all know it's a lie but we pile up possessions in front of them, and honour them. Even Albus honours them.'

'Albus makes the gods bow to him,' Ceinwyn replied. 'He uses them to build his support. He made himself High Priest, but really the gods serve him.'

Titus nodded. 'Impressive. Who told you that?'

Ceinwyn slapped his arm. 'And what makes you think I would not be able to see that myself?!'

'You've not been here long enough, you've not seen him speak in public, and you're not clever enough!' He kept his face completely serious for a moment before bursting out laughing. In retaliation, she stole an oily tomato from his plate and ate it. The oil dripped down onto her chin, and she saw him looking at her hungrily.

'But I don't disagree with you,' he continued, eating the last remaining tomato before she could get it. 'Albus, I think, does use the gods to control people. It's for the best though, better that than having to use the Praetorians.'

Ceinwyn shook her head at him with exasperation. She tried to remember that this was his home. He could not see how rotten it was.

'You don't *really* believe in nothing,' Ceinwyn said changing the subject.

'I don't believe in your God Ceinwyn, sorry, but I never will.'

'I don't mean that Titus,' she said earnestly. 'Perhaps one day your eyes will be opened, and you will, but that's still not what I mean. You see, you believe in yourself. You believe in your strength, and protecting your friends, and keeping us all safe. You're the bravest man I've ever met.'

Titus smiled and took her hand. They stood up together and looked out over Rome. A breeze rippled through her hair and she caught Titus staring at her. He flushed slightly, and then stared back up at the red giant in the Hunter's Belt.

'If the ancestral star does exist, then, one day, we will both be there.'

'Not for a long time husband,' Ceinwyn replied quietly.

'Whatever happens, it is good to know that,' he whispered in the gentle cool breeze. 'Whatever happens.'

'I love you.'

They kissed over the table and Ceinwyn expected his hands to start working away at the back of her dress, but they didn't. Instead Titus was still staring at the star.

'We can sit up there together on the edge of a plume of burning gas,' he said. 'And far away, we can watch our children, and their children, and their children's children. And then, in turn, one day, when they too grow old, they will come to us, and take their places beside us, for eternity, on the plume.'

'That's lovely,' Ceinwyn said.

'Shame it's just a ball of gas millions of miles away,' Titus said.

Ceinwyn laughed. 'We could start by sitting on a mountain and looking down at our children in Luguvalium. Actually,' she glanced at the bed, 'we could start by making one.'

Every part of her longed to just leave Rome now and start their life properly. If only Titus would just let his pride go, surely Rome could find another to serve it?

'One day your son could take over as Governor of Luguvalium,' she said hopefully.

'Or Hispania.'

Ceinwyn suddenly felt slightly sick. The wine was disgusting, and she was a bit drunk, but it was the realisation that Titus was seriously considering Albus' offer that shocked her.

Titus must have noticed because he reached over and took her arm. 'Only if you want my love,' he said reassuringly. 'Only if you want.'

'I want to go home,' she said, it sounded more imploring than she meant it to. She didn't quite know why she felt so strongly about this. If anything, Rome was really her home, but Rome had thrown her out, and she owed Rome nothing. The mountains, the lakes and with her father's people was where she belonged.

'Of course,' Titus said stiffly. 'We will go home then. I'll find this terrorist for Rome, and I'll refuse our reward. Then we will go home.'

Ceinwyn felt the warmth rise inside her again, and she finished her drink. 'Pour me another,' she said and stood up, leaning over the balcony. She arched her back slightly so that her bottom stood out tightly against her dress.

Titus put his arm around her and pressed the recharged glass into her hand. They knocked the bases of the glasses together and made eye contact for good luck before kissing again. Ceinwyn felt Titus' hand start to move down her back. She stared up into his eyes and put her free arm around his neck. 'Before we do anything like that Titus I need to ask you something.'

Titus nodded. His hand had reached her bottom now and was pressing her in towards him.

'If we are going to be staying here for a while then I am going to do some work for Rome too.'

Titus laughed. 'I'll have a chat with Albus, perhaps he can find something for you.'

'No,' Ceinwyn said mischievously, turning around so that he now hugged her around her tummy as she stared down onto the newly built streets below.

'My father has given me a mission,' she whispered over her shoulder. She felt his arms tighten slightly around her. She pushed her bottom backwards into him and heard him gasp quietly.

'I thought your father was a historian?'

She thought back to the year before, in Luguvalium. 'That was when you were a Roman, and I was a Slave. I didn't trust you. No, he's more than a historian—he's our leader.'

'What's his mission for you,' Titus said.

She could feel him against her and she started to wriggle slightly. 'I'll need your help,' she said.

'Whatever.' Titus said, as his hands started to lift up her dress.

She put her hands softly on his, holding them, and stopping him for a moment. 'My father wants me to find out how Albus' family have kept power for so many years.'

'Oh good. I already know that one, let's go to bed! They conquered everything, and then they gave us peace. It's everything the common Roman wants, except bread, and circuses of course, but we've had those on tap for years!'

Ceinwyn laughed. 'Seriously Titus, how does he keep it? No one seems happy with him.'

'But they vote for him.'

'So the vote must be fixed.'

Titus stopped pushing against Ceinwyn. 'I'd be very careful Ceinwyn. That's impossible, and treasonous, if anyone heard you...'

'It's not impossible,' she said shaking her head. 'I've heard about things like that happening in the past from my father. You can tamper with the votes in the ballot box, or you can prevent your rival's supporters from voting.'

'It's all done with the omniajunctus Ceinwyn,' Titus replied. 'It's a completely secure and independent process run and collated through the great omniajunctus servers beneath the Library of Apollo. He's just popular Ceinwyn, that's why he gets in every year.'

She shook her head. 'There's more to it Titus. He's a Slave murderer, we both know that. But he is a Tyrant too, and I'm going to prove it.'

'And I'm not going to stop you Ceinwyn, even though he is my friend, and you are wrong about him, but be very careful.'

'Will you help me?'

'I'll help you by proving to you that your suspicions are thankfully false. Start by going to the library. See where the omniajunctus was born, and where every single piece of data created by a scire is routed through and protected. There is no access to it, except by the librarians themselves. Then you will see how impossible your father's conspiracy theory is.'

'I'll go tonight,' she said, smiling mischievously at Titus.

'You will not,' he said, glancing at the bed.

She reached around and started to untie the straps at the back of her dress. 'Perhaps if I go like this, the librarians will give me a personal tour of the omniajunctus hub?' She let the dress slip to the ground and walked towards Titus slowly. She enjoyed the feel of the cool night air on her breasts and felt her nipples harden under it. His mouth fell open slightly as she reached him. It had been the right decision not to wear anything underneath the dress. She kissed him. 'Perhaps tomorrow,' she said, and led her husband to their bed.

VIII

Quintus woke to the sound of his bleep. He pulled out his scire angrily and called back the number.

'What?' he snapped, still half asleep.

'Good morning Decius.' The voice was calm, and edged with scorn.

Quintus' heart sank at the voice, it was the Archiatrus. His boss. He sat up quickly on the edge of the bed in the on-call room, at the other end of the Aesculapium to his ward. 'I've overslept sir, I'll be—'

'Whenever Decius, don't rush,' the man replied irritably. 'I don't mind. We have all started without you, again.'

Quintus' heart sank even further. It would have been better to have received a tirade of abuse now than to be humiliated on the ward round in front of many others. He hung up and kicked some of the empty beer cans away from the end of the bed; then he held his head in his hands. The word Decius kept flying around his head. It seemed wrong. Over the course of the last two weeks, he had had to get used to being called by his family name again.

There was a knock at the door.

A young medicus that Quintus had met a few times on the corridor put his head in. 'Decius! Have you been on call *again*?'

Quintus nodded. 'At least it keeps me busy.'

The boy looked around the unkempt room.

'Can I help you?' Quintus asked, standing up and starting to pull on his official ward round robes which lay draped over a pile of pizza boxes, they were starched white to protect from infection.

'Are you living here?' the boy asked with concern.

'Fuck off,' Quintus replied.

The boy looked surprised and went red as he backed off, closing the door.

Quintus sighed. How had his life come to this?

He thought of his fine house on the Caelian slowly being packed up, the contents being taken, bit by bit, to an even finer house, just completed, on the Summus. But it wasn't just his house. It was his to share with his wife Gaia, the most beautiful and eldest daughter of the Dolabella family, and her mother, father and younger brother. There was only one problem.

He didn't love Gaia.

That in itself was not insurmountable, he knew of many people who didn't love their spouse, yet they had children and carried on their family lines as they were expected to do. Gaia's father had been so pleased to have married his daughter off to a medicus, especially one who was about to take a prestigious internship at the Great Aesculapium in the centre of Rome, one of the few buildings that extended across both levels, the Aether and Imum. It was also one of the few buildings to stand as part of the wall surrounding the city; even the Summus didn't block out their sunlight.

But there was no internship now. He was a first year junior medicus again; his time working as a mercenary alongside Titus, apparently, had blunted his training.

He spat as he thought about the Archiatri, sneering at him, as they finished his interview and assigned him this job on a pittance of a wage. He was back to where he was a decade ago. His face burnt at what his father would make of this, if he had the spirit to tell him. However, he had a worse shame—the shame that prevented him from returning to Gaia, for she was really no wife to him at all. She was pretty, and he knew that many men had wanted her, but he could not bring himself to touch her. He had told her about his secret on their wedding night, when finally he was unable to maintain the pretence of protecting her innocence any longer. They had cried together all night, and he was sure that she had told her father—it was the way he looked at him, as if he was some sort of pervert, as if he was weak. He laughed at that, as he thought back to the men he had fought and killed. Loving men did not make you weak.

He sped down the corridor towards the Admissions Unit where the Archiatrus would be beginning his round with the rest of Quintus' team. He was finished with mercenary work now. He had wasted too much of his life with Titus and that half-breed that he called a wife. He was going to work his way up through the Aesculapium and make his father proud. Perhaps if he lost himself in work enough, he could even forget about Tiberius; Tiberius who he'd never managed to approach. Perhaps loving men *had* made him weak.

He hit the button for the levator. 'Come on!' he hissed at it angrily. An old lady wandered past slowly with her carer and looked at him quizzically as he cursed the levator again. *Where was the levator?* It was almost as if it was *trying* to get him into even more trouble.

He stamped his foot and ran to the stairs. Charging up them he came face to face with a young nurse from the next-door ward.

'Hi, Decius.'

'Hi,' he tried for a moment to remember her name, then he realised he didn't care.

The young nurse took a stylus out of her hair and used it as an excuse to pull her curls up, away from her face, and play with them. Quintus made some quick remark about being late and started up the stairs.

'Oh, Decius,' she called from below.

His heart sank.

'I was wondering if...'

'Yes,' he half turned back up the stairs, trying to show his hurry.

'If... you'd like to go to Lararium with me tomorrow? There's a big night, I heard you like music?'

Quintus liked it when Tiberius played music.

'Sorry... Look... I'm just really busy.' He knew deep down if he tried hard he could think of a really good excuse, but he couldn't be bothered; his career was on the line, and all this girl cared about was bagging a medicus.

'Oh...' she looked sad. 'Okay then.'

'See you,' he called over his shoulder and bounded up the stairs.

He entered the ward and jogged up to the back of the ward round, slowing his pace at the last minute to quieten his approach. Perhaps he could slip into the group and avoid a public rebuke. He joined the back and smiled at one of the nurses who returned the smile anxiously. The Archiatrus was slowly examining a patient.

Quintus slowed his breathing and tried to look calm. He tried to remember who the patient was. This was his ward; he should know all of this, but his mind wandered. This was all beneath him anyway, by now he should be in the Archiatrus' place. He had been a medicus for over a decade, he had seen things that were beyond anything this Archiatrus had dealt with in his privileged life here in Rome.

'Decius.' The Archiatrus' voice was old and weary, and Quintus felt even more contempt. 'What is wrong with this patient?'

'Simple sir, he has heart failure,' Quintus said quickly, proud that he had remembered the case. Now he needed to show off his knowledge, he could still salvage this day. 'The main ventricle has enlarged as a maladaptive method of trying to cope with the myocardial infarction he had three years ago,' he continued. 'The enlargement is counterproductive and actually makes the heart beat less effectively.' He felt proud, being allowed to show his knowledge to the whole ward round. He looked at the patient as he explained how the fluid, that was building up in his ankles and chest, was due to this process. The patient smiled at him, and Quintus' heart soared, even *he* was impressed.

'Very good.' The Archiatrus nodded. 'Now, Decius. Would you be so kind as to explain to me why he is not getting better, despite these diuretics he is on?'

'His kidneys, they are failing as well.'

'Again, very good. Why?' The Archiatrus fixed him with his penetrating stare. This was a good sign. He had heard that this Archiatrus would just ignore you if he thought you had no ability.

'Well, he's had a myocardial infarction. Vascular damage in one area suggests there will be vascular damage in other areas too. It's probably long term microvascular disease which has suddenly got worse.'

'Perhaps.' The Archiatrus nodded again, the nurse behind Quintus shifted uncomfortably. 'So then, what has suddenly made it worse since he has been on the ward?'

Quintus suddenly felt edgy, the whole ward round were looking at him. 'His heart has got worse, so presumably he hasn't perfused his kidneys as well as usual, so, perhaps he has developed acute renal failure from that?'

'You're right about the diagnosis, it's acute renal failure. In fact, he is going to need dialysis and thankfully for him he can afford it, but you are wrong about the cause.'

'Please enlighten me sir,' he said, trying not to sound too sarcastic. How could the Archiatrus know for sure the cause of this complex, multifactorial process? He was standing there, so smug, Quintus wanted desperately one day to see him humbled.

'Have a look at his drug chart.' The Archiatrus passed it to Quintus and walked to the next bay, the ward round trailing behind like a ceremonial parade.

Quintus scanned the chart. Just the usual sort of medication you would expect for a patient with heart failure. Then his eyes spotted what the Archiatrus was referring to. Suddenly he felt sick and the hairs on his back stood up. 'Shit,' he whispered quietly to himself, his voice hoarse.

He waited outside the bay for the Archiatrus to come out. 'Sir, he was in pain, I didn't think. It was the wrong thing to give him...'

'It's been a long time since you went to the medicus school isn't it, Decius?'

Quintus went red. 'Yes, but with respect I've learnt a lot during my last decade—'

'Not enough,' the Archiatrus interrupted. 'If you are going to work on my ward then you need to remember basic medicine, not prescribe diclofenax to people who have no heart muscle left and shrivelled useless kidneys.'

Quintus opened his mouth to retort back. The Archiatrus was right, he had made a mistake, but the Archiatrus' mistake was to fail to see the extra things Quintus could bring to the ward. *Did he not realise how much trauma medicine he had learnt working alongside Titus?*

His bleep went off again.

Suppressing the silent curse that jumped to his lips, he waited for the lecture to continue.

'Go and answer it Decius,' said the Archiatrus, trailing his retinue down the ward to the next patients.

He wandered over to the ward scire dejectedly, one of the nurses at the desk tried to give him an encouraging smile, but he scowled back at her. How dare she pity him.

'Good morning, is that Medicus Decius?' The voice was informal and youthful. It couldn't be from any of the other wards in the Aesculapium.

'No, not interested in becoming a locum,' he said, knowing it was yet another rep from a locum agency. *How did they get his number?*

'Medicus, give me a second if you can. This isn't perhaps quite the job you expect that we are offering?'

'Really? Let me guess.' Quintus took a breath and prepared his most sarcastic voice. 'I imagine that you are going to be offering me fifty denarii an hour to work in a dead end job, completely unrelated to my capabilities, where the only person who will hate me more than my colleagues, who will be earning half what I will and do twice the work, will be me, for selling out and ending my career before it has even begun.'

He waited for the click as the rep put the scire down. They always put the scire down. But it didn't come.

Instead the rep laughed. 'You sound like just the person we are looking for! I'm phoning from *Coniunctus*. We are a new innovative scire hardware and software company. Our work is... a bit confidential, but essentially its scire-human interface stuff. We need medici to work with us.'

'In what way?' Quintus asked, interested.

'Implanting mainly, but research too if that's your thing.'

'I'm pretty busy,' Quintus said. 'Let me think about it.' The ward round had nearly got round half the ward by now, he'd have so much work to catch up on.

'Well, that's fine medicus. Give us a call back. I'll message my number to you. Oh... I forgot to mention. The Senate is giving us special dispensations at the moment, so that means you'd start on one hundred denarii an hour, and when you return to your Aesculapium the Senate will make sure you don't return to ward level.'

Quintus opened his mouth to speak, wanting to accept right away now. It didn't sound like real medicine, but it would get him higher up, and then he could practise real medicine in a year or too without the interference of the Archiatri.

'Okay, I'll do it.' He waited with trepidation, perhaps they would want to interview him? He wasn't great at interviews. But the line was dead; he'd have to wait for the message. With a heavy heart, he rejoined the round.

'Okay, Decius, time to redeem yourself,' the Archiatrus said grimly. 'Name me eleven causes of pancreatitis.'

It was going to be a long morning.

IX

Ceinwyn caught a glimpse of her reflection in the glass outside the Great Library of Apollo; habit now forced her to stop and examine her face carefully. She moved closer and quickly examined her left cheek, making sure that no trace of the signum was visible through the make-up. The disguise was perfect, although it made Ceinwyn sad that she no longer had any visible freckles. Her long, curly, copper coloured hair still framed her face well though, and she supposed she still looked pretty like this, but she wasn't herself.

The library seemed remarkable to Ceinwyn. The building was modern, all glass front, but with concrete pillars carefully disguised as ancient pillars, to reflect the heritage. This was meant to have been the first library in Rome. It was meant to be almost two millennia old, but like many structures, the original building must have been destroyed to make way for the modern construction. It made her sad to think of ancient history being destroyed.

She pulled her shoulder bag closer in towards her as the doors glided open silently. Inside there was complete silence, and she had a sudden and irritating urge to cough. The atrium was huge. Each wall of the gigantic circle was covered by bookcases on three levels; despite the levels, you would need a ladder to reach any book more than a quarter of the way up any bookcase. A few people sat at tables in the centre of the room, leafing through the books. Flitting around silently, with slippered feet, moved the Guardians. They knew everything about every book in the library, which meant they knew everything about every book in the world.

A banner above the central desk advertised tickets for the 'Omniajunctus Experience'.

'I want to see the omniajunctus,' she said, yawning. It had been a long night.

The Guardian behind the desk nodded. 'Two denarii,' he whispered, and Ceinwyn realised that she had spoken too loudly. 'You've come at a good time,' he continued. 'It's half price in the mornings.'

He gestured towards a holding area where a young couple stood, the only others waiting for this particular tour. She wandered towards them, staring up at the beautiful domed ceiling, half the height of the building and made entirely of a single sheet of glass. It seemed impossible that men could create such a thing.

'Students?' she asked the couple, who shook their heads.

'Holiday,' the young man replied with a heavy accent, explaining that they were from Gaul.

The Guardian at the desk gestured silently to another Guardian, who glided over to them and swept his arms towards the door behind. The couple held hands, and Ceinwyn followed behind thinking of Titus. At least he hadn't been against her investigating her father's suspicions, but she would have rather had him here helping her. He had been so restless over the last week, and Ceinwyn knew it was because his lead against Filii Aquilae had not been followed up. She had tried to persuade him to leave Rome again, but he had refused; he had been given a responsibility that he felt he must discharge, but he couldn't see that he owed Albus nothing. She hated arguing so much that she felt like giving up about it altogether, and she probably would have done if she hadn't been so desperate to leave.

As Ceinwyn passed under a great arch of cables, and into the first room of the exhibition, she resolved to try to see the best in temporarily remaining in Rome. She had her own mission, her father trusted her, and she wasn't going to let him down. Somewhere, in this very building, lay the hub that controlled the omniajunctus. If her father was right, Rome was being controlled somewhere just under her feet.

Now that he was out of the main library the Guardian was able to speak, and Ceinwyn was surprised at how strong his voice was for someone whose job it was to flit around silently and retrieve books.

'The omniajunctus will soon be a century old.' He began to tell them the story of its creation as Ceinwyn looked around at the exhibits on display—she wasn't interested in these old scires, she wanted to get down to the hub room that Titus had mentioned. She shifted her weight from foot to foot impatiently, but the Guardian either didn't notice or didn't care. This was the moment of the day when all attention was on him, rather than the books, and he clearly enjoyed it as he theatrically detailed how the Consuls had handed over responsibility for the 'most powerful weapon in the world,' to the Guardians.

The next room detailed the work to lay cable to the great server room. Ceinwyn yawned and watched the young couple enviously.

Finally, they started down the corridor that led to the server room itself. As they reached the end, the Guardian stopped the three of them and lined them up, before ceremoniously searching them. As he patted his hands up Ceinwyn's sides, he smiled at her disturbingly, she gave him an off-putting frown, and his hands stayed well away from her breasts.

Now searched, the three were allowed to approach the doors at the end of the corridor. Slowly they lifted, and Ceinwyn half-expected dry ice smoke to billow out from underneath. At least they were trying to give her two denarii's worth of fun. The couple certainly seemed to be enjoying their trip at least.

There was no dry ice, but there were more Guardians, armed with sonifi. The young couple gasped at the sight, and Ceinwyn remembered that sonifi were banned in Rome. The only people allowed to carry them were the Guardians—to reflect the importance of the omniajunctus never falling into enemy hands.

The group were ushered in, past the guards, and Ceinwyn was at last able to see the server room. It was even larger than she had expected. Great cables hung from the ceiling and snaked around the walls, and the room was bathed in a faint blue light from their fibre-optics. Cameras stared down at them, monitoring their every move, and around the room, the Guardians moved slowly in an endless parade.

Ceinwyn thought of what her father had said, that the elections must be rigged. If he was right then the answer had to lie here, in this room. There would be no other way to control the vote, but the Guardians were not controlled by the state, and they had the key to the elections safely locked down. She thought quickly, perhaps later she could call Cyric, her old friend in Luguvalium who knew more about machines and technology than her, and ask him if there was any other way for the Senate to control the omniajunctus if they did not control the hub. However, if Titus was right, then everything she did was probably being monitored, *how could she have that scire call secretly?*

As she thought frantically, a realisation slowly dawned on her.

She was cold.

She looked around at the ceiling stretching up nearly a hundred feet above her, row upon row of high stacks of servers and cables humming loudly. *All of the omniajunctus data created in the world came through here.*

There was a small shaft in the ceiling, but no other ventilation. So how could it be uncomfortably cold down here? She walked over towards the nearest server bank and put her shoulder bag down on it heavily. A hollow clank rang out throughout the chamber and all of the Guardians stopped and looked at her.

'Sorry,' she said disarmingly, reaching into her bag and pulling out a hairbrush with which she started to comb her hair, trying to make herself look as empty headed as possible.

'Move away,' the nearest Guardian ordered, gesturing at her with his sonifex. She picked up her bag ensuring that her hand brushed the metal of the server. It was as cold as the walls of the library. At the same time as she picked it up, she glanced down and spotted a gap between the wall and the server. Wedged in the gap was one of many dust coated speakers—the source of the humming? She backed away and apologised again to the Guardian, who shook his head at her in exasperation as he continued his ceremonial patrol.

The tour leader Guardian, glanced at her suspiciously, decided that they had spent long enough in the server room, and beckoned them to return to the library. Ceinwyn's mind worked furiously. Where was the real omniajunctus hub? Had the Guardians put up a sham one to protect the hub? Or were they not as impartial as they were meant to be?

The tour leader sidled up to her as they walked back and Ceinwyn seethed with irritation, the glare from earlier had clearly not been enough.

'I need to talk to you.'

'I'm married,' she said bluntly.

The Guardian shook his head at her. 'Foolish girl! I'm not interested in that, we have vows,' he said quickly, hurrying her back into the atrium and gesturing for her to follow him into a small office. The couple from Gaul wandered away, and Ceinwyn was alone with the Guardian.

Ceinwyn looked around for a good escape route; did these Guardians carry sonifi too? She couldn't be sure. She resolved that if she were captured she wouldn't mention her father, no matter what they did to her.

The Guardian looked around quickly, making sure no one was watching, and Ceinwyn noticed that he was sweating. He looked more afraid than she was. He shut the door to the office in a hurry and gestured for Ceinwyn to sit on the ground, so that she was beneath the line of sight from the windows.

'How did you know?' he asked shakily.

Ceinwyn shook her head, but she was terrified.

'Okay, don't say anything,' he said trying to stay calm. 'I don't work for the Praetorians though and I'm probably the only person here who can help you.'

'How do I know what?' Ceinwyn asked.

'That the server room is a sham. You suspected, you saw our deception,' the Guardian replied nervously.

'What do the Praetorians have to do with this?' Ceinwyn asked, relaxing slightly as she realised she was not being interrogated. 'Did they create the fake server room?' she asked.

The Guardian shook his head. 'No,' he whispered. 'We did that, decades ago: to protect it. The real thing should not be on view to tourists!'

'So where is it?' Ceinwyn asked.

The Guardian paled again and shook his head. 'In the Library of Apollo, where it's always been.'

Ceinwyn was puzzled. They were already in the library. Then she understood.

'This isn't the original library is it? Where is the old one?'

'Where all the original buildings are in Rome,' he replied looking down at the ground.

Ceinwyn realised he meant the Imum, the original layer of Rome.

'Whoever you are, please help us,' the man said, shaking.

'From the Praetorians?'

The Guardian looked around, clearly still worried someone could be watching them, even in this tiny hidden office. 'They moved in last year, they killed my son. They said that they would... kill my wife. I had to obey them, despite my oath. Take these,' he passed her his set of keys. 'I don't know who you are, but please, whoever you work for, help us. The omniajunctus is more important than any of us. Find the room at the centre of the Library. There is a levator in the centre that will take you up to the main servers around the walls. All the proof you need is there.'

Ceinwyn took the keys and stood up. The Guardian opened the door a crack, ensured no one was watching, and let Ceinwyn leave first. As she crossed the floor of the atrium again, her heart beat faster in her chest. She headed for the levator. Pressing the call button, she stood there nonchalantly looking up at a series of books documenting the medical differences between Slaves and Romans. She laughed inwardly as she thought about how the Guardian with the key would not have imagined she could have the ability to help in any way at all, had he realised that she was half Slave and half Roman. Her father was able to create a scire virus to defeat that which Marcus Albus had created to keep himself in power, yet her father was apparently not even human in the eyes of Romans.

The levator opened and a Guardian exited. Ceinwyn reached up, pulled down a book and pretended to study its cover.

'Servus Animalis!' the Guardian exclaimed, impressed at her choice of reading material. She smiled at him, imagining the concealed blade she had in her bag cutting into his smug face.

As soon as the Guardian had passed, she darted through the gap in the closing levator doors. There were four buttons on the panel, ground, middle, upper, and a blank one with a key hole. She inserted the Guardian's key and turned it. The levator started to descend, gathering speed and leaving her stomach behind.

She reached into her bag and brought out the small camera; her father would need evidence of the Senate controlling the omniajunctus. She reached into the lining and brought out the thin knife Titus had given her. He had been training her to use it. She tucked it into her pocket, still in its sheath, which she left unbuttoned.

The levator came to a halt and the door opened. She exited into a brightly lit tunnel of exposed bare metal; in the distance was a faint hum. She moved forwards slowly, there was no noise apart from the hum. She remembered the slippered feet of the Guardians, and imagined how easily they could creep up on an intruder. She would need to stay vigilant.

After a hundred yards, the metal corridor ended at a window. She paused and looked out. Ten feet away, across a gap, lay the rotting facade of an ancient building. Rank air blew in from the window stinging her eyes, and a makeshift, exposed bridge linked the building she was currently in with the original Library of Apollo. She stepped out onto the bridge and immediately regretted looking down.

Fifty feet below lay the streets of the Imum. Curri rumbled beneath her feet, sending their thick fumes up to Ceinwyn who coughed at the stench. The people walking alongside the roads wore no masks and Ceinwyn wondered how they managed to survive. It was no wonder that life expectancy in the Imum was twenty years less than that of Aether dwellers. A roaring sound from behind alerted her to a volacurrus, which swept by, just under the bridge and onwards towards a roof portal, the purple flash from its plasma engines illuminating the side of the rotting Library. A gust of foul wind from the volacurrus' wake buffeted her as she crossed the divide between the two buildings, and she ducked through the opening into the Great Library gratefully.

The brick here was ancient, crumbling at her touch, and the corridor was dark. The smell of damp permeated the air as she descended the gantry before her. A spiral staircase went off to the left. It was partially blocked off but Ceinwyn clambered over the obstruction. She pulled out her scire, and used the light from it to descend the rotten stone steps, damp with centuries of condensation.

She crept down slowly and came out into what appeared to be an abandoned storage tunnel full of row upon row of decomposing books, which were stacked high against the walls in piles that teetered, threatening to rain down upon Ceinwyn. She tiptoed forwards silently. Up ahead somewhere was the omniajunctus hub, and the evidence she needed.

The corridor ended in complete darkness. Ceinwyn felt like she had stepped out into complete nothingness; a huge never-ending cave. The smell inside was grotesque: a combination of mildewed walls, ancient books, and something sickly which Ceinwyn couldn't place. She stepped forwards apprehensively. The beam from her scire cast light for only a few feet into the dark, moist air.

After walking for just over a minute, a horrible realisation overtook her. *How would she ever retrace her steps in this complete darkness?* The thought of being trapped here sucked at her stomach, and her chest felt heavy as she breathed. She turned around and stood completely still, trying to control her breathing. Then, walking quickly, hand outstretched, she tried to walk in a perfect opposite of her outward path.

After another minute, she realised she must have missed the entrance to the cave and she began to panic. Her pace quickened, and she nearly dropped her scire. Her breathing was coming too quickly. Her fingers started to tremble. Suddenly a wall loomed out of the darkness in front of her. She placed her hand on its dank, filthy surface and smiled at the slight security it gave her.

She began to edge around. The sickly smell was stronger now. An opening appeared. *The door*—she thought, and darted towards it, but it was low and she had to stoop. Then, with a growing sense of dread, she realised she was still lost. She ducked under the entrance, continuing to crouch so that she could move forwards. The smell was disgusting. Ceinwyn stretched the scire further out in front of her, but she could not yet see whether this low room led anywhere.

Her foot stepped on a large, round object that gave suddenly under her weight with a soft crunch. She lifted up her foot, and felt wetness up the side of her ankle as she did so. The sickly smell, which permeated this whole area, suddenly intensified. She pointed the light from her scire downwards and gasped with shock and disgust—she had trodden on a rotting skull. She lifted her foot up quickly and took a step backwards. Crouching low and shining the scire all around, she could make out three bodies here, wearing the dress of the Guardians. The bodies were in an advanced state of decomposition, as the Guardian had said, the Praetorians had taken control of this area last year. *Perhaps this was all that was left of the Guardian's son?* Ceinwyn wanted to take these bodies out and ensure they were buried, but she had a mission first, and if it was successful, she knew that the souls of these dead Guardians would be pleased at the part their deaths had played in the fall of Marcus Albus and his dictatorial Senate. For now, she was more convinced than ever that the elections were a sham. She took a photo of the bodies. Along with the other photos she planned to take, showing the hub controlled by Praetorians, this would help prove the conspiracy to the ordinary Romans. But, most of all, she wanted to prove it to Titus. She shook her head angrily as she thought of how he would not believe anything, unless the evidence was put clear in front of his eyes.

She backed out of the low room and into the huge chamber. She followed the wall, bolder now that she had found something to use to keep her bearings. Eventually she came to a section where the wall jutted out slightly. Raising her scire up high she read the inscription above, 'Scientia est Potentia'—'*Knowledge is Control*'. Beneath the inscription was an ornate, partially ajar, door.

This area was not a cave, Ceinwyn realised. It was the original Great Atrium, a mirror image of the one she had been standing in twenty minutes ago, except bathed in darkness and death, rather than light and wisdom.

She slid through the gap in the doors and turned off her scire's light. Bulbs every twenty feet lit the corridor ahead dimly. They had been badly drilled into the old marble, and whoever had done it had had no interest in preserving the building. A cluster of large holes in the wall caught Ceinwyn's attention; leaning in closer she realised they were from sonifex rounds.

Tiptoeing, she reached the end of the corridor. The light was stronger here. The corridor opened up, into a circular passage, which had clearly been completely gutted when the Praetorians attacked it. The ground was dotted with shattered marble, bundles of cable, and in places the inner wall had been torn away, revealing glimpses of the room inside. Ceinwyn glanced in, but could make out little; whoever had set the bulbs up had not illuminated the inner room.

She continued around the corridor, constantly watching her step over the bundles of torn cable. Any noise could betray her in this silence. Eventually she reached the entrance to the inner room, and taking a deep breath, she walked in.

It was extremely dark. There were great gouges in the floor, as if massive objects had been dragged across it. The room was cold and silent. *Where was the omniajunctus hub?* She walked forwards and collided with a metal structure, knocking her head. Cursing silently as she rubbed her head, she began to examine it. It was the levator the Guardian had mentioned. She was in the centre of the hub. She broke into a great grin.

She looked around for the great servers, her camera ready. She needed more light. Reaching around on the levator gantry, she found a switch which she flicked. Lights from the gantry flickered on, and the open levator slowly ascended, with Ceinwyn on it. As the levator rose higher, and light from below began to illuminate the walls, Ceinwyn put her hand to her mouth and gasped with surprise. She looked around quickly but she could not believe, nor understand, what she was seeing. For the omniajunctus hub was not under Praetorian control after all. It was gone. The walls were covered in great scars where the servers had been pulled down, and the ends of broken fibre optic cables loomed out eerily, like the heads of patient eels waiting to strike. Far below, she could see similar devastation on the floor itself. She reversed the switch on the levator, taking photos on the way down too, although she could see little use for them. *What did this prove?* Now it seemed that nobody had any control over the omniajunctus.

As she stepped off the levator she realised, with fear, that powering the levator had caused other lights to go on too. Now ahead of her, opposite to the way she had come in, she could see that a gantry ran gently uphill in the direction that she had originally entered. She wished now, knowing that the place was deserted, that she had just followed that gantry down here rather than using the spiral staircase and traversing the great hall with its decomposing bodies.

She reached the top of the gantry quickly, unsure of whether turning the lights on would alert anyone upstairs to her presence here. She dashed back across the bridge, noticing a small demonstration down below in the Imum led by a tall bald man. Black flags were being swung, and many of the Imum dwellers looked desperate and angry. *'Give us power'*, was the chant, and at first Ceinwyn wondered why the lowest people in Rome would even think to ask for such a thing. Then she realised that they must mean electricity.

Apparently, over the last six months, there had been rolling power cuts in the Imum, and her father believed they would come to the Aether soon. Ceinwyn couldn't believe that a city as powerful as Rome could struggle to obtain enough power. Her father told her that the mines in Dacia were running out of coal. Ceinwyn wondered what would happen in the Aether if they started having power cuts, in addition to having their natural light cut off. Albus was perhaps not as safe as he believed in his palace in the clouds she thought, as she ran lightly up towards the levator.

To her horror, the door began to open as she approached. In a fraction of a second she considered her options. She had dressed in simple clothes and fitted in, just as she had planned, as a student. She also had her knife. The Guardian would hopefully just throw her out.

Then, as the doors opened, to her surprise, out stepped a Praetorian. Ceinwyn resisted the urge to take a photo, it would prove nothing, and of course, it would be guaranteed to get her killed. Instead, she thought of her mother, slowly starving as her desperate father tried to find enough food for her. The tears came almost immediately.

'Thank the gods!' she exclaimed and reached out as if to hug the guard. 'How do I get out of this horrible place?' She wiped her tear stricken eyes with her sleeve, smudging her make-up slightly to add to the effect, but being careful to avoid smudging her cheek where her signum lay under the layer of concealer. She looked up at the Praetorian imploringly.

'You shouldn't be down here,' he said angrily, grabbing her wrist. 'What are you doing down here?'

'I got lost,' Ceinwyn cried. 'I was looking for a history of the invasion of Britannia, but—'

'Stop,' the Praetorian shook his head. 'I don't really give a shit, to be honest, why you came down here. You're not the first idiot student to not be able to read a map.' He paused and took a long look at her before continuing. 'I need to search you, and then,' the way he said it suggested the search would take a long time, 'once I am satisfied that you have not been stealing from the library. Then you can go.'

The Praetorian took off his helmet, and Ceinwyn saw that he was in his fifties and hadn't shaved for several days. He looked more like the sort of drunk you would find under a road bridge in the Imum than someone paid to keep order.

'Give me that bag,' he said, gesturing at it with his fasces.

Ceinwyn reluctantly parted with it, wondering whether he would look at the pictures on the camera. However, she didn't need to worry, he had only the most cursory look within the bag.

'Right, better search you then,' he said swaggering over. 'What's under your top?'

'Sorry?' Ceinwyn asked incredulously.

The Praetorian fixed her with his stare. 'What is under your top?' he repeated slowly.

'Nothing.' She said firmly.

'That's not what it looks like from here,' the Praetorian letched, staring at her breasts. He leant forwards and put his black, armoured hands on her hips. 'Put your arms out to the sides, I need to search you.'

Ceinwyn did as he asked. At least her ruse seemed to have worked. His hands patted firmly up to her armpits and then travelled back down slowly. Ceinwyn fidgeted uncomfortably as his hands intentionally stroked the edges of her breasts. She thought about reaching for the knife, but she had never killed with it before. It would be safer to endure a small amount of this than risk her life.

His hands reached her hips again and patted down her trousers to the pockets. Ceinwyn's pulse quickened and her breath came faster. *If he found the knife...*

The searching stopped, and Ceinwyn realised that the Praetorian was completely engrossed in the movement of her chest as she breathed.

'Take it off,' he said hoarsely.

'What?' Ceinwyn asked, outraged.

'You heard me, take it off,' the Praetorian repeated angrily. 'How can I be sure you haven't got stolen pages in your bra?' he added, seemingly as an afterthought.

Ceinwyn took a deep breath and pictured the structures underneath the Praetorian's neck as Titus had taught her. She could see the pulse of the internal carotid, pulsing faster with his excitement, and beside that would lie the jugular vein. Either would lead to almost immediate, fatal blood loss. She nodded to the guard.

'Okay sir,' she fluttered her eyelids. 'I'm so pleased you are here, it was so scary being down here all alone,' she said softly, and lifted her top up over her head slowly.

The Praetorian smiled and came in closer. 'And the trousers.'

She smiled. 'Whatever you say sir.'

Her left hand went to the button at the centre of the waistband, and she moved her right to sit over the pocket, just above the knife. She unpopped the button. The Praetorian was staring at her hand. She moved her right hand into her pocket slightly, as if to ease the trousers down. The Praetorian reached down to help her. This was the moment.

She pulled the knife out of its sheath, and as she did so, she kicked up hard into the Praetorian's groin. The body armour there was just padding, and her kick was hard and well directed. The guard groaned and fell to his knees. Ceinwyn stabbed in with the blade, aiming for the pulse point in his neck. The guard screamed as Ceinwyn sawed the blade about desperately. Blood sprayed across her chest, dying her light green bra a purplish colour. Then the scream was suddenly cut off as blood spurted out of the Praetorian's mouth; she must have cut through the carotid and the windpipe she realised, feeling sick. She pulled the knife out and stepped back.

The Praetorian fell to the ground, clutching at his throat, and hissing between bouts of blood gushing from his mouth. His eyes were wide and terrified. Ceinwyn stepped forwards and put her hands on either side of his head, just like Titus had taught her. Her hands shook. The Praetorian tried to fight with her weakly; *didn't he realise she was trying to end his suffering quickly?* She let go. She couldn't do it. Sobbing, she pulled her top back on quickly before rebuttoning her trousers and, grabbing her bag from the floor, jumped back into the levator. The Praetorian crawled one step towards her, before collapsing face down on the metal gantry.

Ceinwyn examined her face in the reflective metal of the levator as it travelled upwards. She was pale, but there was miraculously no tell tale trace of blood on her face. She wiped her right hand down the inside of her trousers to clean it as best she could. She looked dishevelled, but there was nothing to show that she had just murdered a man.

She felt sick as the full realisation of what she had done hit her. A man, albeit a horrible one, had until a moment ago been alive; he might even have a family. Now he was dying alone, or already dead, because of her.

Tears came to her eyes again, but she rubbed them away. She would not shed tears for Roman scum. She knew that what she had done was right, and she had a feeling that she would have to do similar things in the future. The feeling made her feel strong.

The levator opened, and she strolled out nonchalantly across the atrium. None of the Guardians seemed to notice her, and none of the students looked up from their books. Every part of her wanted to run, but she made her feet keep their slow, casual, pace. The door to the outside world slid open silently, and she stepped out into the bright midday light. She ran now, across to the fountain at the other side of the street, where she washed her hands. They looked clean, but when she closed her eyes she could still see the Praetorian's blood splashing across them and hear the sounds of his throat as she sawed at it.

She smiled grimly. She was working for her father now.

X

Marcus watched as Antonius picked up his cards, dropping one in the process and nearly revealing it to the rest of the table. Perhaps the drink was getting to him, Marcus wondered, but a careful examination of the empty bottles surrounding his friend showed that he had had no more than Marcus had. Marcus' head pounded, and all he wanted was to go back to the dormitory and sleep, but Antonius was not like him, this amount of drink wouldn't have touched the sides. He was just a clumsy oaf, a clumsy foolish oaf, who somehow was extraordinarily talented at cards.

Marcus looked down at his own cards, a four and an eight unsuited. He sighed and folded his hand. He had once been told, many years ago by a Cornicen in the army, to only play a hand if you held at least one ace. Tiberius told him that he folded too many hands, and that people would be able to notice this and read him as the game went on, but he reckoned he won games more often than Tiberius did, so the Cornicen's advice was probably right, even if it was a little boring. The three legionaries they were playing with stared contemptuously as he pushed the cards back to the middle.

Marcus had lost count of the number of hands they had played now, but he had not lost count of how much money they had lost. They were being paid again, for the first time in over a decade, but he doubted whether when their next weekly salary came in it could cover the losses made in this game. Tiberius caught his eye and smiled grimly. It had been his idea to play tonight. Marcus cursed him under his breath. His mind turned to Ceinwyn, as it often did. Perhaps if he could save up whilst he was here, then back in Luguvalium he could start a business, make something of himself...

He stopped himself, made himself picture another girl at his side, but he didn't know what this imaginary girl looked like. He tried to paint her in his mind, his arm around her back, the two of them standing outside an old stone house—theirs, on a cliff by a distant sea. But her hair kept cascading in crimson, intense, forbidden waterfalls over his skin. He shook his head and waited for the next hand. The hopeless dream was going to come to nothing anyway if they gambled all their money away.

Antonius burped loudly and knocked over his bottle which shattered on the stone floor. A veteran, in the corner of the bar, tutted at them and turned back to staring into the dregs of a well-nursed drink.

'It's your play you drunk cunt,' one of the three legionaries muttered to Antonius. The three men looked no different to the sort of cutthroat you would find hanging around the lower canals of the Imum, Marcus thought, wondering why the army was recruiting people like this. Every day more fresh recruits seemed to pour into the barracks. Having spent so much time and money disbanding most of the armies ten years ago, it seemed pointless to be scraping rogues like these off the streets and making them take oaths that meant nothing to them.

Antonius waved his hand at them angrily. 'I need to look at my cards first.'

He lifted them up and looked at them again; was this the third time? Marcus had lost count. The legionary thumped his fist down on the table in irritation. Antonius picked up the correct amount of sestertii to match the blinds and threw it haphazardly into the centre of the table.

'I've raised you!' Tiberius chipped in angrily, disgusted. 'Just fold already and we can move on.' Judging by his expression, Marcus reckoned Tiberius was ready to give up, cash out what few chips he had, and drink the small amount of money that would bring in. He had never seen him undermine Antonius in a game of cards before.

Antonius fixed him with a glare and pushed all his chips into the centre of the table.

'All in then,' he said pugnaciously, staring around at the others at the table. 'If you can beat pocket aces.' He was so drunk that the word *aces* sounded like *arses*, and the three legionaries all burst out laughing. Then they looked at each other hungrily. Marcus had suspected they had been playing as a team, and now their deception was clear.

'Call,' they said, one after another, pushing chips forward to match Antonius, who was the only one out of he, Marcus, and Tiberius with a decent stack of chips remaining. Not that that mattered Marcus thought, he was about to lose them all. *How had Antonius managed to get drunk off just that?* It came to his mind that one of the legionaries might have slipped some sort of drug into one of the drinks. He glanced at them suspiciously. No, they didn't look anywhere near clever enough for that.

Then he noticed something that surprised him, Tiberius no longer looked forlorn. However, at the same moment that Marcus spotted him smirking, he slipped back into a picture of abject despair. 'Fuck this,' he muttered, got to his feet, and threw his cards back into the middle before storming off to the bar.

The legionaries laughed and looked at Antonius. 'Hope you can afford all those chips we lent you lad,' one said.

'We always get paid eventually,' another chipped in.

'In knees, elbows, that sort of thing, but we prefer cash,' the third added flipping his cards over to reveal a suited king and ten. The other two men whistled at the decent hand.

Out of the other two there was a pair of jacks, and a nine and ten suited. Marcus shook his head. Antonius was the sort of player who would go all in on anything if the mood took him, so Marcus confidently expected a two and seven in separate colours.

'Hang on,' Antonius said, slurring his words. 'I need to finish this.' He reached down to his side and picked up his jug of dark wine. He sipped slowly, clearly savouring the flavour, and then wiped his mouth with the back of his hand.

'Okay then,' he said calmly and flipped over his cards—revealing, as he had broadcast earlier, a pair of aces.

Tiberius came over from the bar and looked over the heads of the three legionaries at the table. 'Ooh,' he exclaimed. 'I'm glad I folded that one,' before walking over to a corner table, around which he arranged three chairs. One of the legionaries turned over the five table cards, one after another, cursing as he turned over a further ace to match Antonius'.

Antonius grabbed at the chips in the middle of the table, scooping them into a drinks tray. Marcus laughed with surprise—this was a month's wages at least!

'Hang on,' one of the legionaries said accusingly, grabbing at Antonius' sleeve. 'You don't look that drunk anymore?'

'You don't look like you've just met each other either,' Tiberius retorted from across the bar as Antonius finished collecting up their ill-gotten winnings.

As Antonius turned to take the chips across to the landlord, to exchange them for a small fortune, the legionnaire grabbed his arm again.

'Give us it back, you cheating fuck!'

Antonius just stared; he was a man of few words. Marcus watched as he swung the tray into the legionnaires face, following it up with a brutal overhand cross that landed in the centre of his collarbone. Marcus heard the bone shatter as the man collapsed back onto the floor, cradling his left arm, screaming.

Marcus stepped forwards to help, he wanted to jump in to the fray, but his cowardly body wouldn't let him. Besides, Antonius could easily handle three assailants on his own. One of the two remaining legionaries struck Antonius over the back with a heavy wooden chair. The chair shattered into firewood and the man stood, incredulous, holding just a splintered leg. Antonius grunted at the blow and turned around slowly, like an angry bear. The legionary swung the leg desperately, but Antonius simply caught it and ripped it from his grasp. Reaching down, he picked up the man by his shoulders and tossed him through the window of the bar, shattering the glass and bringing the other drinkers to their feet. Everyone started to back away as Antonius advanced on the last man.

'Keep the chips, take them all!' he yelled as he shuffled backwards trying to reach the exit.

Antonius stopped, stared, and laughed. He reached down to the floor and picked up one of the many chips that Tiberius was furiously scrambling around, picking up. 'Here you go, go buy yourself a drink,' he said, clapping the legionary on the shoulder as he walked on past to where Marcus stood.

'You'll be able to get plenty of whores now,' Marcus said to Antonius uneasily, partly because everyone in the bar was now staring at them, and partly because he couldn't think of anything worse than laying with a whore.

Antonius shook his head. 'Not sent anything to mother for months, she needs this more than me.'

Marcus smiled, enjoying the fact that someone as coarse as Antonius still sent most of his earnings to his mother.

'But,' Antonius added thinking heavily, 'there will be some left over for whores. And ale, some for ale too.'

They were interrupted by the proprietor, approaching angrily with two doormen. It was time to leave. The three of them darted out of the door as the few drinkers who remained started to clear the final few lost chips from the floor. They ran around the corner, stopped, and collapsed with laughter against the wall at the back of the bar.

'Tiberius!' Marcus exclaimed. 'That was great! The look on their faces...'

'It was pretty good work by Antonius, didn't have you pegged as an actor,' Tiberius exclaimed.

Antonius grunted, ignoring the praise, and pointed down the alley behind them. Four men stood there, three they didn't recognise and the one unharmed legionary.

'Run,' Marcus hissed and they darted down the alley to their left, pursued by the group who were now armed with thick wooden clubs.

Marcus felt the familiar sick feeling in his stomach that always came on whenever fighting was a possibility. He had never wanted to join the army all those years ago, but his father had reckoned it would 'make him a proper Roman', so he had obliged. He didn't want to fight, especially not against a gang of thugs armed with clubs, and presumably promised a reward if they could get the chips back. Why had he let Tiberius drag them down into the Imum for a drink and a game of *'ruber et niger'*? There were plenty of nice bars in the Aether, and far less chance of the evening ending either dead or in the Aesculapium.

They darted past a life size portrait of Gnaeus, and if Marcus' breath hadn't already been blowing raggedly with every step he would have laughed. It seemed he was now the poster boy for Tarpeius' campaign; a slogan beneath the pair of them extolled: 'True Rome, for True Romans'. Gnaeus was dressed in full military regalia.

'Down here,' Tiberius shouted, and they changed direction quickly. Marcus hoped they could slow down soon, his belly ached from the drink and he had developed a horrendous stitch. His pair of friends hadn't yet broken a sweat. He glanced over his shoulder—had the thugs gone?

Tiberius hissed at him to keep running.

Marcus threw himself forwards and tried to pretend he wasn't tired. Would they leave him behind if he ran out of breath? It hadn't even been his idea to cheat the legionaries.

They darted down another alley. This one was populated by the homeless, and they had to jump over piles of rags and emaciated beggars. Tiberius threw a chip backwards in his wake, presumably in the hope that the people there would put their pursuers off the scent, but Marcus suspected that the homeless were more likely to help fellow Imum dwellers than Sursumas like them.

Suddenly, they burst out onto a main Imum street and were enveloped in a cacophony of noise and stench. Across the street was a thick wall which, given their location in the city, was probably to prevent Imum dwellers getting into the Ancient Forum. It would only be accessible from above, by Sursumas. Despite the late hour the streets were full, people wandered drunkenly back and forth, some of them clearly under the influence of things much stronger than drink, wandering aimlessly, just staring, seemingly indifferent to the world and their plight at the very bottom of Rome.

A club to their left blared out fast heavy music which hurt Marcus' ears, but Tiberius seemed to be quite enjoying it. Two men walked past holding hands, and Marcus was surprised to see how well dressed they were compared to the other revellers. *They must be from the Aether,* he thought, realising that if they behaved like that in the world above that they would be outcast from their families. One of them slapped Tiberius on the arse as they passed. He smiled at them sarcastically and walked on, smiling.

'We can't stay here,' Marcus shouted to Tiberius over the music and sound of heavy vehicles approaching. They needed to get back to the barracks before they were reported as missing, but at least they were temporarily safe here in the crowd.

'We're in the wrong direction for the nearest levator,' Tiberius replied.

Marcus agreed. Did the barracks have an Imum entrance? He hoped so—it was likely their only chance of getting out of the Imum unscathed.

'Hey mate,' Tiberius said, to a thin man who was leaning against one of the ineffective streetlights that were permanently on in the Imum.

'Hey,' the man replied casually, 'what d'you wanna buy? I've got velocitas, furor, heroina... take your pick!'

Some curri started to pass, and everyone waited for the noise to die down so that they could speak again. The heavy curri threw up a great cloud of the filthy dust which carpeted every road and pavement in the Imum. Marcus shielded his eyes. A familiar logo was visible, *Coniunctus*. The cargo was plastered with it, and once again, it was heading in the direction of the Void Levator.

Marcus' attention turned back to the conversation with the drug dealer.

'No, no,' Tiberius said calmly, 'I'm looking for the barracks.'

The dealer's hand went to his belt, 'I've got a knife Praet,' he said casually. Marcus believed him, and readied himself to drag Tiberius away.

'I'm not a Praetorian,' Tiberius said, smiling disarmingly. 'Just need a piss, thought their doorway would make a nice spot.'

The dealer laughed. 'You're on the wrong city mate. Entrance is on the Aether. But,' he added, 'the riot gate. That's not far,' and he began to give the directions. 'Piss on it for me!' he shouted after them as they strode off.

The sound receded behind them as they left the main street and approached the area beneath their barracks. Marcus started to become aware of how uncomfortably warm it was. The Imum had almost no natural ventilation, and was therefore kept at a constant temperature by fans in the floor of the Aether, similar to the vents which let rainwater down. He looked up, the fans were not spinning and the lights were dimmer than ever.

They rounded a dingy corner and stepped over the bodies of some dead Slaves. Ahead was the riot gate, rusty iron, bolted firmly into a thick stone wall. To his surprise, Marcus' pass card worked on it—one of the benefits of being friends with Albus' new right hand man was a high-level security clearance. The gate swung open at their approach, creaking on its rotting hinges.

Inside there was a short passageway, initially strewn with the thick dust of the Imum, before giving way to clean, bare metal. Ahead there was a large levator, big enough to carry down a whole century of Praetorians at once in the event of unrest in the Imum. Not that that was needed anymore, not since Albus had brought an end to war over a decade ago, ushering in an era of peace that, he had claimed, would last one thousand years.

The Roman people had been crying out for peace, and loved Albus for bringing it to them. There would never be unrest on the streets of Rome again, not now that there was peace and prosperity for all. That was what had been said at the time anyway, but having wandered the streets of the Imum several times now, Marcus was no longer sure. He could see that as long as rich people continued to live on top of the poor, unrest would be unavoidable.

Tiberius pushed a button and Marcus' stomach lurched as the levator ascended.

Antonius unzipped his flies and started relieving himself in the corner. Marcus shuffled slightly further away and checked to make sure the puddle was not running over towards his boots. Suddenly the lights went out, throwing them into total darkness. The levator came to an abrupt halt and the three of them nearly fell over.

'What the fuck!' Tiberius said, his voice shaking slightly.

Marcus could hear the creak of the steel rope suspending them from above as it adjusted itself. *How far up were they?* Far enough, he reckoned, wondering if the gambling chips found around their bodies would be enough to buy decent funerals. He did not want his mangled body lying for all eternity in the Imum, or even worse, ejected through a chute onto the ground outside Rome, like would happen to the corpses of the beggars and Slaves they had stepped over earlier.

A sharp noise in the corner indicated that Antonius had zipped his flies back up. Marcus heard him lumbering around and then felt his huge hands on his shoulders. 'Lift me up,' he grunted.

Marcus shifted position and linked his hands together low, in a cup. 'Go on.'

Antonius put a urine-drenched boot onto Marcus' disgusted fingers and launched himself up. Marcus heard a crash and felt Antonius lift himself up out of the levator's ceiling.

'Up here.' Antonius' grunt echoed in the vertical tunnel. Marcus could make out the shape of Antonius against the dim light leaking in from high above them, one hand reaching down over the edge of the levator roof. He grabbed it, and the huge man pulled him up to join him.

Soon the three of them stood on the roof together and looked around. There was no sense in waiting for the power to come on; it was the middle of the night, and the Imum power cuts often lasted for over an hour, even during the working day. Tiberius climbed up onto Antonius' shoulders and found that he could just reach the lip of a maintenance doorway above them. He heaved himself up and called down to Marcus to follow.

Marcus tried to get onto Antonius' back, but slid back down onto the levator with a clang. To his embarrassment, Antonius had to squat down so that Marcus could get onto his shoulders. He felt like a child. The levator lurched as Antonius stood up, and Marcus' eyes widened with panic. The power was back on.

Marcus launched himself upwards and grabbed at the lip of the doorway as the levator started to move upwards again. Scrabbling desperately, he hauled himself through the hole and joined the panicking Tiberius.

'Antonius!' Tiberius shouted. 'Get back in the levator!'

But Antonius either hadn't heard, or didn't listen. He charged across the roof of the levator and leapt at the doorway, at exactly the same moment as the levator came level with it. Unfortunately, he hadn't judged his new upward momentum well, and his head crashed into the ceiling of the corridor as he leapt through its entrance. His body was catapulted forwards, and he fell to the ground with a crash that shook the corridor. Blood splashed across the metal floor and down his face from a gash on his bald scalp.

'Antonius,' Marcus hissed, dropping down to the ground in front of him. There was no movement. 'Antonius,' Marcus said again, louder this time. He started to shake him. Was he dead?

'Fuck off,' Antonius replied groggily.

'Where is Quintus when you need him?' Marcus cursed.

Antonius got to his feet cradling his head. A ping from high above indicated the levator had reached their dormitory level. They were far below, probably in the high security research and development wing. They were drunk. There would definitely be trouble.

XI

'Gnaeus, you should be standing up there next week, not me.' Gnaeus laughed and shook his head. The Sun had just risen over the Field of Mars which stretched away before them. The first of the Saepta was being erected: wooden stakes set to mark out where the polling boxes would sit and the thick queues would snake. 'I never wanted to be a politician.'

'You are becoming one,' Tarpeius replied thoughtfully. 'Even if you don't like it.'

'The army is much simpler,' Gnaeus replied. 'We just got paid to kill people and protect Rome. We didn't have to pretend we were doing something different to what our actions declared.'

Tarpeius thought for a moment, staring into the distance. Far on the horizon, the great towers of Ostia rose up from behind clouds of smoke, billowing from the industry there, which was excluded from the Eternal City itself. 'We're not all like Albus,' he said. 'Do you know what the first thing I will be expected to do is, if I manage to win this election?'

Gnaeus shook his head.

'I'll need to go straight to the temple of Jupiter and swear an oath, an oath to protect Rome, and to relinquish my power after my year term in office. Albus has said that oath now twelve times, and not once has he meant it, but that doesn't mean that the oath is meaningless. This is a serious undertaking, many lives could be in our hands. We must win. We owe it to the people to rid them of a Tyrant.'

Gnaeus smoothed his long black hair back over his shoulders; it was longer than Tiberius' hair now, but he would never be handsome with his pale, thin, almost Slave like face. He thought of Vibia, Tarpeius' daughter, and how she had suggested she help him work on the election paperwork in the late hours. He had enjoyed the time spent alone with her. They had kissed, just once, last night. He felt like a different person now.

'It's strange Tarpeius. I came to Rome because my friend was coming here. I never expected to stay, and I didn't know for sure what I would do afterwards. I've just followed him, for as long as I can remember. I don't know why I followed him, except that he, and I, both somehow deserved it. I don't think I need to follow him any longer.' He paused and thought of his patron's daughter. 'I might stay here a while.'

'And I'd value it Gnaeus!' Tarpeius replied. His voice was stronger now, the possibility of victory had visibly changed the man; he looked no more than fifty now, and Gnaeus could swear he had grown some hair back. 'Because of you, we might actually win!'

At that, one of their assistants pulled a cord, and a giant banner fluttered down behind them, casting a shadow over their plinth, where in seven days' time they would have to stand and let the people decide who would rule. *'Three Levels, one Rome, two Consuls.'* It was a good slogan. Gnaeus particularly liked the last bit, playing on the fact that people believed Catula to be nothing more than an extension of Albus himself.

But was it enough? Gnaeus secretly worried that Albus was too popular. Even with his suicidal attack on the hard working middle classes of the Aether, the richer Nobles, who he heaped wealth upon, loved him. And the people in the Imum? They were told what to think. The messages of fear were pumped in daily, onto their screens, on their food packaging, by the fist of a Praetorian.

'How will you control Catula? Or Albus,' he added, suddenly realising the possibility, 'if you win?'

'Why would I have to? Who says one of them will be the other Consul?'

Gnaeus wondered if Tarpeius was losing his memory a bit, there were only three entries to the Consulship this year. Gnaeus had been amazed when he had looked back in the official records, and found that one year there had been no less than nine candidates. It appeared that few people aspired to the Consulship these days, or perhaps, he thought, they did not think they had any chance of winning and feared the consequences of losing.

A man rushed over, dressed in official robes, he was one of the Custodes who was responsible for overseeing the elections and ensuring the process was fair. He smiled at Tarpeius pityingly, clearly suspecting he was another candidate doomed to failure. 'Sir, the voting slips have been finalised. Please check that we have the correct spellings before we go to press.' He handed over a grey piece of card to Tarpeius who studied it.

'Looks fine to me,' he said shrugging his shoulders. 'Would you check you are happy Gnaeus?'

Gnaeus looked down the list at the names of the hopeful Praetors, Aediles and Quaestors. Right at the bottom of the list, humbly, were the Consul candidates. Gnaeus opened his mouth and gasped. Right there, printed in heavy black ink, slightly raised up under his disbelieving finger, were the words *Gnaeus Lartius*.

Gnaeus felt sick. He looked down at his name again. He thought of his family, the Lartii were nobodies. Perhaps he could change that? But he didn't really want to. He prayed to God, quickly asking what he should do, and in return he received an image in his mind, of a short girl with dark brown hair and a wide smile. A girl who made him laugh all the time. The message was clear. Maybe he could do this for Vibia, even though he did not want to do it for himself.

He smiled and extended his hand to Tarpeius. 'For the Senate and the people of Rome,' he said, echoing the S.P.Q.R. initials on the banner which was being erected in front of them.

'Let's rule Rome together,' Tarpeius said, resting his hand on Gnaeus' shoulder. 'Let's turn this City on its head and see what pours out.'

XII

Marcus stepped out from one grey faceless corridor to another, wincing as Antonius stomped up loudly behind him. His hangover was starting to kick in now, and they would most likely be fined, if not flogged, if they were caught in these levels. There was no need for military research anymore, but the labs were supposedly used for medical research now, which was nearly as secretive. His security card didn't work on most of the doors, confirming that they were certainly not meant to be down here, even with a high security clearance.

'Tiberius,' Marcus hissed back down the corridor. 'Stop *looking*, we need to get out of here!'

Tiberius pulled his head away from the small window in the office door. 'Marcus, keep it together! It'll be an hour before anyone comes down here. These research people work a nice cushy nine till five day.'

Marcus gestured to him angrily, and reluctantly he walked over to them. He moved to look into the next office, but a glare from Marcus stopped him. Marcus cursed Tiberius' childishness, imagining the feeling of the flogging rope biting into his back, and the laughter of the soldiers as they watched. It wouldn't matter that he was a guest at the barracks; temporarily he was an honorary officer of the second cohort, he was paid at that level, and he would be expected to act and be punished as one.

The sun streamed in through the long window alongside them as they headed towards the maintenance stairwell, their best chance of getting back to the dormitory level undetected. They were not far now. Outside it was morning, and outside the barracks the usual queue was forming. Most of the people who gathered there each morning were homeless, and would struggle to fill out even an extra small uniform, but some, usually the ones that looked like criminals, could conceivably prove useful to the retained army. They were rounded up, handed some coins, and bundled into basic uniform ready to start training. Times were hard, and even a job as a basic infantryman on a pitiful wage looked attractive currently.

The long window ended, and was replaced by another, equally long, but the interior was completely pitch black. Ahead, at the end of the corridor Marcus could see the first flight of stairs. They had made it. This would take them to a higher level, one that they could use to sneak back to their barracks.

Antonius lumbered up, they had found some toilet paper to bandage his head, and mercifully the bleeding had stopped. He would have a big scar, but he had plenty of those anyway, and he liked them. An oversized black cap, stolen from a cloakroom, covered most of the bloodied paper.

'Let's have a look at what's in here,' Tiberius said, gesturing into the darkened room.

Marcus shook his head, and opened his mouth to bellow exactly what he thought of that idea, but at that moment, a light appeared in the room. Light flickered out twice across the ceiling lamps, before bursting into fluorescent life.

Inside, a scientist, dressed in a thin white cotton suit complete with hair net, crossed the room, oblivious to their presence, and turned on a second set of lights. He turned around and spotted them.

Marcus stared back, aghast. He looked across at the others, not sure what to do, but they were both staring at him. He fished in his pocket for his security badge and tried to look less scared than he felt.

The scientist walked nonchalantly up to the door next to them and swiped it open from the inside.

'Excuse me sir,' he said in a low voice, 'but you can never be too safe.' Marcus, who had been staring around the room, suddenly realised that the scientist was gesturing at his security card.

'Of course, here you go.'

The scientist scanned it, looked down at his scire, and appeared puzzled at Marcus' name and rank.

'General Marius has sent you in his stead?' he asked disdainfully.

'Uh huh,' Marcus said nodding. *Could the scientist smell wine on his breath?*

'That's fine,' the scientist said, his entire appearance suggesting the exact opposite. 'I am sure you will convey back to the General in *great detail*, the massive steps forward we have made.'

Tiberius nodded. 'We will, I have been looking forward to this all week!'

The scientist fixed him with a withering stare. 'No need for the sarcasm. I know you'd rather be out using this stuff in the field, than having to come and see us rats design it, but remember, if it wasn't for us you'd still be using those old bolt action sonifi.'

Tiberius shrugged. 'No. Really, I am quite excited,' he said, and walked forwards. The others followed.

The scientist moved aside at the last moment, 'I imagine you didn't get the memo about 'correct safety dress,' but we'll just have to plod on regardless I imagine. Follow me!' and he strode on across the room and around a corner with the three of them following in tow.

'Let's just run off! Say we need to go straight back to the General. He'll buy that won't he?' Marcus whispered to Tiberius, as they moved at a near jog to keep up with the fractious scientist.

'No,' Tiberius replied. 'And we'll miss out on seeing what happens in the research department. Did you hear? Apparently they have a horse down here somewhere.'

'What?'

'Yeah,' Tiberius continued, 'a horse. They experiment on it. It's meant to be immune to all sorts of neurotoxins now.'

'Tiberius, I know you are excited, but there is not going to be a horse. We are just going to see many boring labs where they are making new medicines.'

'Why did he mention the bolt action sonifi then, and why was he expecting an army general?'

Marcus shook his fists in exasperation, 'I don't know Tiberius, but it doesn't matter! We need to be in our bunks within thirty minutes or we will be officially missing.'

They passed through a corridor with completely glass walls and floor. Marcus tried to focus ahead on the scientist, keen to get things over as soon as possible, but even he found his eyes drawn below to what appeared to be an automated factory floor. Row after row of machine was churning out the same grey and black object, an object which they all knew extremely well, an assault sonifex. Great tubs of sonifi were being filled every minute and dragged away on rail led trolleys.

The scientist reached the end of the corridor and theatrically paused with his security card halfway through the reader. 'What you are about to see through these doors is as secret as it gets.' He drew breath, and slid the card through the reader. The doors parted with a gentle hiss and lights flickered on within. 'Gentlemen, from the Senate's *Minerva Labs*, that brought you the Jupiter machine, I present to you, the Juno project.'

The room was massive, grey and almost empty. However, right in the centre sat a bronze coloured currus. The front was curved, with a seat behind for just one driver. At the back a globe, several metres across, glowed gently with a faint blue light.

'Perhaps I could ask you to stand over by the Juno machine,' the scientist asked condescendingly.

As Marcus approached the vehicle, he could feel a faint warmth emanating from the globe. They turned around to pose alongside it. Marcus' worst fear was that the scientist would want to photograph them there. He would have to live the rest of his life knowing that his knowledge of this project would one day be discovered, and he would need to be permanently silenced by the authorities.

But the scientist didn't want to take their photograph. He raised his hand out over a panel in the floor that, at his command, flipped over and raised itself to waist height to form a cabinet. The scientist reached inside and drew out an assault sonifex.

'Hang on!' Marcus shouted with alarm. 'Let's talk about this!'

The scientist laughed and pulled the trigger. The sonifex tip sparked as it disgorged rounds in their direction. Marcus' mouth hung open, a scream on his lips. He didn't feel ready to die. But, as soon as the scientist started shooting at them, he felt a blast of warmth from behind him, and his hair crackled with energy.

Then he watched, amazed, as the rounds disintegrated several metres in front of him. It was if they had hit some unseen wall in midair. Two metres in front of him the air glittered and shone as it shattered the rounds. Ricochets bounced around the walls and pieces of shrapnel littered the ground around them. Marcus turned around slowly and saw that the great orb on the back of the Juno machine was glowing a deep, reassuring blue colour.

The sonifex fire stopped.

'My apologies sirs, but I imagine you now very plainly understand the aim of project Juno? Does anyone need a change of trousers?'

'Can *I* test it?' Tiberius asked. Marcus couldn't believe he had recovered so quickly.

'Of course,' the scientist said, clearly excited that real interest was being shown.

'Where does its shield reach to?'

'Well, at the moment it's fixed,' the scientist said, pointing out the faint line on the ground which seemed to delineate this point, 'but eventually it will expand as needed. We expect that with enough power it could reach half a mile if need be, by the time of your next campaign we're sure that—'

'Good, good,' Tiberius said, cutting him off. 'Perhaps you could come over here then,' he gestured to the other side of the shield boundary. 'Stand there for me.'

The scientist did as he was asked, a quizzical look on his face.

Tiberius switched positions with him, so that the scientist was behind the shield line. He smiled, and then swung his fist up into the scientist's face. The fist made contact with the side of his jaw, with a soft wet thud, and threw the scientist down to the floor, his mouth bloodied and his eyes wide.

'Oh.' Tiberius said, looking down at his bleeding knuckles.

'It doesn't work on slow moving objects,' the scientist gurgled, spitting out blood and teeth as he sat up.

Tiberius laughed. 'Suspected not. But General Marius will be impressed.'

The scientist nodded, happy seemingly, despite his disfiguring injury.

'But he says you need to work harder.'

The scientist's face dropped.

Tiberius couldn't resist one last dig at the arrogant man who had nearly made them all die of fright. 'No more holidays, get this thing ready soon. Or, you all get reassigned.'

'But...'

'Oh, and your wife is having an affair, with General Marius, he asked me to tell you.'

Marcus put his face in his hands, he could already feel the knots of rope cutting into his back.

The scientist started to cry.

'Come on!' Marcus said, dragging Tiberius away and leaving the distraught scientist on his own with his amazing, but pointless machine. War was impossible, Albus had made promises.

XIII

Titus pressed his fists into the corners of the wall and gritted his teeth. Suspended ten feet off the ground, above a doorway with his hands and feet rammed into the corners, he tried to control his breathing. He could still hear the Praetorians talking just the other side of the door. They had walked under him without noticing, but Titus wished they would move on altogether, before his grip on the rough brick failed.

'There it is again!' one of the Praetorians exclaimed gruffly, and with relief Titus realised they were jogging away, in pursuit of some other prey. Titus got his foot back onto the lintel above the door and swung back down, landing as quietly as he could. He pulled his father's map out of his pocket. The warehouse was just ahead.

He pulled his Dacian headscarf down over his face and stalked forwards slowly. His hand went instinctively to the handle of his gladius, but it was not there. His great ancestor's gladius remained securely stored in the palace basement. He was unarmed. He was going to face Filii Aquilae, unarmed.

He looked down at his hands. He had bandaged his knuckles with coarse tape, into which he had imbedded some metal shards from the floor of the workshop through which he had gained entrance so far; it was the nearest he could get to a weapon. Part of him wished that, rather than moving secretly, he could have the Praetorians with him, but that would dilute the honour, and more importantly, Albus had specifically forbidden him from doing what he was about to attempt.

A few days had become two weeks. Every day the stolen fertiliser was likely nearer to being a useable bomb, but no matter what Titus said, Albus refused to let him move in. He was to wait for Verres, but Verres was doing nothing it seemed. Titus had started to wonder if the young Praetorian was a coward, but one look at Verres told him this was not the case. The whole thing made no sense at all.

Even though Albus had entrusted securing this facility and destroying any bomb making equipment to Verres, Titus knew really that the job should have been his from the start, and if Verres wouldn't make the move? It really left Titus with no choice.

Titus quickly dived behind some empty sacks as the sound of marching feet returned. A torch shone through the doorway and passed carelessly around the walls missing him by a mile.

'She's not in here,' one Praetorian called to the other.

The pair retreated again.

'I've seen her before, skulking around,' the other muttered as they walked away.

'Imum scum, scavenging food dropped by Aether workers. Fucking flood this place and kill the lot of them I suggest.'

Titus listened until the voices passed out of earshot again before getting up. He tried the handle of the next door and found it open. There was no security at all, and Titus started to worry that his father's friend might have been wrong; if he had been building a bomb here, he would have had the place completely locked down.

Ahead was a dingy corridor lined with more dusty sacks. Titus bent down and examined them. There was a small trace of white powder. He dabbed some with his finger and licked, it was foul, but he was still unsure as to what it was. Every part of him hoped it was fertiliser; he could already imagine Albus clapping him on the shoulder and rewarding him. Perhaps he would let him keep Northern Britannia as well as Hispania? Ceinwyn would like that. He sighed as he thought about her and how much she worried. Why did Britannia matter so much to her? He could be so much richer in Hispania. He daydreamed constantly about accepting the new position, and he was sure that Albus would still grant it to him if he asked. Perhaps the head of Filii Aquilae himself would be down here in this warehouse overseeing the bomb making? If not, he was sure that whoever he did find here could be persuaded to divulge more details under the dedicated work of a Carnifex. Torture sickened him, but sometimes it was the only option. If it was the only way to protect Rome, then surely it was necessary.

He froze. Someone was definitely watching him. The hairs on the back of his neck stood up. He turned his gaze back to the sacks, and hummed gently to himself. Then suddenly he swung round. He was sure he caught a glimpse of light coloured hair as someone swung out of view round the corner. He charged back down the corridor and shone his torch back into the storeroom. He caught a flash of loose fabric at the next door, and the sound of extremely quiet but fast footsteps as whoever it was made their escape, too swiftly for him to catch. It had been a girl, he was sure of that. Presumably the one the Praetorians had been after, the starving one.

He sneaked across the room and waited by the doorway, pulling in tight against the wall. Perhaps he would be able to grab her if she made her way back in. He reached into his pack, but he had not brought anything. He would have happily fed her—no one should have to go hungry in the Eternal City.

After five minutes of no sound he realised that she wasn't coming back. He suddenly felt very alone. He shook his head—a veteran general did not need a little girl for company.

Then suddenly he did hear footsteps, but just one person, too heavy to be a girl. He readied himself. A torch beam shone into the room, slowly and methodically checking the corners. He waited. A figure half stepped through the door. In the dark Titus couldn't make out the face yet, but it was a man, and the way he carried himself betrayed that he was dangerous. This was a man who had killed before, many times.

Titus let him step through the doorway before leaping out. He clapped one hand over the man's mouth, the other around the side of his neck, and used his legs to trip him over his outstretched knee onto the ground. The man went down immediately, grunting with surprise into Titus' hand. Titus swung him round quickly, onto his back, and shone his torch down bright into the man's eyes, and onto his bald, bearded head. It was Verres.

'Titus,' Verres said, laughing. 'Thank the gods I've found you.'

Titus was puzzled, and stared at him quizzically. 'How did you know I would be down here?'

'I guessed,' Verres said honestly. 'I came to your rooms earlier to,' he paused, 'ask your advice about this attack, but you weren't there. I know I've taken a long time to attack this place you found.' He reddened with embarrassment. 'I realised you must have run out of patience, so now I'm here.'

Titus laughed. He liked Verres immensely, even more now that he had admitted he needed his help. 'Okay, let's do this together.'

Verres looked surprised, and shook his head. 'No Titus, it's okay. I've got some of our best Praetorians together. We are going to do this tomorrow, in the morning.'

Titus smiled at him smugly. 'You've got a lot to learn Verres, always best to attack at night, they don't expect it.' He stood up, and helped Verres to his feet. 'It's this way.'

'No,' Verres said, staying put, 'the Consul has already agreed the plan. I can't go against him.'

'It's okay,' Titus said. 'I'll take the blame,' and he started to walk forwards.

'I have to insist,' Verres said, looking very awkward, as if he hated himself for saying the words.

He pointed his fasces towards Titus.

'Are you going to use that on me?' Titus asked, amazed.

'Titus, I'm just doing what I've been told to do,' his voice shook.

'And what's that?'

'Take this place down myself tomorrow. The Consul has given me my orders. We cannot go in tonight.

Titus took a step closer, so that his chest was almost against the glowing end of the fasces. 'Then strike me Verres,' Titus said earnestly, 'because I don't care what he says. He asked me to defend Rome, and that is what I will do. We attack now, we surprise them and we stand a better chance of capturing some of them and seeing what they are doing. Albus is a politician now, not a soldier. He employed me to make these sorts of decisions for him.' He stared at Verres, exasperated. Surely he understood this as well as he did?

'I have orders,' Verres said sadly.

'Yes, from a great man, someone who used to be a great general, but it's been years since he fought. He must be rusty. We know better than him.' He reached out his other hand to Verres. 'Come with me, let's make a name for ourselves.'

Verres paused and his eyes glanced to one side, seemingly in deep thought. His hand shook. For a moment, Titus thought he was actually going to get stunned by the fasces, but then slowly a smile broke out over the young Praetorian's face. He reached out his hand and shook Titus', his grip painfully pressing a shard of taped on metal into two of Titus' knuckles. He suppressed a wince.

'Lead on Titus,' Varro said gesturing forward with his gently crackling fasces.

The pair returned to the corridor and walked through a succession of further storerooms. To Titus' irritation, Verres insisted on searching each one systematically, even though there was clearly no one guarding the place.

Finally, inexorably, and extremely slowly, they moved towards the centre of the cluster of storerooms on Titus' map, the one to which the materials had been tracked.

Titus had a sudden fear that it would be empty. What would Albus say? Everyone had told him that Filii Aquilae was a conspiracy of the rich, and that he should be searching on the Aether, but his father had given him this lead, down here in the darkest part of the Imum. He would look a complete fool.

He placed his hand on the last door. 'Ready Verres?' he whispered.

A nod signalled in the affirmative. Verres stood to the side of the door, his fasces raised and his forearms bulging.

Titus pushed. The door didn't move, not even slightly. Titus, puzzled, reached around the edges of the door in the gloom. There was a thin rectangle of metal over the lock. Beneath it, a small nub of metal protruded with a tiny aperture in the centre. A magnetic lock. This was not the security device of a common criminal. They were onto something.

'Ah,' Verres said crossly. 'Looks like we'll have to come back in the morning, after all. We need a universal key scire to crack this. I'll have a word with the quartermaster and hopefully—'

Titus cut him off. 'You mean like this one?' he said, reaching proudly into a pocket in his jacket and bringing out the battered grey plastic box that he had borrowed from Marcus all those months ago in Luguvalium.

Verres looked surprised. 'Yes, like that one,' he said loudly.

Titus gestured for him to quieten down, he was getting carried away, and they didn't want to alert any terrorists on the other side of the door.

Titus' fingers glided over the controls of the scire as he set it to auto mode; Marcus would have known a faster way to crack the code, but Titus would have to trust the box. A small red counter ticked across the screen slowly. As it reached halfway, Verres broke out into a fit of coughing.

Titus put his hand to his mouth and glared at him.

Verres nodded apologetically. 'The dust.'

Titus shrugged, the counter was now at ninety percent. 'Get ready.' He was breathing faster now, he was ready to fight—he needed to.

The lock clicked. Titus flicked his head over his shoulder instinctively to check behind him as he pushed the door forwards. He jumped, as he saw the silhouette of a girl, dressed entirely in black, standing twenty metres behind in the previous doorway. She was brandishing some sort of knife, but before he had a chance to move she had darted out of sight in a flash. For a moment he thought it was Ceinwyn, but then realised that it was far more likely to be the feral girl the Praetorians had been looking for. It did not matter. He had a more important mission than discovering the girl's identity. He dived into the sudden brightness of the room ahead.

It was almost empty. The walls and floor were entirely bare, swept clean, and in the centre was a simple wooden bench. An Arabian man stood there, in shock, staring at them as they charged towards him. The man dropped the two silver containers he was carrying, spraying white dust into the air.

Titus paused as he reached him. The top of the man's head was wrapped in a red scarf, and he was wearing a thin white robe. His skin was dark. He was unarmed.

'Please!' the man shouted, in perfect Latin, which took Titus aback—he looked like he was from Asia Minor. His hands were outstretched before him in surrender.

As Titus opened his mouth to accept his surrender, Verres leapt forwards and thrust the fasces into their captive's neck. The man collapsed onto the ground, spasming from the shock.

'Verres!' Titus shouted angrily. The man had surrendered, and had no weapon.

Verres dived onto the man's chest and started smashing his fasces down into his face repeatedly, as the man screamed wordlessly and writhed desperately.

Titus grabbed Verres' shoulders, but the Praetorian was heavy and strong, and Titus could not stop him. 'We need to question him!' Titus shouted, hoping common sense would get through to him.

Blood started to splatter over the concrete floor as Verres continued his onslaught. The man's screams had stopped, replaced only with a gentle gurgling sound.

As Verres brought the gore coated fasces down a final time, Titus caught it and managed, with great effort, to wrestle it from his grip.

He looked down. The floor was covered in blood. The man's face was in tatters, bone shards and pieces of brain mashed into the floor. He shoved Verres angrily. 'What the fuck?' he raged at the young fool. 'He had surrendered to me. He was my prisoner!'

'He's from Asia Minor, he's a terrorist. Praetorians kill scum like that, that's our job,' Verres retorted angrily.

How could they be sure where he was from? He had spoken Latin well. Now, they had lost any chance to question the man thanks to Verres' brutality. Titus walked over to the window at the far end of the empty room. He poked his head out into the foul Imum breeze and stared down into the canal fifty feet beneath them. The edges directly below were splattered with white powder. He looked back at the dead man—he had been destroying the evidence as they arrived. They had almost been too late.

'We need to report back to the Consul immediately,' Verres said, looking very pleased with himself. 'Even better than catching Filii Aquilae! We have foiled an Asia Minor terrorist attack!'

Titus looked down at the man's ruined face. One of his hands was still twitching. Titus was not sure what they had done, apart from murder a man who had begged him for help. All he knew was that, despite his father's certainty, Verres was right in one thing: this had nothing to do with Filii Aquilae. The lead had been false.

Verres swung around and marched out, with Titus following. As he followed, he began to notice something, something that brought a wave of cold nausea upon him. A thin piece of wire hung down into Verres' collar. He was wearing an earpiece.

XIV

Titus' head ached. He had been awake over twenty four hours now.

'Is it true that Asia Minor have tried to bomb the Eternal City?'

Titus stared back at the reporters over the table. There were two dozen of them, and he had been taking questions for nearly an hour, the answers to which had been broadcast, onto every screen on every wall in Rome, possibly every screen in the World. Every channel had been diverted, so that they had no choice but to watch him. He hated it.

The reporter's eyes bored into him, desperate for confirmation of imminent war. Titus thought back to Albus' victory parade nearly a decade ago—the parade that he had missed, instead spending it starving with what was left of his army on the shores of the Transmaritanus. People had loved peace then, new and full of wonder and promise. It was strange that only a decade later these men could lean forwards, scires outstretched, to hear the first ripples of fresh war, war they clearly longed for.

Titus took a deep breath. He didn't know the answer, so he said what he had been told to say a few hours before as he and Verres had stood in front of a tense pacing Albus. He thought of the look on Albus' face as he had explained what had happened. At first, Albus had looked almost pale with anger, and Titus had been terrified. He had failed to find Filii Aquilae, and he had directly disobeyed Albus' orders to allow Verres to deal with whatever it was he had stumbled upon. However, slowly, as Albus questioned Titus his face had relaxed, and Titus had started to realise that he was not in trouble. Finally, Albus laughed and his face brightened up again. His voice regained its warm, composed glow, and he explained that his Praetorians had been tracking a new terrorist cell from Asia Minor for months. Apparently Titus had accidentally stumbled upon it. He was relieved—Albus seemed to be quite pleased with him, but it didn't make sense.

The reporter tapped his scire on the table angrily.

'Yes,' Titus said, finally, confirming that terrorists were involved.

The reporters stared at each other, open mouthed. Then the room erupted into a sea of questions. Titus imagined the scene all around Rome, in living rooms everywhere, in the squares, in the bars.

The questions came at him too quickly for him to answer.

'Would Rome attack back?'

'Will the army be reformed?'

'Are we ready for war?'

He hoped the army would be reformed. It would bring jobs to many veterans like himself who had struggled to move on after the army was disbanded.

'What proof have you got of this?'

'Why would Asia Minor do this?'

'Have the plotters confessed yet?'

The questions were endless. He felt sick. He opened his mouth again, 'I'm not sure exactly. The situation in the room was, unusual. I haven't got my own mind around it yet really. There was one man there, but before we questioned him—'

'The General is tired.'

Titus looked around, cut off in mid sentence. Albus was striding towards him, dressed in a brilliant white toga, edged with purple and gold. There was an ancient painting of the great Consul, Sulla, which hung imposingly in the entrance hall of the Senate building, which Titus had stared at every day of the six months he had spent learning politics at his father's request—the six months that caused him to leave Rome and join the army. That picture had stared down at him every day. It was a picture of what Roman power looked like. It was as if

Albus had dressed specifically to resemble that picture. No one was listening to Titus any more—all eyes were on the Consul.

Albus stood to the side of Titus and put his arm on his shoulder. 'The General has done a great job. He has protected Rome. He has saved us from a terrible bombing that would have caused great loss of life. Terrorism is a scourge that must be wiped out, erased from the face of the Earth. There is no place for it in a peaceful republic.' His voice boomed out across the hall and Titus imagined the faces of half the Empire staring at their leader through their screens, mesmerised, just like he was.

Then Albus' eyes darkened, and he looked suddenly extremely serious. 'People of Rome,' he called out. 'Terrorists can strike at any moment. We are in constant danger and we must be constantly vigilant. Keep calm, keep out of the darker places of the City. Let us do our work. Let Titus, the saviour of Rome do his work, and our faithful Praetorians, as they protect you.' He looked at Titus and smiled. 'Titus Labienus Aquilinus has done a great thing today, his quick thinking and swift action have saved us from a great atrocity; an atrocity which I am sure would have caused great destruction and loss of life.'

Albus looked at him, and for a brief second Titus caught a glimpse of what seemed like utter contempt, quickly replaced by his usual winning smile.

'For that reason, I now bestow upon Titus an honour not given for centuries, an honour, which his own great ancestor once held. Albus turned to face him. All the cameras were trained on them. Albus nodded, and Titus realised he was meant to kneel. He crouched down before the Consul.

Albus reached forwards and placed his hand on the crown of his head. 'In the name of Juno, the guardian of Rome, I invest in you the power to protect, to do what is necessary: to defend our ancestral Eternal City. Arise, *Protector of Rome*.'

Titus struggled to his feet, shaking: he had not been expecting this. All around him there was applause, everyone was looking at him now. All around the world, he could imagine the People, standing as one, as they applauded him for averting a great tragedy. A huge smile burst across his face and all the worries suddenly evaporated from his mind. He thought about his father, their crumbling ancestral home, and the ruin of his once Noble family, suddenly all made right. His father would be proud of him now. He could do anything, have anything, be anything he wanted. Rome was his. He would answer only to Albus. He reached out and shook his old friend firmly by the hand. He, just like his great ancestor, the man who had murdered the would-be-Tyrant, Julius Caesar, two thousand years ago, was the *Protector of Rome*.

Summus

2765 AUC

'The land may have been fallow, dear husband,' spoke Livia. 'But far better it be fallow, than be corrupted by tobacco.'

'Wife, speak not of what you do not understand,' replied Varro angrily. 'For you did not sow the tobacco, and you did not overthrow the master, and you did not make this place good, and prosperous, and powerful.'

'Oh, not one day passes in which I pray not, that I might once again inhabit a land of stones, and toil, and oppression, if only I had back my husband.' And she dashed the rich possessions, bestowed upon her by him, at his feet.

The Book of Varro, Part 2. 1654AUC

XV

'Let that friend of yours know that there'll be no ill feeling,' Albus said, leaning in so that Titus could hear him over the ancestral music blaring out of the tapestry speakers, which covered every wall of the feast hall. 'When he loses tomorrow,' he added sniggering.

'We'll see,' Titus said civilly. 'I've never met anyone who didn't like Gnaeus, plenty will vote for him. The polls are favourable'. In truth, the polls did favour Gnaeus over Catula, and it was therefore quite likely that Albus and Gnaeus would be the next Consul pair. Titus wondered how Gnaeus would fare facing up to Albus over the Senate floor as an equal if he could usurp Catula as Consul.

'That may be,' Albus conceded. 'But that Tarpeius, he's a wound up bitter old bastard. He would lead Rome into the gutter. Your friend has picked the wrong side, unlike you my old friend,' he added, as he slapped Titus on the back heavily. 'Let Gnaeus know he can run my campaign next year instead if he wants.' He leaned in close, 'and between you and me, I think he'd do a lot better than that old hippo Catula.' They both stared over at the bloated man as he laughed raucously with a group of girls in the corner. One of the girls stood slightly apart from the others, almost embarrassed. She was dressed differently to them, and her golden hair cascaded down over her shoulders in a sort of controlled disorder. Titus realised that, unlike the other girls, she was not part of the entertainment.

Albus saw where his gaze had fallen. 'She's nice isn't she,' he said, slightly amused.

'She's young,' Titus answered, looking around the room for Ceinwyn again. The girl looked no older than fifteen.

'Yes. Nice,' Albus replied. 'She's Catula's daughter you know.'

Titus spluttered the gulp of wine he had just taken. *How could Catula have produced something so different to himself?* An athletic boy, a similar age to the girl, walked up behind her and put his arm carefully round her waist. She smiled and leant her head back to kiss him, as Catula rose to force a cup of wine into the boy's reluctant hand.

'She's taken,' Titus said to Albus.

'So it seems,' said Albus offhandedly, and continued to swing his hand, up and down, in time to the gentle, ancient music.

'Regarding Gnaeus,' Titus said, returning to the original conspiratorial aim of their conversation, 'I will ask him, but I think he has pitched his tent firmly in Tarpeius' camp.' Gnaeus and Titus had spoken several times in the last few days, but never about the campaign. Gnaeus would only speak about Tarpeius' daughter.

'Right,' Albus said purposely. 'I've got some important pre-election business to attend to.' He looked around for one of his many assistants. 'Where's that fat bastard gone?' he called to a man nearby, meaning Catula. The assistant nodded, without hesitation, and pointed to one of the booths that lined the walls. Albus nodded and wandered towards it.

Titus wearily scanned the room again, but there was still no sight of Ceinwyn. She was meant to be here. The pair of them had barely had a chance to talk since the press conference earlier in the week. He hadn't realised how much work being *Protector of Rome* entailed. Endless meetings with the Praetorian Guard continued into the night as they followed countless threads, one of which might hopefully lead to Filii Aquilae. No one had mentioned a new province, or even allowing him to return to govern his current one. He thought back to Albus' words, that he needed him to capture the leader of Filii Aquilae first. He thought of Hispania, it could still be his if he could persuade Ceinwyn to stay a little longer; the cold wastes of Luguvalium, devoid of riches, and leading to obscurity, were no longer in his thoughts. He thought of their children to be—descendants of the *Protector of Rome!* His family, the only one ever to have had two *Protectors* in its lineage. One day surely a child or grandchild of his would be Consul.

A young Roman girl wandered up to him, her breasts exposed, and her whole body painted with thick, lustrous oil.

'General, and *Protector of Rome*, I wondered if you would like any treatments?' her voice was soft, and surprisingly intelligent. She smiled and put her arm on his.

'Treatments?' he replied cautiously.

'Massage,' she replied, pointing over to a series of booths that ran along the bottom wall of the hall, one door was still open, and inside he could see two other girls dressed the same as she was. He blushed. 'I'm looking for my wife,' he said quickly, scanning the room again.

The girl chuckled coyly. 'When you find her, bring her over, she's welcome to join us.'

Titus walked away quickly. He wanted to find Ceinwyn and get out of here, he had never enjoyed parties at the best of times, and especially not orgies.

'General.' An old man blocked his path.

Titus stared at him, waiting for him to move aside, fed up with yet another admirer.

'Oh, I see you don't remember me,' the man replied quietly, blushing a little. He seemed to be very uncomfortable in this environment. 'I fought alongside you in the Transmaritanus.'

Titus tried to remember him without success. He didn't have time for every decrepit old legionary that had followed him across the surface of the Transmaritanus.

'In the Yellowstone campaign,' the man added, trying to help.

Titus suddenly, with embarrassment, placed the man. 'Centurion,' he said, and a great inexplicable sadness overcame him. He remembered the pride he had felt, so long ago, when, as a child really, he had opened his hand and looked down at the Crown of Valour placed there, and then in disbelief, back up into the face of *this* man—a man he had admired more than any other at that time. This was his first commander, the man who had inspired him to become who he was, but he could not even remember his name.

The Centurion smiled kindly, 'I should not waste your evening. I am old, and you are young. You were the best that I ever trained. The best don't always manage to get to the top, but I am glad that you did. You gave a lot for Rome, and I am glad you are happy. Enjoy your evening.' He turned aside, and walked away.

A wave of regret washed over Titus, and he reached out to grab at the man's arm—to drag him away and talk more, but the Centurion had already moved on. He scanned the party, trying to catch sight of the man through the throng of whores, drunkards, and senators. He had no idea why he needed to speak to him, but he felt he had to confess that he wasn't happy. As if somehow, by doing so, he could regain the happiness he had felt twenty years ago. For a brief moment he wished he could give up every moment, from that day under the cliffs of Yellowstone, to now, if only he could be back there as that young boy—that young boy who had loved Rome, and wanted desperately to grow into a hero.

Then he caught sight of Ceinwyn and the regret of the wasted years melted away. Her white dress clung lovingly to her body, and her hair cascaded down onto her shoulders. She was sitting on a bench, across the room, and in her lap, she was comforting the head of a crying girl. At that moment she looked up, their eyes met, and they both smiled at the same time. He walked quickly across the room, ignoring everyone in his path until he had reached her.

Her face was paler than usual with her make-up; she looked beautiful but he couldn't get used to seeing her without her signum.

'What's happened?'

The girl stopped sobbing and turned her head over, and he realised that he recognised her: it was Catula's daughter. Her tears and make-up had smudged all over Ceinwyn's dress, leaving an odd brown patch over the tops of her legs.

'She won't tell me,' Ceinwyn said, sounding slightly irritated. 'I think she's had an argument with Gabinius.'

That must be the name of the boy, Titus thought. He shifted his weight from foot to foot uneasily. He found it difficult enough talking to Ceinwyn about feelings, let alone a teenage girl.

'You should speak to Gabinius,' he said to the young girl. It seemed like sensible advice.

The girl started sobbing again. Then she took a deep breath, rubbed her eyes in Ceinwyn's dress and appealed to them. 'Please, help us! I love him, and he loves me, and they—'

'Sexta! What are you doing? You were meant to go to your room!' Her father, charging across the room at a speed that Titus would not have imagined him possessing, interrupted her before she could say more.

Sexta leapt up from Ceinwyn's lap to confront her father, but before she had had a chance to speak, he grabbed her and started to drag her away, his face completely colourless and his expression empty and broken.

Suddenly there was commotion on the other side of the room. Titus watched as the boy, Gabinius, climbed onto a recliner. 'Stop! I love her!' he called in anguish as the girl was marched from the room by Catula. Then, seemingly from nowhere, two Praetorians appeared and grabbed him by the shoulders.

'Get the fuck off me! I'll be an officer next year, you have no right!' he called out, struggling with the Praetorians.

One of the Praetorians struck the boy hard in the face with his armoured glove, and his protests stopped immediately. He looked around at the room groggily, blood pouring from his broken nose. Then the Praetorians dragged him away.

The room fell silent, and everyone tried to avoid looking at everyone else.

'Music!' called Albus, walking to the centre of the room quickly, and beaming from ear to ear as he climbed up onto a nearby recliner. 'Music!' An assistant nodded to a technician in the corner who flicked some switches. The traditional music of the first part of the evening was replaced by jagged, electronic music. A few of the younger senators started dancing energetically, grinning manically. Titus rushed over to Ceinwyn. 'What the hell just happened there?'

'I've no idea! Ask him!' she replied angrily, pointing at Albus. 'You're meant to be best friends,' she said sarcastically. 'Ask him why he just had a fifteen year old beaten whilst his fiancée was dragged away by her father.'

'Fiancée?' Titus said astounded. The pair were so young.

Ceinwyn just stared at him, waiting. He looked over his shoulder at Albus, dancing away with some high-ranking senators whilst a semi naked girl stood in the middle of the group, openly touching herself. He looked back at Ceinwyn. 'What makes you think Albus had anything to do with what just happened?'

Ceinwyn kept staring at him coldly.

There was no point arguing. 'Okay,' he said. 'I'll see what I can find out.'

He walked over slowly, not wanting to interrupt, but he had to. He started trying to dance to the music. The rhythm made sense to him, a bit, but his body didn't seem able to move in time to it, he just sort of rocked back and forth. He reached Albus awkwardly.

'My wife isn't very happy.'

'Oh, well,' Albus said flippantly, 'if I were you I'd take her home and fuck her. That always seems to cheer women up.'

'No,' Titus said, feeling foolish. 'She's not very happy about what just happened to that boy.'

'No?' Albus said. 'Well, tell her I agree with her. It's fucking awful. Spoiling my party with his teenage spat.' Albus kept dancing. One of the senators slapped the dancing girl on the bottom and she turned around to face him.

Titus tried to think of what to say next that would appease Ceinwyn, and not enrage the Consul of Rome. 'I think it was the...' he paused. 'The Praetorians, the hitting him in the face. She really didn't like that... He looked quite badly injured,' he added.

'You're in charge of the Praetorians,' Albus replied. 'Well, that's not exactly true,' he added thoughtfully. 'I appointed Verres to do that, but, you're the *Protector of Rome*, so you're in charge of Verres, so in a way you're in charge of the Praetorians, if you see what I mean?'

The dancing girl accepted some sestertii notes from the Senator, and sensuously dropped to her knees in front of him.

Titus was taken aback as he realised he now did control the Praetorians. 'Hmmm. I don't want them behaving like that. Perhaps I should speak to them.' He realised that he was actually apologising for something that in no way could be his fault, and caught himself. How did Albus do it?

'Yes, do.' Albus said abruptly. 'And perhaps, whilst you're at it, you could ask if that oaf who smashed Gabinius' face in, wouldn't mind cleaning his blood and teeth off my floor before morning.'

The other senators had moved away from him and Albus now, and were standing in a circle, near to the girl, waiting for their turn.

Titus reddened with anger. The way Gabinius had been treated was wrong. Not only that, but it was not his fault, no matter what Albus said. He looked at Albus, smiling, carefree. He felt sick. He felt lied to.

'Why did you try to stop me investigating the terrorist hide out?' he asked, knowing it was unwise.

'What?' Albus said taken aback.

'This supposed Asia Minor terrorist? I could have attacked the place a full week before I did. Why stop me?'

'I didn't,' Albus replied, as he stopped dancing and turned to face Titus properly. 'I asked Verres to make the assault. I wanted to test him.'

'Clearly he passed the test,' Titus said ominously. Verres had if anything acted like a coward, and yet Albus had made him head of the Praetorian Guard.

'Yes,' he followed my orders. 'Something which you failed to do.'

'If Verres had delayed any longer there would have been no terrorists to find, and some of Rome would have been destroyed.'

'Perhaps.'

Titus, who had partly gained the courage to question Albus under the belief that he was drunk, now realised, with concern, that the Consul was completely sober.

'Titus,' Albus continued. 'Sometimes when you are a General, and I don't mean a sub-general like you were,' he added, 'you have to be able to look at the bigger picture. We now know nothing about these terrorists, or their plans, because we didn't study them for long enough. Your hot headedness prevented us from gathering intelligence. We had been watching them for weeks, learning their plans. You ruined months of work.'

Titus paled at Albus' words and then realised there had to be more to it than what Albus was telling him. 'No,' he replied quickly. 'They were destroying the evidence when we attacked. If we hadn't, then there would have been no intelligence at all, just an empty room.'

'That's not true,' Albus replied crossly.

'And the man we found,' Titus continued. 'We could be questioning him right now. Only, Verres beat him to death before he even uttered more than one word. Why would you order that, if you were delaying the attack in order to gather intelligence?'

'I didn't. I don't control Verres. He chose to beat him to death rather than ask questions. He's young, he'll learn.'

Titus shook his head. 'Why was he wearing a wire then? Who was instructing him?'

Albus' mouth hung open for the briefest of moments. He quickly diverted his attention back to the girl as she finished with the first of the senators and turned to the next.

'Your eyes deceived you that night Titus,' he said very quietly, and very finally.

Titus opened his mouth to protest, he knew what he had seen.

Albus fixed him with a stare. 'Election day tomorrow Titus,' he said slowly and forcefully. 'Make sure you get some sleep.' Then his expression softened and he smiled disarmingly. 'And get some fucking in too!'

He turned back to the group of senators and walked forwards, dropping the hem of his toga. 'Fuck off you lot, it's my turn.'

XVI

Gnaeus had seen videos of the previous year's elections. Tarpeius and he had studied them, the speeches, the dress, the body language. Anything that could give them an edge, but the thing that had struck him most was the apathy. The few voters who had bothered to turn out, trudging around in the mud, barely looking up at the candidates as they carelessly cast their votes. It was as if they realised that Albus would win, yet again, *and why wouldn't they?* His family had been in power for the whole of Gnaeus' life. Gnaeus had practised his speech under the careful tutelage of Vibia. He glanced across his shoulder to where she stood next to him, their hands nearly touching. Like him, she was looking ahead, peering through the white shroud that, for now, shielded them from the field ahead. She was almost a foot shorter than he was, tiny. He loved the fact that, in preparation to stand before the entire world, not only was she keeping all her piercings in, but she had also dyed half her short black hair purple. They had spent every night of the last week together practising for today. He had rehearsed his speech so many times that it filled his sleep and prevented any meaningful rest. Moreover, those nights had tested his self-control to the limit.

He looked down at the ring on her right hand, she had not told her father yet. She saw where he was looking and smiled. Perhaps she would tell her father this evening after the victory? Then the ring could move to its rightful place. He would think it odd that his daughter plan to marry after only knowing a man for a month, but they knew their own feelings, and Gnaeus was looking forward to doing more than just kissing.

He thought back to last night, and how near to giving into temptation he had been. Vibia had wrapped a scarf around his eyes and had him practise his entire speech blindfolded. She had told him it was to practise speaking to a passive audience, however, when he had finished, he removed the scarf to find her standing naked in front of him. She had been embarrassed when he explained that he couldn't, not until they were married. The Roman gods didn't care about what you did with your body, as long as you paid their priests handsomely in sacrifices.

As he thought about her body, the way her small breasts curved upwards towards him, and the beautiful nest of black hair between her legs, he, with embarrassment, had to lean forwards and adjust his toga. He blushed and looked dead ahead, hoping she hadn't noticed.

At that exact moment, to his horror, the shroud separating them from the crowd below lifted. Vibia turned to him, smiled, and took his hand. Tarpeius began to walk forwards, extending his hands outwards towards the crowd who were ahead, just over the lip of the stage. Gnaeus had no choice, he marched awkwardly, bending forwards slightly to conceal his erection, suddenly glad about the horrendously low election turn outs of recent years.

As they approached the lip of the stage, two custodes flanking them signalled five sharp blasts on their cornua. To his left Gnaeus caught sight of Albus, Catula, and their entourage moving towards a separate stage, adjacent to theirs.

Gnaeus took the final step forwards to the edge of the stage and was met by a roar so loud that he nearly stepped backwards onto Tarpeius. The crowd was so large that there was still a half-mile queue to even get into the field. He had never seen anything like it. To his left he heard some boos and watched as the Praetorians quickly intercepted a group of men, who were intent on throwing a large supply of bottles onto the Consular stage. Gnaeus had never seen so many people in one place—it seemed like the whole of Rome stood before him. A louder blast on a cornum brought the crowd to some semblance of order. Gnaeus held Vibia's hand firmly and tried to smile.

Above their head, on the highest stage of all came the voice of the Chief Augur. Technically as it was the elections, the auspices should have been checked by the Pontifex Maximus, but seeing as Albus was currently elected to that title, in addition to that of Consul, this would have been considered a serious breach of protocol.

'By the power vested in me by the Republic, I stand before you to consult the gods as to the suitability of today, and this venue, to decide the future rulers of our people.'

The crowd chattered amongst themselves. Gnaeus noticed a banner towards the back of the multitude with his own slogan daubed across it raucously: 'Three Levels, one Rome, two Consuls'. He grinned, suddenly wanting nothing more than the power of Consulship. He could do so much to change Rome. He couldn't wait to deliver his speech. It was full of details about the economic changes he and Tarpeius could bring. So much money was wasted at the moment. They had even discovered that by diverting only fifty percent of the money used to run and entertain the Senate, they could feed the poorest twenty percent of Imum dwellers for free. They also planned to try to reform the elections to reduce cost. There seemed no need to have annual elections—half the year was spent campaigning rather than administrating Rome.

Gnaeus turned around to watch the Augur as the ceremonial brazier was brought across to him. With a theatrical flourish, the Augur pulled a shroud away from a wire cage in front of him, revealing a flock of woodpeckers. The birds were terrified, ripping at each other with their beaks in the confined space. The Augur produced a small plastic canister from his bag and used it to spray some noxious fluid over the panicking birds. The volatile smell reached Gnaeus immediately; it smelt like some sort of solvent. The Augur reached into the brazier and pulled out a single glowing coal using a golden pair of tongs.

'Juno, grant me your sight,' he said with loud reverence, and cast the stone into the cage.

The woodpeckers burst into flames. Burning feathers cascaded down to where Gnaeus stood in surprise. He had seen birds opened before, to check the omens in the lay of their innards, but this particular pagan cruelty was new to him. The Augur whipped out a pad of parchment and a stylus and made quick notes, glancing up at the woodpeckers as he wrote and drew. He seemed to be using the patterns of their panicked behaviour as some sort of arcane key to Juno's mind.

As the flames started to die down, most of the birds lay still. Gnaeus thought of his own God, and how, rather than expect other things to be tortured for him, he let himself be tortured for Gnaeus. Then, suddenly, one of the birds swooped upwards from the bottom of the cage and somehow flew threw one of the thin gaps in the bars. Aflame, it twirled through the air, flapping ineffectually in its last moments of life.

Its companions had expired together, caged, but it spent its last moments free, coursing down to earth, far below: a dying spark in a dying world.

Everyone applauded the Augur, and Gnaeus realised he was still staring down to where the woodpecker had fallen, far below, lost in a crowd which had not noticed its final, desperate, panicked, valiant flight.

Gnaeus looked up to the Consular stage as a chorus of boos erupted from the crowd. Albus had risen to give the first speech.

'I do not need to extol my virtues. For they are clearly known.' Bizarrely the way he spoke made even the most self-righteous remarks seem compelling. 'Firstly, I am a true Roman, born of true Romans. Secondly, I am a Noble, and my family has been Noble since the first days of the republic. Thirdly, I have fought for Rome against its enemies and been voted the most feared General ever produced by our Eternal City. Fourthly, I am the Pontifex Maximus and have the blessing of the gods. But,' he raised his arms up above his head, 'these things are not that important. What is important now, more than ever, is strength. Romans. Where would you be without me?'

'Richer, you thieving bastard,' a shout rang out from far below, followed by some laughter.

'I'll tell you. Lost.' Albus paused, and let his words echo over the Field of Mars. 'Without me there would be no Rome now, and you would have none of the things you take for granted. Some of you wouldn't even have a roof over your heads.'

'Some of us have got three roofs over us now you cunt!' the same man called out, from near the front of the crowd.

Albus glanced across to his security team, and a Praetorian in the corner of his stage muttered an order into his neck microscire.

'Rome has enemies. You might have forgotten that, after years of peace which I bought you with my blood.' Gnaeus drew breath sharply at this remark, remembering how Albus had feasted in Rome, whilst he, Titus, and the others, had nearly starved on a freezing beach. He wanted to shout a retort back himself, but suppressed the urge. Not only would it have been highly against protocol, but also he had a perfect view of the troublemaker from earlier being dragged away by Praetorians, his newly broken arms hanging crookedly by his sides.

'Our enemies now surround us. You saw how our great Protector Titus Labienus Aquilinus saved us from the terrorists. Vote for me, and enjoy another year of protection. I will keep Rome safe. We will keep Rome safe.'

He ended there, very simply. It was tradition now for the speeches to be short. Gnaeus had read that in the early republic they would sometimes have gone on for so long that there was barely time to complete the vote before sundown. Albus returned to his seat apathetically, as if his speech had cost him nothing and meant nothing.

Catula's speech was even shorter. He had clearly been drinking constantly since the night before and looked awful. The whole bottom hem of his toga was wet, and Gnaeus wondered if perhaps he had wet himself. He mumbled some words about his Nobility into the microscire. At one point Gnaeus thought that he was going to cry. His speech received no response from the crowd at all, as if it had gone unnoticed.

Gnaeus heart beat faster as the cornum blasted a third time. He gripped Vibia's hand tightly for a moment, and then slowly released it. He was on his own now, in front of the world. He stepped forwards to the edge of the stage and tried not to look down; he wasn't too keen on heights.

He opened his mouth to give the speech that he had prepared. Every word was there, imbedded in his mind. Facts and figures, all the information that would define his Consulship: the blueprint to reform Rome. He thought of Vibia, of Tarpeius and his dead garden, of Titus and his starving army, and of the woodpecker dying needlessly as it flew to freedom. He ignored his clever, perfectly worded speech. Instead, he spoke from his heart.

'I am Gnaeus Lartius, and I am not a full Roman, although my father was. My mother is Etruscan. I am not a Noble, and I care nothing for titles men give themselves. I have fought for Rome against its enemies, but I will not dwell on that here because it is irrelevant to why I stand before you today. I am not the Pontifex Maximus, but I believe that that position is nothing but a ruse to create money and wield power. I do not even believe in your gods. On paper I am the worst candidate for the Consulship of Rome.'

There was a sharp intake of breath from the nearly silent crowd, no politician would ever admit to not believing in the gods publicly. Gnaeus ignored their surprise and continued. 'If you don't vote for me, no army is going to come and crush you in response.'

He paused, and glanced behind him. Vibia was staring at him open mouthed with horror. He turned back to the crowd. He knew he was doing the right thing; she would have to trust him.

'So why, if I am the wrong candidate, and I have nothing to scare you into submission with, do I bother standing before you today? It's because, yes, if you don't vote for me, you will not lose your lives, but you may perhaps lose something greater.' He now raised his arms out to the crowd. 'Romans, did you even turn in your sleep as your freedom was taken from you? Why stand here and vote for a man who will build his Consular palace over your very roofs? Over your gardens, over your Harpasta fields. Why allow this man to turn pure rain from the sky into something controlled? Your rain will become the runoff from his sewers, your light will be at the intensity he allows it and your air will be the quality he chooses to afford you. He will not just rule you, but control you, own you—he will bury you.

'If you vote for me, and for Tarpeius, we will, together, root out the corrupt heart of Rome. We will upend this city. No longer will the rich live on top of the poor. The Summus will be torn down, and we will find ways to bathe the Imum in light it has not seen since our ancient forefathers walked the earth. The Imum was once the beating heart of Rome. It was Rome. It should be free again, and the Aether should be free also, and equal, high up, airy and clean.

'People are more important than politics. We do not need a war with Asia Minor. We need to have a war against our system! And I am ready to fight that war.' He closed his eyes and turned around, walking back to his box.

A huge roar erupted behind him; the crowd was going mad.

He embraced Vibia. He wanted to collapse on her, exhausted. Her mouth was wide open with surprise, 'Gnaeus. That... wasn't what we practised!'

Gnaeus shook his head, 'I'm sorry, I just heard that bastard and...'

'Gnaeus it was amazing.' She tilted her head upwards to kiss him.

Gnaeus felt her father's hand on his shoulder. 'Gnaeus', he said softly. 'Listen.'

Gnaeus did, he could hear cheering. They were still cheering, apart from a small part of the crowd that sounded annoyed with his opposition to war.

'They are shouting your name, Gnaeus,' said Tarpeius.

And they were.

The hairs on his forearms stood up as he listened. They were going to win.

XVII

Titus patrolled back and forth at the front of the voting pens. Citizens pressed forwards, hurriedly pressing their voting key onto the pad at the end of each pen; each key had four faces, one for each candidate. The sun was low in the sky now and most of the people had already voted and headed to the nearest bar. The noise was still deafening though. A hard-core group of Gnaeus supporters refused to leave the field of Mars, despite casting their votes long ago, and their cheers reverberated off the walls of the stage, rising in intensity whenever Gnaeus, Tarpeius, or Vibia, (who seemed to have become some sort of idol for the opposition supporters), appeared, in order to wave or shout encouragement to the crowd. Titus looked about. He was pleased to see that Ceinwyn's father had been wrong about conspiracy and corruption in the elections. There was no sign of anything untoward going on at all.

The last few people were coming through the gates now. The vote was nearly finished. He turned and jogged towards the stage and was allowed up the gantry at the back by the Praetorians guarding it.

'Gnaeus,' he called out as he caught sight of his friend.

Gnaeus, who had been talking to Tarpeius, turned around quickly, smiled, and rushed forwards to embrace Titus.

'I think you are about to win,' Titus said happily.

Gnaeus laughed nervously. 'We'll know soon.'

Vibia came running over excitedly. 'Gnaeus! They are marching in the streets for you in Londinium!' She showed him her scire, on it a

Britannic news broadcast showed a huge group of people thronging the streets, banners proclaiming Gnaeus' and Tarpeius' slogans were being displayed all over the omniajunctus.

Titus pumped his fist in the air: his friend was about to become Consul! The global vote seemed likely to favour him too, not just the capital vote. He looked across at Gnaeus and Vibia, so happy together. He imagined his friend ruling Rome and realised how suited to it he would be. He thought of Hispania. Gnaeus would surely give him and Ceinwyn any province they wanted.

The cornua blew again, and the few people who had waited for the result on the field fell silent. As a group, all on Gnaeus' balcony solemnly wandered forwards, to the edge of their stage and looked around in the cool evening air. The field had been torn apart by the footfall of thousands of voters as if some machine had ripped and scarred its surface. A cheer rang up from the minority that remained as they caught sight of Gnaeus. Titus looked across to the left, Albus stood there proudly, seemingly indifferent about his lack of support. It was as if he couldn't accept that he had lost the people. Titus almost felt sorry for him. Catula was nowhere to be seen. Titus wasn't surprised. It was inconceivable that anyone who had seen, or heard, his speech would consider voting for him. He was probably back in the palace, clearing out his office.

The chief augur walked onto the top stage, above both Gnaeus' and Albus'. Complete silence descended over the field now, and Titus could hear his heart beating hard in his chest.

'Romans. You have cast your votes. You speak with many voices, but together they make just two pronouncements. I have the results of both the Capital and the Global vote.'

Titus took a deep breath. The whole of Rome seemed silent, in their homes, their bars, on the streets; they watched and listened.

'Firstly, the Capital Vote: In last place, with four percent of the vote is, Decimus Catula.'

A jeer rang out over the Field of Mars, quickly silenced by the augur.

'In third place is, Marcus Albus with twenty seven percent of the vote.'

Titus grinned, and looked across at Albus who continued to stare serenely into the distance. He looked like he was posing for the carving of a statue, which was to adorn the forum.

'In second place is, Aulus Tarpeius with thirty percent. And the winner, of the Capital vote is,' he paused theatrically. 'Gnaeus Lartius with thirty nine percent of your vote!'

The augur stepped backwards as a huge roar went up from Gnaeus' supporters. Gnaeus hugged Vibia and the pair danced around in circles on the balcony laughing hysterically.

The augur's voice boomed out once again, but it was almost drowned out by the cheers from below. Rome had a new Consul. Rome had a reforming Consul.

'The results from the global vote are as follows...'

Titus strained to hear. Tarpeius popped open a bottle of champagne and passed it to Gnaeus.

'In last place is, Aulus Tarpeius with three percent of the vote.'

The roar below them started to die down as the few that had heard the proclamation began to spread it. Titus listened in disbelief. The foreign results were always a carbon copy of the Roman vote. If anything, Gnaeus and Tarpeius should have been *more* popular abroad than they would be in Rome, as their policies favoured those on the edge of society. The foreign vote was worth exactly the same as the Capital vote. Tarpeius was out of the running.

'In third place, with twelve percent of the vote, is Gnaeus Lartius.'

Titus felt a sickness rise up from his stomach. The bottle of champagne fell from Gnaeus' fingers and the liquid glugged away, spraying off the edge of the balcony in the gentle breeze.

'In second place, Marcus Albus with thirty two percent.'

The Consul did not move at all as the announcement was read, he just stared forwards at the horizon impassively.

'And the winner, of the foreign vote, is Decimus Catula with fifty three percent of the vote.'

The Augur gestured for Albus to move forwards. The Consul nodded his head in deference and came forwards, bowing low before the Augur.

'By the powers vested in me by Juno, the guardian of Rome, I declare you Consul of Rome, alongside your fellow Consul, Decimus Catula.'

Albus had beaten Catula by just a few percent, but they had left Gnaeus and Tarpeius far behind. Titus turned around, expecting to see some Praetorian guards standing behind them. He thought about the cells of the Mamertine, and their excellent power supply. He was supporting the wrong side, but he could not abandon his friend. He hoped Albus would understand.

Albus turned to the crowd who stood in silence now, too shocked, or too afraid to boo. 'Friends, I wish to express my gratitude for the many of you who came out today to vote for me. Many of you chose to not support me, but your lack of faith has been counterbalanced by the many sensible votes of your countrymen spread across the globe. For those of you who did not vote for Catula? Your lack of support saddens me, he is an honourable man, and he has given much for Rome.'

Titus put his hand on Gnaeus' shoulder. He was shaking too.

'As for my fellow candidates...'

Albus looked up at their balcony, and for a moment his eyes met with Titus'. Titus winced, and he squeezed Gnaeus' shoulder tighter. Whatever was about to happen, they would face it together.

'Today was not your day. However, order is the most important thing. I will behave with honour as long as you do also. There must be no fighting on the streets.'

Titus couldn't believe his luck—they had been offered a truce by a man who could have simply crushed them. Gnaeus was still shaking, but he wasn't looking at Albus, he didn't seem to have listened to him at all. Titus watched as he put his hand on Vibia's and pulled at one of her rings. She darted her hand away before he managed to get it off, shouted angrily and stepped back.

'No!' Gnaeus shouted at her. 'I will not dishonour you!'

Vibia glared at him angrily, proudly.'

'Father,' she said sternly.

'Yes,' Tarpeius said wearily, turning towards at her. He looked completely broken.

'Last night, Gnaeus asked me to marry him once he was Consul of Rome.'

Tarpeius said nothing. He didn't look like he was even listening.

'I intend to marry Gnaeus anyway.'

'But Vibia,' Gnaeus replied pleadingly. 'I've ruined it, I'm not... not anything now...' He reached for the ring again, as Vibia hopped back out of reach, her half purple hair bouncing vigorously.

Then she stopped, shook her fists angrily, wiped her eyes with them, and flung herself at Gnaeus, kissing him frantically. 'Don't you understand, you stupid, proud, brilliant man, that I don't care whether you are Consul of Rome, or dying under the Carnifex's blades—I love you! And I always will. And I will hold you to your promise to marry me.'

Gnaeus pulled himself away, shocked, and started to laugh. Then Vibia started to as well, and the pair collapsed to their knees on the floor of the box, laughing and sobbing.

Tarpeius walked slowly over to the pair of them his face unreadable. 'I have lost this election, and now I am to lose my daughter it seems.'

Gnaeus opened his mouth to speak.

Then a smile managed to break across Tarpeius' exhausted face. 'But I am gaining a son—a son who is a better man than I, and one day a son who should lead Rome. A son who will one day stand before the whole of Rome and with his words, either change it forever, or bring it down, so that its power is broken for eternity.' He kissed Gnaeus on the forehead. 'I bless this marriage.'

Titus embraced Gnaeus and congratulated him, before returning to his place on the edge of the balcony to hear the last of Albus' speech. Most of the supporters had gone now, and the few that remained were sitting in silent disbelief. The Field of Mars had started to fill again though, with Praetorians, their black helmets glowing a dull orange in the setting sun.

'Finally,' Albus said. 'I have two announcements. Firstly, I have the sad duty to announce that, due to a sudden failure in Dacia, we will have a programme of rolling power cuts starting from tonight. These will mainly be at night to prevent damage to industry and will be accompanied by a strict, military enforced curfew. The Imum will receive double the length of cuts due to its lack of key business, but the Aether will also need to bear its share of the pain. We are all in this together. A groan went up from the last of the crowd.

'And on a more cheerful note, earlier today I took a new wife.'

Titus laughed involuntarily with surprise, but managed to stop himself before anyone official heard. He had never heard such a ridiculous victory speech. No wonder Albus' mind had not been on the election.

'Sexta Catula will produce a child to continue my family name. She is an honourable Roman from a long honourable family: a family who serves Rome completely. With the help of the gods, our son will one day serve you, as I stand before you today to serve you as your humble servant.'

He stepped back from the balcony edge and disappeared behind the purple drape, behind which, presumably, waited his new, extremely young wife. Far below, the Praetorians began to clap, almost mechanically, and with a deepening nausea, Titus watched the small remaining pocket of Gnaeus' supporters, now trapped in the centre of the Praetorians, start to nervously applaud their victorious Consul.

XVIII

Far below, on the street, a crash of glass alerted Titus to another attempted looting. The Praetorians ruled the pitch-black streets at night, but there were many troublemakers who would risk anything to unsettle their victorious Consul.

'Burn the bastards out!' rang out a cry from far below him, as he sat on the balcony with Ceinwyn. She was dressed much more simply for this dinner, and she looked tired.

Far below, Titus heard the outraged scream of whoever owned the shop carrying up to him on the wind, followed by the shout of whoever it was who had broken in. 'You're going to burn, you treacherous Gallic bastard!'

'I voted for Tarpeius!' came the shopkeeper's terrified, accented cry. The Praetorians were nowhere to be seen.

'Maybe, but your country didn't.'

A flash illuminated the walls of the building around them, followed by the flicker of flames far below. Titus listened in silence as the man's screams grew quieter.

'So,' Ceinwyn said, after a long pause. 'Is this really the city you want our children to grow up in?'

Titus sighed. The interruption from below couldn't have come at a worse time. He looked across at the now nearly complete Colloseum, glowing with power as the final elements of its hurried construction were finished. Its glow was the only source of light for their meal, apart from two candles sitting forlornly at opposite ends of their new table which, like everything in their new room in the palace, was ornate. Titus felt embarrassed to be sad living in such opulence, but they had argued every day now for the week since Gnaeus had lost the election.

'Titus, look at me.'

Reluctantly he did.

'Titus, we have a home to go to, with friends, and some sense of security. You have no reason to remain here anymore. You've lost Albus' trust since you supported Gnaeus—all we have is this horrible room.'

'I'm still the *Protector of Rome!*' Titus exclaimed. It was true. To his relief, Albus had taken him aside the day after the elections and asked him to stay on. 'He still needs me to find Filii Aquilae. He thinks they are more a threat than Asia Minor.'

'Perhaps. Perhaps they are,' Ceinwyn replied angrily. Her gourmet food was untouched. 'Maybe we *should* find them Titus, but join them, fight Rome with them.'

Titus rose to his feet angrily, his chair falling over backwards and clattering on the marble balcony. 'Be careful Ceinwyn,' he growled. 'If we are heard then...'

'Then what?' Ceinwyn screamed. 'We'll be put in prison?' She scowled at Titus and pointed back at the room behind her. 'This room is a prison Titus. It's a prison to keep us quietly content.'

'Ceinwyn, you need to be careful,' Titus said calmly. Anyone could be listening.

Ceinwyn rose to her feet, speaking slowly and forcefully. 'Are you threatening me Titus?'

'No. If you want to oppose Albus then do it. However, I cannot. And I think you are a fool.'

'For seeking justice?' Ceinwyn asked.

'For throwing away this chance. We have this one chance to make something great of our family. I cannot believe you are being this selfish.'

'Selfish?' Her eyes narrowed as she hissed at him. 'My mother died because your people couldn't accept her loving a Slave. I nearly died at the hands of Strabo who would have sold my friends' organs, and mine, to rich Romans. It's your people who are selfish.'

'But I'm different,' Titus implored. 'Come on Ceinwyn, remember! We've spoken about this. I hate what my people have done—'

'I'm not sure,' Ceinwyn said quietly, tears flowing now, 'or at least... I'm not sure anymore.'

'Ceinwyn!' Titus said softly.

'The Titus that I married, all *he* wanted was to live with me and have children in the mountains, to be safe and have his friends around him. He didn't even want to be Governor really.' She looked up at him lovingly. 'He was proud of the honour though when it was given to him, and he would have been so good at governing Luguvalium. He didn't care what people thought of him, and he could probably have told when people were using him. That Titus, could tell when people, who call themselves his friends, were laughing about him openly at parties.'

Titus seethed, Ceinwyn was wrong. Albus trusted him, and the senators respected him as the *Protector of Rome*. Without him the terrorists would have destroyed a large, presumably important, part of Rome, but his wife could only see her own desire to be back home; home where it was cold and rained three hundred and sixty days of the year; home where Cyric was. He tried to brush that distrustful thought from his head, but it would not quite leave.

'Let's leave tomorrow,' Ceinwyn said. 'No, actually, no. I'm not trying to pressure you—a week; a week to get everything in order and do any final jobs for Albus, then let's go home and never come to this terrible place again.'

'But Hispania would be so much better, think of all the things we could have? Our children would—'

'Stop bringing our unborn children into this!' Ceinwyn shrieked. 'How do you know that one of them even *wants* to be Consul some day? What if one of our children, one day, becomes like that monster.' She pointed across towards the huge eastern wing of the palace, which was entirely made up of Albus' private chambers.

'Do you really think someone that you created could turn out bad?' Titus said, amused.

'I didn't,' she said firmly. 'But then that child would only be half mine.' She picked up a fine china plate and took aim.

He ducked as the plate flew towards him, avoiding it easily, watching forlornly as his wife stormed back into their room. The door slammed.

Sighing, he turned around and looked down at the streets. Belatedly, the Praetorians were finally bringing the fire under control, but the shop, and presumably its owner, had been consumed by it. Far below, the Aether stretched below him dotted with fires. Soon the last of it would be covered over, and the view from their balcony would become one of pure, serene marble. Perhaps then they would have control of the streets again? But Titus could sense that that would not be enough; Rome seemed to be quivering with energy as if it was ready to explode. For a moment, he worried that Albus might lose control of Rome; the thought both terrified and excited him. For a moment he let himself believe that that event would lead to Gnaeus taking over, but he knew that, in reality, some mob leader would rule for a short while, before in turn, being deposed by another, and then another. Rome was safer in the hands of Albus. His wife was a fool for thinking otherwise, but a beautiful fool. If she wanted Northern Britannia then she must have it.

He rose from his chair again, downed the last of the vintage wine and went off to find Albus. It was time to get his province back.

XIX

'Titus, you oaf, I need you—stay!' exclaimed Albus, pouring another glass of the palace's best wine down his throat and refilling both their glasses.

Titus shook his head and tried to avoid drinking anymore. Ceinwyn had drunk almost none of the bottle of wine they had shared earlier that evening, and the Consul seemed set on forcing a whole amphora more down his throat. Albus stared silently, watching him drain the glass, before himself following suit.

'It's good isn't it?'

'The best, of course, Marcus.' Could he get away with using his praenomen? Albus called him by his, but then he was Consul.

'Well, it's not the *best*,' Albus said honestly. 'But really not many people can tell, including you it seems. It's the sort of skill one loses, I suppose, the longer you are away from Rome. Like loyalty?' he added, after a slight pause.

Titus suddenly felt cold. 'You mean like the Governor of Asia Minor, turning to the side of the rebels?' he said, deflecting the question, which he was sure was aimed at him.

'Hakim Shariff?' Albus spluttered. 'No, I always suspected he would be a traitor. It was my father who appointed him. I never agreed that a native man could lead a province, you can only trust a true Roman. No Titus,' he said matter of factly. 'I mean you. Why should I trust you?' Albus stared at him, his eyes unblinking.

Titus looked around fearfully, but there were no Praetorians about to grab him. What was this?

'Trust me? My old friend, well... remember the Transmaritanus...' he tailed off as the memories of what he had done to prove his loyalty flooded back. 'Okay, not that, but... I am here! I came back when you asked and served you. I foiled those terrorists...'

'Hmmm, we've spoken about that already. But I have now come to believe it was an honest, yet of course foolish, mistake of yours to disobey my orders that night.'

'So why do you doubt my loyalty?' Titus asked.

Albus looked at Titus as if he must be mad to ask. 'Well, you're *leaving*?' He rose and collected another jug of wine before returning to their recliners set out in his reception room. The air was full of hashish smoke from the pipes in the centre of the room. Titus had tried not to inhale, but he felt very unusual.

'It's Ceinwyn, if it wasn't for her I would stay, but she's homesick.'

'Ah. I knew it Titus,' he said, wagging his finger at him. 'Fratres supra meretrices,' he said chidingly.

Titus felt a flash of anger. Ceinwyn was not a whore, but perhaps he was indeed guilty of putting her before his friends. He suppressed his feelings and instead laughed. 'We can't do without them though!'

'We can. Or we can just marry a younger one,' Albus said, at the exact moment that Sexta walked in. She immediately looked down at the floor, walked quickly across to Albus and bent to whisper in his ear.

'At this time!' he said angrily, and Titus saw his fist clench. But he seemed to catch himself, slowly relaxed his fist, and gently caressed Sexta's hair. Titus watched her head jerk back suddenly at the first touch, before she remembered to let him. Albus grasped the back of her hair and guided her mouth to his, kissing her firmly in front of Titus. She gasped, and Titus looked away. He tried to think of something to say to interrupt, but no words came. At last, Albus released his wife and with relief, she darted away.

Albus stared at the ceiling for a moment, lost in what seemed like utter delight. 'I'm going to have a proper heir you know?' he said dreamily. 'A child who is mine and who I can be proud of: a Roman child, from two strong Roman families. Rome will be safe.' It was as if he was talking to himself, but then Titus realised he was staring up at the roof mural as he spoke.

'Who are they?' Titus asked, pointing up at the couple, who looked down at them from the ceiling, depicted in bright amaranthine and scarlet, standing on the edge of a great City, presumably Rome.

Albus paused for a second, still lost, and then suddenly looked back at Titus.

'Sorry?' he said. 'What did you ask?'

Titus realised Albus had genuinely been talking to the mural—the hashish must be stronger than he thought. 'Who are they?' he asked again.

'My father and mother.'

'Your father would like Sexta?' Titus asked.

Albus nodded. 'He would be pleased with me. It was he that showed me the truth about Slaves. I must confess, I was not always this... pure.'

'Your slave child?' Titus said thoughtfully, before he could stop himself.

Albus' mouth dropped open and he sprung up, so that he now suddenly sat on the edge of his chair.

'How the fuck do you know that?' he said, his eyes wide with paranoia. He leapt to his feet and crossed the room in an instant. Titus tried to stand up, but it was too late. Albus was standing over him, his face terrifying and his pupils so wide that his eyes were dark, disquieting pools.

'I thought...' he was about to say that he thought everyone knew, because from what his father had said, they did. However, he realised that that would be completely the wrong thing to say. 'I just heard,' he said softly. 'I'm not sure where, maybe at one of the briefings? When we were looking for Filii Aquilae, a lot of intelligence people were there. I think it was mentioned then?'

Albus looked away and nodded silently, clearly filing this information away. Titus wished he had prepared a better answer, he was sure that someone was going to suffer for the lie he had just told.

'Titus, I can trust you as a friend can't I.'

Titus nodded, trying not to look as terrified as he felt.

'When I was young I did stupid things, I was impressionable. I had to be taught. We are all like that, are we not?'

Titus continued to nod.

'Back then, I didn't realise that there is a reason humans and Slaves don't mix, don't breed,' he drew the word out in a way that dripped with contempt. 'I was seduced really, by one of them. She sought a baby of Roman blood I think, and she got it.' His face darkened, and a tear dropped from his eye. He drew the sleeve of his toga angrily across his face to wipe it away. 'That bitch took some of my seed from me, and created a monster, a thing, a half-breed.' He looked up at the ceiling, his pitch black eyes almost inhuman, 'I never loved her! I never loved her!' He was shouting now, clutching his fist and staring up at the mural, into the face of his father.

Titus put his hand out, took a deep breath, and grabbed hold of Albus' shoulder to calm him.

Albus paused, sighed, and looked straight at Titus. 'I didn't order it Titus,' he said earnestly. 'It was my father, he made them do it. I did not have the child killed! I didn't love the girl! I didn't have the child killed!' he shouted at Titus imploringly, desperate to be believed.

'It's okay,' Titus said, moving the hashish pipe out of Albus' reach before any further harm could be done. 'I believe you.'

Albus fell back onto his recliner, chuckling with his eyes closed. Then Titus noticed that the copper table next to Albus was half covered with lines of white powder; the Consul was not just under the influence of hashish.

Albus sat up again slowly, licked his finger, shovelled half a line onto it and sucked it, grimacing at the taste. 'Titus?' his voice was calmer now.

'Yes Consul.'

'You will stay won't you?'

Titus rolled his eyes with frustration. 'No!' He had nearly shouted. He calmed his voice, 'Consul, as I was saying—'

Albus cut him off. 'I need you to destroy Filii Aquilae.'

'Verres can do it,' Titus replied. 'He's better than me anyway.' It was true that Verres seemed much more suited to that sort of work; the work that now churned Titus' stomach.

'No, Verres is Imum scum,' Albus said. 'He's good, but he's from the Imum originally, whatever he tells you. You are a proper Roman. I need you. I trust you.'

'My wife...'

'Will love her new province, and the limitless splendour and bounty of Rome whilst you remain here as my guests. Hispania is rich, Titus, it will fulfil your wildest dreams, and you can do and have anything you want, both here and there, forever. Or you can leave for the freezing wastes of Northern Britannia, beset by Reivers, and not blessed by my favour.'

Titus knew then, for certain, that Ceinwyn was wrong. He understood why she wanted to go back to Britannia, but her thinking was flawed. By doing this first, by performing his duty now, they could have whatever they wanted afterwards. It was worth the wait. Then he had an even better idea; an idea that was sure to win her over. 'We need both provinces.'

He thought of her beaming face proudly, as she realised they could have the riches of Hispania *and* keep the home she loved.

'Of course,' Albus said happily.

Titus shook his fist in silent triumph. He quickly thought of whether there was anything else he needed to ask for whilst the Consul was under the influence of the various drugs he'd taken, but then realised he had been given everything he wanted in the world: two provinces, and anything he wanted in Rome whilst he remained there. All he needed was to find the Filii Aquilae leader in return. The man they called the Aquila.

The door to the reception opened and Sexta reappeared. She bowed and hid her face from him, but it was clear that she had been crying. Behind her, she led in a pair of men dressed in suits, carrying sheaves of documents and a projector.

'*Coniunctus* are here,' Sexta said quietly, and gestured to Titus to leave.

Albus sat up, trying to regain what he could of his composure. 'My old friends, let's have an update then.' He gestured to the man with the projector, who flicked his hand and showered the wall with images of stock graphs and pictures of microchips and satellites.

Titus ducked out of the room. 'Thank you,' he said to Sexta, and reached out to put his hand on her arm protectively, but she was already walking away.

XX

Titus rose at first light and turned over to look for Ceinwyn, but she was not there. He coughed and his parched throat cracked painfully. Clutching his painful head in his hands, he reached for the glass of water Ceinwyn always brought up to bed, but of course it wasn't there. He clattered around the bedroom, tripping in the thick carpet, almost pleased Ceinwyn wasn't there to see him in this state.

The wall screen blinked into life by itself, and a giant eagle appeared in the centre. Titus proudly thought of his gladius, the flag he had followed across the World, and his old body armour, all emblazoned with that same eagle. The volume of the screen increased automatically, heralding an important announcement from the Senate—the post election speech, due today in the Senate building. Titus cursed, how could he have forgotten? At least he didn't have to give a speech, but he should be present with the Praetorian Guard. Then he laughed, at least he was going to be in a better state than Albus, who was meant to be giving a full speech about his plans for this year in office. Titus suspected that, far from preparing to speak to the World, the Consul would be soundly asleep, recovering from his drug binge.

It was past midsummer now and well into the month of Sextilis, but if anything, it was even hotter and Titus felt oppressed by it. He hung his head low, sweating, as he walked across the deserted, sun-baked streets of the nearly completed Summus. In the distance, he could hear the rumble of machines; work on the Colloseum seemed endless.

He reached the levator that eventually would carry thousands of people daily between the upper two levels of Rome: Albus had decided that no levator that granted access to the Summus could also go to the Imum. Just like the streets, the levator was also deserted and Titus felt very alone as he was swallowed by the floor of the Summus. The walls of the levator were glass and the ride down was extremely disconcerting. Only a month ago this area of the Aether had been open to the sky. The Aether's new lights were much brighter than those installed in the Imum, and Titus could see signs of a sophisticated sprinkler system on the ceiling to create artificial rain, but there was something very strange about looking down on the Senate building from above, and seeing it lit entirely artificially in the height of a summer's day. Of course, a far grander Senate building, in new gleaming marble, was nearly complete several hundred feet above him, but for now the original building remained the seat of government and the seat of great announcements. As the levator dropped below the level of the tallest buildings, Titus saw streams of citizens heading towards the Senate building, flanked by a large number of the Praetorian Guard. The building was surrounded by the large press curri, adorned with their satellite dishes.

Titus leapt out of the levator and gathered his ceremonial robes around him closely. He hadn't shaved, but the stubble looked like it was intentional, he'd get away with it. He nodded to the Praetorians lining the route, as he marched past with the rest of the crowd. He caught sight of Verres, his bald head glowing under the lights, and his beard now threaded with gold rings and diamonds. His black body armour was polished, gleaming in the floodlights. He looked one hundred percent the head of the Praetorian Guard, and Titus felt acutely aware of how unprepared he was for today; Verres had probably been planning this for weeks. Titus made a conscious effort to stand up as straight as possible, and puff out his chest. Even if he didn't feel like being the *Protector of Rome* today, then he could at least try to look the part. He wished Ceinwyn was here with him. Or, was it that he wished that he was with Ceinwyn? Wherever she was.

The great cornua blew loudly, announcing the start of the assembly, and the noise took Titus back to his youth. Pride for his city, and people, rushed over him, dispelling the dark clouds. He rushed forwards to take his place in the building, and the crowd parted before him.

Albus caught sight of him as he entered the assembly hall and raised his hand in greeting. Titus smiled back, remembering the night before and how he had been promised two provinces. He needed to tell Ceinwyn the good news, if she ever came back he thought sadly. As Titus came to a halt at the end of a line of Praetorians, Albus shook his head, instead gesturing to an empty place next to him. Titus was taken aback—the right side of the Consul? He crossed the room happily, and took the seat. Two huge cameras pointed down at them. This was being screened all around the world and he was sitting next to the Consul himself. Catula was nowhere to be seen, it was as if he himself had just been promoted to Consul.

Albus rose and the assembly fell into silence. 'All that I needed to say has been said yesterday,' Albus said quietly, clearly also feeling the effects of last night. 'As I mentioned we have a power crisis, and the rolling power cuts will be continuing for the foreseeable future. However,' he added playfully, 'I may, in my infinite wisdom as Consul have found a solution. I have some very interesting people to introduce to you, with some very interesting ideas. You will gain far more from listening to them, than you will from hearing anything else from me.'

Titus was pleasantly surprised. He had never heard Albus be self-deprecating in his life. This was his floor, and traditionally the speech given by the winning Consul was at least an hour, not under a minute. Perhaps it was the comedown from the drugs last night, but the Consul looked quite well, bright and smiling. He looked better than Titus did. Every screen in the World was forced onto this one channel for now, why pass up on the opportunity to speak into every home?

The lights dimmed.

Titus turned around and saw stars projected onto a giant screen behind them. Epic music rose in the background. A spotlight twirled from the ceiling, and came to focus on a giant silver shape that had appeared, as if by magic, in the centre of the Senate building. It was a giant silver tube, about thirty feet long, and on each side it had what appeared to be a massive wing. Fifty feet long and six feet wide, they extended out, lattices of thin, black panels. Titus realised he had seen the panels before on that day he had been searching for Filii Aquilae in the Imum. The trucks had been carrying them in sections. There had been endless trucks.

The screen behind suddenly became almost unpleasantly bright. A huge image of the sun was projected, followed by a montage of ordinary Romans flicking light switches, watching screens, making calls on scires, and driving curri. Then the music quietened and became very solemn as images of Dacia flooded the screen; radioactive filth pouring from pipes over huge fields of dead animals and plants; the sky yellow-grey with the thick smog pouring from the power factories. Titus knew the images were a true likeness of Dacia, for he had spent over a year there as a mercenary. In fact, they were tame. He had far worse on his own scire. Some of the animals he had seen there were like nothing elsewhere on Earth, as if they had evolved differently, or the destroyed landscape somehow caused them to grow differently.

The screen cut out, and suddenly the only light in the Senate building was the spotlight, shining down on the machine at the centre.

A deep voice rang out loudly through the speakers.

'Clean power.'

'Limitless power.'

'Secure power.'

The lights slowly came on, and two smartly dressed men walked forwards to stand by the machine. Titus realised they were the men he had seen last night in Albus' quarters.

'We are *Coniunctus*,' the first man said.

'You are *Coniunctus*,' the second added, addressing the camera—addressing the World.

'We are all *Coniunctus*,' they spoke together. The room fell silent.

'A new era has begun. No longer do you have to rely upon dirty, unreliable power. Infinite, cheap power will soon be here. Your great Consul has given us the honour of this great contract with you. We will, starting next month, begin to fill the void above our Earth with these.' He gestured to the machine next to him: 'These state of the art satellites and their state of the art solar panels. The Consul has given us permission to use the Void Levator, and we are very grateful. In return, from next month, from the moment we start producing your power, your energy bills will be reduced, not by fifty percent, not by seventy five percent, but by ninety percent.'

They paused to let an expectant silence build, but a great hubbub of animated conversation from the crowd prevented the effect from properly developing.

'We ask little in return. We simply ask that you give us time and space to help you. We need a calm Rome to allow our curri to move freely, to allow our people to work safely. We appeal for calm. Thank you Rome. We are here to serve you. We are *'Coniunctus'*.'

Silence fell for a brief moment as people absorbed what they had just been told. Then, suddenly, everyone was on their feet cheering. Albus nodded and looked up at the camera, smiling magnanimously to his crowd around the world. Titus started to clap too but was distracted by his scire vibrating in his pocket. He drew it out, and to his surprise, the number calling was his father's.

He answered it. He could barely hear his father over the crowd.

'Titus, I can see you on my screen.'

Titus smiled. 'Yes father, isn't it amazing? I think I've done it, I think I've restored our honour!' His heart soared, and he looked up at his friend Albus and thought about the two provinces he and Ceinwyn would have, and the children they would have, and the wonderful privileged lives they would all lead. He was at the right hand of the lord of the world.

'I need to speak to you now.' His father's voice sounded grave.

'Father, look, you can see I'm busy.'

'Rome may depend on this.'

Titus stopped smiling and crouched down, where it was a bit quieter.

'I'm not sure if I can leave father. Can't this wait? This is amazing news! I can't believe Albus has managed to get this company to, basically, give free energy to Rome, things are looking great—'

His father cut him off. 'Titus, I need to speak to you now, in person, not over the omniajunctus. Make your excuses and get here now if you truly consider yourself to be *Protector of Rome*.' Titus winced at the sarcasm his father held in his voice when using his title.

He started to leave, deflated. His father cared nothing for what he had achieved.

'No,' his father said, over the scire, as he started to cross the floor glumly. 'Smile, keep applauding.'

Titus' hairs rose up on the back of his neck, and he started doing as his father said. Looking around he saw the other happy smiling faces and wondered how many others were acting. He thought of the applauding crowd on the Field of Mars the evening before, with the Praetorians, and their fully charged fasces, surrounding them.

'I'll come straight to the house.'

'No, Titus. I'm at the Great Aesculapium.'

Titus frowned for a moment. 'The Aesculapium?' he said with surprise.

'I'll explain when you get here.' The scire went dead.

Titus hurried out, trying to look both happy, and on important *Protector of Rome* business at the same time. At the door, he gestured to one of the Praetorian curri, and one of the five ceremonial guards quickly threw him his key card without a moment's hesitation.

Rome was still deserted as he drove to the Aesculapium. Everyone was still inside their houses watching their screens and celebrating Albus' generosity, but he could no longer be happy; he had no idea what had happened to his father. He was in the Aesculapium, and from the tone of his voice, it sounded serious. The deserted streets let him use both sides of the road.

XXI

Ceinwyn paused outside the entrance to the Colloseum construction site and watched as a huge earth mover crawled past, its bright manoeuvring lights shining like the eyes of a lumbering insect. The Senate gathering was the perfect moment. Her father had packed her a small bag and helped her with her disguise, as Thana looked on angrily. Thana said that she was concerned for Ceinwyn's safety, but Ceinwyn could see through her; she was jealous that her husband's daughter was back; she was jealous that she could not herself bear a child to her husband, and she was jealous that Ceinwyn was more important to her father than she was. Ceinwyn despised her. Thana was so obvious.

She had come close to simply leaving after that meal with Titus, and returning to Luguvalium, but the truth was that she wasn't yet ready to leave without him. She still loved him, and to her horror she had discovered two nights ago that she had not needed to use any of her sanitary towels since she had arrived in Rome. She had carried the secret for two days now, too long. She had tried to share it with Titus last night, but the meal had turned sour. She knew that he wanted children, and she did too, but the timing was completely wrong now, and she wondered now how she ever would tell him. At least she had managed to share her secret with one other person though she thought, as she remembered the angry scire call to Cyric that she had made last night, and how serendipitous it had been. Cyric had tried his hardest to convince her to leave, to come back to him, but in doing so had unwittingly given her information that made it even harder for her to leave.

She had mentioned her father's suspicions about Albus tampering with the vote, and her attempts to prove this by finding the omniajunctus hub under the Great Library. She had spent hours since then trying to work out where it might have been moved. Surely it was too big to move secretly out of Rome? Also, it would have to have been removed carefully in sections, or the omniajunctus would have had to go offline. Cyric had been eager to help. He had asked about whether any new buildings were being built, taking an age, and using huge amounts of power. As soon as she mentioned the Colloseum, he had suggested she look there. It made sense. The intensive building work here would be perfect cover to move the hub slowly over the course of months. Albus would retain control of the omniajunctus, but also have the advantage of an even securer long term location for it.

The small satchel on her back carried stolen official papers, which her father and other resistance Slaves had obtained. Her smart suit marked her out as wealthy, important, and official. She marched up to the gate and flashed the ID at the guard. She was allowed past easily, which made sense, as the ID showed her to be a member of the Senate Office, and the documents she carried authorised her to carry out routine inspections at the facility. She glanced behind the guard hut as she passed and noticed a large portacabin. Visible through the window were half a dozen Praetorian Guard uniforms hanging on the wall. She would do well to avoid capture.

She took a deep breath and approached the building itself which gleamed in the sun. The outside, like everything else in the Summus, was constructed from a mixture of white and rose marble. The final level was nearing completion, and a fortress of cranes surrounded the structure, heaving blocks to the highest level, whilst an army of workers swarmed across the top, hammering and mortaring them into place. Ahead of her was an opening twice her height and ready to take two wooden doors, which leant up against the side of the Colloseum, still wrapped in protective plastic sheeting. Through the sheeting, she could make out a diorama showing the history of Rome etched into the wood. The history stretched from left to right, top to bottom, all the way from Aeneas, through Romulus and Remus and their wolf, through the time of the Tyrants, and the Great would-be-Tyrant, Julius Caesar, and finally to the Republic. She liked the way the wood changed colour as the diorama proceeded, the lighter wood at the bottom for the more enlightened modern times. However, she disapproved of the choice of sun baked, white wood for the last line at the bottom, which depicted the construction of the Summus overseen by a giant smiling visage of Albus. She would have had that carved out of blackest ebony should the choice have been hers.

Through the gate, everything was lined in plastic sheeting to protect the marble. A second security guard appeared from what would one day become a ticket booth and sat her down in a waiting room.

To her horror, the room contained five other suit clad Romans. She shuffled across to a spare chair and sat down, trying not to draw attention to herself at all. She reached into her satchel quickly and drew out some of the documents, making sure she didn't disturb the compartment beneath them, which contained a tiny camera and her knife, amongst other things she didn't want discovered. She thought of the basements below the Mamertine which her father had told her about, she did not think she could cope with torture. A small part of her wished that she hadn't tried to be brave when her father had offered her a special capsule, sewn into the lining of the satchel, which she could take in the event of capture. Thana had run upstairs when he had suggested it to her, and she had refused it, laughing at her father, a laugh that had not been returned. Whether capture was likely or not, she needed to try to complete her mission, she needed to get out of here and start exploring the building, but it seemed she now had no choice but to take part in some sort of official tour with these other people.

'Which department are you in?' a Roman woman asked, from across the room.

'Which one are you in?' Ceinwyn asked, thinking quickly and trying not to sweat.

'Hospitality, of course. I've not seen you before,' she said suspiciously.

'Oh,' Ceinwyn said haughtily. 'Hospitality.'

She looked back down at her documents, trying to look extremely important. At that moment, to Ceinwyn's relief, the final person that they were waiting for arrived.

The guard returned and led them quickly down the rest of the plastic sheet-lined corridor, before pausing in front of some metal doors. 'Ladies and Gentlemen, through this gate lies the floor of the new Colloseum. When the facility opens next year people will entertain, fight, and die, for your pleasure, on the very floor you stand upon.'

He pushed the gate open and the sun rushed in. Ceinwyn was surprised to see that there was already sand on the floor of the arena.

The group moved quickly to the centre. Ceinwyn looked around. The first thing that surprised her was how small the arena itself was, no more than three hundred feet from end to end. It was remarkably similar in size to the ancient one below, in the Imum, which it was replacing, but the seating amazed her. Almost vertical tiers of seating reached into the sky, so high that she noticed mirrors installed at the top to ensure that sunlight would always reach the arena floor. Above her, work continued quickly; they would be finished in weeks she suspected. At one side of the seating, half way up, was a huge screen and an enormous contraption of plastic tubes, within which sat huge orange balls painted with numbers, the purpose of which was not clear.

The guard had been joined by two pretty girls, a similar age to Ceinwyn, dressed in white dresses. They wandered amongst Ceinwyn and the government officials, handing out leaflets.

'Without Senate funding none of this would be possible, so remember to tell your managers how important this all is to Rome!' one of the girls said. The other gestured behind them. Ceinwyn turned to watch as the screen flickered into life.

The numbers '2766' flashed up onto the screen, slowly darkening in colour, from a light scarlet to a deep crimson. That was next year's date, when the Colloseum was due to open. A great sound rose from unseen speakers, a low rumble that shook the ground. Suddenly, the numbers were replaced by a montage of the various events that would be shown here. Scenes of Harpasta, and Follis finals were interspersed with bloodier sports: criminals fighting to the death, Slaves being drowned in oil whilst spectators gambled on who would live longest. Ceinwyn felt slightly sick, and suddenly had a great idea of how to slip away and explore the facility. No one was looking, so she put her fingers into her mouth and made herself retch.

The others turned around at the sound of her gagging, looking surprised. She gave an apologetic look and dashed back towards the entrance. No one followed her, engrossed instead by the violence on the screen. As soon as she was behind the metal door once again, she pushed it gently to. She took a corridor perpendicular to the one she had entered from. The plastic sheeting continued to protect the walls as she ran. As she dashed past the rooms, she scanned left and right for any sign of cabling, but there was none. The lights were all fed power by induction coils, but there was no way that would work for the omniajunctus hub; it would need miles of thick cables. Perhaps Cyric had been wrong?

Suddenly a staircase appeared to the right. The steps descended downwards, where surely no spectator would wander. Carefully she began to descend, taking small steps as quietly as she could on the marble. Within one turn of the staircase, the ornate marble was replaced by hatched metal. Ceinwyn smiled to herself. This was an area that the spectators were not expected to see.

At the bottom, the staircase opened out into a dingy corridor. She jogged along, noting that it was lined with cells. Her sense of direction suggested to her that she was directly below the arena now; this was where the animals, Slaves, and criminals would be kept. The cells were tiny, and somehow already looked squalid despite never having been occupied. Ceinwyn wondered what it would feel like to be locked down here in the dark, wanting one last glimpse of light, but knowing that with that would come death. She shivered, even though it was boiling hot beneath the baked sands of the arena. At the far end of the corridor were two larger rooms, with hooks on the walls and showers. These must be the team changing rooms, for Harpasta, and Follis games.

Ceinwyn looked around for another route, but it was clearly a dead end. She turned around, ready to retrace her steps and try another staircase, if there was one, but then she noticed the showers again. The whole changing room was tiled, a giant wet room, and in the centre was a large grating. She knelt down and peered through it. A metal sluice slanted downwards at a forty-five degree angle, deeper into the bowels of the building. It was lucky she was slim. She pulled the knife from her satchel and used it to prise up the edges before clambering through.

Lying on her back, she found she could control her slide on the warm metal using the soles of her shoes. As the dim light from the grate receded, she wished she had packed a torch. Suddenly the incline steepened, and with horror she realised that she was no longer in full control of her slide. Within seconds, there was no metal under her at all and she shrieked as she fell through the air. She landed on a thin metal ledge which dented and rang out deafeningly in the confined space.

She groaned and rolled into a sitting position. Her left hip hurt every time she moved it, but she found she could just stand. The ledge she was positioned on was faintly illuminated from above, and as she looked up drops of muddy water from a grate, at least a hundred feet above, landed on her face. She cursed herself for her stupidity in assuming this vent would lead to some sort of secret facility; she was in a sewer, a far more sensible place for a water drainage shaft to lead to. She was probably going to be flushed all the way down to the Imum before she found a way to escape. She shivered. Her suit was soaked with filthy water. She peered over the edge, where the water landing on the ledge was gently cascading off. There were rungs below, leading down into darkness. She started to descend, slightly happier: if there were rungs, this must lead somewhere.

She had no way to time her climb, it felt like a kilometre, but she knew in truth it could be no more than two hundred feet, or otherwise she would have climbed down into the Aether itself. She knew of no direct connection between any buildings in the Aether and the Summus level, there were just the levators and the road link—Albus wanted to regulate entrance to his palace district.

A warm blast of air below gently buffeted her, telling her that she must be near the bottom. She peered down and saw a disc of white light at the bottom of the vent. With trepidation, she climbed the last of the rungs. She paused, with her foot on the last one and looked down, working out where she would fall to, and what the landing would be like. The room below looked odd, bright and hazy at the same time. Then she realised with panic that it was no room at all.

Far below lay the deserted streets of the Aether, hazy, as she was seeing them through the cloud that today was hanging just below the Summus level. Her arms ached. She looked back up, dreading the climb.

Then a realisation came that sucked her strength away, and she nearly fell. There was no other way off the ledge above, except this ladder to nowhere. Another gust of wind sucked at her. She lowered herself down into nothingness, until at last she hung from the last rung. She looked around desperately in the thin mist for anything that she could use to help her escape. To her surprise, the tiles that made up the metal support of the Aether roof, were not closely fitting and were made of a metal lattice. Twenty yards away she could make out another drainage vent, like the one she was hanging from. Did it too lead to a metal ledge with no escape? Probably, but she had no choice but to try. That, or fall hundreds of feet to certain death. She had to try. She had two lives to look after now.

XXII

Titus left the Praetorian currus carelessly slewed across the road in front of the Aesculapium. He jogged into the great Atrium and headed straight to the reception desk. In front of him were a queue of young men and women wearing white coats. Titus waited impatiently as, one by one, they posed in front of a small white screen set to the side of the desk and had their photo carefully taken.

'Excuse me,' Titus said, leaning around the queue of new medici and trying to catch the eye of the reception girl.

She fixed him with a glare and continued her work.

It would be at least another ten minutes to get all the photos done and Titus didn't have ten minutes: his father must be terribly ill to interrupt him whilst he was sitting at the right hand of the Consul of Rome himself.

Titus turned around and jogged back across the atrium, finding the back door to the accident and emergency department. He peered through the door. There was no way to open it from this side. He knocked twice, the second louder than the first. Then a porter, pushing a trolley with a bloodied patient on it, caused the door to open and Titus slipped through.

He rushed down the main A and E corridor, glancing in at the cubicles. The place was teeming with the sick, but his father was nowhere to be seen.

He ran up to the nurses' station and was greeted by a frosty stare from the senior matron.

'Can I help you, sir?' she said, inhospitably.

'My father, where is he?' Titus blurted out.

'Well let me see.' She put her hands on each side of her head and pushed firmly, closing her eyes as if in deep thought.

Titus stared at her, had she gone mad?

'Hmmm, no... Sorry... My psychic abilities are sadly weak today,' she said sarcastically. 'Perhaps you could start with giving me your father's name?'

Titus glared at her. 'Aquilinus, Lucius Aquilinus.' He pushed his official ID across the desk. 'I'm Titus Labienus Aquilinus, *Protector of Rome*. Who are you?'

The nurse didn't seem especially impressed.

'Are you a patient?' Titus turned to look at a scrawny unshaven medicus approaching him from the side.

'No,' Titus said irritably, 'I'm looking for my father.'

'We're a bit busy, sit over there, and we'll have a look later,' the medicus said quickly.

'Hang on,' Titus replied. 'I'm the *Protector of*—'

'I don't give a shit,' the medicus said, turning back to face him. 'I don't give a shit who you are. Sit down over there, or fuck off.' He looked exhausted.

Titus shrugged his shoulders, ignoring the medicus' order, and continued to search the department. He heard shouting, and general commotion emanating from some double doors up ahead. He pushed the doors open and strode through, ignoring the protests from the nurse and medicus.

There was blood everywhere. Three men lay on thin, plastic coated, metal beds in the centre of the room, screaming, while nurses did their best to keep them in place. Three medici were working furiously on them, trying to get needles into their arms. The nearest man's skin was blackened from head to toe, he only moved a little and his cries were weak. One of the other two men had crumpled legs, one of which seemed to be attached backwards. Titus gagged as he realised that the toes of the man's foot, hanging off the end of the bed, were pointing down at the floor. Thankfully none of the victims was his father.

The medicus grabbed Titus' shoulder roughly and pulled him back into the main department.

'Get out of my department!' he shouted.

'No! I'm not leaving till I've found my father.'

The medicus reached for his security alarm button, but then looked up at Titus' desperate face. 'Okay,' He said wearily. 'Fair enough, I probably wouldn't leave in your situation either. Was your father involved in the disaster at the Colloseum construction site?'

'No,' Titus said, looking back into the room. 'What happened?'

'There was an explosion, a gantry collapsed. They fell.'

The man with the broken legs was still now, and the team looking after him looked even more agitated, feeling desperately for a pulse.

'Into what?'

'Beats me,' the medicus shrugged. 'Something hot.'

Titus looked at the nearest man and his blackened skin. There was something about the pattern of his burns that seemed unusual to Titus. He had seen burns like them before, in the Transmaritanus. He felt an icy chill creep down his back, and the deep, unsettling hum of a Jupiter machine filled his ears. He closed his eyes and drove the memories away.

'Go back to the desk,' the medicus said. 'I need to help these people. The nurse will have a look on the screen for you and find your father.'

Titus nodded thanks and wandered back. 'He's not here,' the nurse said bluntly.

'But where...' Titus said. 'He called me, he's ill.'

'Yes, well—this is an Aesculapium. There are many ill people here, why do you suspect he is in accident and emergency?'

'He called me!' Titus said, exasperated. 'It must be an emergency, he must have fallen ill suddenly, or something horrendous happened to him. Please look again,' he implored.

The nurse tapped away at the keyboard quickly. 'I'll search the ward computers,' she said before sighing. 'Omniajunctus is so slow today!' Eventually she managed to get a result for her search, 'as I thought, your father is on Larch ward. Next time just go straight there, all the cancer patients are there. They don't come here.'

'Cancer?' Titus said feeling sick.

'Shit,' said the nurse quietly, looking down at a file of notes and trying not to catch his eye again.

Titus, in shock, backed away to the chair that the medicus had offered him earlier, and sat down.

XXIII

Ceinwyn took a deep breath and let go of the rung with her left hand, taking all her weight with her right. Her arm ached, but she was strong and light, she knew she could do this. She swung forwards and grabbed the edge of the roof lattice with her free hand, and then released her right. She was now hanging from the roof alone. She laughed for a moment as the wind whistled by, starting to dry her clothes. She felt so free up here. She swung forwards again and began to move towards the next hole.

The last few movements were torture on her arms, but she knew she could make it, because she had to do it or drop to her death. She paused at the edge of the vent to recover her strength. When she was ready, she took a deep breath again. Hanging from her right arm, her left reached into the vent to take hold of the ladder, but it touched only bare, smooth, metal. She started to panic, and could feel her grip slipping. The hold on the sharp lattice of metal was cutting into her skin. She felt like screaming, but there was no one to hear her. She wondered what passers-by below would make of her mangled body lying in the middle of a street or park. They would have no idea of where she had come from, let alone what she had died trying to do: getting evidence to unmask a Tyrant.

She threw her body forwards in a last, desperate attempt. Her grip slipped. She started to fall, but as she did so her left hand closed around a ladder rung above her.

The momentum of her slip swung her wrist painfully against the edge of the vent, but she just managed to keep her faint grip on the rung. Throwing herself upwards, she got both hands onto it, and pulled herself up until she could use her feet as braces against the sides of the vent.

She paused for a moment, panting, her breath ragged, as she stared down at the city below. Then she looked up. She had to climb upwards, into the dark sewer system beneath the new Colloseum. Her hands ached, but she made them hold onto the rungs, and her legs shook as she took tortured steps upwards. There was a constant drip of dirty water from above, and she tried to keep her gaze downwards as much as she could to avoid it.

It was so hard to gauge distance in the dark, but she was sure that she had climbed further up now than she had descended in the first tunnel. She hoped desperately that she was right, for she knew that most likely the vents were identical, and that despite her long climb beneath the Summus, she would probably end up stuck on an identical metal ledge with nowhere further to climb. If that happened she would just have to try another vent, and then another, until she found a way out, or through weakness fell to her death hundreds of feet below.

Then she caught a glimpse of a new light. A glimmer of faint white on the metal in front of her. She twisted her head round and laughed with joy. A small tunnel joined the shaft behind her, and at the end of it, she could see a small metal grille. Bright light, from an as yet unseen room, shone brightly from between the bars. She twisted round and managed to get her legs into the tunnel and, with one final push, she finally lay on her back in the shaft. She stayed there for a moment, enjoying having no weight on her aching legs. Then she began to shuffle forwards, feet first.

She rested again with her feet against the grille and listened. Cool air blew gently up her trouser legs. She could hear two men talking, but couldn't make out what they were saying. She waited for them to go. The shaft was too narrow for her to turn around to get her head to the grille. There was now silence. She waited another minute. Still nothing, just a faint whirring sound in the background.

She kicked hard. The grille flew into the room beyond, and she used her hands to push herself forwards. As she fell into the room, she narrowed her eyes against the sudden brightness, making out rows of metal tables and chairs. She landed awkwardly, but managed to stay on her feet. She was in a cafeteria, but it wasn't empty. Standing at the other end, one hand in the dispenser of a chocolate vending machine, was a fat young man in white overalls. His piggy eyes stared at her, and his mouth flopped open.

'Intruder,' he yelled, in a high-pitched, whiny voice, and started to run towards her. Then he stopped half way across the cafeteria, clearly changed his mind, and charged away before hammering on a door across the corridor from the cafeteria. Ceinwyn turned the other way and fled. She tore along the corridor's concrete floor, looking desperately for any open doors that she could enter. Perhaps she could find another vent to hide in? The corridor turned a corner. She sped round it, acutely aware of how noisy her impressive heeled shoes were. She could hear pursuers behind her. Was she still under the Colloseum? Was this where the Omniajunctus hub was now accommodated? The rooms on either side of the corridor had windows, but the interiors were pitch black and the doors locked.

The pursuers were closer now, and to her horror she could see ahead that the corridor was a dead end. She panicked, kicking at the doors as she ran. Three men, all in white overalls, rounded the corner. One of them was the fat man she had seen in the cafeteria.

She kicked the door again, and threw all her weight against it. It burst open, throwing her to the floor in a pitch-black room. She got to her feet and ran into the darkness, but almost immediately she caught her leg against a hard cold metal object. She screamed with pain and rolled onto the floor.

She lay there, trying to control her breathing. Looking up, she could make out some faint light in the room now that the door was open. There was row after row of scire banks. She smiled despite the pain, and the inevitability of her capture: her father had been right— Albus had moved the omniajunctus hub. Now all she needed was photos to prove it, and proof that there was a malicious intent behind it being moved. She crouched down and started to run along the bank of scires, keeping low. She thought of Titus. She would need him to get that final piece of the puzzle somehow. He would be able to steal something of use that could prove what Albus was doing; that was, if he would help her at all. She thought back to waking that morning and seeing him lying drunk next to her, and for the first time in their short married life, she had not had the desire to wake him. She had no idea where he had been all evening after she had stormed off. She had returned, half an hour later, after a walk and he had been gone. *Would he help her?* she wondered—when he had so much to gain by staying loyal to Albus. She was sure that Hispania was simply a lure to get Titus' loyalty, but Titus didn't accept that. He believed Albus over her. She wanted to cry.

Above her, the lights started to flicker on as the men started to cross the room towards her. She stood up straight now, there was no point trying to hide anymore. She ran, as fast as she could, towards the end of the scire room, her breath catching in her throat painfully. She was exhausted already from the terrifying climb she had done earlier. She reached for the knife that she had earlier moved to her pocket. The Praetorian's dying face flashed before her, but she would not let these Romans capture her. If need be she would kill herself first, she knew that she could never withstand torture. She would never let herself give her father away.

She flicked her head round and glanced over her shoulder. The men were no more than twenty yards behind her now, gaining on her quickly. She charged towards the end of the room and leapt through a window at its edge. She landed on a thin metal gantry, and her mouth opened in awe.

She stood in a silo, fifty feet across, and in the centre was a huge bank of scires. The bank was shaped like a giant upright torpedo, a hundred feet high, and the scires were connected by tubing, which glowed blue with energy. She was staring at the omniajunctus hub. She needed to take a photo, but there was no time, and no point if she was then captured. She looked up; there must be a way to escape. There were around twenty levels of gantry to reach the top, and the first was just within reach. She leapt up, caught the edge, and with the last of her strength, hauled herself up just as the first of the three men appeared.

The man tried to jump up too, but Ceinwyn stabbed down into his knuckles with her knife, and he leapt back, screaming with anger. She ran around the gantry to the other side of the silo and leapt up to the next gantry. The men were slower than she was over this terrain, she thought to herself that they should leave the fat man behind, but they didn't seem to want to reduce the size of their group. It was almost as if they were scared of her.

After ten minutes of running and climbing, with a last effort, she pulled herself onto the highest gantry and looked down at the glowing hub below her, crackling with energy. She pulled out the small camera her father had given her, the men were a whole level below her. She took photos, at every possible angle and of every section of the installation that she could. The scire tower was so close now that she could feel the intense heat coming off it. She thought about the blue glowing connections between the scires, just fragile plastic tubes, and started to have an idea. The men were close now and the drop was massive, over a hundred feet.

She stood at the top gantry, looking down as the men reached the same point on the gantry below her. She smiled and held out her bag over the top of the scire tower.

The men paused and looked up at her. The fat man looked behind him at the scire tower, looming so close behind, and then back at her heavy satchel, poised to throw. He shook his head frantically. 'No! Please!' he implored.

She let go of the satchel and leapt from the gantry, into the safety of the topmost corridor encircling the hub silo. The satchel collided with the hub, shattering some of the connections. The lights above her flickered and the hub spluttered, arcs of power coursing up and down it in light blue lightning bursts. The three men backed away, unable to escape as smoke started to rise towards the roof of the silo. At the point of her satchel's impact, the hub now glowed red as it melted and started to bend towards the men. Seeing what was about to happen two of the men leapt from the gantry. Ceinwyn watched as one made it to the gantry below, before being lost to view, but the other fell, end over end, right down to the bottom of the silo. The final man stood, rooted to the spot by fear, as the hub split in two only a metre in front of him. Ceinwyn was temporarily blinded by the flash as more power arced forth, and the man's screams were abruptly drowned out by the crackling of electricity. Her nose filled with a smell just like roast pork, only slightly sweeter. She checked the camera was safe in her pocket, smiled to herself, and jogged towards the levator at the end of the corridor, hoping that one day the pictures she had taken could help bring Rome to its knees.

She reached her father's house quickly, taking backstreets where possible. However, the streets were still mainly deserted and she needn't have taken the precaution. Then she was sitting at the kitchen table again, exactly as she had that morning, except now she was no longer afraid. She had succeeded in her mission. She looked up proudly into her father's eyes as he scanned through the pictures she had taken. He smiled grimly saying nothing as he examined them, but she could tell that he was pleased with her.

'Good,' he said eventually. 'This is very useful. We just need proof of intent now.'

'What do you mean?'

'Proof of why they moved it. We need conclusive evidence that they used this to influence the elections, and then we need some way of making it public.'

Ceinwyn thought about the screens in every house in Rome and in almost every house around the world.

'No,' said Devin realising what she was thinking. 'We looked at that. All the broadcasts are run via the omniajunctus, so we would need to control that in order to control the broadcasts. If we were strong enough to do that, we'd be strong enough just to *take* Rome.'

Ceinwyn thought for a moment. She didn't have another idea yet, but she realised that it was a waste of time to worry about that yet. Before she could show proof to the world, she needed to find proof. She needed proof of what Albus was doing, and that would need someone, on their side, within the highest ranks of Rome. She needed her husband.

The screen flickered on in the corner, and Sentius, the old Roman who was Devin's master, chuckled to himself and opened his eyes to stare at it. Her father hated screens and turned it off as much as possible, but there were some announcements where the screens would turn themselves on and Devin would have to find the controller and turn it off, if that was permitted. He suspected that doing this was logged somewhere, in case it turned out to be useful evidence in the future.

As her father reached for the controller, Ceinwyn caught sight of something which made her feel terribly sick, and as angry as she had ever been at the same time. There, on the screen, was Titus standing next to Albus, happily applauding. The voiceover spoke about power, and satellites, and something called *Coniunctus*, but she barely heard it.

'Have you still got a spare room?' she asked miserably.

'Why?' her father asked brightly and looked up at the screen. 'Oh,' he said quietly looking embarrassed, realising why she asked. 'Yes, of course,' he said, sadly.

Both of them sat in silence for a moment after her father had turned off the screen.

'He may not have had a choice you know,' her father said, trying to cheer her up.

'It's not that father,' Ceinwyn replied bitterly. 'Last night we talked about leaving, and I really thought he was considering it. But,' she added, 'he has made his choice.'

'And you should make yours,' came the dry creaky voice of her stepmother who at that moment appeared at the top of the stairs.

'Thana,' her father said. 'I don't think this is a good time...'

'Yes, you were right!' Ceinwyn shouted at Thana, interrupting her father. 'You were right, you dried up selfish bitch! I should have listened to *you* from the beginning. You must be so happy that my husband has betrayed me! But you know something? I'm coming home now, so you'll have to put up with me for weeks, months even, whilst I help my father defeat these Roman bastards. So don't start gloating too soon Thana, you won't be rid of me easily.'

'You ungrateful girl!' Thana said bitterly. 'I really am pleased. I want you to come home, this is your home!'

'Don't lie to me, Thana,' Ceinwyn said. 'The day I was expelled from Rome was the happiest day of your life—the day you got my father all to yourself!'

'Ceinwyn!' her father shouted. 'Calm down! Thana has cared for you since you were a young child. She loves you.'

'Don't worry, Thana,' Ceinwyn continued sullenly. 'I'll be gone soon enough, and hopefully you'll never have to see me again.'

'Ceinwyn,' Thana said, her voice breaking. 'Yes, it's true that I am very happy that your marriage to this Roman bastard has collapsed, but I am not going to gloat, because I know how much it must hurt. However,' she added very seriously, and with tears in her eyes, 'there are things that hurt more than the loss of a husband. You... you, know so little—'

'Thana,' her father said calmly, 'I think you need to rest.'

'Yes,' Thana said, quietly and distantly, 'I do.' She turned to Ceinwyn. 'Please stay as long as you like.'

Ceinwyn wanted to continue to curse her, but for the first time in her life, she felt sorry for her stepmother. 'It must have been hard for you,' she said. 'Not being able to have any children yourself.'

Thana nodded, walked out silently, and shut the door.

She got up and hugged her father, and the tears started to come. She couldn't stop them, didn't want to. She sobbed, her head buried in his chest.

'It's okay Ceinwyn, it's okay.'

'I want to destroy Albus. I want Titus back!'

'We will Ceinwyn,' he replied softly, 'one day we will be free. Thana loves you dearly and just wants you to be safe, but in one thing she is wrong. There is no good in you and Titus falling out.'

'He loves Rome more than me,' Ceinwyn said quietly.

'He has been tricked by Albus—remember who it is we are dealing with. Please Ceinwyn, don't write him off completely yet.'

'But for now,' Ceinwyn replied, 'we have no one we trust who can get the information we need.'

'We'll find a way,' he said. 'We always have.'

Ceinwyn walked upstairs and sat down at the top of the stairs alone. Her hands drifted down to her tummy and she hugged herself, imagining the tiny life growing beneath her fingers; a tiny life that might never know its father. She started to cry.

XXIV

Titus galloped up the stairs of the Aesculapium towards the cancer ward, his mind completely jumbled up.

He had known his father had been ill for some time, but cancer? Why had his father not said something?

He tapped on the ward door and a young nurse answered it politely, leading him through. She gestured towards a small sitting room, with two battered sofas and some chocolates on the table in the middle. There were no windows. He could hardly think of a more depressing place.

Somewhere in the distance, he could hear the sound of retching. The nurse came back. 'Your father is having his treatment, you'll need to wait.'

'I can, but I'd rather see him now. Would you ask him?' The nurse nodded and wandered away. Titus sipped the cup of weak coffee they had given him. At least they had been kinder to him than in accident and emergency. He wondered how many people had sat in similar situations on these sofas.

His father had pretty much ignored him when he was young, and he had been proud of how he had managed to make so much of himself without his parents. Now, he wondered how he would cope when his father was gone.

The nurse came back and nodded. 'He's not well, but he's happy to talk.'

Titus was ushered down the ward. He looked into a bay as he went past and saw four men, all yellow and emaciated, staring into space from their reclining chairs. The room was utterly devoid of hope. His heart sank.

He rounded the corner and found that his father was in a private bay. 'He's a Noble,' the nurse said. 'We give him the best room when he comes for his treatments.' Clearly, Strabo's words a year ago, about the fate that would befall his father if he didn't work for him, had been lies.

Titus paused outside the room and tried to make himself feel brave. He would have far rather defended Marcus from the Transmaritanians again, with one arm broken, than face what lay in this room. He stepped forwards. His father was sitting up, reading his newspaper, and you could only tell there was something wrong by the drip connected to his arm. Titus sighed and walked forwards.

'Father, why didn't you...'

'Titus!' his father said happily. 'Something has happened today that makes no sense at all. We need to discuss it urgently.'

Titus stared at him. 'What? You mean *Coniunctus*?' he said incredulously. 'I've just discovered my father has cancer, and you want to talk about some satellites, and who provides the power in Rome?'

'Naturally,' his father replied quickly. 'Because I think that this is the key to it, the key to who has the *power* in Rome.'

'When did you get diagnosed? What do you have? What is going to happen? Are you going to die?'

His father laughed. 'So many questions. First of all, an apology. I should have told you, but you were far away and I didn't want to make you come back. There really is nothing for you here, and I still think you should leave before it's too late.'

'But what is it father, is it curable?'

'Perhaps. They say it can be, in some cases. But the cure is, amusingly, poison,' he said chuckling and gesturing at the glass drip bottle. 'I think you know this poison better than I do.'

Titus looked up at the bottle connected to the tubing. A slightly yellowish substance sat within, dripping slowly through a line wrapped in metal foil. Titus looked at his father's arm, and saw bright red lines coursing upwards.

His father saw the direction of his gaze. 'It damages the vessels when it enters, hurts a bit, but it's necessary. That's not really important though, we need to speak of *Coniunctus*.' Suddenly he went green and retched. The nurse rushed back in, moved Titus back and injected a very small amount of another liquid into the drip. The retching slowly subsided and the nurse left. Titus waited whilst his father got his breath back.

'Sorry Titus, at least it's only once every two weeks, you feel fine for a few days between, a bit fluey the others.'

'What have you got?'

'It's called Lymphoma, my immune system attacking itself. I've had treatment for over a year, but,' he paused, 'there is always hope.'

'And what's that?' Titus asked, pointing at the treatment.

'Oh, the poison? Well, it's blistering gas really, or an extract of.'

Titus paled, and thought of the towns he had destroyed in the Transmaritanus by launching canisters of blistering gas over the walls. 'But it kills people!' he said appalled, wanting to pull the drip from his father's arm.

His father laughed. 'Titus, it's not pure blistering gas, it's just derived from it!' His voice quietened to merely a whisper, and he seemed very distant all of a sudden. 'Isn't it funny,' he said, 'we create weapons to destroy others, but then we learn that some of our weapons can actually cure. You know, what I have was thought to be incurable fifty years ago, until we found that people we used the blistering gas on, who also happened to have this incurable disease, went on to recover from the disease, if they survived the gas that is. So, we have to make better weapons! But that's your forté. I'm just a writer who wanted to change the world, but I couldn't even help my own son.' He slumped back in the chair.

Titus was struck by how old he suddenly looked.

He reached forwards to touch his arm.

His father brightened up a little. 'Titus, I did not call you here from the right hand side of your new powerful friends to discuss my illness. It's far more important we discuss *Coniunctus*, especially if you really do count Albus as your new friend.'

'I count Rome as my friend,' Titus said proudly.

'Very loyal Titus,' his father said sarcastically. 'And I imagine that you would go on to spout that Albus, 'is Rome', or something equally helpful in justifying your support of an evil dictator. But of course, we can be overheard and I shouldn't use words like that, or is that not what you were going to tell me?' he said, fixing Titus with his intelligent stare.

Titus stared back, not sure what to say. His father risked much by speaking so openly, even here.

'What do you think is wrong with *Coniunctus*?' his father asked him.

'Nothing,' Titus answered honestly. 'It sounds good, didn't you hear the applause? Everyone thinks it's great.'

'Exactly, everyone is happy. That can only mean one thing: too good to be true.'

Titus shook his head. 'No, it just means that this company have found a way of making energy cheaply, and it's going to save everyone a fortune.'

'Oh yes, and save us from this 'energy crisis' too. Odd that we have only had an energy crisis for about two months though Titus, isn't it? All of these power cuts? It's almost as if it was all planned isn't it? No, Titus,' his father said earnestly. 'Not everyone is happy, someone is losing out here; for every thing that is given, someone else has to give. But who is it?'

'The only people I can see losing out are *Coniunctus*,' Titus said. 'If they've messed their sums up...'

'Exactly!' his father said excitedly, 'I knew I hadn't raised a complete idiot after all! *Coniunctus* stand to lose out greatly.'

'But only if they get the pricing wrong,' Titus added.

'I think the pricing is completely wrong, but who's to say it's a mistake. Imagine, if in one stroke you could make everyone in Rome happy, what could you do? You could clear the streets, you could restore public order. Who else loses out from this Titus?'

Titus shook his head. Everyone was happy with cheap energy from the sun.

'All our energy is made in Dacia. Who owns that?'

Titus shrugged.

'Well, actually a lot of people own shares in it,' his father said, 'but principally there are two major senators who have large stakes in the Dacian power mines, and both stand out in the Senate because they often oppose Albus on major votes.'

'Could be co-incidence,' Titus said quickly.

'Could be,' his father conceded. 'But think of this: to make solar panels you need a large quantity of an ore called tellurium. Now Titus, my maths will not be perfect, I don't even have a calculator in this cursed place, but just in my head, the whole thing cannot add up. That ore is scarce, it's expensive to process, then you have to get satellites into the Void, granted the Void Levator makes it cheaper, but it's still vastly expensive. Power costs should, by my reckoning, at least double. So, even if I'm very wrong, *Coniunctus* will make a massive loss. No company is going to do that unless it wants to put someone else out of business, before pushing prices up dramatically.'

'To ruin these senators?'

'I don't know for sure, perhaps you could find out. But this is indulgence really because it is my problem not yours.' He sighed, looked out of the window, and then back at Titus. 'How are you getting on with the Book of Varro?'

Titus went slightly red with embarrassment. It was just like his childhood—he felt like the little boy who, once again, had not read the book his father had recommended.

'It's okay Titus, I didn't really think you would read it. I told you that when I gave it to you!'

'No father, I did read some. I got to the point where Verres overthrows the governor and starts to make all the improvements he dreams of.'

'Good. Did you understand it?'

'I...' Titus thought, 'I think so, I don't follow all the bits where the gods talk, but it's an old book—'

'Old yes, but important,' his father interrupted. 'Titus, I want you to do something for me.'

'What's that?' Titus asked, expecting to be asked to investigate *Coniunctus*. Would he do it? Would he go against Albus if his dying father asked him too? He wasn't sure.

'Finish the Book of Varro.'

Titus laughed with surprise.

'Okay,' his father said. 'You clearly see no point in reading it. If you really can't be bothered then I'll tell you what happens. You see, it's about whether people can change. Jupiter and Juno have an argument over this: Jupiter thinks it's impossible, he thinks that all of his creation are set on their paths and cannot change. The weak remain weak. The strong remain strong, etcetera. Juno thinks otherwise. So, they play a game, and they play the game on a man called Varro, a subsistence farmer.

'Varro hates his master but does nothing about it. He does his little job, tending the fields, and although he has really amazing ideas that would mean everything was fairer and more efficient, he just lives out a life of quiet desperation. But then Juno visits him, and changes everything. Verres gets the villagers together and overthrows the governor. Then he sets about changing the way the town is run, and suddenly the place is prosperous. The people end up hailing him as some sort of saviour. They install him in the palace, even though he initially refuses it, then they start to call him governor, even though he hates the term.

'Over time though, he starts to get used to the love of the people, and he realises how much more he could make of the land. He changes the crops to ones that make money, and he starts to treat those he leads with contempt, much like the old governor.'

'So Jupiter wins the bet,' Titus said sadly.

'You need to read the third part for that. Finish the book, see how the story ends.' He closed his eyes, and for a moment Titus thought he had fallen asleep. He turned to go.

His father's eyes opened again. 'Titus, I want you to read the third part of the book when you are far away from Rome. I think you should leave soon, today if possible. Don't get drawn in any further.'

'Or I could keep working for him, get my province and then leave.'

His father did not reply.

'Or, I could get the extra information you want about *Coniunctus*, complete the puzzle for you?' he offered, not sure if he could really carry out this promise.

His father shook his head. 'You could find out,' he said. 'The solution for this puzzle is in Albus' mind, no doubt, but he is a clever man and I suspect that, no matter how much he trusts you, you will get little of the truth from him. Besides, getting close enough to him to learn anything would be so hazardous for your own soul that I would not advise it. This isn't even your fight. I simply suggest that, having learnt that your friend is likely up to serious non-good, you cut your losses and leave this broken city, this city utterly lost to the gods. And when you leave,' he said sincerely, 'for goodness sake, take the only good thing in your life with you.'

'She wants to leave,' Titus said, 'but Albus will give us so much if we just stay a short while longer. It's only a short time, and it gains us so much. But she cannot see.'

'No Titus, you fool!' his father said angrily, before catching himself and holding out his hands in apology, almost to himself, as if he had promised himself he would not let himself get angry. 'I'm sorry Titus, I know you are no fool, but you are *acting* a complete fool. You cannot see: it's not *her* who's wrong. It's you. The longer you stay here, the less likely you are to leave. Albus knows that, it's just a game to him. Get out before you cannot.'

'But Hispania!' Titus said imploringly. 'My children, your grandchildren,' he added, 'could be rich and powerful.'

His father laughed.

'Things,' his father said. 'These riches, and titles, and provinces you speak of are just things you know.'

'Things?' Titus exclaimed with irritation. 'Things are important! They can make life comfortable.' He pointed to the drip in his father's arm. 'They can cure, and they can prolong life.'

Titus' father shrugged. 'Of course, they can be very useful. But you need to remember what they are, and why they are.'

'What do you mean?'

'Do you know how things began?'

'Sorry?' Titus asked confused.

'The first 'things' were simply tools. You look at a chimpanzee in Africa, trying to get some termites out of a mound and it uses a specially cleaned and prepared stick; a stick that it keeps and looks after, treasures even. Because in truth that stick *is* a real treasure to it: because that stick can be used to get termites, and they can be used to make the chimpanzee full and happy; because that stick has a true *use*.

'So, the natural order of things is thus—that people are made to be loved, and that things are meant to be used.'

His father paused, and looked sad. 'The problem Titus, with the world today, is that *things* are loved, and *people* are used. There is nothing wrong with things when they are used properly and respected, and you remember what and why they are. That is why I worry about these things you long for, because it seems that perhaps you would rather have these things than you would have Ceinwyn.'

Titus felt like he had been punched in the stomach. 'You're just like her,' he said angrily.

'No,' his father replied, seeming amused. 'She wants you to do what she wants you to do. My agenda is far more straightforward— I simply want you to be happy. But,' he added, 'I do think she is right this time.'

'I think it's too late,' Titus said sadly. 'She was not there this morning.'

'She'll be back, and when she does...' he paused and smiled at Titus, 'when she does come back, please for the gods' sake take her in your arms and leave Rome. This is no place for young people who have a future ahead of them. Leave it to old, bitter people like Albus and I, to fight to the death over this dried up shell of a city that we both once loved, until every reason that we once loved it has been destroyed by the battle to own it.

Titus laughed. 'You fight with words! He fights with his Praetorians. What chance do you have?'

His father smiled again. 'Perhaps,' he said, shrugging his shoulders. 'But it's not your fight, it's mine, it's Albus' and we both use the tools we have. Get Ceinwyn back, leave, and don't trust a word Albus says. He's a better liar even than me!'

Titus laughed, 'I'd still like my wife back, and a new province.'

His father looked at him sympathetically. 'And I don't particularly want to die. But, we don't get to choose a perfect life do we. We just get the life we are given. You have to choose Titus, because I don't think you *can* have both.'

His father opened his mouth to continue, but suddenly turned green and started to vomit into the bucket by the side of the bed again. Titus reached over to help him, but he wasn't quite sure what to do, so he patted him gently on the shoulder.

As the spasms of vomiting stopped, his father groaned and lay back on the bed. 'Stop wasting your time here!' he shouted, flecking Titus with his vomit. 'Go home and speak to Ceinwyn.'

Titus rose and obeyed.

He walked out of the Aesculapium in a daze, and as he looked around at the floodlit streets of this section of the Aether, he saw cracks in the stone pavements he had never seen before; he smelt a foulness to the air, where before it had smelt sweet and homely; and he saw how almost everyone walked by with their heads downwards, desperately, quietly, going about lives that were essentially miserable. He walked back to the Summus, his eyes finally open.

He started to plan his words to Ceinwyn. He resolved to leave, to tell her how foolish he was. However, when he got to their room her things were gone, a bottle of the finest passum was sitting on the bedside table, and a brand new uniform hung on the wall. Notes on the table written by Albus himself thanked him for his help, and there was another note from Verres, asking for his advice tomorrow in following a lead about Filii Aquilae. He had everything he wanted, everything he had wanted until one hour ago. He sat on the bed and wept, then rose and thought seriously about leaping from the balcony.

He showered, put on the uniform and looked in the mirror. His heart filled with complete emptiness. The uniform was black from head to toe, edged in dark purple. He looked powerful, menacing even—the second most powerful man in Rome. He opened the bottle of passum. Ceinwyn had either left Rome, or gone to her father's, but he had no idea where that was. She was lost to him, perhaps forever. He took a sip, and enjoyed the way the liquor burnt his throat, it made him feel slightly better. He was the *Protector of Rome*, Albus had promised to look after him. He didn't trust Albus fully, especially after what his father had said, but what other choice did he have now? He took a longer draught from the bottle.

XXV

As darkness fell, Quintus picked up his coat from the ward office and pulled it on, exhausted. It had been two weeks now since he had handed his notice in, and the Archiatrus had ensured that they had been the worst two weeks of his life. Quintus had expected to be overworked, to be punished for leaving medicine, even if only temporarily. But, far worse, he had been given almost nothing to do. He had written some drug cards, and he had written discharges for patients. He had even been asked to take some blood once, but he wasn't involved in the ward rounds any longer, and he had forgotten the last time he had been allowed to make a decision.

As he opened the door to the ward for the last time, he thought about saying goodbye to the nurses he had worked with. They had been mainly kind to him, unlike his senior medici, but he didn't have time. He needed to move house as well. Almost penniless on his junior medicus wage, he was about to have to swallow his pride and ascend the Caelian hill with the small bag that contained everything he owned. His wife did not even know he was back in Rome; she would be extremely surprised when he turned up at their door tonight.

For a moment he cursed Albus, who had given barracks quarters to Marcus, Antonius, and Tiberius. He thought of Tiberius every day, yet he had not seen him since the day they had returned to Rome, now nearly two months ago—the worst months of his life. Strange, because he had dreamed of returning to the Eternal City every day he had spent in the Transmaritanus, or Dacia, or Brittania. But then, his dream of return had always been at the side of Tiberius, not living in a tiny on call medicus room whilst pretending he didn't. Everything about him was pretence, and he was fed up with it, but he couldn't change the laws that made his deepest desires illegal.

As he reached the halfway point in the foyer, he saw the blonde nurse again. She had already seen him, and carefully looked away as he passed. He had not meant to snub her that day on the stairs, he had just been busy. If he had had longer to talk to her that day perhaps he could have told her the truth, like he had eventually told his wife Gaia—although she had said that her wedding night was too late to find out that your husband could not consummate his marriage. She had a point he thought, but it was not his fault; it was the fault of Rome. Perhaps he should have stayed in the provinces, where he could be true to himself, he thought, but then he remembered how empty the provinces were, how far from Rome, and how he had always been meant for great things. Great things like his work with *Coniunctus*, work that he still had no idea of the details of. But one hundred denarii an hour? He would be happy to do pretty much anything for that.

As he approached the revolving doors at the end of the atrium, a figure entered them from the other side, dressed in a thick, black overcoat, white coat underneath. It was his Archiatrus.

Quintus tried to think of something to say to the man on his last ever meeting with him. He thought of trying to shame him for the way he had treated him—an overly deferent, 'thank you sir,' would probably suffice for that, but would the man understand the sarcasm?

He was still thinking of the perfect line when he drew level. The Archiatrus looked him in the eyes and then pointedly turned his head away as he passed, just as the nurse had done. Quintus walked on three paces, stunned. Then he stopped. How dare the man not acknowledge him? Rage rushed up inside him.

'Who the fuck do you think you are?'

The Archiatrus stopped and turned around slowly.

Quintus matched his gaze. He remembered who he was: one of Titus' band of six. Mercenaries who had taken on everyone they had met and won; hardy survivors who had lived in the most terrible parts of the empire. He was not a child, unlike the other juniors this man was used to dealing with.

'What did you just say?' the Archiatrus replied, his eyes terrible.

Quintus looked down at his feet. 'I asked you,' he said quietly, before looking straight back up at the Archiatrus, 'who the fuck, you think, you are.'

'That's the end of your career!' the Archiatrus said and started to walk away. 'Not that you'd have had one anyway of course,' he called over his shoulder. 'You are the worst medicus I've ever encountered. They could have dragged any fool in from the Imum and dressed him in a white coat and I'd have been better served.'

Quintus followed him back into the Aesculapium, wanting to continue their exchange. The Archiatrus heard his footsteps, and looked back over his shoulder. He looked surprised, most juniors would have broken down and fled, but most juniors were twenty three and easily bullied.

'You hate me,' Quintus said, 'because I have seen something outside of the world that you inhabit. You hate me, because I am proof that you do not have to inhabit your little world in order to make something of yourself. You hate me, because I abandon so lightly something that you have worked at for years. Yes! I discard it as if it is nothing. You think that makes me useless at it...'

'It does,' the Archiatrus said angrily, speeding up. He seemed almost afraid. Quintus increased his pace too. A small crowd had formed in the atrium now to watch the altercation.

'A hundred denarii an hour Archiatrus!' he exclaimed. 'That's more than you earn. I'll have a much better job, and I'll be much better paid. Don't you ever fucking sneer at me again.'

'You'll never see me again Decius,' the Archiatrus said, his voice shaking, as he reached the levators. 'I don't have rude, incompetent fools, working with me. Even if these charlatans you are about to work for promised you promotion, once they are finished with you, I will never let you back in this place.'

'Perhaps it will be me, one day, deciding your fate Archiatrus,' Quintus replied.

'Weak,' the Archiatrus said scornfully, 'mentally weak. You never had the time and application to learn. You lost all of your skills out in those woods, you and those ridiculous mercenaries. At least your leader made *'Protector of Rome'*. Straight into politics!' he said sarcastically. 'Mark my words Decius, even politics won't have a homosexually perverted incompetent like you.'

Quintus raised his fist. How did he know? The Archiatrus stepped back, with real fear in his eyes. Quintus would have struck him had it not been for the levator behind them, opening that moment and disgorging a man covered in blood.

The Archiatrus jumped back from the man, trying to keep his coat clean, and the man staggered forwards, falling to the ground at Quintus' feet. A paramedicus leapt after him from the levator and tried to get him back to his feet, they had obviously just entered from the basement admissions route. Quintus looked up and noted a trolley in the levator, covered in blood.

'Hit by a currus on the Appia fifteen minutes ago,' the paramedicus said to Quintus, as they both kneeled down by the writhing man. 'Head injury definitely, really confused. But I reckon internal bleeding too.'

Quintus looked down at the man's abdomen, slightly swollen, the paramedicus was probably right. He looked at the bag of gear the paramedicus carried.

'Right,' he said confidently as he stood up. 'Get some oxygen on. You,' he said, pointing at another junior medicus he knew. 'Call the recovery team, we need some people to help get this man to accident and emergency once we've stabilised him.'

The medicus ran off to call for help. Quintus started to rummage through the bag and found a huge cannula needle. He picked one of the brown ones and started to tap away at the writhing casualty's arm for a vein. He was definitely losing blood internally somewhere—his veins were collapsing, but this was the sort of thing Quintus had dealt with every day in the Transmaritanus. The needle went in perfectly, and the cannula slid across it into the vein.

'Saline!' he shouted to the junior medicus, who had returned from making the call now.

Quintus looked down, the man was writhing less, but it was clear that despite what they were doing he was slipping into unconsciousness. It was probably the head injury. Quintus knew there was still a chance to save him, but he would need theatre to sort the internal bleeding, and probably head cooling to prevent long lasting brain damage. He needed to stabilise him now so that these things could happen.

'Get me the RSI kit,' he shouted to the paramedicus. He rubbed his palms together, and felt a thin film of sweat. He hadn't done this for a long time, and it wasn't easy.

He injected the first of the drugs into the line. The man jerked less, starting to go to sleep. Quintus knew he had only moments to complete the procedure. He injected the muscle relaxant and picked up the laryngoscope. The point of no return had already passed: if he failed to intubate, the man could not breathe by himself anymore. He had just put him to sleep, and paralysed him. He had to succeed.

He bent the man's head back and inserted the scope, the grating of the metal on the man's teeth set his own teeth on edge, as it always had. There was a good view, minimal blood in the trachea. The paramedicus handed him the ET tube. He passed it, first time, and inflated the cuff.

'Pass me the bag,' he said, his voice hoarse from his dry mouth. Fumbling slightly, he attached the bag to the tube and squeezed. The man's chest rose slightly. He felt his heart soar. The junior medicus leant forwards and listened to both sides of the chest with his stethoscope as Quintus continued to squeeze.

'Good air entry,' he said. 'Both sides.'

Quintus stood up.

'We'll take it from here!' a man in scrub pyjamas said, rushing up with a trolley and a team of medici and nurses. Quintus stepped back and smiled at the perfect timing—he hadn't been entirely sure what to do next.

He looked around at the huddle of staff around him who had watched the last five minutes unfold. The man might not survive, but he had the best chance he could possibly have now. He had given him that chance. The crowd started to applaud. All apart from the

203

Archiatrus, who stood separately from the rest, against the wall by the levator, still glaring.

Quintus stared at the Archiatrus, standing back and looking on, impotent. He caught his eye, thought of some more words to say, and then realised there was no need. He simply smiled, turned his back, and walked away.

The applause faded as he left the Aesculapium, but it remained with him, keeping him warm despite the cooler night, as he ascended the bay tree-lined streets of the Caelian district. The Caelian had once been one of the most beautiful parts of the Aether, with its lush parks, but was now covered by the Summus like the rest of Rome. Apparently, he had a new family home on the Summus now, but the family had not moved yet, so he walked to the Caelian and to Gaia, his heart feeling heavier with every step.

He reached the gate, which he had last seen over a decade ago. He opened the small, black, iron gate and walked up the drive. A gentle breeze rustled the leaves of the ornamental trees, and he could hear the sound of water from within the large compound. The Dolabelli were rich, that was the primary reason why his family had been so keen for him to marry into it.

The guard at the gate didn't recognise him. Quintus tried to argue his way in quietly but to no avail. He felt ridiculous, prevented from entering his own house by his own guard.

'I thought you were dead,' he heard a voice come from high above, a soft, painful voice from his past—the sound of his argument must have carried to Gaia upstairs. He couldn't tell from the tone whether she had hoped for his death, or worried about it. Perhaps both.

'I have returned,' he said. What else was there to say?

'Clearly,' she said and her head disappeared back into the room. Quintus looked at the guard, who shrugged and allowed him in.

Quintus walked into the first reception room and glanced around, hoping against hope that his parents-in-law would be out. He could handle the family in turn he felt, Gaia first, then the in-laws. The reception room was almost devoid of furniture now, some fine paintings remained on the walls, but most were wrapped in sheeting against the wall, waiting to be transported to their new marble house on the Summus. The Dolabelli would soon be back under the sun.

A Slave arrived, carrying a tray of dormice, Quintus acknowledged him, then realised that outside of his group of six this was highly unusual behaviour. He stuffed the dormouse, dipped in garum, into his mouth. He sat down on one of the old recliners that he remembered from courting Gaia; she had always tried to touch him on it, and he had always tried to make himself enjoy it.

'Quintus.'

He glanced up from his thoughts. A vision in white and jewels appeared at the bottom of the stairs. She glided over towards him, and sat down. She had clearly just washed and got dressed for him. She looked beautiful.

'Gaia, I...'

He tailed off, having genuinely no idea where to start.

'I always hoped that one day you would come back,' she said sadly. 'My father still to this day says he hates you, and my mother thinks whatever my father wants her to think.'

'Gaia,' he said, 'I should have written, I have been a terrible husband. I am a terrible husband! No woman could want a husband like me. I should have told you before we married, but...' he nearly stopped again, 'I couldn't tell myself really. I couldn't tell my parents. I don't think they even know to this day.'

He looked down at her legs. She was wearing stockings.

'That doesn't matter Quintus, you are back now. I read about some of the things you did in Dacia and Brittania. I think you were very brave.'

Quintus smiled. 'It was really hard. I am pleased to be back. I would like to stay, if that is okay? At least until I find somewhere of my own. I have a new job. I won't be in your way for long. But I'd understand if—'

He was interrupted by Gaia reaching over, and squashing her beautifully painted lips onto his. She lifted up one of her long, slim legs and placed it over his lap. Her skirt rode up as she moved, and he saw the curve of her bottom above the tops of her stockings, with the clips that held them up digging very slightly into her firm body. Gaia was beautiful, but he couldn't respond to her, and even if he could, he didn't want to. He pushed her back, gently.

'Gaia...' he said, frustrated. She still did not seem to understand.

'Quintus, I was thinking while you were away, every night, about how I could please you.' She spoke quickly, and he could see tears forming in her eyes.

'Gaia, please!'

'I am your wife Quintus, we must have children. My father... if he doesn't get a son...'

'Gaia...'

She lifted her skirt right up, revealing that she had shaved completely. Then she rolled over onto her hands and knees, her skirt in the air. 'I wondered if maybe you... started there.' She sounded ever so slightly disgusted by her own idea, as she gestured to her bottom, 'then you could finish...' her finger moved down a couple of inches. She rolled back over and sat down, looking up at Quintus desperately.

Quintus was shocked. 'Gaia, do you not understand? That's not the problem!' He was so surprised by her lack of comprehension, that he was almost speechless. 'The problem is that you are a girl. Lots of men and women do what you're suggesting, that doesn't make those men love men!'

Gaia looked hurt. 'Can't we just try?' she asked frantically.

'No, I don't... I can't find you attractive. I didn't come home for that. I came home because I wanted to be back in Rome. I'm sorry to seem so uncaring, but at least I'm being honest now. I don't expect you to let me stay.'

'But what am I to do?' Gaia said holding his hand, and looking up at him.

'Take a lover,' he said, 'I don't mind, I'll even say the child is mine if I have to.'

Gaia's face darkened. 'You would have your wife sleep with another man?'

'I'm sure you won't be the first to do that amongst Noble families.'

'Quintus look at me,' Gaia said, holding his chin, and turning his face so that he had no choice but to look into her eyes. 'I've waited a decade Quintus, a decade, and this is all you can suggest? When I kept myself pure for you, alone for a decade, with my father constantly nagging me to register you as dead so that I could remarry?'

'Gaia, I'm sorry. Perhaps you should have.'

'Perhaps,' she said bitterly,' perhaps you should have died! At least then I'd be left only with a memory of you, rather than the real, selfish thing. I do not just want a baby Quintus—I want a baby with you. I want a baby with the man I loved.'

She got up, turned around quickly, and started to sob as she walked out of the room. Quintus heard the door to the house slam, followed by the metal gate as it clicked open and shut. He took his bag, found an empty, unmade bed and settled down to sleep.

XXVI

Titus awoke with the worst headache of his life. Groaning, he reached over for Ceinwyn. The awareness that she was still not there brought back memories of the day before, the revelations about his father, and then his realisation that it was too late to leave now—Ceinwyn had left him. He looked up, with eyes partly glued shut from dehydration and saw his new uniform hanging on the wall. Beneath lay an empty bottle of passum.

There was a knock at the door. 'The Consul is coming,' a voice said brightly. 'Be ready in two minutes.'

He hastily got out of bed, there was no time to shower, and pulled the new uniform on. It fitted perfectly. He barely had time to adjust the black peaked cap by the time Albus arrived.

'Titus,' he said thoughtfully, 'let's walk.'

Albus led him out of his room, in silence, keeping a few paces ahead. He started to worry: Albus had said many strange things when he had been under the influence the night before last. Titus suspected he wanted to gauge what he had heard, and how much he understood. The truth was, Titus was still mightily confused. All that he had learnt from Albus' unusual outburst was that Albus had had a child with a Slave when very young, (but his father had told him that anyway), and that Albus' father had ordered the child's death, seemingly against Albus' wishes. He started to sweat at the lengths the Consul might go to silence him, then realised that the best way to deal with this was to bring it up before the Consul did.

'It was a very heavy night, a couple of nights back, wasn't it?'

Albus remained silent for a few moments as the pair continued to walk upstairs towards the roof. 'Yes, it was fun though.'

'I don't remember much of it.'

'You're clever Titus,' Albus said, 'I remember it as clear as day, and I was far worse off than you. You are my head of security, I trust you. What I told you... I'm happy with you knowing.'

Titus didn't know what to say. Was this some sort of test?

'Did you never do anything that you regretted when you were young?' Albus asked him.

Titus thought for a moment. It hadn't sounded like Albus had regretted the Slave. He remembered Albus' words, aimed at the roof mural depiction of his father:

"I never loved her."

'My father was wrong to have the child killed though,' Albus said. 'The Slave girl seduced me, but I was fourteen, and I didn't know how wrong what I did was at that point. The child would have been half Slave of course, but he would have been half me too, surely that would make up for all the foul genetic weaknesses inherited from his mother!'

Titus made himself laugh too. 'But you have Sexta now,' he said, kindly. 'You'll have an heir eventually, I'm sure.' They had reached the roof of the palace now and Albus led him across to the edge.

'I hope so, but if not my family will die out with me, and my father killed the only possible heir I had. Not that it matters really, I am sure that had the child lived, he would have turned out to be more Slave than Roman anyhow.' He put a hand on Titus' shoulder. 'That's not why I brought you up here Titus. I wanted to talk to you in private about something more important.'

Titus took a deep breath and stared out at the beauty of the nearly completed Summus, and the view that seemed to stretch across the whole of Italia. 'Go on,' he said, waiting for a test of loyalty that he did not feel fully ready to try to pass. Loyalty to Rome? No problem. But loyalty to Albus? He thought of his father's words yesterday.

'I wanted to talk about Ceinwyn,' Albus said gravely.

'I don't want to,' Titus replied sullenly, but Albus didn't seem to notice.

'It's okay, I already know. I'm really sorry. She seemed like a nice girl.'

'I'm not sure it's actually over,' Titus said hopefully. 'We just had a bit of a falling out.'

'Now then Titus,' Albus continued, as if he had not heard him. 'As a good friend, who fought alongside you many times, I see it as my duty to help you through this difficult time. Of course you may have any of the women in the palace that you choose, except for Sexta of course. But I think really what you need is to throw yourself into work.'

Titus shrugged, he thought of Ceinwyn, probably journeying back to Britannia. He hoped against hope that she was still in Rome with her father, but even then he wondered if he would ever actually see her again. He had been foolish, he knew that, but she had not given him enough time. Now it was too late.

'My offer of Hispania stands Titus, I'll give you it, and you can keep your position here in Rome too; you'll be one of the most important people in Rome. But I need you to destroy Filii Aquilae: Verres works very hard for me, he gives everything, but he's not got it all up here,' he said, pointing to his head. 'Titus, you need to help him, both for himself and yourself, it will give you time away from your thoughts.'

'Let me think about it,' Titus said gloomily, looking down in the vain hope that he would catch sight of Ceinwyn far below somehow.

'No time to think,' Albus replied, 'we believe that they are planning something big this time—civil unrest. The streets are getting worse every night; I'm sure they are behind it. Go with Verres, help him investigate.'

Titus opened his mouth to reply, but at that moment, the bald figure of Verres appeared from the stairwell onto the roof behind them. As usual, he wore the full Praetorian body armour minus the helmet, his dark glasses firmly welded to his bearded face.

'Titus!' Verres shouted, his smile beaming, revealing perfect teeth that Titus didn't remember—had he had them replaced? 'It's time to kick some terrorist arse! Let's get moving.'

Verres loved Rome, and his enthusiasm was infectious. Titus nodded, and the pair headed together down the stairs, towards the Imum. Perhaps Albus was right—he should throw himself into work. It was too late to make any other choice.

XXVII

Ceinwyn was halfway between the Caelian and the Palatine Aether districts when she heard the crying.

The great park was free of the noise of curri. It still smelt of summer, but Ceinwyn could see that the late flowers were drooping, and the grass beneath her feet was a yellower shade than it should be. She suspected the banks of high intensity lights mounted to the Aether roof were not quite bright enough.

The sobbing was coming from the centre of the great maze. She paused for a moment. She was already slightly late for a secret meeting between two groups of Slaves that her father had arranged. It turned out that her father was not the only Slave leader in Rome, and not the only one who wanted to oppose Marcus Albus directly. She felt privileged to be invited to attend, and she had been asked to present evidence too—the photos of the omniajunctus hub—but she couldn't ignore the crying, so she entered the maze.

The lack of natural light had done little for the condition of the hedges in the maze, and Ceinwyn could easily tell which way the centre lay.

She rounded the last corner of the maze quickly, and saw, in the centre, a Roman lady lying face down on the memorial bench. She was dressed in white, and it looked like she had been there all night. There was something very odd about her clothes Ceinwyn thought. The dress looked extremely expensive, suggesting that she was perhaps a Noble, but her skirt had ridden up, nearly to her waist, and what she was wearing underneath suggested she was a prostitute. Ceinwyn edged forwards.

'Excuse me,' she said quietly, trying to disguise the Britannic lilt to her voice and sound Roman.

The woman turned her face to Ceinwyn, the bright artificial lights from above made her face look even more puffy and blotched than would be normal from a night of crying. Ceinwyn moved forwards, pulled the shawl from her own shoulders, and draped it over the girl's legs to cover her. She studied the girl more closely; she was probably no older than she was and had a tangle of golden curly hair. If it hadn't been for the tears, and the running make-up, she would be beautiful.

'Leave me here,' the girl said. 'I need time alone. Don't tell anyone.'

'Who are you?' Ceinwyn asked.

The girl's expression suggested that it seemed odd to her that Ceinwyn did not recognise her. 'It doesn't matter, I'll be alright,' she said.

'Who did this to you?' Ceinwyn asked, concerned.

The girl laughed—it was a bleak sound. 'My husband, but I don't think he meant to.'

'What did he do? Cast you out onto the streets? Rape you?'

'I wouldn't have minded the last...' the girl replied sarcastically.

Ceinwyn thought for a moment, she needed to get to the meeting. Perhaps she could just leave the girl her shawl. She turned to go.

'Stop!' the girl said, clearly changing her mind. 'Please wait!'

Ceinwyn turned back and waited.

'Could you sit here for a moment, I don't...' she went red with shame, 'I don't actually want to be alone right now.'

Ceinwyn walked over and sat by the girl, she could smell her perfume now; it too seemed expensive.

The girl sat up and pulled the shawl tightly around her lower body. 'My name is Gaia Dolabella.'

Ceinwyn opened her mouth and was about to tell her hers, but then a fantastic idea burst into her head. 'Tita,' she said, 'Tita Sentius.' She proffered her hand in greeting. 'Good to meet you.'

She picked that nomen because it was the nomen of her father's master. She had no idea why she picked the name Tita; it just flew into her head, like the idea had in the first place. She was immediately pleased with it, and made a promise to herself that she would use it well. For her actions now would have to be the actions she would have wished from Titus, the actions that she still wished from Titus, and that she hoped one day Titus would perform; the actions he would perform if only he would wake up to reality.

'The Sentia are an old family,' Gaia replied, surprised. 'I've not seen you before, but then, I have spent many of the last ten years in the family compound,' she added sadly.

'Your husband doesn't let you out?' Ceinwyn asked, trying to work out what the problem was.

'I thought he was dead, I spent ten years waiting and hoping. What else is there to do, if you marry a man when you are fifteen, and then he disappears for a decade?'

Find someone else, was the phrase that appeared in Ceinwyn's mind, but she thought better of it.

'So he's back? This husband of yours,' she asked.

'Yes, but sadly, he is no different.'

'Does he hurt you?'

'No,' Gaia said exasperated. 'I shouldn't say—it's not something I can say.'

Ceinwyn got the impression that she was meant to be getting some sort of Noble society hint, but she had no idea what Gaia's secret could be. She shook her head.

'He's a homosexual,' Gaia whispered, looking around to make sure no one could hear.

Ceinwyn opened her mouth to laugh, unable to believe that this was the source of all this trouble, but she, once again, thought better of it. 'I'm sorry,' she said sincerely.

'It's alright,' Gaia said, 'I feel a little better already because of you. There's something quite odd about you isn't there?' she asked.

Ceinwyn didn't know what to say and shrugged instead. She had no idea how a young Noble lady should behave. She should probably have giggled.

'I've never met anyone like you,' Gaia continued. 'I don't imagine you'd let something like this stand in *your* way.'

'I don't know,' Ceinwyn replied, 'nothing like that has ever happened to me.'

They sat in silence for a moment, and Ceinwyn built up the courage to start working on her plan. 'Gaia,' she said, 'I hope you don't mind me calling you Gaia do you? I need to get to a meeting, but I wondered if we might meet again some time?'

Gaia's face brightened up, and she smiled, before quickly hiding it behind the cold Noble face she was meant to portray to the world. Ceinwyn realised then how lonely she was and her heart soared—this was playing straight into her plan.

'Perhaps we could have some drinks?' Gaia said brightly. 'There is a good Popina that I used to visit. Maybe we could find you a husband too?'

'Already got one,' Ceinwyn said, and immediately wished she hadn't. The whole point of inventing a new name was to invent a new identity, one that would help get information from Gaia whose father was clearly an important Noble.

'Oh,' Gaia said, and Ceinwyn could tell that she was questioning whether a married woman would make a good drinking friend to share sorrows with.

'But,' Ceinwyn thought quickly, 'he's dead.'

'Oh, I'm so sorry,' Gaia said, her hand flying to her mouth.

'Yes,' Ceinwyn's mind thought quickly. 'He was in the army, but then, when it was disbanded, he went to Dacia to put down an uprising that was threatening the power mines.'

Gaia's eyes opened wide. 'Your husband protected my father's mines?'

'Yes,' Ceinwyn said. 'Yes he did!'

Gaia looked sad again. 'It's a shame he's dead, we could use his help now.'

'Why?' Ceinwyn asked, her heart beating faster. She hadn't even got the girl drunk yet, and she knew that she was about to hear something that could help her father fight Albus.

'Our mines are going to shut this year. Half of the mines in Dacia. We'll have to shoot all the Slaves, close the pits and the factories, and extinguish the fires.' She started to cry again, 'I need to figure out what I am going to do very soon, before everyone else knows. My husband only married me because my family was rich, but soon I won't even be rich. Even if I leave him, I won't be able to get a new husband. Why would anyone want to marry me?'

Ceinwyn looked at Gaia's face, pretty despite the blotches, her long legs, and the shape of her body. People would surely want her? But then, this was Rome, and being a Noble was something Ceinwyn knew almost nothing about. Family, wealth and titles meant more than anything it seemed. She thought of her dead mother, killed because Rome forced her to become an outcast; her poor father fighting a seemingly hopeless battle against the, far more powerful master of Rome; and her own face, disfigured by her makeup-concealed signum. She wanted to hate Gaia because of what she represented, but she couldn't quite bring herself to.

'We'll drink it over, we'll talk and we'll figure it out,' Ceinwyn replied. The meeting would be over by the time she got there she thought, so she needed a little bit of useful information from today, to prove to her father that the delay was worth it.

'Why are you shutting the mines in Dacia?' she asked, hoping that this wasn't pushing Gaia's trust too far.

Gaia looked sad again, and said a word that Ceinwyn had heard too much of recently, a word that was stuck to the side of every public currus and emblazoned in banners across streets, with phrases such as: *'Keep calm while we carry on,'* and: *'Stay off the streets while we fix them'*.

'Coniunctus.'

Ceinwyn thought for a moment, and had an idea that would make her original plan much more effective, but it was much riskier. She took a breath and thought hard. She had to do it—she needed to find out what was going on. The truth was, she didn't just want to pass information on to her father, but she also wanted to pass it onto Titus, to make him see that the man he was fighting for was a monster.

'My father,' Ceinwyn said, 'he has some influence himself. Perhaps we could help your family.'

They both sat in silence on the bench and Ceinwyn could feel Gaia's fear.

'What you suggest could be seen as treason,' Gaia said very quietly, as if they might be overheard even here.

'Why?' Ceinwyn asked, confused. 'Why would it be treason to plot against a company?'

Gaia's face looked grave. 'When the company you consider plotting against is owned by a Consul of Rome.'

XXVIII

Verres jogged down the ancient steps between the Aether and the Imum, humming merrily to himself. Titus kept pace easily, but found no desire to hum; he had no zeal for what they were about to do today. The sun was already well up, but of course none of that penetrated this deeply into Rome. The artificial lighting on the stairs was dim, and a foul draft of air blew up at them as they descended.

'Welcome once again Titus,' Verres shouted, as a cloud of dust blew into their faces, 'to where I once came from, and where I vowed never to return.'

'I thought you were from the Aether?' Titus asked, sure that Verres had told him this when he had first met him.

Verres stopped and smiled. 'And that's how I feel. I adopted the Aether as my home the moment I left this filth encrusted hole we are about to enter; the moment that I became a Praetorian.'

Titus nodded. It made sense. He wondered how many other Aether dwellers were lying about their past.

Verres bounded on, taking the steps two at a time, fasces outstretched. 'Brother,' he called back at Titus, 'not many people know the truth, keep it silent my friend.'

Titus affirmed that he would keep Verres' secret. 'Brother', he had called him. He had never had a man respect and trust him the way Verres did.

'I never wanted to return to the Imum,' Verres shouted as he continued his run down the dark, slippery, stone staircase. 'But to return like this, to the seat of all the scum in Rome?' He swung his fasces back and forth manically. 'It's like a dream!'

He leapt down the last flight, alighting agile as a cat on the street below.

Titus moved to his side, and together they peered into the darkness around them. This was one of the great staircases that connected the Aether and Imum, and it came down into, what was once, the original Forum of Ancient Rome. Columns lay in heaps, exactly where they had fallen in antiquity, and what remained of the old Senate building was still covered in scaffolding. Titus remembered that same scaffolding from his childhood, but he had never seen any work undertaken on the building: the Senate clearly had forgotten the building their ancestors had argued in.

A crowd of people surrounded them, some dressed in rags, all looking hungry. There must have been at least a hundred in this space. They huddled together, staring in fear at the pair: Titus dressed in his black uniform with the peaked cap; Verres in full Praetorian body armour, minus the helmet, his fasces glowing. Despite the gloom, he had not removed his dark glasses.

'Get a job you worthless scum!' Verres shouted at the nearest group. 'I got out! I live on the Summus now! Learn to do a day's work in your life and you might too.'

Someone mumbled a sarcastic sounding reply, and Titus was thankful that neither he nor Verres could fully make it out, or identify exactly where it came from.

Verres cleared his throat so that he could project his voice further, 'Romans!' He paused, letting the word ring out, which somehow exaggerated the scorn with which he had said it. 'It is just as your eyes tell you. This is the *Protector of Rome*, and you know who I am. But,' he added, menacingly, 'keep calm, go about your daily business, and you have nothing to fear from us.' He paused, waiting for the groups to disperse. Then the pair started to walk.

'Did you know,' Verres said amused, 'that they have a name for me down here now?'

Titus laughed quietly. 'What is it?'

'The *Nothus*,' Verres said smiling, and stroking his thick beard.

The word meant bastard.

We need to get deeper in,' Verres said, 'the troublemakers aren't going to be just standing out in the forum.'

Titus nodded in agreement. Verres had eventually accepted Titus' arguments that Filii Aquilae would surely be found based in the Imum, where the street violence was emanating from.

After twenty minutes of brisk walking Titus was completely lost. 'We're on the Aventine hill,' Verres said, 'nastiest place in Rome. My childhood home was only five minutes from here—you should see my new one...' He stopped talking and listened. In the distance, they could hear shouting and the sounds of a fight. Titus looked around. They were standing on a small track covered in dust and gravel, and on each side of this road were tiny dwellings that looked like they had changed little for hundreds of years. Their thin walls were patched up with rusting sheets of iron, the roofs were patchy too, and Titus realised that for many, the Imum receiving no rain would be a blessing. The water that came from the taps down here though could hardly be described as such—recycled a number of times on its journey down from the aqueducts that fed the Summus and Aether. Door after door slammed shut as they passed, and Titus could hear the cries of a baby, silenced suddenly, in a building to their left. Verres laughed. 'See how scared they are of us!'

Titus nodded, saddened as he realised that the hungry Imum people reciprocated the fear that the people of the Aether and Summus had of them. Rome was truly broken.

They were near the source of the shouting now, but it had quietened, someone was clearly going ahead of them and warning everyone. Verres' heavy boots rang out on the street as they broke into a jog. Titus' sweat started to run in the stifling, constant and unventilated heat of the Imum. It dripped down from under the peak of his cap and onto the lapels of his black jacket, soaking into the insignia of the eagle, and the letters *'SPQR'* underneath.

A small courtyard opened ahead, and the pair jogged into it. At first it seemed deserted, but then Titus spotted two men sitting under a small corrugated iron shelter. The men drew back, watching cautiously. Verres approached.

'I heard fighting,' he said, and waited for one of the men to reply.

One shrugged. 'Lots of fighting in the Imum,' he said casually.

'Are you spreading disorder?' Verres asked accusingly.

'No,' the thinner of the two men replied firmly. 'I work for a living, I want peace.'

'I don't believe you,' Verres said. 'Our sources implicate this district of the Aventine as the source of several planned riots on the Aether.'

'Nothing to do with me,' the man replied. Was there a trace of fear to his voice? It seemed so to Titus.

'So who was fighting, and why have they stopped?' Verres said, continuing his interrogation.

The man shrugged again.

Verres gestured to Titus to watch the men closely, as he started to search the courtyard. Titus watched him stoop, pick something up in the gloom, and start to chuckle as he walked back.

'What's this?' he asked, showing the other man a wooden club he'd found.

'It's a club,' the man said, 'for killing chickens.'

'Then,' Verres said slowly, 'why is there a pile of ten of them over there in the corner, along with sheets of metal with leather hand straps riveted on?'

Titus smiled. They were on to something now: a collection of riot equipment, and two people who had likely just been training others to use them. 'Good work Verres!' he exclaimed. 'Let's take them upstairs for questioning.'

Verres laughed. 'Nice joke Titus,' and he swung the club at the nearest man's head. The man jerked his head back, almost in time, taking a glancing blow to the temple instead of what, probably, would have been a fatal blow.

'Verres!' Titus shouted, as the man fell back, his companion scrabbling away desperately. 'Questioning! Remember the terrorist?'

Verres laughed, grabbing the stunned man, and pulling him out from under the shelter. 'Get the other one Titus. We might need him if this one doesn't talk.'

Titus grabbed the other man and held him. The man was thin and weak from malnutrition and Titus had no trouble preventing his escape as Verres punched the other man twice in the face to subdue him.

'Verres! We have trained interrogators upstairs who can get information—'

'They are weak Titus. Constrained by the media as to what they can do. Much better to do things properly down here!'

Titus snapped some handcuffs onto his suspect, attaching him to the shelter; he tried to avoid the man's eyes, but the terror in them sought him out and he felt sick. He walked over to Verres.

'Come on,' he said to the man hopefully. 'You heard what my Praetorian said. I'm the *Protector of Rome*, and he, as you probably guessed, is *'the Nothus'*.'

The colour drained from the man's face as he heard the word.

'Just talk and we'll let you go.'

Verres looked at Titus, raising an eyebrow in surprise at this promise.

'Fuck you!' The man said.

Verres smiled knowingly at Titus, 'I told you so.' He asked Titus to hold out the man's arm.

The man started to scream.

Verres brought the club down on the side of his elbow, and Titus felt the power of the blow, transmitted down the forearm, into his own hand. The man bellowed and tried to wriggle out of Titus' grasp. Titus looked down and saw shattered bone protruding from the elbow joint.

'Next side,' Verres said to Titus who moved across carefully, trying not to be sick.

The man's cries increased in volume as Titus stretched his other arm out across the dusty gravel of the courtyard. Verres struck twice this time, once at the shoulder, and then at the elbow.

The man writhed and shrieked, his useless arms flailing around, as he tried to kick at his tormentors. Titus tried to think of anything he could do to end this quickly. He was sure that the interrogators upstairs in the Aether could have got information in a more humane way. Verres seemed to be enjoying himself for Titus heard him humming an old Saturnalia song as he rolled up the man's trouser leg, searching for a knee

Titus suddenly had an idea. He ran over to the man he had handcuffed. 'Why are you letting this happen to your friend?' he asked. 'Just tell us who is organising this. Who is the leader of Filii Aquilae?'

Behind them, Verres brought his club down on his victim's knee. The man shrieked again, and then lay still, unconscious. Verres got up and looked for something to revive him.

'I don't know!' Titus' man said desperately. 'She never told us who was in charge.'

'Who's she?'

The man's face crumpled as he realised that he had already started to give away the secrets of those he worked with. 'I can't tell you any more!' he begged.

'She's the one who is arranging the riots isn't she?' Titus asked softly.

The man nodded.

'Okay,' Titus said. 'I just need her name, and then you are free, and your friend is free. I'll even arrange for medical care for him. Just the name!'

Verres wandered back over with a bucket he'd found in the corner of the dirty square. 'Communal toilet!' he said laughing. 'Should have got a plumber out!' he quipped as he poured the congealed faeces and urine into the face and wounds of the tortured man, who woke with a gasp, choking on the detritus.

'Tiberia Murena!' the restrained man screamed into Titus' face, appalled by the scene. 'Let me go, just let me go!' he shouted, fighting so hard against the handcuffs that blood trickled down his forearms.

Titus smiled at Verres who, with regret, put down the club.

'You're not really going to let them go are you Titus?' Verres said. 'What about our reputation?'

'Verres, you are meant to be learning from me, remember? Learn from this. You can get more from someone by showing some mercy than by only showing power.'

Verres turned his hands over, in a gesture of acceptance, and backed away from the tortured man, who still writhed on the ground. Titus wished he hadn't promised Aesculapium care for the victim, now he was probably going to have to carry the man, and the filth that coated him.

A stone hit Titus hard on the back of the head and stung him. He turned around. 'Verres!' he shouted, pointing at the entrance to the courtyard where a group of other men now stood, arms crossed; a few were armed with clubs, but most had nothing but their hands. Another stone was thrown towards them. There were two dozen at least, and more joining at the back all the time.

'Come on!' Verres shouted, and charged. Titus followed swiftly as Verres made contact with the pair of men blocking the gateway, pushing them back.

Titus leapt forwards, armed with one of the small clubs the men had been using to practise fighting. He hacked left and right with it at the angry Imum residents as they surged forwards at them. A man tried to claw at him from the right with what appeared to be a modified rake, but Verres smashed the weapon away with his fasces, before burying the lethal tip in the man's chest.

Verres marched ahead, swinging his fasces back and forth like a scythe, forging a path. Energy coursed from the fasces' tip, and people were thrown back by its force whenever it touched them. The air smelt of static and roasting flesh. Another stone struck Titus on the forehead, dazing him, and he felt blood trickle down, closing his left eye. He slumped down onto his knees, his vision swimming. Attackers surrounded him, kicking, punching. He felt his sight start to fade. 'Why have I died for this?' he thought as he fell, face down in the dust. As he looked up, he caught a glimpse of a girl dressed in black, with light hair. She stood apart from the crowd, neither attacking nor protecting him. 'Ceinwyn,' he moaned and lunged towards her.

He awoke slightly from his stupor at a shout from Verres, and saw a blurred image of the Praetorian charging towards him, knocking men aside as if they were straw. Verres forced him to his feet, and started to drag him along.

'Come on Titus!' Verres shouted. 'We can make it to the Aventine levator.'

The crowd started to back away, aware of the danger that Verres' fasces posed. Most started to pick up their dead and wounded and retreated into their hovels, but a determined group followed, at a safe distance, and as they followed they began to chant.

'Death to the Consul! Death to Rome! Let's eat the rich. Let's rape them all!'

More and more people joined the group, gaining courage and falling in behind. Men and women of all ages, some working people, some clearly from the streets, all Romans, all Imum dwellers, and right at the back, Titus kept catching glimpses of the girl. He was sure she was watching him. 'Ceinwyn!' he bellowed, as Verres kept dragging him forwards, away from her. Feebly he started to fight against the Praetorian. He had to get to her.

They reached the levator, and Verres pushed the call button. He stood waiting, with Titus at his side, still slightly dazed as the levator lowered itself. A few men tried to move forwards and Titus watched as Verres flicked his fasces from side to side. The men backed away.

The levator arrived and they leapt through the door. There was room for at least fifty people in the levator, so they stood at the doorway, blocking the entrance, as the crowd surged forwards. As the crowd reached them, the people at the front tried to stop, lest they be forced onto the end of the fasces, but the crowd kept pushing them forwards as they turned and struggled. The door started to close. Titus punched a young man's contorted face and pushed him back, leaning against him with all his weight as the door edged shut, finally closing the crowd out.

Then, at last, there was quiet, except for the faint sound of hammering on the other side of the thick door. Titus felt a judder as the levator started to rise, leaving the angry mob far below.

'When we get to the top we need to immobilise this levator,' Verres said gravely. He checked his arm communicator for signal, and with relief, noted that he was high enough up to communicate with Praetorian Headquarters again. 'We need back-up!' he shouted into it.

'We need to secure the Imum. Shut down the levators, don't let anyone out!'

Rome was at war with itself.

'Oh,' said Verres as he noticed the time, 'my wife is doing a lunch barbecue at our house about now. Do you want to join us?'

Titus looked at him blankly, then realised he was serious, and nodded in dazed agreement.

XXIX

As Titus bit into the huge steak, drowned in spicy sauce, he felt some of the fear he had felt that morning subside. Partly this was the effect of the delicious meat, but it was also because he could see the sky again; clearly being head of the Praetorian Guard had its privileges.

They sat in a lush garden, surrounded by the sound of birds. Far below, chaos was likely breaking out in the Imum, but Praetorians had been stationed by all the levators, and the problem was contained, for now. Titus looked up, the palace stood nearby, and he could see the balcony of his own apartment. They were two of the most powerful men in Rome now. He sat back, closed his eyes and tried to enjoy himself, but he could only see the terrified faces of the men they had interrogated, and his mind was filled with the reproachful words Ceinwyn would have had to say if she knew what he had done in the Imum. He had achieved what he wanted, but at the expense of the person he had achieved it for. It was hollow, completely meaningless. He felt like crying.

'More potato salad?' Verres wife asked, walking over, 'I made it myself.' Her accent was straight from the Imum, but her beauty was well placed in the Summus. Dark, straight hair framed her golden face, and her low cut top revealed the top of firm, tanned breasts.

Titus nodded and she doled some of the salad out onto his plate. It was simply mayonnaise and potato, but Titus thanked her anyway.

She sat down next to him and looked around her new garden, visibly glowing with pride.

'You've done well,' Titus said.

She smiled at him. 'It's all him,' she said, pointing at Verres. 'We're so proud of him. He worked hard, got us from the Imum up to the Aether, then up here with all the rich who have had money for generations. I can shop anywhere I like, I can do anything I like. I love him.'

Verres walked across, from the other side of his beautiful lawn, and embraced her, nearly smudging her thick layer of make-up. 'We didn't imagine all of this when we met at school,' he said.

Titus had an image of a strong, sixteen year old Verres, loyally protecting and caring for the most beautiful girl in the year. He turned around at the sound of Verres' two children who had been playing in the house, opening the door and running out into the garden—a three year old and a one year old, playing and rolling around in the sun laughing.

'You should invite Ceinwyn to our house,' Verres' wife said to Titus. 'I hear she's beautiful and very funny, I'd love to meet her.'

'Perhaps,' Titus said, thinking how much Ceinwyn wouldn't get on with Verres' wife. 'But she isn't too happy with me at the moment. I don't think she likes Albus' direction currently.'

Verres' wife laughed. 'Who cares what direction he's going in?' she looked up at her husband, 'as long as it's putting food on the plate. It's put us onto the Summus, and you as well. She should be proud of you.'

Titus nodded politely, but he didn't agree anymore: some things were not worth what they cost you. Titus turned back to his steak, but it had gone slightly cold and tough.

He excused himself soon after and wandered back to the palace, hoping there would be another bottle of passum in the room. As he wandered, he thought of the girl he had seen earlier. He was still certain it was Ceinwyn, in which case she was still in Rome! But in the Imum. He cursed his stupidity, but it was too late. He had picked this path and, even if it meant working for Albus, at least he was still fighting for Rome. If he left now he would genuinely have nothing.

No Ceinwyn, no power, and none of his friends, who he hadn't had a chance to see properly now for weeks.

The guard at the side entrance to the palace backed away in good time as he approached and didn't even consider checking identification. Titus greeted him, but he looked down at the ground instead and avoided eye contact. As he wandered through the palace, Titus noticed the same response from most of the staff—they were terrified of him. He hated the feeling as much as he knew that Verres loved it.

He reached his room, found the passum, and poured himself a big glass. He drank half of it straight away, to try to remove his headache, then he sat and stared at the screen for a few minutes, but there was nothing of any value to watch, although he was amused by yet another advert for *Coniunctus*, this time announcing a free upgrade service for Slave identification chips. He wondered what his father would make of that, another example of the company seemingly throwing money away. He thought for a moment of going to the Aesculapium and speaking to his father about it, but he thought about what he and Verres had done to that man in the Imum, and couldn't bear the thought of what his father would say. Then his scire rang. He paused for a moment, planning to not answer it so that he could drink, fall asleep, and forget the day, but he glanced at the number first and his heart soared with joy. It was Ceinwyn.

He grasped at the scire, fumbling with the buttons, nearly hanging up accidentally, but finally he managed to push the right button. He held the handset up to his head, his hand shaking.

'Hello,' he said hoarsely. There was no sound from the other end at first.

'Titus,' Ceinwyn spoke, her voice sounded sad and tired. '*Coniunctus* is owned by Marcus Albus. You are being deceived.'

Titus tried to speak over her, 'Ceinwyn, please, come back, I'm sorry...'

There was a click, and looking down at his scire, he saw that she had hung up.

He threw the scire at the wall in frustration, roaring in anger.

He sat and thought desperately. He tried calling her back several times, but she didn't answer. He paced the room angrily, before trying again. There was still no answer, so he left a message saying he loved her. Still she didn't call back. Then he started to think more rationally—there must have been a reason that she would call to tell him this. As he started to understand, a faint ray of hope began to spread its glow through his heart. She had told him because she still felt there was time for him to redeem himself—if Albus owned *Coniunctus*, then there was indeed great deception going on.

He left his room for the corridor and started to search the palace for Sexta, he needed to know if Albus still stood for Rome.

He found her eventually in the garden room where he had first seen Albus on his arrival in Rome two months ago. He cursed that day now, wishing that he had stayed in Britannia, wishing that he had listened to Ceinwyn. Sexta was sitting alone, reading. Her face looked drawn, very different to two weeks ago when she had been dancing with her young fiancé. Titus wondered if her face was slightly bruised, but it could simply have been the mottled light filtering in through the plants.

'Sexta,' he said as quietly as he could.

She jumped, nearly dropping the book.

'Yes,' she said quickly, clearly terrified at the sight of him.

'Sexta, you don't need to be scared of me,' Titus said.

She backed away slightly as he sat down next to her. He was more scared of *her*: what if she revealed to her new husband what he was about to tell her? But he had no choice—she was the only one who might have an idea of what Albus was up to.

'Sexta, I need your help.'

She shook her head.

'Wait, it's about *Coniunctus*. Today I learnt something, that it's actually owned by Albus. I wonder if you know why?'

'Stop!' Sexta hissed quietly. 'You'll get us both killed.'

Titus sighed with relief. He was definitely on to something.

'It's alright Sexta, tell me what you know, I can protect you.'

The girl looked at him with pity in her eyes, 'Titus, you can't protect me. Not from him.' She got up and started to walk away.

'Sexta!' he called after her.

'Don't follow me Titus, or we will both end up dead. Just do what I do, do what he says, and maybe one day you will be able to escape before you lose anything else you love.'

She walked away to find another quiet place, and Titus realised that following was futile for she was too scared to help him, and he could think of no way of earning her trust. He called Ceinwyn one last time, but there was still no answer. He had no choice but to take Sexta's advice—wait, listen, and keep himself safe. He resolved to find out as much information as he could. He thought about leaving, about trying to find Ceinwyn now, but three things stopped him: firstly, the fact that she probably hated him now, and secondly he had little idea where to find her. If she was with her father, then she was in the Imum, but exactly where was a complete guess. The Imum was probably still rioting. He hoped she would be safe.

But thirdly, every time he thought of deserting Albus, in his mind he had an image of his great ancestor plunging a gladius into the back of Caesar whilst he slept. True, many people had called the great Labienus a hero for that act of murder—a murder which had saved the Republic from the predations of a would-be-Tyrant. However, Titus knew what most called his great ancestor, for it was a phrase he had heard many times at school, always behind his back.

'Traitor.'

He was a true Roman. He could not desert Rome, no matter who the leader. Ceinwyn would never understand that.

XXX

Quintus put down the suture needle, and nodded to his assistant to wheel the Slave out of the small operating office. He sat down at his workbench, placing the used tools into a yellow bin so that they could be taken away for incineration. Finished, he turned to the wall behind him and looked through the one-way glass. The glass brightened slightly, permitting him to see the silhouettes of the panel of supervisors. He waited patiently whilst they conferred and ticked away at boxes on their clipboards. The head examiner then glanced up, caught his eye, and gave him a nod. Quintus punched the air with joy and left the office.

The corridor outside was warm after the air-conditioned environment of the office. He wandered down to the recreation room, which as usual he had to himself. The walls were lined with entertainment consoles, and in the centre was a Latrunculi table, which had stayed set up, waiting for nonexistent players, every day of Quintus' trial period. It seemed that despite the generous wage, they were having difficulty recruiting medici for the job. There were two others that he had seen, but they were from Dacia, stank of tobacco, spoke poor Latin, and kept themselves to themselves. Quintus sat down on the large recliner and pulled out his scire. He took a deep breath and dialled Tiberius' number. His heart started to beat faster.

There was no answer. He wasn't surprised: the last time he had spoken to Tiberius what was left of the army were on standby to reinforce the Praetorians at the Imum gates if need be. Quintus laughed at the idea of scum from the Imum trying to bring about the downfall of Rome. They were outnumbered by the good, upstanding, people from the Aether, and unlike the Praetorians' weapons, the rioters clubs could not kill with a single blow.

Quintus picked up a sample of the leaflets that this clinic, and many others identical to it, had been distributing around Rome for the last few days. On the front was a picture of a smiling family with their Slaves working industriously behind them. His job was simple, cut into the Slave's signum, remove the identification chip, and replace it with a new one that had longer battery life, could track the Slave, and apparently reduced the need for sleep—increasing productivity.

His first procedure on a live Slave had gone very well. The Slave had struggled at first, but the cuts were superficial and the clamps had held the Slave's head in place quite firmly during the delicate work. The family had even tried to pay him afterwards, but he had refused. Even just one year here would make him rich, he didn't need tips, and he had been told from day one of working here that the work they were doing would be entirely free. The banner, hanging over the front of the clinic, made it clear why. Sandwiched between pictures of *Coniunctus* engineers happily building satellites and bringing power to Rome, were the words, *'Bene Facis!'*—'Thank you!' Rome had allowed *Coniunctus* a lucrative deal to supply power—upgrading every Slave in the city was their way of thanking the citizens.

He thought about the money again, a thought that dominated much of his dull work in the clinic. He suspected that, now fully through the assessment process, and being expected to perform the procedure one hundred times a day, his life would become even more drudgerous, but, for that money, he could cope. He planned to buy a new house first, on the Caelian district of the Summus near to Gaia, so that he could easily say that it was simply that they needed more space. Perhaps he could take a lover? Even if she would not. He thought about Tiberius again, and resolved that this year he would find a way to ask him. He knew Tiberius had slept with men before, but he slept with women too, and Tiberius was so handsome it was highly unlikely he would be interested in Quintus. Besides, Tiberius thought that he was devoted to Gaia, it was the excuse he had used every time they had visited whores. Would he be rejected if he told Tiberius of his true feelings? He burned with embarrassment just at the thought, yet he knew that if he did not ask he would never know.

The whole far-away dream was close to jeopardy though, and his hands became sticky with sweat as he thought about Gaia's mentioning of divorce last night. He had felt sick when she said the word, because there were not many grounds under which divorce was possible. Now that he was definitely not dead, there was only one other possible avenue she could use—non-consummation. His parents would die of shame. Why would she not just keep up the sham? Take a lover as he had suggested? Since she had run off that night, a week ago, she had had a new confidence about her and it scared him. At least his secret was safe for now. He wondered what he might do if that secret was threatened? Could he kill Gaia? The idea was ridiculous, he could never do something like that, but his secret must stay safe—he tore at his hair in frustration.

A voice boomed out over the intercom system, interrupting him from his dark thoughts. 'Quintus Decius, report to main operating office immediately.'

Quintus sprang up, eager to give a good impression. He bustled back up the corridor, white coat flying behind him. He saw one of the Dacian medici come out of a side room, slowly extinguishing a foul smelling black cigarette. He had left his scire screen on, still displaying a pornographic film of dubious legality. Quintus shook his head. He believed that only true Romans should be allowed to practise medicine in Rome.

A long line of families, with their Slaves, stretched through the complex now; the doors had just been opened for the morning. Most of the families seemed relaxed and happy, even if their Slaves looked apprehensive. Quintus reached the door of the office and opened it, greeting the two assistants who would help with the rest of the morning's procedures.

He was about to sit down, to get the first set of equipment ready, when he heard an altercation at the front desk. He poked his head out to listen, expecting to see a Slave trying to escape. Instead, there was a whole family arguing with the reception girl.

The head of the family, a thin man in his forties, was pointing his finger at the reception girl. 'She doesn't want it! She has never needed new batteries for the chip before. We'd rather just leave her as she is. She's seventy years old! We were a bit shocked to be interrupted by the Praetorians and herded down here.'

'You missed your slot, it was yesterday,' the girl said offhandedly.

'Yes, we missed it on purpose,' the man said, slightly exasperated now. 'We would have called to cancel, but there was no number to call. It's a free service anyway. We simply choose to decline it, but thanks anyway.'

'I know it's free,' the girl said. 'But it's compulsory. Orders of the Senate. Get back in line, and be grateful your Slave is getting a free upgrade.'

For a moment, the man looked as if he was going to ignore the reception girl, and take his family and Slave away, but then he spotted the Praetorian overseeing the queue, thought better of his plan, and meekly joined its tail, their seventy year old Slave quivering with fear. Quintus shrugged his shoulders and called for his first case as a fully qualified *Coniunctus* technician, thinking of how each one brought him a step further towards his fine house, and freedom from those who might judge him. It was a small price to pay.

XXXI

'Come on!', Titus shouted to Verres, encouraging him onto his feet yet again. 'First position.' He waited whilst the young Praetorian steadied himself and brought his gladius out in front of him, elbow half-bent, wooden gladius slightly up pointing. 'No, not quite,' Titus said, moving forwards and making a slight adjustment.

'Fucking pain in the arse!' Verres cursed. 'What's the point?'

Titus shook his head, laughing at him. *'What's the point?* History Verres! History! Rome was built on legions armed in this way. Sometimes in battle, close quarters battle, there is no better weapon.'

'I use a fasces,' Verres replied simply.

'Yes, yes you do,' Titus conceded, 'but you can learn a lot from the way we used to fight, and it's good exercise too...' He tailed off, why *did* he like gladius fighting? He thought for a moment, truthfully speaking it was simply that he enjoyed it and was good at it. Surely that should be reason enough. Most Roman Nobles could use a gladius, but few of them had practised as much, or were as good as Titus was.

Titus coached Verres through the positions again, and once again, in vain, tried to get him to join them together to make a basic *Tripudium Mortis*. At least he knew the nine positions now.

'Right,' Verres said, clearly bored, 'time to make an arrest I think.'

'Tiberia Murena?' Titus asked.

'Yup.' Verres took a sip from of pomegranate juice, walked over to the balcony, and looked down at the parade ground where, months ago now, Titus had watched the Primiles going through their paces.

'I wonder what she is doing now,' Titus said. She was a senior senator, with a young family and Titus hoped they had been misinformed by the riot leaders they had tortured, but it was highly unlikely. Filii Aquilae seemed to have links not just to the Aether, but to senators as well. 'Could be out with her children,' he continued, having no desire whatsoever to make the arrest, but little choice. He couldn't let terrorists thrive in Rome, but he would do anything to avoid a repeat of the scene in the Imum earlier. He wondered for a minute if Verres would tone things down in the event of capturing a woman, but he knew in his heart that there was little chance of that. He felt sick as he imagined what he would likely have to assist with.

'Okay,' Titus relented, 'we'll go to her house in a minute, but I want to see you connect these positions first.'

Verres roared, and leapt forwards with his wooden gladius, nearly catching Titus by surprise.

Titus laughed and started to fight back, easily countering him and knocking his gladius from his strong grip with an expert riposte.

Verres chuckled. 'Right boss, show me how you did that then.'

Titus glowed with pride. His pupil was at last interested in learning some skills.

An hour later, and the sun was directly above the palace, but they remained sheltered in the room behind the balcony. Verres finally, not only managed to string the nine positions together, but also managed to disarm Titus once, although Titus knew that he had let him to some extent. Verres had strength, but he lacked Titus' speed, learnt through years of extra training with the gladius. They stood together, sweating and laughing, and were both about to sit down to further pomegranate juice and a lunch of oiled sardines, when the door burst open to reveal Albus, but Albus in a light Titus had never seen before, as if he was on the verge of losing control of himself.

'Drink!', he shouted to the assistant, who poured him a glass of the juice. Albus sniffed it and chucked the glass onto the floor where it smashed. 'Fucking proper drink you idiot!' he snarled, and the man ran off to get some wine for the Consul.

'Albus,' Titus said trying to calm him. 'What's going on?'

'You should already know Titus, as *'Protector of Rome'.*' He sighed and walked to the balcony, signalling Titus to follow. 'While you've been playing centurions with your head of the Praetorian Guard, his men have had to fall back, there is rioting on the Aether. Can you believe it?' His voice was high and outraged. 'The Aether! And that's not the worst of it. Some people from the Aether are actually joining the Imum scum!'

'Maybe we should close off the Summus,' Titus said, thinking quickly.

'And lose two thirds of my city?' he looked at Titus as if he was mad. 'Perhaps you are working for them Titus, with ideas like that?' he gave Titus a sideways glance that unnerved him, as if his statement about loyalty was in fact a question. Titus ignored the comment and concentrated on maintaining an expression of deep thought to avoid further accusation.

'I'll take the Praetorians from the Summus,' Titus said at last. 'We'll break up the groups, disperse them. Get them back into the Imum.'

Albus shook his head. 'Already in progress Titus,' he said sarcastically. 'Don't worry yourself, we've got it covered. You and Verres are clearly doing something more important.'

Titus reddened with embarrassment. 'We're about to make an important arrest.'

The servant returned brandishing a brimming glass of dark red wine.

'Ah!' Albus exclaimed, finishing the drink in one draught, the moment it was placed in his hand. 'Good,' he said, much brighter as he turned to Titus, 'an arrest is good progress. We need to find the Aquila himself soon and put an end to this nonsense before they blow something up or have one of us killed. Rioting we can put up with!'

Titus signalled to Verres, who nodded, and the pair moved to leave.

'Hang on a moment,' said Albus, calmer now after his glass of wine. 'Were you sparring?'

'Yes,' Titus said proudly, 'I thought your head of Praetorians should know some basic moves.'

'Spoken like a true Roman,' Albus said, clapping him on the shoulder, all trace of the earlier animosity gone.

Titus turned to go once more.

'Show me.' Albus said imperiously, walking to pick up one of the two discarded gladii.

'I'm not sure if we've got time,' Titus said. There was something odd about the way Albus' mood had changed so quickly, it unnerved him.

'I insist,' Albus commanded.

'Okay,' Titus said, resigning himself, and took position at one end of the mat. He brought his gladius into the first position and watched Albus as he did the same. They bowed their heads imperceptibly to each other, neither taking their eyes off their opponent's wooden blade.

Titus lunged forwards, ducking to avoid the swing he expected from Albus. He felt a breeze from Albus' gladius as it passed just over his head, so close. Albus was much faster than he had expected. He swung upwards to catch him as he recovered from the swing, but Albus had anticipated it already, as it was the standard response to his previous attack, and Titus' gladius swung meekly into thin air ready to be countered. But no counter came.

'This is boring,' Albus said, off handedly. 'Proper gladii,' he called to the assistant, who looked confused.

'But sir,' the man said, 'there are none.'

'Of course there are, you idiot! They are just locked away, down in the basement, bring me mine, and see if you can find Titus'. It should have been brought here when he took up residence.'

Titus felt slightly nervous—he had not expected the Consul to be so fast. And now real gladii? Hurting the Consul would surely be punished by death.

'You're not bad at this,' Titus said, trying to make conversation while they waited for the gladii. The sun was beating down even harder now, and the balcony was stifling. He wiped his palms, trying to keep them dry for the upcoming contest.

Albus laughed. 'You should try to fight a Primiles.' Titus remembered the demonstration he had seen on entering Rome when Albus had been attacked by one of his own generals. 'I've been training with them every day for two years now, and I'm nearly there. But there are still several of them who are too quick for me.'

Titus wiped his palms once more. The sweat had formed again.

'Ah!' Albus exclaimed. 'Good, good, pass them over.' The servant passed Titus his great ancestor's gladius with the ivory hilt, and he swung it round twice, remembering its balance.

'That's a beautiful weapon,' Albus said, waiting, 'I'd like to have a look at it later if I may.'

'Perhaps,' Titus said, feeling strangely possessive of his family's gladius.

They took the first position again, and this time Titus waited for Albus to make the first move. Albus started to step sideways, and Titus followed, edging, always just out of the gladius' reach. He jiggled his shoulders slightly as he moved, trying to keep his muscles moving, maintaining his focus. Verres stood at the side watching on. Titus needed to put a good show on for him, he couldn't look foolish in front of his new pupil.

Despite his intense focus, Albus' attack was so fast it nearly overwhelmed Titus. He was nearly too late with his first and second parries, and ended up on the back foot, fighting desperately. He tried to use his superior bulk to push Albus back, but the Consul slipped to the side of him. Titus parried to his side, as a reflex, not expecting a blow there during a training match as it would be extremely dangerous. The parry connected with a blow, so vicious that it nearly knocked Titus sideways. He swore and leapt away, knowing that if it hadn't been for his parry, that strike would have likely punctured a kidney.

He backed away, Albus advanced, menacingly. Titus readied himself. Perhaps the attack had been a reflex from Albus, in the same way his own defensive stroke had been? Most of the *Tripudium Mortis* was performed by reflex and muscle memory, which was why it could be performed so quickly.

This time it was Titus' turn to attack. He threw his full weight behind every blow, trying to break down Albus' defences, but to no avail. The Consul was faster than he was, and with fear, he realised that he was tiring in the searing heat. He longed for the bout to be over. He had neglected his training these last months, and he was embarrassed by how much it was showing. Then suddenly Albus was on the attack, and without warning, Titus found himself on his back, Albus' gladius at his throat.

He made himself laugh as he sat up. 'Very good,' he said to Albus, trying to sound magnanimous. 'I need to get back into training! This has been a big wake up call.'

'On your feet,' Albus said coldly. 'This isn't over—we're fighting to first blood.'

Titus rose slowly, subconsciously looking for an escape route, the new tone of the Consul's voice disturbed him deeply.

'Titus,' Albus said coolly, as they circled each other, gladii outstretched. 'Are you still in contact with your wife?'

'No,' Titus said truthfully, she still refused to answer his messages.

'Pity, because if you were, you might have a word with her about meddling in business which is not hers.'

Titus' arms suddenly felt like lead, and sweat burst from every pore. 'I'm not in contact,' he said, almost pleadingly.

'Forgive me for not believing you Titus, but I am a pragmatic man. Control your wife, or both you and her will no longer be friends of mine.' He struck, immediately after speaking, and Titus was completely unprepared. Within seconds, he was on his back again.

Angry, Titus swung his gladius up at Albus who leapt back laughing. 'Now we're fighting Titus, come on!' He signalled to Titus to attack.

Titus leapt to his feet and bellowed, trying to put out of his mind the threat Albus had just made to Ceinwyn, trying to remain calm so he could fight rationally. He struck desperately, blow after blow, ducking, dodging, and leaping back and forth. Twice he nearly cut Albus. He knew that any other opponent he had ever fought would have been in ribbons by this point, but Albus seemed almost superhuman. He didn't even look tired.

'Oh, Titus?' Albus said calmly, as he parried a blow.

Titus nodded to show he was listening, with no energy left to speak. The pair circled each other again, looking for a weakness.

'Let your wife know that there is no point in her phoning her friend in Northern Britannia again.'

He let it hang. Titus felt sick. He wished he hadn't drunk so much pomegranate juice.

'And Titus, you'd better catch the Aquila, because if you don't, and I don't award you Hispania, then you're going to have a few issues with accommodation when you return to your shit hole of a province.'

'Why?' Titus asked, thinking of Cyric and Decimus, and his other friends, with a growing sense of dread.

'Didn't you hear the news?' he said, suddenly sounding very concerned. 'Oh, Titus! I am sorry. The Governor's complex in Luguvalium burned down last night. Apparently there were no survivors. So sad, so very sad.'

Titus stared at him, rage rising up inside him. The Consul was clearly trying to keep a straight face, but the faint edge of a smile crossed his expression. It was more than Titus could bear. He leapt at the Consul, gladius raised above his head. He didn't care if Albus ran him through, he would still make his overhead strike connect. Albus stepped to the side neatly at the last minute, nicking his back with the tip of his gladius as he passed.

It stung no more than the bite of a mosquito, and when Titus reached around there was only a speck of blood.

'I win,' Albus said softly and walked away, leaving Verres, Titus, and the servant, alone on the balcony. Titus sat down on the mat and put his head in his hands. He had never felt more alone.

XXXII

Ceinwyn was already feeling quite drunk by the fourth Bibesian Field cocktail, and she felt heavy too, each one contained a whole layer of gold leaf, a layer which she could imagine congealing in her stomach. Gaia continued to laugh and enjoy herself; Ceinwyn was sure she had had at least six of the potent drinks by now. The Popina was starting to get busy now as the sun was setting. There was something very unusual about the atmosphere, as if she was drinking at the end of the world. People were throwing shots and cocktails down like it was their last night on Earth, or perhaps more precisely they were worried that the bar would not be open tomorrow. The streets here were still quiet, but Ceinwyn had heard that the trouble from the Imum was spreading. Yet Gaia remained unconcerned.

'Not the first time the rabble has risen up,' she said indifferently, 'and last time they lined the Appian Way with crosses.'

Ceinwyn shuddered at the thought of her father hanging from a cross, but she pushed the thought away. She hoped the uprising would succeed. It had been mainly her father's idea, apparently a diversion for something much bigger that he wouldn't tell her about, yet.

She had spent the last two days getting to know Gaia better, but had learnt little else of use except that *Coniunctus* was owned by Albus, and that Gaia thought it was a direct ploy to ruin her father's business. Ceinwyn accepted this, but knew it was too narrow an explanation on its own. *Coniunctus* wanted people to love it and it seemed to be working. Every day she saw more and more people proudly wearing their t-shirts and holding free items that had been handed out. It hadn't stopped the riots though, despite *Coniunctus'* pleas for everyone to clear the streets.

Ceinwyn's main problem was that she was getting drawn further and further into Gaia's life, and that of her husband, who apparently now wished to move out completely. Ceinwyn thought this was a great idea, but had been rewarded with a look of complete astonishment by Gaia at declaring this view.

Ceinwyn sighed as she looked up at her new friend—she was crying again, in public; she would be so embarrassed in the morning.

'Gaia,' she said softly, and reached over with a napkin to wipe her face, trying her best not to smudge her make-up further. 'Maybe we should get you home, back up to the Summus, before the riot comes.' Her family had moved just in time.

'I don't care Tita!' Gaia moaned. 'I'd rather be dead than stuck with him.'

'Why not divorce him?'

Gaia sobbed louder, 'I know, I asked him, just like you suggested. Even though I don't really want to, but he laughed, said it wasn't possible.'

'It is.' Ceinwyn said. 'You just need to say that he's a homosexual and wouldn't sleep with you.'

'It would embarrass him though,' Gaia replied, clearly still deeply in love with her uncaring husband.

'Do we care?' Ceinwyn asked, still unable to believe the amount of loyalty Gaia showed this arrogant and selfish man. 'He should have had the decency to tell you the truth before he married you.' Ceinwyn had the faint suspicion that Gaia would have probably married him anyway.

'He's said he won't allow it.'

'It's not his choice,' Ceinwyn said, finishing her drink. The bar was really filling up now and she was worried about being asked to dance; she pulled her coat around her shoulders tightly.

'Tita?' Gaia said softly. 'I'm scared. I think he really might... you know... do something bad if I divorce him.'

Ceinwyn felt a sudden wave of anger against this cruel man she had never met. 'Then we should do it all the more, and if need be my family will protect you!' She regretted it as soon as she had made the promise, as there was really nothing she could do. But she resolved to at least confront the man herself if need be, to protect Gaia—a child really, purposely kept that way by her family, despite her age being the same as Ceinwyn's.

'Would you, really?' Gaia said, with a look of amazement on her beautiful face, as if she'd never had a friend before. 'I love you Tita, thank you,' and she embraced Ceinwyn, who felt a little burst of warmth run through her. She realised for a moment that she had felt the first inkling of how it might feel to hold her own child in her arms. An experience that she had been dreading ever since her periods had stopped—it was an experience she only wanted to have with Titus at her side.

She looked back at Gaia, as the girl reached down for her beeping scire. 'Message?' she asked.

'Yup,' she said, her fingers moving with lightning speed over the scire's screen, replying much quicker than Ceinwyn would have been able to.

'What's he asked?'

'Just checking on me.'

'Why do you reply then?' Ceinwyn said angrily, grabbing the scire.

She looked down at the captured device, the last line was Gaia's reply, it read:

'*In a bar with a friend, don't worry—a girl!*' (there was a strange icon with a smiley face here that Ceinwyn thought looked crude, and was pleased she didn't know how to produce), '*I'm about to—*'

Her eyes were drawn to the line above—his message to her: '*Where are you? We need to talk.*'

But it wasn't the chauvinistic text that surprised her—it was the picture alongside it, a picture of a man she recognised.

She paused for a second and thought hard. She had already felt she was meddling in something that was not her business, but now she knew it for sure. She suddenly felt very bad for criticising Quintus so much, but at the same time angry that he could treat his wife like this.

'I'm going to go,' she said, handing the scire back. 'Do you want me to walk you home?'

'No,' Gaia replied offhandedly, still replying to the message. 'Plenty of men here, I might take my husband up on his suggestion, and sort 'my frustrations' out.'

Ceinwyn shrugged and left the bar, alone. The streets were oddly quiet now, and as she walked, she noticed many of the doors were barred. There was a distant rumbling sound, and pausing she realised that the ground beneath her feet was shaking slightly with it. Rome was in uproar below her, and this night she would likely see that spill onto the Aether if the news was correct. She started to hurry, trying to get home quickly. Her father's house was in the Aventine district in the Aether, and she knew trouble would probably start in that area sooner than the others, it being the poorest Aether area, and directly above the least salubrious district of the Imum. She started to jog.

After a few minutes she paused at a crossroads to check the way. The air was cooler now and she pulled her shawl in tightly around her shoulders. She cast her glance both ways, remembered where she was, started to walk, and then noticed a dark figure move a hundred paces behind her. Other than that, the streets were deserted. She quickened her pace. The figure followed.

XXXIII

Titus and Verres paused for a moment outside Tiberia Murena's door, in the Capitoline district of the Aether. The sun was nearly down now, and Titus could hear sounds of unrest in the distance. He wanted desperately to be over there now, protecting his city, rather than be about to do what he had to do. However, after Albus' outburst earlier, he needed to prove his loyalty even more if he was to survive. He resolved to restrain Verres as much as he could, but they both knew this woman would know the identity of the Aquila, and somehow they needed to get her to tell them. Titus had seen the museum of interrogation in the Mamertine many times, it was now the Praetorian headquarters, and he wondered what implements would be used nowadays to break people beneath those dark, lonely floors. He didn't want her to end up there, but first he had to prevent Verres from torturing her in her own home.

They didn't bother knocking, Verres simply pushed the door over and they charged upstairs. Murena was cooking supper for her children, two boys; one looked around five, and the other was a baby, perhaps just over one. The youngest was holding onto the side of a dining chair, trying to climb up.

Murena screamed as they charged into her kitchen, and rushed over to the eldest child, trying to get between him and Verres.

Titus put his hand on Verres' arm to try to keep him at his side. He wanted to run this his way, keep Verres under control.

'Tiberia Murena,' he said in as formal a voice as he could muster. 'You are under arrest for conspiracy against Rome itself, for inciting violence, and for leading revolt. You may answer now, or to a Carnifex. Do you wish to speak?'

Murena's face paled as she heard the word Carnifex, as would anyone's. Titus wanted to walk forwards, hug her, and tell it would be okay. He wanted to take her and her children away from here and hide them, but he couldn't: he had thrown his lot in completely now, and besides she *had* plotted against Rome. He thought about all he had been through, but he had remained loyal, she should have done too. Yet she didn't deserve what would happen to her.

Murena shook her head. 'Please! Don't hurt my children.'

Titus nodded and walked towards the eldest. He would ensure he was passed to a good Roman family, and hopefully Murena would be able to take him back if she was ever released. He knew it was unlikely, and from her expression, so did she.

He had an idea. 'We are having an amnesty today,' he said.

Verres looked around quizzically, and Titus frowned at him, trying to make sure he didn't interfere.

'As *Protector of Rome*, I may be able to overlook certain crimes, if we are properly recompensed.'

'We're paid well enough!' Verres laughed.

'Not money!' Titus said, glancing across at Verres. 'With information.'

Murena paled again.

'So a choice,' Titus continued. 'The Mamertine and never see your children again, or names. Or *a* name, for that matter. The Aquila.'

Murena stared at her two children. She walked towards them, and in turn picked each up and kissed them as tears rolled down her cheeks, splattering on the tiled floor. The smallest one began to scream, crawling around her feet, crying to be picked up again.

Verres walked around to the other side of the kitchen, found a clothes iron and switched on its induction coil, before resting it back in its holster menacingly.

'Have you made your decision?' Titus asked, hoping desperately that his plan would work. He hadn't agreed the amnesty with anyone, but surely as *Protector of Rome* he could make rules up like this if need be. As long as they got results.

Murena stood back up, stared at him with rage in her eyes, and to Titus' amazement, shook her head. 'I refuse your terms.'

Titus was speechless. He tried to think of another plan, but it was too late. Verres had become bored. Titus watched as he marched forwards and grabbed the youngest child by one of his ankles.

Murena screamed and darted forwards to hammer at Verres with her fists. Titus grabbed her, holding her tightly as she screamed and fought. Verres took the baby and moved closer to the open window, they were twenty feet above the ground.

He extended his arm, dangling the terrified infant upside down, suspended above the hard concrete below. Murena was shrieking, and even Titus was struggling to hold her. He looked into her face, screaming and contorted, and across at Verres', smiling as he held the child. He knew that Verres would drop the baby. He would drop him as proof of his ruthlessness, and use the five year old as a negotiating tool afterwards. The iron was hot now—Titus could see the induction coil glowing angrily.

Suddenly some of the grey mist that had filled Titus' head for the last months lifted and he saw the scene clearly. What had he become?

'Verres, for fuck's sake. Put the child down,' he said commandingly.

Verres smiled at him. 'It's for the best.' He looked down and Titus was sure he was about to drop the baby.

He let go of Murena, who fell to the ground shaking, and leapt forwards, grabbing Verres' arm. 'I said: put - him - down!' he said firmly, staring into Verres' heartless eyes.

Verres stared back, and Titus saw a hint of fear there. The young Praetorian slowly flexed his arm, bringing the child into the room. Titus took the child from him and, unsure how to cradle him, he returned him quickly to Murena who was busy cursing both of them by every god she knew the name of.

'Verres! Go outside and keep watch. I need five minutes alone with the prisoner.'

Verres opened his mouth in protest.

'Go,' Titus said firmly, and Verres obliged.

After Verres had left, Titus turned to Murena. 'I'm sorry.'

'Fuck you, you bastard! Get out of my house,' Murena shouted, trying to push the five year old further behind her for protection. The veins on her forehead were bulging, and she looked like she would scratch Titus if he came any closer.

'We're both trapped,' Titus said, 'I have to get a name. I can't stop him! I don't want any harm to come to any of you. But I need a name!' He felt himself start to cry with anguish.

Murena sat down as she saw the terrifying sight of tears falling from the *Protector of Rome's* eyes, and turned even more pale, if it was possible.

'Please just get him away, get him away from my children!'

'I need a name,' Titus insisted. 'Who is the Aquila?'

Murena sighed angrily. 'You are stupid aren't you. It's called Filii for a reason, there are many.'

'I need one. A leader.'

'I know the most powerful one,' Murena said quietly, sobbing.

'Tell me.' He could hear Verres moving about outside and knew he didn't have much time. 'Come on,' he hissed, 'tell me.'

'His name,' her voice stuttered as she gave away the leader of the resistance. 'Is Lucius Labienus Aquilinus.'

The foundations of Titus' world crumbled, and he sat down on the tiled kitchen floor. He did not doubt the word of a mother protecting her children, and so his father must be the leader of Filii Aquilae. Verres could never find this out. He heard him on the stairs. He had only moments, and two stark choices. Kill the trembling Murena to silence her, or kill Verres. He wondered how he would manage to kill Verres unarmed, the man was much stronger and younger than he was, but he would have to try. Either that or see his father arrested and killed.

He turned to face Verres, making sure Murena and her children were safely behind him.

'Boss,' Verres called as he rushed in.

Titus readied himself. He might be able to break his neck if he took him by complete surprise. His father was head of Filii Aquilae, what did that make him? Was his father a traitor? Or was he himself fighting for the wrong side?

'Headquarters!' Verres shouted. 'We are being called back. The riots, we are needed to defend the Summus.'

'What about the prisoner?' Titus asked, ready to strike at Verres if need be.

'Leave her!' Verres shouted, gesturing at Titus to move down the stairs. 'They fear the Summus itself will be overrun.'

Verres dashed down the stairs as Titus leapt up. 'Flee!' he hissed back, to Murena and her family, as he charged out of the house after Verres. In the distance, the roof of the Aether was illuminated orange.

Rome was burning.

XXXIV

Gnaeus waited patiently at the end of the garden room for Vibia to make her entrance. The altar to Jupiter had been set up in front of the dead garden and flowers had been obtained from outside Rome to strew across it, ready for the wedding. Tarpeius had ordered every room of the house decorated.

Gnaeus looked around the room at the witnesses. Another explosion in the distance made the floor shake, and a tile fell off the roof into the garden behind him. The witnesses looked around quickly, trying to pretend they were not terribly afraid. There was not a single person there that Gnaeus knew well: they were all friends of Vibia or distant members of the Tarpeius family. He thought of the friends he had invited, but none had been able to attend. Quintus had said he was working, and of all the excuses, Gnaeus did not believe this one. Titus, he knew, was actually working, although he disagreed with his work fervently. They had spoken little in the last week, and as Gnaeus thought of the empty seats in the room, he felt a pang of sadness for his old friend and hoped he would not be lost forever to Albus and his tyrannical regime. Marcus, Tiberius and Antonius had been due to attend, but at the last minute they had been refused leave from the barracks.

Another explosion rang out. His friends were probably fighting on the streets right now. Part of him wanted to be there, but his friends were fighting on the wrong side.

He thought about what he was about to do—marry into a family actively opposed to Albus, who was every day strengthening his grip on Rome. He would surely either end this year dead, or in the Mamertine. He thought of Vibia. He didn't care what happened to him. Nothing mattered except her.

The speakers from behind the altar played a song Vibia particularly liked, it was loud, fast, and shouty—like all the music she enjoyed. As the song reached a slow, chuggy, part, the doors at the end of the room opened and everyone turned to watch. Gnaeus' heart beat harder as he caught sight of his wife to be. Her floor length tunic was simple woven cotton, as was traditional, but the flowers in her bright red veil, strewn through her beautifully arranged hair, were amazing. She looked more beautiful than he had ever seen her.

She walked briskly up the aisle towards him as the music drowned out the sound of rioting, which was getting closer every minute and the priest of Jupiter started the service, rattling through the preliminaries at an alarming speed. Gnaeus could see him sweating and glancing around, afraid. The priest had wanted to postpone the wedding, but Gnaeus and Vibia had refused. The wedding date had been set for weeks, and they weren't just going to change it because of a riot, Gnaeus wanted to say to him. Besides, if this was the end, better that it come married to the one you love, than alone.

Vibia took off the bulla, her special necklace that she had worn since childhood, from around her neck, and handed it to her father standing beside her, then she turned and took Gnaeus' hands. Her fingers were cool, but they did not tremble.

Gnaeus looked down at the knot of Hercules wrapped around the centre of her tunic, which only he was allowed to untie. He thought about untying it later and how her tunic would unravel. He looked up and saw that she had seen where his eyes had been, and she smiled at him mischievously. She still had her lip and nose piercing in. She laughed with joy as the priest of Jupiter stated that they, as a couple, had come together today to be married forever and as she laughed, Gnaeus could see that she also had her tongue piercing in; she was still Vibia. He loved her even more.

The service was much shorter than the Christian one they were going to have next week, secretly. Gnaeus still could not tell Tarpeius the truth about his beliefs, although he suspected that once he had been in the family for some time these would be grudgingly tolerated. Vibia didn't mind at all, and was quite looking forward to having two wedding services. This first one was so short it was already almost over.

'And now,' the priest of Jupiter said, 'the giving of consent for marriage.' He gestured to Gnaeus, whose turn it was to speak first. Gnaeus stared into Vibia's eyes, thinking about their first kiss and the confidence she had in him. She thought he would be Consul one day. He loved how much she believed in him, but a part of him was scared of letting her down. He opened his mouth to speak the words said for centuries, the words that declared the marriage. He would love her forever. That at least he could promise.

'When and where you are Vibia, I then and there am Gnaeus.'

His voice trembled slightly as he spoke.

Vibia looked up from under her, short, beautiful, black hair and smiled at him, 'when and where you are Gnaeus, I then and there am Vibia.'

'You are husband and wife,' the priest said, and cut into the cake sacrifice the moment he finished the pronouncement. A small portion was immediately sacrificed onto one of the incense lamps, which spluttered and nearly went out. The rest went away to be divided for the guests. Gnaeus looked at Vibia. 'I love you,' he said.

They kissed.

The floor shook so hard it nearly knocked them to the floor.

Plaster fell from the roof and some of the guests screamed, running for the exit.

'Quick onto the street!' shouted Tarpeius.

Gnaeus held Vibia's hand tightly as they dashed out. A huge ball of fire hung in the sky to the south.

'The oil stores are burning!' Tarpeius shouted, with no glee in his voice. He had always promoted peaceful protest.

'We'll be safe here,' Gnaeus said to Vibia. 'They are far away, the other side of Rome, and the Praetorians will hold them off.'

Tarpeius took a few of the guests, and started to walk down the street in the direction of the explosion.

'Father.' Vibia shouted. 'Come back!'

'Child,' he said calmly, 'my people are going to get themselves killed, and they are going to ruin everything that we have fought for. I have no choice but to try to stop them.'

Vibia ran over to him, with Gnaeus following. 'Please,' she said, crying, 'it's not safe, stay here, stay with us.'

Tarpeius shook his head. 'I cannot let my people kill themselves. Particularly as many of them think that they are fighting for me. Don't worry about me, I'll be fine, they wouldn't dare harm me openly on the streets.' He started to walk away, then turned back and took his daughter in his arms, his expression betraying a trace of fear. 'Besides,' he whispered to her, 'if something does happen to me, at least I saw my daughter marry one of the last good men in Rome.'

Gnaeus walked up and put his arm softly around Vibia's tiny waist, comforting her as she watched her father walk away.

They stood in silence and watched. Minutes passed. Gnaeus thought about going inside but he could tell that Vibia didn't want to. She stood there, on the step, staring out over the city. He realised that she was planning to stay there until her father returned. They waited a few minutes more. The floor shook again, and a further gout of fire spurted into the sky from the direction of the oil stores. Gnaeus looked down at the knot of Hercules around Vibia's waist; he had longed for his wedding night for years. Then he looked down at her tear strewn face as she stared out at the devastation on the other side of the City. He cursed the bad timing of the riot. 'Come on,' he said to Vibia, knowing in his heart there was no other course of action. 'We'll go after him.'

Vibia looked at him, her face serious. 'Gnaeus it's out wedding night.'

'Yes, but how can we enjoy ourselves knowing that your father is out there trying to save Rome.'

Vibia's face broke out into a wide smile and she kissed Gnaeus, over and over again. 'Brave husband,' she said amused at using the term. 'Thank you.'

Their wedding night would have to wait.

XXXV

Ceinwyn reached her father's house and hammered on the door, but there was no answer. The man who had been following her had disappeared for now, but she suspected that he was nearby. Was he watching her from a nearby window or alley? The house her father had lent her was one street away. A resistance Slave safe house. It was a sparse place, but all she needed was a bed and a desk to work from. She had no desire to go back to it alone now. Why wouldn't her father answer?

There was still no reply so she peered through the windows, but inside all was dark—even Sentius was out, and that never happened. Something was definitely wrong. She started to feel panic rising up inside her.

A huge explosion nearly threw her to the ground and fire filled the sky. Panicking, she started to run. She was at her door in under a minute.

Her hand shaking, she got her key into the door and started to turn the handle when she felt a hand on her back.

She froze.

The streets were still deserted, and there was no noise but that of the burning oil stores nearby.

She would not allow herself to be raped. She had no knife, but Titus had taught her something of how to fight with her hands. She turned around, ready to fight, and looked into the eyes of her would-be-attacker.

She jumped back with surprise, smacking her head into her unlocked door.

It was Quintus.

'Hello, Quintus,' she said surprised, but she could tell from the look on his face that he was equally, if not more, surprised than she was.

'Ceinwyn?' he said, 'I... sorry, I thought you were someone else.'

He turned to go, but then turned back as he understood: 'You called yourself Tita didn't you,' he said accusingly.

Ceinwyn nodded.

'Why are you trying to turn Gaia against me?' Quintus asked, sounding very hurt.

'Why did you follow me?'

'I wanted to talk to you, to ask you to stop meddling.'

'You followed me through dark streets, during a riot, waiting until I'm entirely on my own, to then *ask* me to stop meddling?'

Quintus went red.

'You would have done more than just ask, wouldn't you?' Ceinwyn asked accusingly. 'Would you have killed me if I'd been some meek Roman debutant, to stop me meddling?'

Quintus shook his head quickly. 'No, I... I'm not sure what I was planning to do,' he admitted.

Ceinwyn believed him, he just looked desperate. 'It's you that needs talking to anyway,' she said. 'You need to sort yourself out and divorce Gaia.'

Quintus grabbed her by her top, and shook her angrily. 'I can't divorce her Ceinwyn!' he shouted, his eyes wide.

She pushed him away, opened the door a crack, and squeezed through it. She tried to slam it, but he managed to get the end of his boot jammed between it and the frame. She leant against the frame hard, but he seemed content to talk through the gap rather than try to force his way in.

'Ceinwyn, please!' he said. 'You have to stop! If she divorces me, then my father... I can't tell my father.'

'That you love men?' Ceinwyn finished his sentence. 'So you mean that you'd rather that a young girl lives her whole life unloved than you tell people what you are? You utter coward.'

'Ceinwyn!' he said anguished, 'I can't do it!'

'It's not your father,' Ceinwyn said accusingly. 'It's you. You can't admit it to yourself. Grow up, or you are going to ruin more lives than just your own.'

'So your mind is made up is it?' Quintus said through the gap.

Ceinwyn couldn't see his face, just his foot. 'Yes.'

'You'll continue to oppose me, and you'll help Gaia divorce me?'

Ceinwyn thought for a moment. She had befriended Gaia simply to get information from her, and not because she was truly interested in her problems, but this was the right thing to do and it would help Quintus in the end. As soon as she had learnt the truth about him from Gaia, she had realised what the looks between him and Tiberius had meant. She needed to free both him and Gaia from this stupid charade so that they could move on. 'I will,' she said finally.

'So be it,' Quintus said, removing his boot from the door.

Ceinwyn pushed it shut quickly, ready for him to try to push it open to attack her, to force her to change her mind, but nothing happened. She stayed leaning against the door for a few more moments—still nothing, no noise at all.

A few minutes passed. She couldn't stay here all night. She opened the door a crack and peered out.

The oil refinery burnt in the distance, lending an orange glow to the street. Quintus was gone. She sighed with relief.

XXXVI

Marcus was pleased that his time training with the reformed army regiment had caused him to shed two stone. The riot armour only came in three sizes, and the largest assumed that your forearms were the size of a small tree. His were not. He wriggled into the medium one, and to his pleasure found that he could still breathe. Tiberius joined him, with Antonius in tow.

'I hope that Quintus is safe out there,' Tiberius said earnestly.

'He will be,' Marcus said kindly. 'He's probably holed up on the Caelian, balls deep in that gorgeous wife of his.'

Tiberius looked sad. Clearly still worried about the possibility of his friend being killed by rioters.

'Or perhaps the Summus,' Marcus continued offhandedly. 'They may have already moved there. He could be fucking her on the Summus. Either way I'm sure he's safe.'

Tiberius didn't look very reassured. He hadn't been quite the same person ever since they had arrived in Rome. He had tried to dissuade Quintus from returning to the Aesculapium, and when that had failed, he had seemed to retreat into himself.

'Come on!' one of the centurions shouted at them. 'Time to move out.'

Marcus nodded to his friends and, fully armoured and equipped with Praetorian fasces, they joined the long line of new soldiers pouring out onto the streets. It was late summer, but the streets were scorching hot and close that night. The power was on very low, so most of their useable light was the orange glow provided by the burning oil works which had scorched the roof above it as it reflected its terrible inferno down upon them.

Looking around, Marcus saw that most of those with him were recruits he had trained. There were no ranks yet, they were new soldiers, and he, Antonius, and Tiberius were their trainers. An old gnarled Centurion led their group. He would keep the new recruits out of trouble, and give Marcus the space to train them on this, their first ever taste of real action.

But Marcus wasn't looking forward to this night at all. He didn't want the men he had trained to kill other Romans. Every step they took, marching down the cleared streets, took them closer to the forum at the centre of the Aether where it seemed they were likely to meet the front of the riot. They had been told to set their fasces to the highest setting. They had been told to protect Rome with their lives if necessary.

A soldier next to him whooped something about killing scum from the Imum. Marcus cuffed him with the base of his fasces, quietening him. Rome was about to fight itself, and Marcus had no stomach for that battle. He wondered where Ceinwyn was. He hoped Titus was protecting her, but knew it was highly unlikely. The last time he had spoken to Titus, he didn't even know where she was. They had nearly fallen out then, even though he had tried to be civil, but he had been so amazed that Titus could simply let her go that it must have shown. He had felt bitterly angry towards him. If Ceinwyn had been his, there was no way he would have let her go, no matter what riches had been offered to him. He had thought about going to her, and he still dreamed about the possibility; taking her in his arms, comforting her, but his dreams always ended with a memory of that night in Luguvalium, where she had told him clearly that she did not, and could not, love him. She had chosen Titus, and far from being so overwhelmed by her love that he had devoted the rest of his life to her, as Marcus would have done, he had let her down. Why had she chosen him? He would never understand women.

They burst out onto one side of the forum and rushed to take up position in a long line across it. The line was made up of Praetorians and other new army units like theirs; half the forum was now full of soldiers and Praetorians. Through the smoke that drifted across the large open square, figures moved towards them slowly, carrying makeshift weapons. Marcus gripped his fasces tightly and waited. Antonius started to beat his fasces against his shield, and the rhythm created was taken up by the others along the line so that the noise spread.

Marcus resolved that if he ever saw Ceinwyn again he would dedicate his life to her, promise to protect her, even if there was no hope of love ever being returned. He started to cry at the thought, no one could see behind the helmet, but she was likely far away, perhaps back in Northern Britannia, and here he was in his birth city about to watch it tear itself apart. A stone hit him in the midriff, jerking him out of his daydreams. The rioters were approaching. He roared with anger at the attack, and took up Antonius' beat with his own fasces. Romans or not, he would kill them if they tried to kill him.

'Vibia,' Gnaeus shouted, his voice hoarse. The crowd was packed tightly around him. He scanned the crowd desperately, trying to pick her out, but he could not see her. The crowd had pulled this way and that and eventually their hands had been torn from each other's. He kept seeing glimpses of what looked like the top of her head. He was panicking now—she was barely five foot and was at great risk in the crowd.

There were no more explosions now, but the crowd seemed stuck. He could hear chanting up ahead. He needed to move forwards. He knew that was what Vibia would be trying to do—her father must be somewhere up ahead.

He started to push, working his way forwards, but many others were trying to do the same and the progress was terribly slow.

'Let me through!' he shouted as he pushed at the mass of rioters, but his voice was lost in the din of chants and screams. A great fire burnt behind him where the oil works had been. Looking up, the flames were licking the roof of the Aether now, leaving great soot marks upon them. He wondered whether the heat was being transmitted through the roof to the Summus where the rich sat. Were they beginning to feel afraid of the mob beneath them?

The apartment block to his left was open. He pushed across the crowd instead, finding it easier, and reached the door. Darting inside, he stepped over a family huddling for shelter in the stairwell and ran up the stairs to the first floor. He peered through the window, but couldn't get enough of an angle to see to the end of the crowd. He looked around, saw a small broken desk in the otherwise abandoned apartment and smashed the window with it.

He stuck his head out again, looking up and down the street for Vibia. His heart sank. There was no sign of her. Was she lying somewhere, trampled beneath the feet of the crowd? He despaired and thought for a moment about climbing to the top of the building and using the roofs to get to the front, but at that moment he caught sight of something that disturbed him.

It was right at the front of the crowd, where a gap had appeared, of about twenty paces, between the rioters and the army line. Each side had been standing, challenging the other; the Praetorians beating their fasces against their shields and shouting commands for the rioters to return to their homes; the rioters throwing stones and brandishing knives and hammers. Now, both groups had stopped to watch a man who dared cross the line, and who now stood directly in the territory between the two groups. A man who would now surely be killed by one side or the other.

It was Vibia's father.

XXXVII

Titus stood in the front of the military line with Verres and tried to look menacing. They were in the middle of the Aether's forum. Behind them stood what they must die, if need be, to defend: the last entrance road to the Summus. Every other access had been shut off on Albus' command to protect his palace district. Somehow, they needed to drive the rioters back down to the Imum and secure Rome. Rome needed to be protected at all costs. Then he needed to find his father and somehow either persuade him to stop fighting against Rome, or get him to safety. Every time he thought about his father, he felt ill. How had he not realised that his opposition to Albus went far beyond the books he wrote? He was angered by him for his secret war against their City, but very proud of him too. His pride brought with it sadness and regret; regret that he had dismissed him and his writings as nothing, spending years bemoaning his father's inaction when in fact he had achieved much. Most of all he felt sick because he agreed with so much of what his father said, but he could not oppose his birth City, the Eternal City, even if he was no longer sure about its leader. He was no traitor, and that was the true source of his sickness—for if opposing your City was treachery, what did that make his father?

Another stone flew across and struck Titus on the helmet. He ignored it—his body armour was strong. They had had it fitted quickly, by the armourer at the palace, before rushing back onto the streets. Verres had been called to see Albus, whilst Titus was shown how to operate a fasces. He clashed it now against his plastic, unbreakable, shield, like his colleagues in the line around him. He didn't like the balance of it and would have preferred a gladius. He looked at the men who faced him across the smoky open square, armed with almost nothing. He wished he wasn't here—he had no desire to hurt any of them. If only they would simply return to the Imum. However, Titus could put himself in their shoes. He could imagine himself, desperate and hungry, in the front of that line, outraged that his Consul would prioritise the building of his pleasure palace over providing him with food, water, and clean air. If he was on the other side of the forum, he knew it would take more than threats to make him leave.

The clamouring quietened for a moment.

A man was allowed forwards by the rioters, who seemed to part for him. Titus stood and waited. They were off to the far right of the line, and Titus only realised that it was Tarpeius once he had left the ranks of the rioters completely.

He stopped beating his shield and waited. Around him, his colleagues did the same, and the quiet spread like a wave.

Tarpeius stopped in the centre of the forum, ten paces from each line. The rioters opposite Titus edged forwards slightly for a better view, but the Praetorian line ignored them as the entire crowd paused to listen to what the man, who could have been Consul, had to say. Titus was scared. One word to incite the crowd and people would die in this place. He glanced up at the temple of Jupiter to his right and said a quick prayer to the god he didn't believe in. 'Keep Rome safe. Don't make me kill any innocent people.'

To Titus' surprise, Tarpeius turned around suddenly and began to address his own people rather than shouting at him and the Praetorians.

'Romans,' Tarpeius bellowed. 'Why are you here?'

The crowd cheered him, shouting out a cacophony of indecipherable reasons as to why they were there.

'Who asked you to risk your lives, and my ideals, on this foolish riot?' Tarpeius said angrily.

The crowd started to quieten down. They had clearly not expected to be rebuked.

'I spent years working on keeping our opposition legitimate. Not all of my friends agreed with me, some wanted to fight Albus the same way he fights us, but not me.'

He spoke quieter now, with great sadness. 'You should be ashamed of yourselves. Go home, and I'll try to salvage something from this so that I can stand again next year and try to help you properly. I supported you. I stand for you. Listen to me. Leave now, return to your families, and wait for next year's elections.'

The crowd didn't move, but they were not chanting anymore. Titus hoped desperately they would listen to their leader.

Tarpeius now turned to face Titus and his line. The rioters were standing almost alongside them now. The two lines had become an elliptical circle, and all eyes were inwards on the bald, elderly, medicus-turned-politician.

'Praetorians, army, Albus—who I know will be listening-in from your earpieces. I pray that the gods help you. You lost people who just help yourselves, never thinking about anyone else. Your minds are closed, you've missed the point.'

Titus felt a great melancholy sink over him, and could see that the whole line felt chastised by his words.

Tarpeius gestured behind him to the rioters who stood watching. 'And I pray that the gods help these people, who would give to others, if they could, rather than store away as you do, so that you can build a kingdom on the heads of others. I pray that one day their burden will end. They can't stand up for themselves, someone has to stand up for them, but it needn't be one man. I call on you all to help me. If you believe, even with just the tiniest part of your heart, that something is very wrong with this world, then go home. Leave my people alone, and think again about how you treat those below you.'

There was complete silence in the forum. The only sound Titus could hear was the roar of the fires in the distance. Titus looked at the rioters, and the rioters stared back at them. He realised that both his line and theirs were waiting to see what the other did. He got ready to take a step back. Perhaps the others would follow him? He smiled at the possibility and the thought that the night could end with peace; the day could be saved. But then, to his amazement, Verres dashed forwards towards Tarpeius.

'This is a public place!' he shouted, his face inches from Tarpeius'. 'Take your men from here now, or we kill you, and all of them.'

Titus put his head in his hands, this was completely the wrong thing to do, Verres had misread the situation horribly.

'Son,' Tarpeius said kindly. 'Go home, and I will take my people home too. We all want the same thing.' He turned back to the rioters and spread his arms wide, ready to address them, and once more implore them to start moving backwards.

Then something happened that took Titus completely by surprise. Verres grabbed Tarpeius by the shoulders and spun him around, so that they faced in to each other, but with Verres' back to most of the rioters. Verres raised his arm to strike the old man. Titus tried to lunge forwards, to intervene, but at that moment, some of the rioters moved too and he was blocked in by them.

'No Verres!' he shouted over the crowd, trying to move forwards, but it was too late.

As Verres brought his arm down, Tarpeius raised his own to protect his face from the armoured fist. Verres grabbed Tarpeius' forearm in his fist, and in a very quick movement, and to Titus' surprise, swung his other hand up to Tarpeius' trapped hand, holding it tightly also. Then he completed the move by twisting Tarpeius' arm up into his chest.

Titus watched as Tarpeius' mouth opened in a silent cry. He stood transfixed, his arm held across his body, his hand gripping the base of something now firmly lodged in his chest. Verres punched Tarpeius' elbow, driving whatever it was further in and knocking him flat at the same time. Titus pushed at the surging crowd again, desperately. Tarpeius was still moving. He had to get to him.

Verres moved forwards to stand over him. The rioters, too scared to intervene, stood their ground and looked on, horrified.

Verres brought his fasces up to strike, to finish him off. 'No!', Titus shouted again, but either it didn't carry, or the Praetorian was no longer taking orders from him.

Then suddenly, a girl stood over Tarpeius' body, blocking him from Verres.

It was Vibia.

Titus scanned the crowd, watching as a figure leapt from a first floor apartment window and started to punch his way through the riot crowd towards them. Titus too kept trying to push forwards, but the line of rioters in front of him remained firm.

'Move aside girl!' Verres snarled, and raised his fasces to strike her father. Tarpeius was still moving, but weakly. A pool of blood was spreading beneath him, congealing in the brown grass of the forum square.

Vibia looked up at Verres' masked face with her pale, blue eyes. 'You don't scare me Praetorian', she said quietly as she stood her ground, protecting her father.

Verres lowered his fasces for a moment and the pair stood, staring at each other. The nearly seven foot tall, body armour-clad Praetorian, facing a tiny girl in her wedding dress. Verres waited, then he put his hand to his ear, clearly receiving a message. Titus pushed hard at the man in front of him and managed to move forwards slightly. He pushed again, harder, and started to make some headway towards the pair, yelling all the time at Verres to stand down. But his voice did not carry.

Verres kept his fasces lowered, but swiped at Vibia with his fist. The movement was sudden and unexpected, and Vibia had no chance to avoid it. His fist connected with the side of her head, and she was thrown several feet through the air, landing in a motionless heap next to the rioters, who backed away as Verres advanced towards her.

Titus pushed again, reaching the front of the line at last. There was now nothing but empty ground between him and the pair. He sprinted as fast as he could move. Verres raised his fasces, ready to bring it down on Vibia's unprotected head. Tarpeius lay, unmoving now, a few metres away from his daughter. His hand had slipped away from the implement Verres had clearly forced into it. The object was ornate and unknown to Titus. He had nearly closed the gap, but he was too late—Verres was about to kill Vibia, and there was nothing he could do to stop him.

Then a man leapt from the rioters, covering Vibia with his own body. Verres hesitated for a moment and Titus jumped forwards, covering the last few yards in the air. His hand caught the centre of Verres' descending fasces, inches from the man's back. The fasces spluttered and hummed with charge—it was set to its maximum killing setting.

He stood up slowly, his grip on Verres' fasces firm. Verres tried to jerk it away but Titus held on. He looked around, the man on the floor was sobbing and trying to move Vibia—it was Gnaeus. Verres ripped the fasces from Titus' grasp and lunged again, at Gnaeus this time. Titus moved quickly so that he stood between his friend and the Praetorian.

'No, Verres,' he said.

'He's obstructing justice,' Verres said emotionlessly.

'He's my friend, and he works for me.'

'He interrupted my official work, I must kill him.'

'Verres,' Titus said calmly. 'Perhaps you must, but if you are to do so, you must first kill me.'

Verres paused, clearly waiting for new orders through his earpiece. Titus waited. For once certain about what he must do. He could not allow Verres to kill his friend. Behind him, he could hear Gnaeus sobbing and calling Vibia's name desperately.

Slowly Verres lowered his fasces, nodded, turned, and walked away. Titus crouched by Gnaeus to help him with his new wife.

But Vibia was dead.

He reached out to touch her face, still partially veiled.

'Don't you dare touch her!' Gnaeus snarled, slapping his hand away, his face beyond grief and anger. 'You chose your side!' He picked up her body easily, and walked away. The crowd parted for him.

Titus got back to his feet, but he was not alone in the circle. Behind him, Verres crouched over Tarpeius' body. As Titus watched, he pulled out the item that he had thrust into Tarpeius' chest and held it aloft, gazing at it as if in amazement.

'Romans!' he bellowed. 'We have proof of our enemies' treachery!'

The item was indeed some sort of knife as Titus had suspected, but its design was highly unusual: the blade was slightly curved, and the handle was ornate with two thin bars protruding backwards from it. It was the sort of weapon carried ornamentally by high-ranking officials in the rebelling province of Asia Minor, in much the same way Titus would carry a gladius.

'He was a terrorist! He was in the pay of our greatest enemy!' Verres continued. Titus' heart sank as he began to understand what was happening.

'He would have assassinated me! This is an act of war!'

The Praetorians and the army cheered. The soldier standing next to Titus clapped him hard on the shoulder before raising his fist in the air, and to Titus' surprise some of the riot crowd started cheering too.

'Go home. There will be war!' Verres continued. 'Marcus Albus has just informed me that he will hold a special announcement tomorrow morning. Be ready. The conscription stations will open at dawn, at double their usual initial payment on conscription. Be ready to fight for your City. I command you one last time, clear the streets.'

The crowd started to back away, some ran, but most walked back to their homes. Most looked dejected at the death of their leader, but some looked genuinely pleased that a terrorist had been unmasked and thwarted. War would bring jobs and money to the desperate who had neither.

Slowly, silence descended on the emptying forum.

Verres walked by, on his way back up to the Summus, speaking to Titus without stopping. 'Party in the palace tonight. Albus says be there.'

He barely glanced at Titus who stood staring at the dead body of Tarpeius.

Titus looked up, and then around for Gnaeus. He wanted to grieve with him, wanted to apologise to him for not being able to reach Vibia sooner, but Gnaeus was gone. The Praetorians and army were filing away too, back to the barracks. There would be a huge party there this evening as well. Titus didn't want to attend either party. He had had the best view of anyone, except Verres, of what had happened. He knew that the weapon Verres had just plucked out of Tarpeius' dead chest had been planted by Verres himself; that must have been why Albus had wanted to quickly see Verres whilst Titus was shown how to use a fasces. It had all been planned.

This was all so that they could go to war, and that meant his Consul was a liar. He thought through his options, and then realised the full extent of what Albus had done over these last months. Because now, everyone who cared about him, who could help, was either dead, dying, or had deserted him.

Titus started to weep. Gnaeus and Ceinwyn hadn't deserted him—he had deserted them.

He started to walk up towards the Summus, tears flowing. He didn't care who saw the *Protector of Rome* crying. It didn't matter anymore—his life was over. The streets were strewn with rubbish left behind by the rioters, and the occasional body of someone crushed to death in the throng. One of the bodies caught Titus' attention. He walked over and rolled the man's body, sure that he recognised something about him.

His face was old and his hair grey, but with a shock, he did indeed recognise him. It was the old Centurion from the Transmaritanus, killed for nothing on the streets of his own City; the City which he had spent the best years of his life defending.

Titus' breath caught in his throat, and he reached for his golden Crown of Valour. He wasn't carrying it, but he knew where it was. He could picture it sitting on the bedside table, forgotten, next to an empty bottle of passum.

He still couldn't remember the man's name.

XXXVIII

Titus wandered aimlessly around the edges of the reception hall in Albus' palace. The whole Senate was there along with some of the most important Praetorians, and in the middle of them all, laughing raucously and drinking the best wine, was Albus himself with Catula at his side.

Titus felt his legs wouldn't hold him, so he flopped down onto a bench at the side of the room. He was drunk, but it wasn't just that. He felt weak and broken. Albus had won.

The booths at the edges of the room were doing heavy business, with a near constant flow of guests heading inside, hand in hand with one of the many semi-naked girls who wandered the hall plying their trade.

Albus had won, he had just had his greatest opponent murdered and quelled a riot at the same time. Ceinwyn was gone—Titus had discarded her, to fight for a man who had lied about everything. He thought about simply getting up and leaving, but where would he go? At least he had some position here, and he would still be doing something for his City. Better that than the streets.

'Titus!'

He looked up from his lifeless stupor.

'Titus!'

It was Albus, smiling like a snake from across the room. He rose wearily and crossed to him.

'Well done Titus!' he said, grinning and flushed. 'We haven't got Filii Aquilae yet, but I gather from Verres that you are close. I'd never have believed senators were in on this!'

Titus barely heard him, and turned to go—he couldn't face the Consul now. He just wanted to go to his room and drink until he fell asleep. Albus grabbed him by the shoulder as he started to walk away.

'Titus, there will always be a place in Rome for you with me.' He held him firmly by the shoulders, speaking earnestly. 'We have a war to fight. I would like you to be its general. Would you control my forces for me?'

Was this what it had all been about? Albus had never wanted him to be a governor; he wanted his general back.

Titus pulled away.

'Will you?' Albus asked insistently.

Titus nodded indifferently—at least as a general he could be away from Albus most of the time, and he wouldn't have to do any more beating and torturing with Verres. Numbly he started to wander away. Everything he had had was gone, and nothing that could ever come could make up for what he had lost.

'Titus!' it was Albus again. 'Come here,' he said slyly, 'I think you might enjoy this.'

Titus felt his heart sink. He had no choice but to walk back over to Albus. He owned him now. The Consul gestured for the music to be turned down and made a signal to a group at the far end of the room who marched towards him holding a prisoner. As the man neared them, Titus realised with surprise it was a Slave, the only Slave he had ever seen in the palace—Albus wouldn't have them anywhere near him.

The group stopped in front of Albus, and the two Praetorians on either side of the Slave shoved him to his knees in front of the Consul. He looked up, defiant but scared, with blood leaking from one side of his mouth and his face bruised.

Albus got a small scire out of a fold in his purple ceremonial party toga and showed it to Titus.

'You were a great Slave killer in your day Titus.'

Titus shook his head. He couldn't kill this man, even if Albus made him. Over the rushing of blood in his head, he could hear the sound of the sea, gently breaking on a warm sandy beach.

'No, don't be modest,' Albus said, not understanding. 'I remember you back in the day. So you are going to like this piece of kit.'

'What's his name?' Albus asked the Praetorians, pointing to the Slave.

'Alcaeus Kleiniou.'

The Slave looked down at the ground.

'Right,' said Albus examining the scire closely. 'Bear with me, I'm new to this. First of all let me show you this.'

He entered the name and received a page of details: suspected birth date, address, and parent names. 'The usual stuff,' he said, 'that you'd have always found encoded in a signum identification chip. But,' he continued. 'Now watch this.' He scrolled down to the next screen.

Titus watched the scire screen, and saw materialise a grainy image of the floor in front of them. At that moment, the Slave glanced up at them, and Titus saw an image, in black and white, of Albus and himself standing side by side.

'Titus,' Albus said proudly, 'I've been having the signum chips of every Slave in Rome upgraded. Now we can see everything they see, hear anything they hear. This will make catching Filii Aquilae much easier, an unwitting spy in every household.'

Titus thought of his father, and his insistence that it was wrong to keep Slaves. Titus was very pleased for this resolve now.

He thought of Ceinwyn, had they upgraded her chip too? She would have fought them hard before she let them touch her.

'And there is one last feature Titus,' Albus said proudly. 'Forgive me, but I came up with this one myself and I am very pleased with it. I think you'll like it too, given your past history with these animals.'

He turned to the Praetorians. 'What is he guilty of?'

'Theft,' the one on the right said, carelessly.

Albus nodded. 'Death then.'

The Slave looked down at the ground again. Titus heard a sob escape from his tightly clamped lips.

'But you see Titus, erecting a steel cross, nailing him to it, waiting for him to die... It takes so long, and it's so boring. So, I give to you...' he paused. 'Crucifixion for the modern age.'

He touched a green button at the bottom of the screen on the scire, and as he did so the Slave's head suddenly jerked upright.

His eyes rolled back, and his arms jerked out to his side. His mouth opened but no sound came.

'Wait,' Albus said, 'here comes the best bit.'

As the Slave's arms stretched out further and further, he started to scream; clearly the chip didn't control every one of his movements. Titus started to pale, the Slave was able to feel and scream, but that was it. He thought about his own torture at the hands of Strabo. He wanted to stop this, but it was already done. The button had been pushed.

The Slave's arms started to bend backwards, forced by muscle contractions outside his control. Titus heard a tearing sound, and the intensity of the Slave's scream increased. Suddenly the front of his chest burst open, and blood splattered across the floor. Titus realised that he had torn his pectoral muscles. They had snapped with such force that they had broken the skin. He watched with horror as the Slave's forearms now bent to forty five degrees and his fists clenched. The Slave's biceps start to bulge, and he wobbled slightly on his knees, looking like he was going to pass out, but sadly that mercy was denied him. Perhaps there was something about the chip that prevented it.

The muscles in his arms bulged further, starting to change to a dusky colour under the skin as the vessels within and over them ruptured. Then, once again, the skin itself burst open under the pressure and blood sprayed onto the ceiling of the room. The cries of the Slave cut into Titus' heart; he thought about grabbing the scire off Albus, but the process was already in motion. What could he do to stop this?

The Slave's scream was suddenly shut off as his mouth clamped shut. Titus could hear him trying to scream behind his closed jaws. Then he heard the sound of crunching from within the Slave's mouth, which jerked open again, revealing fragments of broken teeth and pieces of his ruined tongue. His clothes were soaked in blood now, and there was a pool surrounding him. Some of the nearby senators backed away, lest his blood soil their expensive formal clothes.

'And finally,' Albus said, watching carefully. 'Death comes at last.'

The Slave's tortured body writhed once more, and his head started to move backwards so that he was looking up at the ceiling. It kept bending backwards, further and further.

The Slave's screams, with barely any tongue, and blood spurting out of his mouth, now sounded truly like those of an animal. Albus stood there smiling as fountains of blood sprayed into his face and across his chest and arms. He seemed far away, as if thinking about something that had happened years ago.

Then there was a sudden click and the screaming stopped. The Slave stayed frozen for a moment, on his knees, head bent backwards, torn arms outstretched—and then, like a puppet whose strings have been suddenly cut, he fell forwards, finally released from life and torment.

Everyone stood in silence, staring at the pool of blood and the broken Slave in the centre. Titus thought he was about to be sick and looked for the nearest exit. As he did so, a ripple of applause rang around the audience, followed by cheering which reached a crescendo.

Albus walked forwards so that he was at the centre of his adoring crowd.

'So, we can use them as unwilling spies and kill them at will. One day, when we have no further need for them, we can kill them all at the push of a button. Romans, we have complete control over the animals in our midst.'

Titus fell to his knees at the edge of the room and retched. Most of the crowd were so busy cheering they didn't notice, but Albus did, and he walked over to him.

'Come on Titus!' Albus laughed. 'You're going to need a stronger stomach than that in Asia Minor!'

Titus glanced up at him and hoped the hatred in his eyes didn't show.

Albus looked across at one of the semi-naked girls as she walked past. 'I know!' he exclaimed. He called the girl over and handed her a wad of sestertii notes. 'Ensure our general has a good time. He's going to be busy for the next year or two. Give him some memories to warm his bed in the long desert nights.'

Titus looked up and tried to mumble a refusal, but Albus was already gone, returning to his adoring crowd. The girl led him, stumbling, to one of the booths. He looked down at the girl's bum as she walked in front of him seductively, covered in fake tan, with a thin thong between her tiny buttocks. He thought of Ceinwyn.

But she was gone.

'Enjoy yourself Titus!' Albus called across the room, as he ducked through the narrow doorway behind a thin curtain. 'See you at the Vulcanalia party tomorrow!'

Titus felt shattered already, more so as he realised that he would be expected to be present at a similar party tomorrow.

'That one will be even better, and there will be cake!' he heard Albus call faintly from behind the curtain.

It was surprisingly quiet inside the booth, but inside his head was just roaring. Albus was a monster. He was fighting for a monster. The room was warm, and smelt slightly sweet. It was dark inside but he could see the girl clearly enough—the girl who was meant to make up for Ceinwyn whom Albus had driven away from him. The girl was beautiful, far more so than Ceinwyn even, and very young, no more than twenty. Her hair, like Ceinwyn's, was red, but straight and cut just to her shoulders. She sat on Titus' lap.

'General,' she whispered confidently. 'I like Generals. Very powerful. Very strong.' She reached down to his groin and squeezed where his erection was starting to form, 'very big.'

She leant back and undid her bra, lifting it away slowly and letting it fall to the ground. As she did so, her two small breasts stayed exactly where they were. Titus stared at them; her nipples were slightly smaller than Ceinwyn's.

She stood up and slipped the thong off completely before turning around and bending over seductively in front of him. She reached around and started touching herself as Titus sat and watched. He reached out to touch her but she slapped his hand away and made him sit on it.

'Not yet,' she said softly, before getting up and sitting across his lap.

He looked into her beautiful face. He wondered what Ceinwyn was doing at this very moment.

But she was gone.

The girl leant forwards, so that her breasts were in front of his face. Outside the party hummed away gently, but he was safe in here, away from the death and the truth of what he had become.

His mouth opened, and his tongue circled one of her nipples. He wondered for a moment if he was going to be rebuked again, but she moaned softly before pulling back and giggling. She was clearly faking her pleasure. He wasn't sure whether he minded or not.

She bent down to kiss him. Their lips met and she tried to put her tongue in his mouth, but he resisted. He thought of the first kiss he had ever had with Ceinwyn back in Luguvalium, and the night it had led to.

But she was gone.

He buried his head in her shoulder. Her hair felt coarse, as if it had seen too many products, and over the smell of her perfume, he could now smell the stench of tobacco. He started to cry.

She stood up, took a step back, and knelt down in front of him, slipping his trousers down. 'Don't worry General,' she said in her soft, common accent, misreading the situation. 'You've seen terrible things, but I'll make it all better.'

She opened her mouth and slipped the end of him inside. Her mouth was warm.

Ceinwyn was gone.

Then the roaring in his head subsided and was replaced instead by a sudden calm.

Ceinwyn was gone.

He had chased her away.

So, it was up to him to get her back. He had to believe he could or there would never be any hope, ever again.

He looked down at the girl, her head bobbing up and down in his lap and felt no pleasure at all.

Ceinwyn had left, yes, but she had been right to do so. Even if he never saw her again, what he was doing here was completely wrong.

He stood up.

The girl overbalanced and fell gently, ending up sitting down on the cool floor of the booth, looking surprised.

'Did you not like it?' she asked, looking up at him. She looked afraid.

'Everything I've done for the last three months has been a terrible mistake,' he said, pulling his trousers up. 'But I've got one night to put it right.'

'Okay?' the girl said backing away, clearly suspecting that he had gone mad. She pulled her bra back on and made sure the sestertii she had been given were safely stashed away.

Titus pulled the curtain across gently and surveyed the party. Albus was at the far end of the room, lying on the altar of Jupiter with two of the girls and a crowd of senators cheering him on. The girls were perched on him, one in reach of his mouth, and the other riding him. They were kissing each other as he pleasured them both.

No one noticed as Titus slipped away.

He fell to his knees as soon as he was outside the room and started to cry once again. This time there was no one to stop him. He crawled up to the nearest wall as sobs racked him uncontrollably. Sobs for the girl he had lost, and for his own soul, forever tainted and destroyed by the man he had lost everything to fight for. The man who still stood for the Rome he loved—betrayal of whom would be treachery.

'Titus.'

The voice was quiet and soft, and for a moment Titus thought it must be Ceinwyn's, but of course it could not be.

'Titus.'

The voice again. It cut through his grief and he opened his eyes, to see a girl, also crying, sitting beside him. It was Sexta, Albus' wife.

He reached out his hand to hold hers, and this time she didn't pull away.

'I hate him,' she said, glancing to the entrance of the hall where her husband was busy with the whores. She was shaking. She looked terrified, desperate to confide in someone but still not sure whether to trust him. Could he trust her for that matter?

'Why did you marry him?' he asked.

She looked at him as if he was mad. 'I didn't have a choice, my father made me. It was the price of him getting a repeat Consulship.'

Titus shook with rage. Everything Ceinwyn had said about Albus had been true.

'I want to fight him,' he said, no longer caring if he was overheard or if Sexta betrayed him. 'But I can't fight my City. I don't know what to do.'

Sexta laughed hollowly. 'You think Albus cares about Rome? He only cares about himself and his family line. Just like his father, who ordered Albus' child killed because it was the child of a Slave girl. Albus loved that girl, despite what he would tell you. Albus doesn't fight for Rome at all,' she continued, 'and you shouldn't fight for him.'

She stood up and wiped her tears away, before taking him by the hand and helping him to his feet. 'Let me show you.'

She led him towards the basement, and to Titus' amazement she knew all of the codes to the doors. Soon they were in the centre of the scire bank that lay under the palace.

'Everyone's at the party,' Sexta said, pausing by the central console. 'Titus,' she said, her voice trembling, 'I can show you things here that could bring down Rome. Things that if Albus knew I was showing you would surely lead to a horrendous death at the hands of the Praetorians. If I show you these things will you help me defeat him?'

Titus thought for a moment. He thought of his father, his life dedicated to a secret battle that even his own son hadn't seen; he thought of Tarpeius and Vibia murdered needlessly; he thought of Ceinwyn, betrayed by his own selfish pride.

'I will.'

He hoped his words would carry to Ceinwyn wherever she was. He wanted her to know that he finally understood her, even if it was too late.

Sexta's hands inputted a password, and images appeared on the screen that did not immediately make any sense to Titus.

There was a map, showing Rome, with several different coloured rings drawn around one area of the City, a flurry of concentric circles radiating out. At their outermost, the circles enveloped about a sixth of the City. Next to it was a picture of a metallic device, which looked like a very basic bomb, and alongside, on the next screen, Sexta had called up some images from the newspaper archive.

Titus leant forwards to read the print. His mouth fell open with surprise as he did, and he could feel his heart hammering in his chest. The newspaper was undated. It was a proof, ready for publication, but as yet unpublished. Its date of creation was dated to just a few days after their arrival in Rome, earlier in the summer. However, the reason for his shock was the headline:

'Terrorists kill thousands in the centre of Rome!'

The story told of a bomb going off in the main forum, killing thousands, and ended with the proclamation that war would surely soon be declared on Asia Minor.

Titus thought back to the warehouse and the man caught emptying evidence of the bomb he was creating into the canal. He thought of Verres' quick despatching of the man, and the way he had called out once, in perfect Latin, before being silenced forever by the Praetorian.

Sexta scrolled though more articles, prepared but never published, about impending war, conscription, and how important it was to get behind the national effort and keep the streets peaceful.

Next Sexta brought up a link to the central stock market, which showed the price of *Coniunctus*. As of this evening, the stock's value had jumped by over a hundred times. She gestured with her hands over a section of the screen, bringing up a mineral chart of Asia Minor, showing the abundance of tellurium there, and another showing that this was indeed, as his father had said, a key ingredient in the manufacturer of the solar panels that *Coniunctus* was going to be placing into the Void. 'Of course,' she added, 'you probably already worked out that he owns the company.'

Titus sat down quickly on a soft leather office chair, completely stunned. 'Just for money?' he said, thinking of Strabo, and his ultimate confession to trading Slave organs and how it had just been for money.

Sexta laughed. 'No, it's all about control with Albus. The money's just a nice extra for him.

'You ruined his plan,' she continued, 'and set him back months by discovering that bomb he planned. I don't think he's ever forgiven you. You see, he can control the elections but not the people,' she explained. 'So he blows up some of Rome, he says terrorists did it. People are scared, they stay off the streets, his grip on Rome tightens. Let's take it a step further, he says that they are Asia Minor terrorists—now he can invade a province which has been rebelling for years and his people will actually want war, whereas a decade ago they were bored of it. War, in turn, keeps a generation of would be rioters off the streets. War brings money to *Coniunctus*, and *Coniunctus* brings more control. It brings spying through Slaves, it brings death to Slaves, and it brings a benign face to his regime. He's very clever,' she said grudgingly, 'but he should never have married me.'

She paused and stared hard at the floor, Titus could see her eyes welling up again as a painful memory returned. 'He should never have had Gabinius murdered under the Mamertine. He should never have ruined my life.' She looked up again, and despite the tears she was smiling, clearly pleased to have given up Albus' secrets to someone she hoped could destroy him. Titus felt a huge amount of responsibility, and for the first time in months actually relished it. He wanted to destroy Albus, the Tyrant, but he needed to get some allies back first. He knew who he wanted to approach first.

'Sexta,' he said urgently, 'you were friendly with Ceinwyn. Do you know where she went?'

Sexta looked worried. 'She told me not to tell you,' she said, clearly holding Ceinwyn's secrets in higher esteem than her husband's.

'Sexta,' Titus said earnestly, 'if I am going to fight your husband, I need her help.'

Sexta nodded slowly, making a decision. 'Very well,' she said. 'She is staying with her father, but I do not know if she will take you back.'

Titus smiled and embraced Sexta. His mind was clear and made up for the first time since he had arrived back in Rome. He was going to see his wife again. He had no idea how he was going to defeat Albus, but that didn't worry him. He would find a way. He had to, before it was too late for them all.

They left the room.

'Good luck,' Sexta hissed, rushing back to her duties as they reached the ground floor again. Titus quickly jogged to his room and gathered his things.

The palace corridors remained empty—the party was still in full swing. He hurried to the exit, but as he passed the reception hall itself, a man staggered out into the corridor directly in front of him. It was Verres. As Titus watched, he collapsed to his knees in the corridor and vomited, completely drunk.

He started to walk past gingerly, hoping Verres wouldn't see him. But he had no such luck.

'Titus!' Verres called as he passed. 'My old friend!'

Titus paused.

'Where are you going?' Verres said, slurring his words.

'Leaving,' Titus said.

'Why?'

Titus thought for a moment, it would be so easy to lie. Then he thought of Verres' wife and children. Verres had done terrible things, but he was under the same Tyrant that Titus had been, and he was younger and more impressionable. He thought about yesterday in the Imum, when Verres had told him his greatest secret, about his origins, when he had called him brother. He felt a huge wave of sadness that Sexta had just freed him from Albus by telling him the truth, but here was Verres, equally lost, with no one to open his eyes.

No one but Titus.

He could do what Sexta had just done for him. Perhaps Verres would even help him fight Albus. He had to try—he couldn't leave him here without trying.

'I'm leaving,' he said, building up courage, 'because our master is a Tyrant. He planned to blow up Rome and blame Asia Minor for it. He would have killed his own people. He's manipulated the elections for years.'

Titus waited to see Verres' shocked expression, but instead Verres looked up at Titus as if he was insane. 'Of course! He told me that months ago. Titus, you can't have all the good things we've got here without some bad things. It's all for the good of Rome.'

Titus took a step backwards, dazed. Verres had known the truth all along, yet still fought for Albus? He looked down at the young man and realised that he did not understand him at all. Here was someone beyond saving. Verres vomited again. Titus turned and walked away briskly.

The night air felt cool up on the Summus and Titus could feel the filth of the palace drifting away from him with his every step. He was free now. He gave a little whoop of joy and began to jog down towards the Aether, and Ceinwyn.

Imum

2765 AUC

'I am a fool,' said Varro to his wife. 'I have destroyed all that I sought to create, and I have created what should never have been mine. I have created for the benefit of myself only, and my creations have been to the detriment of those I sought to protect with my creations.'

'And now we are cursed across the face of the whole Earth,' his wife replied angrily.

'We will start again, with nothing,' Varro replied, thinking his wife more beautiful than ever before without her fine make-up and jewels. 'I need only you.'

'And I too you may lose,' his wife replied quietly, 'for hidden we may feel we are, and protected for now we may be, but mark my words—one day, even these woods will not be safe for us.'

The Book of Varro, Part 3. 1655AUC

XXXIX

The streets of the Aether were deserted and stank with thick oily smoke. The refinery fires had died away now, instead replaced by near darkness, as the inadequate lighting from the Summus roof failed to penetrate the black smoke that continued to billow from the site.

He had never been to Ceinwyn's father's house before, he didn't even know where it was, but Sexta had told him, and now, thanks to Sexta's bravery, he was about to see his wife again. He had no proof that Ceinwyn was still there, she could have lied to Sexta, or by now lost all faith in him and simply moved on. He could only hope, and trust, that she had not completely given up on him.

There were no lights on inside, but that was no surprise as it was two in the morning now. He felt sober after the long walk but realised he would still smell of drink. He wished he had something to cover up the scent; he would just have to do his best to argue his way in. He knocked lightly on the door, trying to sound like a friendly visitor rather than a group of looters or a Praetorian.

He waited a couple of minutes, but there was no answer. He hammered harder now, again and again. He took a few steps back and shouted up at the curtained, dark, windows. 'Ceinwyn!' he called. 'Ceinwyn!'

He shouted until he was hoarse, his voice reverberating around the streets, bouncing off the roof high above and ringing eerily throughout the whole district.

He fell to his knees, slumped in the street. He would wait until morning if need be.

Then the door opened, and a middle aged, thin man, with dark hair and a long pale face opened the door; there was something odd about his mouth, it looked twisted at one side.

'Devin?' Titus asked, trying to peer in, but inside was dark, and the man kept the door held only slightly ajar.

'Who are you?' the man asked, staring at Titus. 'Actually, I think I know who you are,' he said. 'She doesn't want to see you. Goodnight.' He pulled the door closed quickly and Titus could hear two other locks being done up. He rushed forwards.

'Please, I need to see her!' He hammered on the door again, 'Devin, please! I must speak to her.'

There was no answer. He had probably gone back up to bed. He thought about leaving, but Devin had said: *'She doesn't want to see you,'* not: *'She's not here.'* His heart leapt as he realised she hadn't left Rome. He started to hammer on the door again, but it was useless, there was no answer, and smashing the door off its hinges wouldn't help his cause at all.

He sat down by the door, facing out to the street.

'I've been such a fool,' he said to himself quietly. 'I've let the only good thing that's ever happened to me leave me. I drove her away because of my pride, and because I was determined to fight for the wrong side. Now I have no side.'

Titus closed his eyes, he would sleep, and in the morning try to speak to Devin again. But then, Titus heard a sharp click as a lock was undone. Then another, and the door suddenly opened, so quickly he nearly fell backwards into the hallway.

'What's that,' Devin asked him amused, 'can you say it again?'

'I fought for the wrong side?' Titus said thoughtfully.

Devin laughed. 'Never heard that from a Roman before. Who are you going to fight for then?'

'I don't know. Who do you want me to fight for?'

'Ceinwyn,' he said. 'Just Ceinwyn. Keep her safe.'

'Where is she?'

'If you've truly changed sides I'll take you to her, but first step inside.'

Titus did as he asked; the room was dingy until Devin turned the lights on properly. As Devin turned around, he revealed a crimson line on his cheek by his signum, a mark that stretched right up to the side of his mouth, disfiguring him. As Titus stared at it, he realised Devin had noticed him.

'Your people marched me out of this house yesterday, me and my wife, and made me have my identification chip changed. Why?'

Titus thought about the Slave he had seen on the floor of Albus' palace, tortured to death by his own nervous system. 'I don't know,' he lied. He could not bring himself to tell Devin what fate could now befall him at the simple push of a button.

He sat down at his desk and gestured to a chair opposite. 'Titus, if I'm to take you to Ceinwyn, I need to be able to trust you completely. I need to know the truth. There's no need to protect me, you already know the danger I'm in, you know who I am.'

'It's for spying,' he said. 'They can watch you through it.' He wanted to say more but Devin interrupted him.

Devin reached up to it as he spoke, touching his fresh scar. 'Then I must remove it,' he said thoughtfully, a drop of blood oozing out from between the stitches as he played with the lethal chip under his skin.

'And it can kill you, horribly,' Titus added.

'All the more reason then,' Devin replied quietly.

Devin's hand trembled slightly as he reached down for a set of knives in his desk. 'It's times like this', he said, as the first of the knives touched the skin of his cheek, 'that I wish we could drink alcohol without feeling awful.' The knife bit into his skin and his lip trembled slightly—the only sign that he was in pain.

Titus watched as he worked the knife deeper in, trying to find the tiny chip.

Devin groaned, and took the knife out, taking hold of the smaller one, 'I'm going to have to work it a bit deeper,' he said. A thin film of sweat had formed on his forehead.

'Let me,' Titus said getting up.

Devin looked at him for a long time, trying to decide whether to trust him. 'Are you any good at things like this?'

'Not really,' Titus said.

Devin smiled at his honesty. 'Okay,' he said, resting his head back, his cheek and neck exposed.

Titus moved the knife closer. Here was the leader of the Slave resistance, and he had a knife at his throat. He couldn't believe Devin trusted him. Then he understood—this was a test. Ceinwyn's father was trusting him with his life, to see if he could trust him with his daughter's.

His hand trembled slightly as he widened the incision. 'Sorry,' he said pointlessly, it was inevitable this was going to hurt.

The knife probed deeper and Devin groaned again. Titus thought about stopping. Maybe Quintus could help? But he had no idea where he was now, and he couldn't exactly take Devin to the Aesculapium to illegally remove an identification chip.

He twisted the knife upwards, probing the incision deeply. Devin cried out but stayed still. Titus felt metal against the end of the knife. 'Sorry,' he said again, and twisted, hearing a gentle pop as the chip came free. Sweat was pouring off Devin's pale face now as Titus withdrew the blade. On the tip was a tiny chip, like a miniature, twelve legged, square, metallic insect, coated in congealing blood. Devin reached up, took it from the edge of the blade, and tossed it onto the open fire in the corner. Sentius, seated in a rocking chair in front of the fire, spluttered in his sleep but didn't awake.

'Thank you,' Devin said, dabbing at the wound on his cheek with a piece of cotton wool. 'We are both safer now.' He rose, 'I'll take you to Ceinwyn. Keep your head down. Protect her. Don't try to leave yet, they'll have people watching for it. A few months' time perhaps, then the pair of you may be able to escape.'

'I'll look after her,' he promised. Perhaps he and Ceinwyn could somehow bring Albus down; he had made promises to Sexta which he wanted to fulfil. He reached into his pocket. 'One last thing,' he said, handing over his scire to Devin.

Devin looked at him quizzically.

'Some very interesting information and documents on here Devin, proof of the level Albus was planning to stoop to control Rome, taken directly from his own intelligence centre.'

Devin looked down in awe and smiled. 'Thank you, Roman.' He reached out and shook Titus by the hand.

As they reached the hallway, Titus saw a figure standing on the landing in a dressing gown.

'Devin!' she called down. 'Who is this?'

'No one dear,' he replied matter of factly.

The woman laughed, her hair was grey, but she looked as if she had once been beautiful and that some great sadness that befell her had torn her looks away, along with all joy.

'Thana,' Devin said, 'Ceinwyn must be allowed to make up her own mind.'

'She doesn't want to see him,' Thana said. 'She mustn't see him. Make him leave.'

'Thana,' Devin replied, 'it's not up to us what she does. She chose to stay here and help me. I didn't make her. She never told us to keep Titus away. She still loves him—you can see that easily. She cries every night.'

'He will kill her!' Thana said, her eyes wide, almost mad. 'After everything! Everything we have suffered. She will die because of him.'

Devin shook his head. 'She must be free to choose.'

'Devin!' Thana shouted desperately, and started to rush down the stairs towards Titus.

Devin pushed Titus out of the door, darted out onto the street after him, pointed down the street saying a number, and then dashed back inside. As Titus walked down the street to Ceinwyn's house, he could hear the argument continuing loudly behind him. He now understood why Ceinwyn found her stepmother difficult, but then, she had good reason to hate him. He was a Roman, and the things that he had done to her people were terrible. He didn't deserve to be forgiven by her, or by Ceinwyn for that matter.

A few moments later and he was standing outside Ceinwyn's door. The street remained deserted. The door was bright blue and centred in a darker blue arch, also of wood. He thought that perhaps on a bright summer day it would look beautiful. He thought about waiting for morning rather than waking her, but he couldn't. He tapped on the door.

It took a minute, but the door did open. He looked up, and into the eyes of his wife. Immediately he felt a wave of complete regret envelope him, and he wanted to fall into her arms and weep for his stupidity, but he had to stay calm.

'Ceinwyn,' he said desperately.

'Titus,' she replied sternly.

He studied her. How angry was she? 'I...' he started, the words were hard to find. He decided just to tell the truth. 'I remember, the first day I met you. You bit a man on the hand and ran away. I liked you.

'I remember saving your life later that night, and even messing that up because I insulted you. I am a fool. I continue to be one, and I'll probably always be one.

'I remember our wedding day, the way you looked at me, and the way I knew we would be together forever. I had a dream then, and it was a simple one. I wanted a house on a hill, maybe some animals, and children running around. I wanted that and you, and that would not 'just be enough', it would be more than anyone could ever want.

'But there is something odd about this City,' he continued, 'or perhaps odd about me. Somehow, I woke up this evening, from a terrible dream, and realised that I had sold you, and most of my soul, to fight for an evil man. This is no excuse Ceinwyn, but I just tell you it to try to explain. I wanted to fight for Rome, Ceinwyn, but Rome is dead, I know that now. I fought for a dictator in order to pursue dreams that I should never have even had—dreams that are just shadows of the real thing; the real thing that you actually offered. Even if it's too late now, I need you to know that, and I need you to know that I love you. That I always did. I am sorry. I deserve, and expect, nothing from you.'

Ceinwyn stared at him. Her eyes were that wonderful deep green that he loved, and her hair, all tousled from her pillow, stuck up at all angles. Her face was freckled, and pale, and beautiful. He could see her signum again, for the first time in weeks without her make-up, and with joy noticed no fresh scar—she had managed to avoid the upgrade so far.

'Husband,' she said softly, 'you are indeed a fool. A big stupid fool. But, there is something enthralling about Albus isn't there? Evil indeed, but enthralling. I felt it too, as if you've known him all your life. You won't have been the first to be taken in.

'I remember when I first met you,' she continued. 'A big Roman bastard, sitting with his friends, laughing and smoking, whilst I ran for my life.

'I remember wondering whether I would ever find a man who I liked, when all I had was Cyric, dancing around trying to get me to like him. I didn't realise it then, but what I really wanted was a Roman. A strong, brave, foolish, stupid Roman.'

She started to speak more quickly now and life came back into her voice. Titus started to realise that she did indeed still love him. He could feel his heart pounding in his chest.

'I remember when I thought I was going to be raped and murdered, and then you were there.

'I remember the way you fought those two men and beat them easily, even though you were drunk.

'I remember how you had no idea what to say to me so you accidentally insulted me, but I never really minded.

'I remember how you risked everything to protect me in Luguvalium, from Strabo and from your friends who you nearly lost in doing so.

'I remember how your heart is just a little bit bigger than your head, but I love you for that.

'I remember that you are the first, and only, person I have ever slept with, and how that will remain to the day that I die.

'I choose you Titus.'

Titus leant in and hugged her, tears of joy running down his cheeks. She smelt clean and fresh and her hair was soft and beautiful. He felt her perfect breasts pushing up against him through her thin pyjamas.

'Oh, and one last thing,' she said, amused. 'I'd have been quite happy living in Hispania. I just didn't want you to lose what you'd have to have lost in order to achieve it.'

'Too late,' Titus said solemnly, 'I should have listened to you.'

'What makes you think it's too late?' Ceinwyn asked, taking him by the hand and leading him up the stairs to her bedroom.

XL

Dawn came slowly that morning—what little light could filter down to the covered Aether was still obscured by the oily smoke. They lay together, her cool naked skin against his.

'Are you awake?' Titus asked.

'Of course,' she replied quietly.

'I love you,' Titus whispered.

They kissed, and she rolled onto her side so that he could hold her around the middle. He could feel her tummy moving slightly with each breath. She smelt familiar, and for the first time in months he felt truly happy, despite their predicament. Her red hair glowed orange in the unnatural light radiating in from outside, and he longed to see her under the brightness of the sun again, standing free in the warmth of it. He thought about Capri. It would have made a much better honeymoon than this.

'What are we going to do?' Ceinwyn asked thoughtfully.

Titus started to move his hand downwards, stroking gently.

She reached down and held his hand firmly in hers. 'That's not what I meant!'

'I know,' he said sadly. 'I guess I don't know the answer to your question.'

'Do you think we would be able to escape? We could go somewhere new, somewhere where Albus' reach is weak and where your name is unknown.'

Titus shook his head. 'We've no chance at the moment.'

The main problem was that the Pomerium beam would identify them as they left, and even if Titus hadn't been reported missing yet, it wouldn't take long for Albus and the Praetorians to realise what had happened. They would maybe be free for a day at most.

'So we're safer here?' Ceinwyn asked, irritably. 'I don't want to hide.'

'Neither do I, but it's what your father wanted, he made me promise I'd keep you safe. Whatever we do, we can't leave now, maybe in a few months, a year, perhaps then we'll have been forgotten.' Secretly, he suspected that even if they waited a decade they would be arrested the moment they walked under the scanning beam, and there was no other way out of the city. It was a fortress.

'So what then?' Ceinwyn asked.

'There is,' he said with trepidation, 'another option.'

Ceinwyn turned around so that they were staring into each other's eyes. 'Go on,' she said, sounding almost excited.

'We could stay, as your father suggests, but we could stay to fight.'

Ceinwyn smiled and kissed him. 'Yes,' she said bravely.

'But, I suspect we could end up facing the same fate as Tarpeius and Vibia.'

'I don't mind dying now,' Ceinwyn said earnestly.

'Don't say that!' Titus said, horrified.

'No, Titus it's okay. I got you back from Albus, and that is all that matters. I think I can face this now. I can face it with you. Albus is responsible for the death of thousands of my people—we have to bring him down. I don't care what my father wants us to do. I want to kill Albus. I want us to kill him. I know that if we try they will probably catch us, but when they catch us,' she whispered with horror in her voice. 'Whatever they do to me, I will always have a refuge in my heart where I can go and be safe with you, whatever they do Titus, whatever they do to me, I'll be with you.'

Titus stared into her wide eyes, appalled as he realised that she was serious. She truly believed her decision could easily lead to her capture and torture, yet she still wished to oppose Albus. He couldn't believe how brave she was, but then his race hadn't been the victim of systematic genocide. 'I'll never let them catch you Ceinwyn, I'll keep you safe,' he promised.

'That's not a promise you can make Titus. You can't fight the whole of Rome.'

'I'll die before I let anything happen to you,' Titus replied, meaning every word. 'I'd rather we stayed hidden here like animals for the rest of our lives than risk your life.'

'But even then we wouldn't be safe,' Ceinwyn replied. 'Even if we hide here for months they will come eventually, and we'll die for nothing. Besides,' she added, 'why did you teach me to use a knife, fight, and shoot a sonifex straight, if you didn't want me to use any of it?'

Titus laughed. He stared at her beautiful, strong face. 'You're the bravest person I've ever met,' he said.

She shook her head, 'I'm not as brave as my mother was.'

'I'll help you avenge her,' he said.

He hugged her again, pulling her in close. He wanted to wrap her up forever and keep her safe, but he knew that she didn't want that, even if he could do it. He released her gently and she rolled onto her back, staring up at the ceiling, her perfect breasts rising and falling rhythmically with her breath. Her face was flushed and he could tell she was imagining the next few weeks. She looked excited. He would be there, right beside her. He felt excitement rising inside him too, and suddenly he realised that the task they faced wasn't impossible. They could kill Marcus Albus—they would just need help. Devin was the obvious candidate. They could join the Slave resistance, but Devin seemed already opposed to it, and would they even accept a Roman? Then he had an idea.

'My father,' he said. 'I'll speak with my father. We can join Filii Aquilae!'

Ceinwyn nodded, sat up and started to pull on her underwear. 'And I've got a contact in the Senate now, through a senator's daughter. I'll go and see her again, try to get some more information about Albus' plans to pass on to Filii Aquilae.'

They dressed quickly, hugged, and headed out onto the street, ready to plot the downfall of a Tyrant.

They paused together at the door. A cool wind was blowing outside, kicking up dust and ash, which floated down the street like snow, speckling Ceinwyn's beautiful red curls and landing on her perfectly made-up face. Titus felt a sudden urge to drag her back inside and change their plan, to stay hidden for as long as they could, to spend their last days living like rats, waiting for a hunter to come, but at least to spend them together. He cursed his cowardice: there was no other real option but that which they had decided upon. They could not hide indefinitely. He kissed her. They were doing the right thing. He had to pretend he wasn't afraid for her.

'I love you forever, whatever happens,' he said as they stood hand in hand.

'And I you.'

As Titus looked at her, she opened her mouth to speak. It hung open for a moment, words unspoken on her lips, and then closed.

'What?' Titus asked gently.

Ceinwyn shook her head. 'Nothing,' she replied. She looked preoccupied. Titus wondered if she was scared—he certainly was.

They kissed, and let go of each other's hands. Titus felt her finger's slip reluctantly through his. Then she turned and walked away.

He headed straight to the Aesculapium.

XLI

Titus burst onto the ward. 'I need to see my father,' he said quickly.

The nurse looked sad. 'He's been moved,' she said.

Titus looked confused. 'It was only a few days ago he was here? Has he been allowed home?' It would be a miraculous recovery if he had.

She shook her head and gestured upstairs. 'It's more comfortable there,' she said.

Titus left, puzzled, and climbed the stairs. The ward above looked more like someone's house. There were armchairs in the sitting room occupied by people with drips attached. They were right on the edge of Rome and occasional squalls of rain lashed in from under the roof of the Aether, shaking the plate glass windows. Everyone was intently watching the screen at the end of the room—Albus was giving his promised speech. War was coming.

The place looked comfortable and homely, but it smelt odd, a mixture of disinfectant and stale food, and there was something about the place that unsettled Titus. The nurse led him to a room at the far end of the ward. The room was nearly the size of the sitting room, and against one wall was a recliner bed. Lying on it was his father, and immediately Titus noticed a difference in him. His flesh was stretched across his face, and it no longer had any colour. His breathing was so shallow that at first Titus thought he was dead. A drip remained in his arm. Two walls of the room were plate glass from floor to ceiling—if it wasn't for the smoke, which lay thickly under the Aether roof, he would have had one of the best views in the City.

He backed away. 'No,' he said quietly to the nurse, 'I will let him sleep.' He had never seen his father look so ill.

But, as he tried to creep out, the figure on the bed awoke, seemingly with great effort. 'Titus,' he said hoarsely, sitting up. It seemed to use most of his strength.

'Father,' Titus said quietly, walking up to him.

The nurse left them in private. 'Father, I came to tell you something.' He thought about how to explain it. For the first time in his life he and his father would be able to see things in exactly the same way. He could imagine the pride in his father's eyes as he explained what he planned to do. He could do what his father had been trying to do his whole life. End Albus' family's regime. They would work together for once.

'Tell me in a minute Titus,' his father said, his voice barely audible. 'First, tell me. Did you finish the book?'

'Father!' Titus hissed, 'I've got something to tell you.'

'It can wait.' His father said peacefully. 'The book. Did you finish it?'

'No,' Titus admitted. 'I never got time.'

'The young never have enough time—they are always too busy to learn what will help them.'

'Father, this is important...'

'So, if you can't read it yourself perhaps, again, a précis will do.'

Titus sat down. He had no choice but to listen and wait.

'So, Varro was weak, he rose up and changed something, overthrew his master and changed how things were done, for the better initially, but then started to become just like his old master. However, the villagers had had enough. They dug up his tobacco and burnt it. They isolated him and his wife in the great manor house and threatened to burn it down. Varro manages to escape with his wife, into the wild places of the island, but they know it's only a matter of time until they are found.'

'So Jupiter does win the bet then?' Titus asked. 'Men can't change?'

'But then,' his father said, staring into the distance and ignoring the interruption, 'Varro returns, he pleads with them. He says he will go back to tending the land as before if only they are allowed to live.'

'And what happens to them?' Titus asked.

'His bravery saves the life of his wife, they let her live. Remember,' he added with a trace of colour returning to his lifeless face, 'she never wanted him to grow tobacco and treat the other villagers like Slaves.'

'And what of Varro.'

'No-one really knows. He ends the third part of the book at the bottom of a well, thrown down and discarded. Nepos never finished his novel, he died of laryngeal tuberculosis; his throat closed to the point where he could no longer eat and he starved to death. The Book of Varro ends midsentence.'

'What do you think happens?' Titus asked, enthralled now.

'I think that Varro gets out of the well, fights for his wife and gets his land back. I think that Nepos was trying to make a point that it's possible to change inwardly without changing outwardly, but that that is still valid change. Varro changed in order to overcome the land owner, but changed so much in doing so that he wasn't himself anymore. He needed to go through trials in order to realise that, and return to a better version of who he had been in the first place; not the person he thought or wished he should be, but the person he truly was all along. But of course I don't really know, and who wins the bet then if that's the outcome, Juno? Or Jupiter? I suspect Nepos didn't know himself; he was famous for writing as he went along without making any plans.'

'Why did you tell me the story?' Titus asked his father, the answer slowly becoming apparent.

'Because I want to know how you think this famously ambiguous story ends.'

Titus took a deep breath. 'It ends like this father: Varro realises he has been an utter fool. He has been fighting for a dream that was never his to have, and has lost everything. He climbs out of the well and is ready to right all his wrongs.'

'Pleased to hear it,' his father replied earnestly, 'but you're not in the well yet I suspect. That is probably to come. Are you ready for it?'

'Ceinwyn and I are back together. We are going to kill Albus. I need your help. I want to work with you. I know who you are.'

'Thank you,' his father said. 'You spared Murena and her children, that was brave. I wondered when you'd come here for me, and I wondered whether you would come as my son or my captor, but I prayed, and Jupiter answered. Welcome to Filii Aquilae my son.'

Titus glowed with pride. 'I have plans. I think I could assassinate him, he trusts me.'

'Trusted,' his father said firmly. 'You've left. Don't expect that he will just let you carry a weapon to him now.'

'My gladius is in the palace, if I could get it...'

'Yes, get it, carry it to him, and kill him. That's a lot of ifs, and he's not a bad fighter.'

'I know that,' Titus said, remembering, 'but I know I can beat him.' In his heart he wasn't sure, he had never fought a man who wielded a gladius as well, but he had to try. He could think of no other way that could succeed. There was no means to get other weapons into Rome.

'There is another way,' his father said quietly as his body was racked by another wave of retching.

Titus waited patiently, wanting to help but not sure what to do.

'Today is Vulcanalia. This evening a great sacrifice of a red boar and a red bull calf will be made to the god, in the Vulcanal, at the foot of the Capitoline hill. The Pontifex Maximus, Albus himself, will be there, with all his most trusted people. You must make the sacrifice there, with your gladius, and then when you are close to him, performing his duties as High Priest, you can kill him. Only then, in the ensuing panic, might you and Ceinwyn escape this Infernal City.

'But how,' Titus asked, 'would he trust me enough to give me the honour of the sacrifice?'

'Because you are the man who captured the leader of the terrorist organisation Filii Aquilae.'

Titus was stunned. He felt sick as he realised what his father was suggesting. 'They will kill you,' he said gravely. His father had lost his mind. There was no way this plan could work, and them both come out alive.

His father smiled kindly. 'Of course they will my child.'

Titus turned to leave. 'No, I'd rather we flee, I'll never speak a word of this. I'll never betray you to him.'

'I'm dying Titus!' his father said. 'I've got days, if that; look where they have moved me to. This is the end! Listen to me.'

Titus shook his head and paced the room. He could not believe it. Didn't want to accept it.

'Titus,' his father called, his voice weakened by the treatment. 'You forget everything I have tried to teach you.'

'About balance, about being myself?' Titus shouted. 'This is me, being myself. I'm not going to let you sacrifice yourself for me.'

'But I have chosen to do this. Titus. Let me ask you, what separates us from animals?'

Titus shook his head—he had no time for his father's riddles now. His mind was turning over and over. There must be another way.

'Let me tell you,' his father continued. 'It is to do with death. Namely our response to it. You see, an animal may see death many times in its life. However, a man, when he first sees or hears of death... with that first glimpse of it comes the realisation that, one day, he too must grow old and die. That realisation that his life is now set on a course that will one day stop, and that at that moment, even the illusion of control that we currently feel we hold over our lives will be extinguished. It is the fear that holds us, the fear that binds us our whole lives.'

Titus stared at him, eyes wide, as his father's words dug into his soul.

'When?' his father continued, staring, mesmerising Titus. 'When will it happen to me? Will it hurt? Is there anything after it?' he paused. 'Are you scared of dying Titus?'

Titus was transfixed and felt the hairs on the back of his neck rise. He nodded slowly, not breaking his father's gaze.

'I'm not scared of dying,' said his father earnestly. 'Titus, I have faced death for over a year.' He lifted up his hand, showing the little cannula needle that fed in the extract of the blistering gas. 'My whole life I wanted to build something separate, to be able to see who I really was, not what the world said I should be. I have tried, vainly, to rely on myself, but that doesn't work. We need each other to survive.

'You know, I used to get so scared when you were young: that something might happen to you, that perhaps I wouldn't be able to provide for you. I was anxious the whole time. So I tried to deal with it. I read about how others dealt with it and discovered that really anxiety is just something we feel when we are trying to chase security—security that doesn't, and cannot ever exist. Isn't that a lovely idea? That we can't change anything, so there's no point in trying? But you know Titus, I never really fully believed that fallacy of idleness. I just told myself I did, and that made me feel better. It justified my powerlessness to change even the smallest thing in this world.'

He closed his eyes, and took a deep breath in. 'Titus, it's only when you know that the end is near, that you can actually throw away all of those crutches that prop up your mind, and you can actually face your fears. You know, really face and understand them. I have faced death Titus, I am staring at it right now, and I can honestly tell you that I do not care when it comes. I know it will. I accept that it must and will happen, but I have one final power over it and I will exercise that power. I will choose how, and why, death comes.'

'It will come here, peacefully.' Titus said. 'I'll find another way.' But he could not think of one.

'No, what would happen then is that I would die here, in anguish, in the knowledge that I had a chance to save my son and his wife, yet did nothing. You have one chance of escape, and that is in the ensuing uprising following the death of Marcus Albus, and for that to happen you need to kill Marcus Albus.

So,' he took a deep breath, completely exhausted, 'I choose to die today at the hands of my greatest enemy, in order that my son may live. I have got nothing left to live for, but everything to die for.' His hand shook ever so slightly. 'You must hand me in, disown me in front of the Praetorians and in front of Albus and the rest of the Senate. You must watch me die and show little remorse. Then, when they have made you into a hero, and you are above reproach, when he invites you to carry your gladius to make the sacrifice—you can spill his blood onto the floor of the Vulcanal and down the streets of the Infernal City.'

'There must be some other way,' Titus said, horrified.

'There is not. You know this. Unless I die then you and Ceinwyn surely shall, and I will die soon anyway.' He held out his shaking hands imploringly. 'You have captured me, *Protector of Rome*. Now save yourself, save Ceinwyn: my life, in return for yours.'

Titus wept.

As he put the handcuffs onto his father, disconnected the drip, and led him through the dingy corridors of the Aesculapium, he mouthed silently to himself. *'Protector of Rome.'* The words were so hollow, but the title that followed was real, and hot, and satisfying—'Slayer of Tyrants.'

XLVII

'Father...' Titus said, as they mounted the thin gantry that led up to the main entrance of the Mamertine prison.

His father shook his head brusquely at Titus' attempt to say some last words to him. He had made him keep up the act the whole way from the ward. He kept his head down, dejected, and Titus had to somehow make himself look proud.

The building had once stretched into the sky, but now its roof almost kissed the Aether roof above them. The building was deep too, and Titus knew that its dark basement extended far down into the thick floor that separated the Aether from the Imum—an underworld of pain and loneliness. The building was made of dark granite to survive the weathering it no longer had to endure. Two huge Roman Eagles were carved into the walls above the main gate, and banners proclaiming Albus' family hung around the walls. It served as both prison and Praetorian headquarters, and there were few places in Rome Titus wanted to be less right now.

He reached the top of the stairs and poked his father in the back so that he stumbled forwards towards the guard.

'Got another Imum terrorist bastard?' asked the bored young man on the gate.

Titus' father looked up slowly.

'Aquilinus!' the guard exclaimed as he recognised him. He looked beyond, at Titus, and his face paled as he realised what Titus had done. 'Your father...' he said, backing away.

'My father...' Titus said, his voice quivering. He coughed to disguise it. 'My father is the leader of Filii Aquilae,' he paused, gathering strength for what he had to do. 'He's a terrorist, and he's a traitor.'

The man on the gate nodded slowly. 'Come inside, I'll call the legate.'

'No need.' Titus said. 'Call the Consul.'

His father shook at this and emitted a thin whimper. Titus' nails bit into his knuckles behind his back, all he wanted to do was leap forwards and break the guard's neck. Then they could run away, and his father would be safe. He took deep breaths. His father was right— this was the only way.

They were led inside, and his father was taken into a side room. The young guard made a panicked, stuttering, scire call through to the palace, and it seemed, after a long time, did manage to at least get a message to Albus. He came back through to Titus bearing two cups of coffee.

Titus took his and sipped it. It was foul and clearly from a machine that had seen better days. The guard walked towards the side room inside which his father was manacled.

'Is that coffee for him?' Titus asked.

The guard flushed, 'Titus... trust me, your father will be treated with respect while he's here, whatever he has done, he's your father.'

Titus had heard tales of the Mamertine. He knew only a little of what happened in the floors below, but respect was not something accorded to most prisoners. The guard seemed terrified of Titus, and well he might be, it was not every day you met a man who was willing to give up his own father for the good of the state.

Titus remembered the ruse he was trying to portray. He shook his head. 'He wouldn't have afforded respect to his victims.'

The guard's hand shook even more as he placed the coffee down on the desk instead.

The pair sat in silence, waiting. Titus wanted to go to his father but then the illusion would be spoiled.

Then, after nearly an hour, there came a familiar voice, as Albus himself marched through the door and into the small waiting room.

'Titus!' he said, 'I had heard terrible rumours; rumours that you had left us.'

Titus stayed silent.

Albus stared at him. 'No matter,' he said eventually, 'you have proven your loyalty now, beyond all doubt.'

He walked onwards towards the cell, the guard darting ahead to unlock it before moving to stand guard over Titus' manacled and weak father. As if he was in any state to hurt the Consul.

'Aquilinus,' Albus said quietly, 'so it comes to this.'

'Marcus,' his father said, using his praenomen sarcastically, as if they had been the best of friends. 'My books just weren't causing enough harm anymore.'

'They say the pen is mightier than the gladius. But those that say that have clearly never held a gladius.'

'Perhaps,' his father replied, 'but then, I would rather die at your hand than wield a gladius in your service.'

'If your wish is death then I can assure you that that will be granted, but you deceive yourself as to your own importance if you think that you will die at my hand.'

Titus watched as his father bowed his head in submission.

'I want a news crew in ten minutes,' Albus said to the guard. 'Have them come to the central waste centre, and bring the prisoner.'

He turned on his heel and walked away. Titus got up to stand by his father.

'Titus!' Albus called at the door. 'Leave him. Walk with me.'

Titus looked at his father and started to smile. He needed to say one final word, but nothing seemed appropriate.

'I'm sorry father,' he said, hoping his father understood what he was truly sorry for—a lifetime of misinterpreting bravery for weakness.

His father curled his face up in a snarl. 'You dare call yourself my son!' he snapped.

Titus recoiled from his father's anger, for a moment completely taken in by his perfect act. He followed Albus out of the door, unable to take anymore.

'Betrayer!' his father screamed at his back as he left.

XLVIII

'Cock!' Marcus shouted at the scire's screen, as a huge banner proclaiming the word *'Defeat!'* spread across it.

Antonius roared angrily from across the table as he slammed his great fist into the thin metal counter, denting it. Their scires leapt into the air and Marcus had to grab at his to stop it smashing on the floor of the barracks.

'Careful Antonius, these don't even belong to us!'

'Learn to play then!'

'It's your fault Antonius,' Marcus replied back angrily. 'Attack as a group, that's the tactic, and what do you do? Send your *Immunes* in a whole minute before my army is even ready!'

'Build faster,' Antonius said, loading up another game. In the corner, Quintus shook his head with exasperation. Normally he was the first to want to play *Astrumbello Duo*; something was wrong, it had been all day. The strange thing was, Marcus thought, today was, if anything, the most exciting day since they had arrived in Rome. They were about to go war.

Albus had announced it that morning. Just after the speech, they had been told to prepare their kit and wait in the barracks. The Legate had hinted that they might be moving tonight to a training camp on the outskirts of the Field of Mars. This was real. Of all of them, he had the least reason to want this to happen. He was the only one who had never learnt to love battle, but even he had to admit a slight excitement that he would get to hold a sonifex again and perhaps even use it to defend his City. It certainly beat being a mercenary. But the day was tinged with sadness for all of them—they had lost a brother. Gnaeus had left them, probably never to return. No one had seen Gnaeus since last night at the Forum. Marcus could still see his face, shouting at Titus, holding his dead wife. He suspected it would be the last time he ever saw him. Gnaeus would never fight for Rome now.

The game loaded and an alien world materialised before him, his fingers glided over the keys and tapped on the screen as he started gathering resources, ready to build an army. Antonius' base was next to his, but he couldn't rely on him, they might as well be fighting their opponents independently.

'Where the hell are the others?' Quintus asked from the corner, he looked genuinely worried. His concern made sense, if they were to move out later today then there was a real chance they would be separated. Titus and Tiberius didn't have long if they were to join them.

'Titus will probably be allowed to leave the Praetorians,' Marcus said quickly. Should he build attacking units yet or gather more resources? It was always a difficult balance. Titus would have known the answer. Across the table, Antonius pushed buttons thoughtfully, slowly. Didn't he realise that speed determined the victor in this game?

'Titus will waltz in when he feels like it,' Quintus said sarcastically, 'but where is Tiberius?'

'He was out all night,' Antonius said, to Marcus' distress seemingly paying little attention to the game in front of him.

'Where?' Quintus asked.

'No idea.' Antonius replied. 'Where were you?'

'Oh, me? Working,' Quintus said quickly. Marcus wondered how he managed. He seemed to have to work every night these days. Quintus looked stressed and clearly in need of sleep.

An enemy unit scouted around the edge of Marcus' base but, he ignored it—it was a weak one, just a resource collector, and he needed all his concentration to keep resources flowing in. He'd be able to build some defence around his base soon, then he'd be safe to build an army. He scrolled up to Antonius' base; a small army was forming of basic ground units at the edge of the ramp that led to his base—as usual he had collected almost no resources. Marcus cursed—he had been trying to teach him how to play properly for over a month.

The door to their barracks room opened slowly and Tiberius walked in quietly.

'Tiberius!' Quintus exclaimed, rising to his feet and embracing his friend.

'Quintus,' Tiberius said quickly, walking to the side of the room and sitting down. He looked exhausted.

Marcus realised, with horror, that the scouting unit he had seen was in fact building cannons in the back of his base, his resource gatherers were being destroyed. How had he missed this? 'Antonius!" he shouted. 'Get your army over here now and help me!'

Antonius shook his head. 'Just need a few more and then I'll attack them.'

'No!' Marcus said, exasperated. 'Help me, or it's one versus two!'

'I can beat two, no problems,' Antonius said confidently.

Marcus held his head in his hands as his base was slowly destroyed. 'Have you seen Gnaeus?' He asked Tiberius hopefully, giving up the game as lost.

Tiberius shook his head. 'Not since he ran off last night. He'll blame Rome for what happened to Vibia no doubt.'

'Did you see what happened to her?'

Tiberius shrugged his shoulders. 'No, the crowd was so thick. She was crushed in it I suppose. Shouldn't have been rioting.' he added sadly. Vibia hadn't deserved to die, and Gnaeus didn't deserve this tragedy.

Marcus felt sad too, regardless of fault it was not fair that so many had died last night. He wanted to go and find Gnaeus and try to bring him back. He'd need his friends now, more than ever, but he knew deep down that Tiberius was right: Gnaeus now opposed Rome. He could imagine him replacing Tarpeius and continuing his fight, then he too would surely die. It was so frustrating.

He was interrupted from his thoughts by Quintus rising from his seat and walking over towards Tiberius. He paused, seemingly unsure of what to say, as if he needed to build up courage for something.

'Tiberius?'

'Yup?' his friend replied casually.

'I need to talk to you about something? Could we err... go for a walk outside the barracks?'

Marcus looked across confused. Quintus seemed really worried about something.

'Of course!' Tiberius said. 'When?'

'Now?'

Tiberius rose.

'Hang on a minute,' Antonius called to him, turning away from the screen as the familiar image of *'Defeat!'* appeared, yet again, across his and Marcus' screen. 'You haven't told us what you got up to last night!'

Tiberius laughed. 'Not much,' he said modestly.

Antonius laughed. 'You're broken! Who kept you up all night?'

Tiberius smiled. 'Oh, just some girl I met in a bar, can't remember her name, began with a *G* I think. She was hot though. I'm knackered.'

Antonius laughed again. 'Sounds like fun,' he said, seemingly indifferent to them just losing the game. Marcus knew he had a lot more teaching to do if they were ever going to win any tournament games.

'She was,' Tiberius said before turning to Quintus. 'Come on old friend, let's walk.'

Quintus didn't move. Suddenly he looked very pale and Marcus wondered if he was about to be sick. 'It's okay,' he said. 'Perhaps later.' He walked back over to the side of the room and sat down as Tiberius watched him quizzically. He looked awful. Marcus tried to cheer him up; perhaps he was missing Gnaeus?

'Three versus three?' he asked, gesturing at the third unoccupied scire and empty seat.

'Fuck off!' Quintus shouted, jumping to his feet and storming off.

The three men looked at each other, confused. Then the wall mounted screen flickered on behind them.

They all turned to watch, and Marcus stared in horror at what he saw there.

XLIV

Titus and Albus walked in silence towards the waste disposal facility as Titus tried to suppress tears. Part of him thought it would be okay to shed them. Surely Albus could understand what handing his father over would mean to even his most devoted acolyte?

'Your father is scum,' Albus said. 'But he's still your family. You have been a brave man, *Protector of Rome.*'

Titus nodded. 'I serve only you, Consul.'

'I know,' Albus said, 'you and Verres and me, together we control Rome. A triumvirate, just like two thousand years ago. But which are you, Crassus, or Pompey?'

Titus suppressed a gasp, unable to believe what Albus had just said. He had just, plain as day, declared himself as a modern day Caesar, the arch Tyrant. 'I'd rather be Crassus,' he said offhandedly.

'He was rich,' Albus said, 'but I suspect you would have been a better Pompey, he was a good general.'

'He was also disloyal.'

Albus looked at him and smiled. 'In which case I will allow you to be Crassus.'

They walked on and neared the great centre where Rome's rubbish and recycling was sorted. There was remarkably little smell: the waste was mainly kept inside and much of it was burnt in high temperature furnaces on arrival.

The news crews had arrived before them, having been forewarned as Albus had requested. Titus felt uncomfortable at the glare of the lenses as he walked alongside the Consul towards the centre of the incinerator floor.

An assistant ran up and quickly fitted safety helmets onto their heads whilst they remained in the work area. A small metal levator carried them up to a gantry overlooking the floor and the cameras followed them. They now stood twenty feet above the ground. The walls were lined with pallets containing waste, and in the wall behind them was the entrance to the incinerator, a square hole around twelve feet across. The place smelt of filth and ash.

A cheer went up outside. His father had arrived. Titus was surprised that so many spectators had managed to get there. News travelled fast in Rome.

Titus' father was led manacled, hand and foot, into the centre of the room. His gaze remained downwards. He stumbled as he walked forwards and fell to his knees. The two Praetorians escorting him hauled him to his feet roughly, and one of them cuffed him hard around the head. Titus' hands tightened on the gantry bar and he tried to catch a glimpse of the man's face beneath the helmet, in case the chance for vengeance should ever present itself. He looked up at Albus, who was smiling at the attention and the knowledge he was about to rid himself of one of his greatest enemies. Vengeance would come to him—Titus promised himself that. He would avenge his father this very day.

'Romans!' Albus boomed loudly next to him on the gantry, making Titus jump. 'Long has the threat of Asia Minor terrorism loomed over our city, but only recently have our true enemies, our closer enemies, felt bold enough to creep from their shadows to attempt to murder us in our beds.

'First we had Aulus Tarpeius, a man who dared to stand for the position of Consul himself, when truly he was no more than a puppet of our enemies. Rome is a safer place for his foolish attempt to murder one of my brave Praetorians. He didn't expect to have his own foul, foreign blade plunged into his chest!'

He gestured at Titus' father. 'And here we have Lucius Aquilinus, a man of words!' he said sarcastically. 'A man of weakness. A man who thought he could bring me down by his pointless musings. Surprisingly that didn't work, so he eventually did what all traitors do: he showed his true cards, by setting up the Filii Aquilae terrorist organisation. An organisation that killed your brave Praetorian protectors, an organisation that tried to assassinate your Consul!' his voice rose with anger. 'I curse him and I refuse to give him the honour of a true Roman burial. In fact,' he said, pointing behind him to the incinerator, 'I refuse to give him the honour of any burial at all.'

The Praetorians started to drag his father across the floor towards the closed hatch as Titus watched on in impotent horror. He thought of calling out a protest, but what good would it do? It would ruin the only thing that his father's death could hope to achieve. It would spoil his father's last dying wish. His hand squeezed the railing so hard he could feel the skin of his palm splitting.

The Praetorians paused at the hatch. One held his father by the shoulders, rooting his emaciated body in place, whilst the other worked the controls to slide the hatch open.

'Marcus Albus!' his father called with a new power to his voice, which carried over the crowd to Titus' surprise. 'Albus!'

The Consul turned and sneered at him. 'Are you ready to die, old man? Your ashes will mingle with the filth from the City you hated so much.'

His father nodded. 'Yes, I am ready, but Albus you have still much to learn. You still think that ideas can be killed as easily as people.' He stared into the nearest camera and addressed the entire world, desperate to use his last moments wisely. 'Consul you can kill people, but you cannot kill words and ideas. Equality, honesty and liberty, are more than just words—they are principles. What I have said in my books will live on, far beyond the span of years Jupiter and Juno will allow you. Long after your bones have turned to dust and blown far from this City that you love, and exploit—my words will carry on. My ideas will live, and people will be safe from Tyrants like you.'

His father spat on the floor as his final speech ended. He stood there, arms folded by the hatch, and waited for Albus to end his life. He looked strangely peaceful.

Albus smiled. 'Words. Just words. Let me show you what real power is.' He gestured to the Praetorians and the hatch opened. As Titus watched, the Praetorians pushed his father in so that he was standing between two crates of waste ready to be incinerated. Albus gestured for the door to be closed.

As the doors slowly edged together, Titus mouthed words to his father. He had no idea if he could read them, or see them for that matter, but he had to hope. 'Thank you.'

His father's mouth moved once as the door closed, but to Titus it was clear what he had said, and it gave a glimmer of warmth to his breaking heart. 'Son.'

The doors slammed shut. The Praetorian pushed a large red button and a loud whoosh was heard from the far end of the room. It lasted only a few seconds. Titus felt a great emptiness open up inside him as the Praetorian opened the hatch. The grating beyond was empty. The rubbish was gone, and so was his father. He was more alone than ever. Albus put his hand on his shoulder.

'*Protector of Rome*, I owe you a province.'

Titus shook his head. This was the moment. 'I already have one,' he said, trying to sound proud.

Albus laughed and shook his head, 'Northern Britannia is a shit hole! I can't have you living there, no, no! Hispania is much more...'

'No,' Titus said firmly. 'Rome. This is my province. I want to stay here with you. I want to serve you. I will be your General as you asked, and then when the war is over I want to live here and continue to serve you as Rome's Protector.'

Albus beamed. Titus could see the look of victory in his eyes.

'So be it!' he said. 'That dream is yours!'

Titus turned to go. He had to time this perfectly. 'Oh,' he said, as if he'd forgotten something very minor. 'One last thing. I wondered if I could have the honour of the sacrifice this evening?'

'You'll come to the party?' Albus asked, seemingly astounded. 'You've escaped the last two I had very early. I thought perhaps you didn't enjoy them?'

Titus made himself laugh. 'No Albus, I want to see that girl again from last night.'

Albus smiled. 'The one with the amazing breasts?'

'Yes,' Titus said, forcing himself to return the smile. 'What do you think she'll give to the man who makes the sacrifice to Vulcan?'

Albus nodded, his smile widening. 'She'll do whatever you want Titus, anything. Make the sacrifice, be my guest.'

Titus shook his hand. 'Until this evening then?'

'Until this evening.'

He left the building head held high, proud for the cameras, but once outside he started to run, away from the view of the cameras.

He ran out of strength within moments of leaving their view and collapsed to the ground sobbing. His breath tore his lungs and he lost all control. His father had paid for Albus' death with his own and seen it as a fair bargain, but Titus knew that Albus should never have been allowed to get this powerful, and the guilt for that rested on everyone in Rome, including him.

Slowly he rose to his feet. He would need time to prepare for the sacrifice, and the sun, beyond the dark walls of the Aether, was starting to set. He headed for the palace ready to wash, dress, and retrieve his father's gladius. A gladius that had never been drawn without spilling blood. It would be drawn tonight, and the blood of a Tyrant would once again spill onto the streets of Rome.

XLV

Titus for once did not circle the party; he was right in the middle talking to the senators, laughing with them. He consoled himself with the thought that he needn't wear this mask much longer; his gladius would be in his hand soon. He glanced up from feigning interest in a boring discussion with two senators who were clearly hoping that he would help support mineral rights claims in Asia Minor after the invasion. Albus was readying himself on the dais at the far end of the temple, which was shrouded in darkness for the night's festivities. The only light was that of the fire lit to honour the god—a huge fire burning at the entrance, across two braziers, illuminating the great statue of Vulcan which stared down upon the scene impassively.

Albus was dressed in his Pontifex Maximus robes. Pure white, no purple despite his rank, but his face was painted to ward off any evil spirits who would dare intrude into the ceremony: a dark, brownish, oily red, and his eyes were circled with deepest black. His long golden hair, now sticking out in sharp angles, looked as if it had been treated with wax. He stayed apart from the crowd as befitted his role as the High Priest here. Titus waited.

Eventually Albus mounted the highest step of the dais, with the altar and throne chair behind him.

'Romans,' he intoned. 'Rome has been saved by our *Protector of Rome* and my guiding hand. Tonight a great enemy has been cast into flames, forever destroyed. Let us remember this as we thank Vulcan for his protection and his gifts of fire.'

Titus thought of his father and his acceptance of death. He longed to get his gladius in his hands.

Albus took a step back and stood by the altar. It was covered in hot coals and a huge hammer lay across it. 'Bring out the first sacrifice.'

Vulcanalia was celebrated with two sacrifices, first a young bull and then a boar. Titus looked behind him, expecting to see one of the Vestal virgins bringing his gladius to him. The virgins had been brought across from their temple to assist Albus. Everyone knew that few of them had remained virgins for long after Albus had become Pontifex Maximus; Titus suspected it was the only reason Albus had taken the position in the first place. The virgins stood in a small group at the back of the temple, but none moved forwards. Instead, Verres who had been standing to one side, drinking with two of his most trusted Praetorians, was ushered forwards.

He opened his mouth to complain. This was his honour: Albus had promised him it only hours before, but at that moment music rose from the floor, a strong pulsing throbbing sound that filled the room. Verres walked solemnly up the steps and picked the hammer off the coals. Albus nodded, and two priests in white dragged in a red-skinned bull calf. The bull roared and fought them, but they had it tightly held through a ring in its nose and quickly brought it, still struggling, to the front of the altar.

'Vulcan,' Albus said staring up at the statue above him, 'accept our offering.'

Titus watched as Verres brought the hammer high into the air and down onto the bull's head with a dull, wet, thud.

The bull collapsed to the ground immediately, its legs thrashing uncoordinatedly. It bellowed once as it died, its sunken eye from the fractured skull seeming to stare accusingly up at the statue of the god above it.

Albus waited a few moments after its movements ceased, his gaze never leaving the statue's face throughout. Then he nodded, 'Vulcan has accepted our gift.' At that moment the braziers roared, and thick red sparks flew into the air for a few seconds. A gasp of wonder went up from most of the senators. Titus looked around and saw them utterly under the spell of their high priest-Consul-Tyrant. He looked around again for the virgin bringing him his weapon, which had been brought specially, under Praetorian Guard, from the palace earlier.

What was Albus doing? Had he been lied to? His eyes fell to the hammer again. He resolved that he would use that instead if need be, but his eyes fell also onto Verres. He would need to go through Verres to get to Albus and he would struggle to do that without his gladius. He waited.

To his dismay, the second sacrifice was also led out towards the waiting Verres. The ochre painted boar roared with fear as it smelt the bull's blood, but it was once again easily controlled. The hammer rose and fell, and red sparks dusted the crowd again.

Verres put the hammer down and began to retreat into the crowd. Titus readied himself—this was the moment. He had only seconds to act.

Albus moved forwards to the front of the dais again.

'Now,' he whispered to himself, getting his courage. He felt sick.

He took a step forwards. He would dash for the hammer, act before Verres could stop him.

'Finally, Romans,' Albus spoke grandly. 'We come to our third and greatest sacrifice.'

Albus' words stopped Titus in his tracks. He turned and saw a virgin gliding towards him, her white veiled face unreadable as she bore his great ancestor's gladius, with its ivory hilt, towards him. Her silk dress brushed his bare arm as she stopped beside him and made the hairs stand up. His mouth was so dry he couldn't even mumble an acknowledgement. He reached down to the white silk pillow, and picked up the blade that had killed so many from its surface. He let the blade hang down by his side, looked up at his greatest enemy and smiled. Albus grinned widely.

'Romans! Our *Protector of Rome* is here!' He gestured warmly to Titus. 'This man has saved us from two terrorist threats. Rome is safer thanks to him and his loyalty. He has given up much to stand here today, more than any of you know.' He smiled at Titus, and Titus realised he was trying to commiserate with him over his father's death. He forced himself to smile once again, but readied his blade. He could imagine it already. Walking up to the dais, standing by Albus, the animal being led out, readying the blade, then at the last minute, turning and butchering the Consul. His father had suggested he would be able to escape in the confusion, but he wasn't sure, the senators in the main part seemed to be so taken in by Albus that they would likely fight for him even after his death. But even if they did, and he too died here, then he would die completing his father's work: freeing Rome; and the land that he left behind would be free—free for Ceinwyn to live in. That would be something he could happily die for. His father had taught him that at the last.

'Romans,' Albus said, his voice severe now. 'There are taxing years ahead for Vulcan. Years of fire and war, years that will test our loyalty to him.' Albus stressed the word in a way that unsettled Titus.

At a further nod from Albus, a vestal virgin was led forwards from the same side entrance that the animals had emerged from. The virgin was dressed from head to toe in silk like the others, and her face was veiled so that she was simply a figure of pure white, but unlike the other, this vestal virgin shook as she approached the dais.

Titus' sickness intensified; Rome hadn't sacrificed people to the gods for over a thousand years. He looked over his shoulder at Albus and with a growing unease noticed that he had moved around the altar and now sat in the great throne chair—the chair reserved for Vulcan himself. The smile remained welded on his horrific, painted face.

The priests moved the virgin to the centre of the dais, to the point where the animals had died. Titus looked at the crowd, staring in rapt awe at the scene. With a growing sense of dread, he saw that they were actually thirsty for this girl's blood. He lifted his gladius. Albus was out of reach and behind the altar, he would have to charge at him and leap over. It would be awkward but he had no choice. As he glanced round, he noticed that Verres had moved closer with his two bodyguards. The odds of success kept diminishing. He felt sweat gathering on his forehead and his gladius arm felt heavy.

The first priest moved around to the front of the girl and took the edge of her veil. He lifted it slowly, revealing a pale, freckled, beautiful face. A face adorned with a signum, but which other than that seemed almost Roman. Titus retched as he realised what Albus had done.

The priest lifted the veil high and pinned it behind Ceinwyn's head, amongst her copper curls. The gladius fell from Titus' numb fingers, clattering on the stone floor.

He turned around in shock and stared at Albus. 'No... I...' he mumbled.

'The *Protector of Rome* has dropped his gladius,' Albus said impassively, 'Verres, pick it up for him. We must complete the ritual.' He rose, and walked slowly towards Titus. 'Didn't I say there would be cake?' he whispered into his ear, before returning to his seat behind the altar.

As Verres walked over, Ceinwyn turned her head slightly to look at Titus. She was terrified, her lips quivering and her sweat drenching the silk she had been made to wear.

Titus wanted to speak, but no words came except for a croak. He moved closer to her, as if somehow he could protect her, when he himself was the one meant to kill her.

Verres bent down, picked up the gladius and placed it back in Titus' hand. He took one pace back and stood firm, completely blocking any attempt Titus might make to cover the ground to where Albus sat in Vulcan's throne chair.

Titus took a deep breath and formed one final desperate plan. Its chances of success were minimal, but there was no other option with three men with fasces so close by.

'I'm sorry,' he said to Ceinwyn, and began to raise the blade towards her neck.

'I love you,' she said urgently. 'My last words: I love you.'

Titus shook his head, trying to reassure her. There was one chance to save her; he would take it. 'I love you too,' he whispered. He steadied his grip on the gladius and brought it up to her soft, white, trembling neck.

'I'm sorry,' he said again.

'Get on with it!' Albus ordered from his throne chair.

Titus pressed the blade as firmly as he dared against her neck. His heart was pounding and he felt like he was about to faint.

He looked out, at the crowd.

'Vulcan!' he shouted. His voice seemed not his own, and he had a strong sense of no longer existing in his own body. 'I give you this girl. May you bring success to our war, and may you smite your enemies with your mighty hammers!'

He turned around and stared at Albus, who simply smiled back at him from behind his make-up. Titus readied his arm.

The distance was twenty feet.

His arm shook, but he controlled it.

He tightened his grip on the hilt of the gladius, as if to draw it back across Ceinwyn's throat, emptying her blood for Vulcan and the expectant crowd. But instead, in one sudden movement, he swept the gladius through the air towards Albus and released.

The blade sung as it spun through the air, straight and true, the best blade in Rome. Titus' heart leapt with hope as he saw it home in on Albus' unprotected chest. He watched Albus start to move, but he had surprised him, and he had no time to escape. He readied himself to leap forwards into the crowd. He reached for Ceinwyn's arm.

Then to Titus' horror, one of the priests leapt forwards, directly into the path of the spinning blade. The blade caught him in the side of the abdomen, the force of the throw knocking him over sideways.

There was silence in the temple except for the sound of Titus' heart in his ears.

Albus rose from the chair slowly, and walked over. Titus could sense Verres close behind him, and the bodyguards were on either side. He was trapped.

Albus walked slowly, paused by the body of the injured priest and bent down to pull Titus' gladius from his twitching, groaning body.

'The gods will reward me in Elysium!' the priest muttered, dying, staring up into the eyes of the statue of Vulcan.

'There are no gods you damned fool!' Albus scoffed quietly, before rising, and walking towards Titus menacingly.

He moved gracefully as if he had not a single care on his mind, until finally he stood in front of Titus and held his own gladius up to him. Titus took a firmer grip of Ceinwyn's hand. At least they would die side by side.

'This is a nice gladius,' Albus said. 'I might keep it. Shame that it's been so contaminated by the hands of traitors over the years.'

'How?' Titus asked, needing to know how Albus had known the truth about Ceinwyn.

'You fool! You even gave up your own father. I wondered how far you would go. You should have believed Strabo.'

Titus felt like he had been punched. Ceinwyn had been right. He had come to Rome to alert Albus to the corruption in his midst, but Albus had only wanted to silence him.

'Titus,' Albus said with exasperation, 'it was too little too late. I gave you every chance to prove your loyalty, but you went back to your father, to this half-breed. I promised you everything, and this is how you repay me? You could have been my greatest General, one of the richest and most powerful men in our world, but no—you chose to oppose me. Now I will show you how I repay treachery.'

His voice was quiet, not a trace of anger, as if he was simply stating fact.

Verres walked up behind Titus, wrenched his hand from Ceinwyn's and dragged him a few paces back, struggling vainly.

'Vulcan needs blood spilt if we are to succeed in Asia Minor,' Albus continued, 'and this gladius, if I understand, cannot be sheaved until it has shed it.' He lifted Titus' gladius, holding it to Ceinwyn's neck. She struggled and screamed, but one of the Praetorians and the surviving priest held her firmly.

Titus lunged forwards desperately, but Verres' vicelike grip held him. As he fought, the second Praetorian came in and grabbed his legs, bringing him to the ground.

Albus turned to the crowd, 'Vulcan! Accept this sacrifice...'

'Verres!' Titus shouted into the young Praetorian's face.

Verres did everything he could to avoid eye contact with Titus.

'Verres!' Titus screamed again, struggling but unable to move. 'Think of your wife! Your child! Please, don't let him do this.'

'Sorry,' Verres blurted out. He stared down at the ground, still unable to meet Titus' desperate, accusing gaze.

'Verres,' Titus continued, solemnly now. 'This is your last chance. Let me go or I promise that one day I will kill you.'

Verres laughed now, but the laugh was empty.

Albus finished his speech. Titus looked up at the Consul, holding his own blade to the exposed neck of his wife and lunged forwards one last, desperate time. But the Praetorians held him firmly. He looked at the faces of the two bodyguards, one holding Ceinwyn, the other helping Verres hold him. He let their faces be burnt into his memory. He would bring vengeance upon them.

Albus drew the blade across Ceinwyn's throat quickly and stepped back. She stood there for a moment, unchanged, just as she had been, and Titus thought for a second that he had not cut her. But then, bright crimson blood flooded down her neck into the white silk of her vestal virgin robe, and she collapsed forwards.

Titus roared, his body shaking violently. Verres shifted his grip and for a moment Titus was free. He leapt forwards, but Verres caught his foot and he tumbled over, landing on the side of his cheek with a crash that dimmed his vision. He lay on the ground, Ceinwyn's face inches from his; her eyes stared, open but empty, into his.

'I love you! I love you!' he screamed, over, and over again at her lifeless face, as the other Praetorian tried to roll him over onto his back. Verres grabbed him and hauled him back to his feet.

He thought of his attempt to save Verres the night before, and how it had failed. He lunged at Verres, every part of his body desperate to kill him, but the bodyguards held him firm.

'Why?' he shouted into Verres' face. 'Why did you betray us?' his voice broke and he coughed, tasting blood in his mouth.

Verres' face fell as he realised what he was being accused of. 'No!' he replied in outrage. 'No! It wasn't me.'

Titus stared at him, blood dripping from his mouth where he had bitten his tongue during his fall. 'My promise stands Verres,' he said hoarsely, 'I will take your life for this.'

He saw Verres' face pale slightly. Then he felt a huge jolt to the back of his head and there was only darkness.

XLVI

Titus was not sure how many floors underground his cell was located; he wasn't even sure how many floors there were. At first, he had counted the days by the dimming and brightening of the lights, but eventually it became apparent that this happened simply at random, and he had lost any sense of time. He felt like he had been down there for weeks, just a few weeks, but it could have been longer, months even. The endless cycle of brightening and dimming was interrupted only by breaks for a thin porridge, and for questioning.

But for Titus every minute was pain anyway. Ceinwyn's face was always in his sight wherever he looked, his love, the love that he had failed. Devin had asked him to keep her safe; instead he had tried to bring down Rome and in doing so, had condemned Ceinwyn.

A silent tear dripped from the end of his nose and splashed on the soft, white, rubber floor; the walls and ceiling were made of the same material except for the recessed lights, which were too high to reach. There was no bed, he simply slept on the soft rubber. The only furniture in the room was a thin white radiator which emitted almost no heat and was firmly fixed to the wall. He had spent most of, what he had thought was the third day, trying to find a way to end his life, but the room was well designed. He would die when they chose to let him.

The corridor outside was similarly white. Toilet trips were unaccompanied, every three hours. Plastic doors opened and allowed a solitary trip lasting no more than five minutes. Titus didn't know what happened if you tried to stay after the beeping started, but he didn't want to find out. The only time he met anyone, or saw anything that wasn't the same shade of white was during his interrogations. It was meant to make him start to long for them he supposed, to make him side with his interrogators, to break him, but Titus was already broken, and neither the loneliness nor the torture were any worse than the thoughts in his head.

The door slid open. It wasn't time for a toilet trip and there was a man there, dressed in white, carrying a fasces, powerfully built, and clearly a Praetorian. Interrogation time it seemed.

'Get up traitor,' he said.

Titus nodded and followed automatically, the same routine every cycle of the lights. As they filed down the corridor, he saw a fellow prisoner fighting weakly with a similar guard at his door, his hands gripping the door frame desperately as the guard tried to haul him away. He had seen this man a few times before; the other prisoners he saw were all new. It occurred to Titus that no one else he saw had been there as long as him. No one seemed to last long down here.

'Please!' the man screamed, his eyes rolling and spit dripping from his mouth. 'No more! I'll do anything! I don't know anything! Please!'

The guard, failing to release the man's grip from the door, let go before chasing the man back into his room. As Titus was led away, he could hear the sound of metal fasces breaking bone, and further screaming.

He walked on blankly. At the end of the corridor, a door slid open, leading into a grey concrete area that was familiar to him. The guard left him in one of the grey rooms, manacled to a metal chair which was itself bolted down to the ground.

He closed his eyes for a moment out of pure exhaustion, it was almost impossible to sleep down in the Mamertine. This suited Titus, his dreams were worse than anything that they could do to him.

He must have fallen asleep for when he awoke the Carnifex was seated in front of him, dressed smartly as always, in black, a young man with pale skin. He never touched Titus—the two white armour clad guards, stationed on either side of him, were for that. Titus had never seen the young man flinch once during these sessions, it was if he had no soul. Titus suspected that, much like he himself, the young man had once had a soul and took some comfort from the realisation that he had beaten Albus in one way at least—he had got out of his service before he ended up like the Carnifex in front of him.

'Who let you into the Consul's intelligence centre?' the Carnifex asked calmly.

This was a new question. Normally all they wanted to know was whether his father had any associates, or who the leader of the Slave resistance was. Titus wasn't going to give Devin away, not after getting his daughter killed, and he truly didn't know any of his father's associates in Filii Aquilae, although he suspected there would be many. How did they know he'd been in the intelligence centre though?

They must have logged his scire in some way when he took the data. He thought of that scire left with Devin. He hoped it was safe and one day its information would bring the arrogant Consul down.

He shook his head. He would never give up Sexta, just as he wouldn't give up the others. The secrets in his head would die with him: it was the only victory he could still cling to over the man who had killed his wife.

The Carnifex made a silent gesture and Titus took a deep breath, ready. Suddenly the masked guards advanced and slid a lever, which caused the floor section under his chair to tilt backwards. The first time it had happened, it had taken him by surprise and he had shouted, using up his breath. He didn't make that mistake this time, he knew about the water behind him, and he knew as usual it would be cold and salty.

He peered up at them through it, ice floating on the surface. He couldn't see their eyes through the masks, but he stared at where they were. He kept staring the whole time even though the salt burnt his eyes. He deserved every minute of this for failing Ceinwyn. He mouthed the words sorry, repeatedly, as his vision started to fade, the guards' faces were replaced for a moment by an image of Ceinwyn, turned around endlessly, never showing her face, just orange curls cascading to the ground and turning to crimson blood. He longed for dreamless unconsciousness, but they were too proficient to allow him that.

At the last minute they lifted him back up, coughing and spluttering up the water he had inhaled. His breath came in gasps.

'Had enough?' the interrogator asked serenely. Titus ignored him. In his mind he was walking the hills of Northern Britannia with his dead wife. He hoped that eventually they would realise that he would tell them nothing, and then finally, at last, he would be executed. Then he could be with Ceinwyn again.

But the book of Varro was in his mind too, and his dreams contained his father speaking words from it in place of his death speech outside the incinerator. He was in the well now, he had no doubt, but he had no strength to climb out. He wished he did. He wanted to find Albus and throw him in the well in his stead, but it was over, Albus had won now. He cursed the priest who had gained nothing in losing his life for Albus by stepping out in front of the blade. He had ended not only Ceinwyn's life, but Titus' too, and any hope for the Eternal City with his foolish act of loyalty.

His body was dripping wet now from the salt water, so they stripped him and brought over the cables. He felt the slight sting of the clips as they hooked the electrodes onto his ears and the soles of his feet—a different part each time, but the effect was much the same.

The Carnifex asked him the question again. He didn't even bother shaking his head this time. The same charade had been carried out so many times now and he was amazed that they hadn't become bored yet. He certainly was.

The Carnifex had control of this particular torture himself. Titus knew what to expect. The machine had numbers from one to ten. They would work up as high as they dared. They had gone too far one day and Titus had woken up with a medicus staring down at him—it had been the best sleep he had had in days. He could only hope the same mistake would be repeated today.

As the Carnifex pushed the button on the desk in front of him, pain exploded into Titus' body from his head and feet. His arms jerked against the restraints in uncontrolled spasms, and his mouth opened to emit a scream that didn't seem to come from his body. He remembered the Slave at Albus' victory party: a puppet with no control over his strings. The strange disconnection from his body that he had started to feel in the temple of Vulcan still persisted: he felt the pain, but it didn't feel like it was happening to him. The feeling was odd, and extremely unpleasant, perhaps worse than experiencing the pain normally.

They got up to seven.

This was the furthest they had ever managed, and Titus smelt his own flesh burning. The air above him was full of steam from the saline on his body as it boiled. Every movement was agony, and his muscles seemed unable to relax even when they turned the power off for a few moments to ask him questions. Titus thought about the people making the power in Dacia. Did they know that the power was being used for this? They probably didn't care; they had their own problems—there was no worse job in the world.

The Carnifex asked him again. 'Who helped you?'

Titus looked away, staring at a corner of the room intently. For a moment, a shadow cast there by one of his tormentors had cast a thin willowy silhouette, and he had nearly called for Ceinwyn. Was it possible? Could she be in the room with him?

The Carnifex suddenly stood up and started shouting, his pale face growing red with frustration. He had never raised his voice before.

Titus turned around slowly, staring at him. It took a moment to focus and concentrate before he could speak. 'Could you be quiet?' he asked, his voice hoarse from screaming and disuse. 'I think I just saw my wife.' He turned back to the corner, and continued to stare.

'What do you want?' the Carnifex yelled at him. 'Tell me, what do you want?'

A thin smile came to Titus' lips as he realised that the Carnifex was more broken than he was. He must be under pressure to get results. Would he end up here himself if he didn't get answers?

'Two things,' he whispered from torn lips. His voice sounded completely alien to him, he'd not heard it properly for weeks. His body was not his own.

The Carnifex craned forwards, thin white hands at his sides. 'Yes, anything, we will do it. Just tell us who helped you?'

'Closer,' Titus whispered.

The Carnifex moved in, Titus could smell him, so clean, and Titus could tell he was repulsed by being so close to a traitor.

'Firstly,' he whispered,' I want to kill Marcus Albus.'

The interrogator took a step backwards, his lip quivering with rage.

'Then,' Titus said slowly, 'I want to die.' He laughed to himself; it was so simple.

The Carnifex punched him in the face. Titus kept laughing as the attack continued, even as his teeth were knocked out, and his vision turned to black. The punches kept coming. The interrogator was screaming at him, and the guards were trying to drag him off.

Eventually they succeeded. Titus lolled back in the chair, semi-conscious. Blood was streaming from his mouth and nose, and he could tell that something was wrong with his face—one side seemed slightly sunken in. The pain still felt illusory.

'He's mad!'

Opening his eyes a crack, he could make out the Carnifex talking into a scire. 'No, there is no hope,' the Carnifex continued. 'Anything he knows will have to die with him. We've tried everything.'

The scire was replaced on the desk. 'Back to the cells,' the Carnifex said. 'List him for execution.'

Titus smiled. The first smile since his incarceration; he would see Ceinwyn again soon. The Carnifex stared at him as he was dragged away grinning, and Titus watched as all remaining colour drained from his face.

Lying on his cell floor, he let himself daydream. He could see Ceinwyn's face clearer now. 'I'll see you soon my love,' he mouthed. His only regret was that he would be unable to avenge her.

But then, there was a new noise.

There were three noises that Titus recognised in the cell: the squeaking sound that his body made on the rubber as he moved around; the whooshing sound of the doors when they opened to allow toilet trips; and the sound of his own blood pumping in his head when no other noise was present.

But this sound was new.

It came from somewhere high up. The cell above him perhaps? Presumably there were layer upon layer of floors just like this. The sound was unmistakable; the sound of a girl sobbing. It was so faint he could barely hear it; the cells were so heavily sound-proofed. She must be crying loudly.

The sound started to wake something inside Titus' dying mind. The girl's crying continued, turning into screams, before returning to the baseline sob, as he tuned in he realised he could hear it more easily. It was the sort of cry someone would make when completely alone and terrified, a hopeless and heart wrenching sound. Titus lay and listened to it.

For a moment he tuned out of it and focused on Ceinwyn again, standing there every time he closed his eyes, waiting for him to die. She held out her hand towards him.

But then the sobbing cut through again. His face suddenly hurt, much more than before, and his body felt heavier, more real.

He closed his eyes, trying to see Ceinwyn again, but she was faint now, and every sob he heard pushed her further away. The screaming started again in earnest and Ceinwyn disappeared for a moment. The girl was begging for someone. He couldn't make out who. He wanted to call out to her. He tried but his voice was still broken from the temple of Vulcan, and he only emitted a hoarse sound; a sound that could never carry through the rubber walls of his cell.

He heard the screaming above intensify suddenly before abruptly cutting out; the guards must have silenced her.

He waited. He could hear crying now, but no more screaming. The guards must have gone. He walked over to the radiator, his legs hurt so much now and were mottled purple; he wondered if they would ever work again. He wanted to retreat back into his mind again to ignore it, but found that he no longer could.

He sat down by the radiator and tapped it hard with one of his knuckles. The sound was barely audible in the room. He tapped again, slightly harder. He didn't want to alert the guards.

He waited. Then, with joy, he heard the faintest of replies echo from inside the radiator.

He tapped twice.

Two taps echoed his. Above, the crying quietened.

He sat by the radiator, knowing that somewhere above him a girl sat doing the same thing, suddenly no longer alone. He didn't know what her crime was; perhaps she deserved her punishment, as he did; perhaps she did not, but he resolved that he would sit here as close to her as he could and do the only thing he could do to help: keep her company. He closed his eyes and willed Ceinwyn back, but she wouldn't appear, only his memories of her, and these were too painful for him to see now. He closed his eyes and tried to sleep. Suddenly the lights came on, at full brightness again; the cycle was being repeated. He tapped the radiator, and received a reply once again. He closed his eyes against the lights and after a while managed to sleep. For once, his dreams were bearable.

XLVII

Titus lay on his back in the cell. His face had started to heal and the bone in his left cheek no longer moved quite as much when he pushed it. There was no mirror, but he imagined he would be almost unrecognisable now. He consoled himself with the thought that there would be few people in the world now who would have recognised him anyway. He hoped his friends lived, but supposed they would probably also have been tracked down and killed by Albus; his victory seemed almost complete.

Today was execution day. His guard had broken the rules to inform him of it, but only so that he could gloat, knowing that Titus was aware of the last hours of his life stretching before him.

Titus waited. The signals shared with the cell above, which had sustained him over the last days, had stopped an hour or so ago. This worried him, and he wondered what had happened to the girl; he wanted to know her fate before he died. Other than that, he was ready to see his wife again.

They came for him at what they said was twelve noon, but the lights were almost off in his room and he had drifted off to sleep.

They marched him quickly down the white corridor and then to a white levator. From the way his stomach lurched, Titus could tell it was taking them up. He stared ahead and waited. The levator disgorged them into the back end of the Mamertine Praetorian headquarters, and Titus walked old wooden corridors that he had trod many times before as *Protector of Rome*. They walked through the garden room that he and Verres had planned missions in during the earlier part of the summer. Previous colleagues saw him and averted their eyes, partly he thought because he was a traitor, but also because of his appearance. He was thin now, his face was broken, and the white overalls he had been issued with on arrival had not been changed, and were now heavily stained with his own blood and yellow vomit.

They passed the garden room and he was led out into an open courtyard. The door behind was closed firmly. There were two windows in the courtyard behind him. He knew that behind those windows lay an area of waste ground and beyond that the Capitoline district of the Aether. Titus thought for a moment of running and trying to get through—the window was certainly wide enough—but it was twelve feet off the ground and the brick of the wall was very smooth. It would be impossible. Besides, Ceinwyn was waiting for him.

They took him to the centre of the courtyard and tied him to a thick wooden stake. The guards left, and for a moment he was alone. He looked up, wishing that he could just see the sky one last time, but instead there was just the Aether roof a few hundred feet above, staring down at him oppressively.

The small group of Praetorians filed back in, carrying sonifi now. Titus wondered where they had got them: they shouldn't have been allowed them in Rome. He noticed marks in the wall behind, clearly they were regularly used within the walls for executions despite Albus' law.

He refused the blindfold that was offered to him. Death was so close, and he could sense Ceinwyn just the other side of it, waiting for him to join her.

Then, the Praetorians paused as a second victim was led in. It was a girl, and Titus could tell immediately from the sound of her sobbing that it was his companion from the cell above. To his surprise, she was a child—she looked no more than fifteen. She was bent double as she walked, as if her stomach ached terribly. Titus wondered what horrors she had experienced in the Carnifex's rooms. Blood drenched her white overalls, and her dark brown hair was matted, plastered to her vomit covered face. Half way across the courtyard, she collapsed, and unable to walk any further, she was carried over to the stake. Once tied, she was so weak that she used the ropes themselves to support herself, simply hanging forwards against them to stay upright.

'Please! Please!' she begged as they blindfolded her. 'Please don't kill me!'

Titus saw with surprise that she had a signum—she was a Slave.

Titus wanted to stand by her, to put his arms around the child as she died, but he was firmly tied to the stake. The Praetorians raised their sonifi. Titus looked across at the girl, ignoring the weapons. Soon he would be with Ceinwyn, and she would be back with her family or wherever she wanted to be.

'Child,' he said softly, 'you're not alone.'

She whimpered, her body trembling.

'Be brave,' he said to her, glancing back at the weapons pointing at them both. 'This is nearly at an end.'

He took a deep breath, and he could hear her doing the same.

He stared at the sonifi and waited. He opened his mouth to whisper one last word.

'Ceinwyn.'

He was ready.

The ground shook with a great explosion and the Praetorians dropped their sonifi in shock, staring up over their heads. Titus craned his neck and tried to turn around, but he could see nothing. The Praetorians all reached for their earpieces at the same moment, clearly received an order, and ran away to act on it. Titus and the girl were left alone, tied to their stakes.

At first Titus waited. He was so close to being back with Ceinwyn, and the guards would be back soon to finish their work. But then he heard the girl's cries, and the sound of her struggling faintly against the ropes.

He looked down at his ropes, saw a weak point in the knotting and started to work at it. In under a minute he was free. He limped over to the girl, lifting her head up with his hand so that he could look at her properly. He lifted her blindfold away.

She was in agony, and her eyes were almost closed by bruising. He wiped away some of her tears with the arm of his filthy overalls. 'I'm

Titus,' he said, 'let's get out of here.' Ceinwyn would have to wait, this girl still wanted to live, and only he could save her.

He undid her ropes, and as he did so she fell into his arms—she was too weak to run anywhere. He carried her over to the door but found it locked. They wouldn't have long before the Praetorians returned. He looked up, there was an ongoing rumbling in the distance and the floor continued to shake, but the Aether roof blocked out any view of what might be going on.

His gaze fell to the windows again. There was a chance. He rushed over, his limp improving as he used his legs.

'Stand on my shoulders,' he said urgently, as he reached the wall.

She tried, teetering on them. He supported her weight easily on his bruised, tortured shoulders, but she couldn't stand straight, and her hands were still inches away from the top of the windowsill, twelve feet above the ground.

'Come on!' he croaked. The guards would surely be back at any moment.

She started to cry with frustration and fell. Titus just managed to catch her.

He sat her down in the dirt, holding her head in his hands.

'What's your name?' he asked softly.

'Hercna,' she replied after a pause.

'Hercna, if you can get up there, then you can escape—you can get back to your parents.'

She shook her head. 'Orphan,' she said.

'Well,' Titus said, 'you can get back to whoever you care about.'

She nodded. 'I want to keep fighting. With Devin.'

'Devin?' With shock, he realised that she must be a member of the Slave resistance, but she was just a child. 'Come on then,' he said, getting back to his feet, 'we need to get back to him.'

She tried again. He helped, standing on tiptoe even though it hurt his bruised feet terribly.

Her fingers reached the lintel and she managed to hang on. He pushed up with his hands, helping her, and with one final, desperate scrabble, she pulled herself up and sat on the edge of the open window, exhausted. Titus smiled. He had managed to save her. She reached her hands down for him. He jumped up, grabbing hold of them, but his weight nearly pulled her off. She screamed and he let go.

'Sorry,' she said, when she had recovered. 'Come on! Try again.'

He leapt again, trying to reach the lintel himself, but it was out of reach, and she was too weak to help him.

He tried three times before realising it was not possible.

He heard the sound of boots in the garden room—time had run out.

'Hercna,' he said calmly, staring at her face, 'I need you to do something for me.'

'What?' she said, her voice shaking with fear at the sound of the boots approaching.

'Go back to Devin. Tell him that Titus Labienus Aquilinus is sorry.'

'No!' she shouted frantically, 'I can save you, try again.'

Titus shook his head, 'Hercna,' he said gently. 'It's not possible. I'll be okay. Cross the wasteland beyond, and you will be in the Capitoline district. Disappear, return to Devin.'

She turned around and looked out of the window at the route. Titus sat down and waited contentedly for the guards. The girl would be safe.

'One last thing,' he shouted up to her, as he heard her scrabbling through the short passage window between the courtyard and freedom. 'Can you see what's going on out there?'

'It's the Void Levator,' she called back in awe. 'It's collapsing. A bomb.'

And then she was gone.

Titus imagined the scene: the one hundred mile high structure collapsing, just outside Rome; the thing Albus was most proud of; the greatest achievement of the Roman people—falling from the sky. He smiled. 'You clever bastard Devin,' he muttered to himself.

The Praetorians returned. He stood and started to limp back to the stake.

'Not today,' the first one said to him. 'You've earned a reprieve. But trust me, you'll regret it.'

Titus tried to duck, as the second Praetorian reversed his sonifex to strike him with the butt, but he was too slow. The world faded once again, and he felt himself being carried, the sound of roaring continuing far away in the background. His last thought, as he drifted into unconsciousness, was the realisation that he no longer wanted to die. Instead, he could see a vision of Albus' livid face as he watched what was happening to his beloved Void Levator. He smiled at Albus' first taste of mortality. He had to kill him. He had to avenge Ceinwyn. He must find a way.

XLVIII

But first he had to find a way to survive. The new cell was much smaller, and there was no light at all. It was four foot by four foot and reminded him of the prison box in Strabo's compound. His heart raced constantly, and he felt terrified in the confined space. There was just enough air, but never enough that he could breathe easily. Instead his breath came quickly, fast but never satisfying.

He lost track of the days again, but before long realised that they had stopped giving him food and water.

Hunger he could live with, he had been hungry for so long anyway now in the Mamertine that he had stopped noticing, but the thirst was new. By the end of what must have been the second day he found himself crouching in the corner licking his own urine off the floor of the pitch black cell. He screamed then, yelled, hammering on the walls, desperate for someone to save him, but there was no answer. He started to sob and then realised that it was pointless. He was completely alone in the dark.

He came to realise that this was in itself an execution, but a worse one. Albus must have suspected that he was involved in the attack on the Void Levator. He laughed at that, Devin would never have trusted him with something like that. Devin had never trusted him at all.

He thought of the girl, hoping that she had somehow managed to cross the broken wasteland and reach safety. The journey would be almost impossible with her wounds, and even if she managed it, he suspected that she might die anyway. He didn't want to think of what could have been done to her during those weeks of torture. 'She was a child!' he shouted into the darkness at her unseen torturer. 'A fucking child!'

His voice was starting to recover its strength, just as his body was weakening.

By what he estimated was the third day he was nearing the end. His mouth was beyond dry and all the urine he had produced had been lapped up. He lay down and in the darkness saw a shape at the far end of the tiny cell. He crept over to it, astonished as Ceinwyn looked up at him with her bright green eyes. She was curled up in the corner of the cell. His mouth opened, but his cry of joy came as simply a cracking sound in his parched throat. He reached to embrace her, but she disappeared in the dark, and he simply fell forwards against the wall. In desperation he searched all around looking for her. She was on the other side of the cell now. He lunged forwards, but again she moved just as he got to her. He started to panic. Why was she trying to get away from him? He leapt from side to side in the tiny box until he could no longer leap, and then he crept, around and around the tiny cell's walls, searching fruitlessly for her, until eventually he lay in a ball in the centre, weeping. She had deserted him now, just like he had deserted her.

He closed his eyes, perhaps he would die in his sleep? That would be release, but that would leave Ceinwyn unavenged.

Suddenly he woke. The cell door was open, and bright light was flooding in. In truth, it could have only been light from the corridor, but he recoiled in fear from its brightness as it seared the back of his dark-accustomed eyes. A figure stood in the doorway. A thin figure dressed in black, with long curly blonde hair. She turned to look at him and the light caught her face.

Immediately he was transported back fifteen years to the beach. He felt the warm sand on his knees, and grief to match that of the last weeks.

The Slaves were dead; piles of corpses, torn and bloody in the bright midday sun, blood soaking into the sand. Marcus Albus clapped Titus heartily on the shoulder and laughed. 'Well done my friend, well done.' Turning sharply, his cloak flashing purple in the wind, he strode back to the command tent leaving Titus alone on the beach. The volacurrus that had been waiting for the Slaves hissed angrily as it rose from the sand and headed back to Rome, its presence no longer required.

Titus wandered silently amongst the dead. Many were still holding hands, even in death, their hollow expressions cutting into his soul. 'Animals, slaughtered animals,' he kept repeating to himself, but he still couldn't make himself believe it. He had to believe it. He had to stay sane.

Then something, but he was not sure what, caused him to linger by the contorted body of a woman. He knelt down upon the warm sand, conscious of the sea lapping calmly close by, the only sound on the now eerily quiet beach. It was just him and the dead. A small part of him suddenly envied them. He pushed the thought aside angrily; he had so much to live for. The new command he had just earned for a start. Beneath the woman's body a small leg stuck out, the leg was attached to a head, and the head was covered in golden curls. He gasped involuntarily, for beneath the curls was a dusty face, streaked with tears. His hand flew to his mouth in sudden realisation of what he had just done.

He was twenty one, a general of Rome, and he had just murdered a young girl. His sonifex fell from his shoulder, thumping onto the sand with a muffled crash as a sob burst forth from his tightly clamped lips.

The girl opened her eyes.

She stared into his face and made not a sound as her bright blue eyes bore into Titus'. He reached for the sonifex. He knew what he had to do. He had his orders. He raised the sonifex and brought it up to his shoulder, examining her blue eyes down the sight.

She simply stared back, waiting.

A tear dripped from his eye onto the sight, temporarily hazing his view of her.

His finger tightened on the trigger. His whole body shook.

He relaxed his finger and dropped the weapon again, waiting to be denounced by an observing soldier.

But the beach was deserted.

'Go,' he whispered quickly.

She didn't move.

'Come on!' he hissed. If only he could just save this one... then perhaps he could... he didn't know; save his soul? But he had just been following orders.

He looked at the bodies again. The girl started to move, terrified.

'I'm not going to hurt you,' he said. The girl looked at him in a strange way. Why should she believe him? He had just killed all the others.

'I'm sorry,' he said. It was pointless, meaning only something to him. His words couldn't give back the people he had just taken from her. She started to back away. He stayed completely still. Then she turned and ran.

At the edge of the beach, where the sand met the scrub, she turned and looked at him one last time, her golden curls blowing gently in the warm breeze.

Then she leapt backwards, and was gone.

'Titus!' he awoke from his memory, staring into the eyes of the adult girl.

Not only was she the girl from the beach, but he realised that this was also the girl he had seen that night he had infiltrated the warehouse with Varro, and discovered Albus' false flag terrorist attack. It was the same girl he had seen during the riot in the Imum. The girl who, in his stupor, he had briefly mistaken as Ceinwyn.

'Devin sent me,' she said authoritatively in her Transmaritanian accent. 'Quick, we haven't much time.'

He crawled forwards towards her and took hold of her outstretched hand. Her skin was cool.

He tried to stand, but his vision swam and he collapsed back down on the floor. Behind the girl, the corridor was littered with dead Praetorians. He looked up at her and the blood drenched blade she held.

'Sorry,' he said as he tried to stand.

'Earn the right,' she said quietly, offering him water from a bottle, and the corridor drifted away.

XLIX

He woke to the cool touch of a cloth on his forehead. The room he was in was pleasantly cool, and there was plenty of air. The window was open and a gentle breeze blew in. His eyes opened slowly, still feeling stuck and gritty from his dehydration.

'Come on, you need to drink,' a woman chided him, and brought a cup to his lips. He sipped. It was cold tea, slightly sweetened. He only managed a few sips before slipping back into unconsciousness.

The bed he was in was warm and he felt safe, but inside he was still broken—Ceinwyn was dead, and all hope was gone.

As darkness fell over the city he woke again, this time to the smell of some food. 'Try just a little,' the woman said as he tried to open his eyes, expecting to see the girl from the beach, but she was gone and a woman who hated him even more was in her place. Thana.

She was holding a plate of pasta covered in some rich sauce. There was a pile of cheese about a foot high on the top. He shook his head. 'Too sick,' he croaked, and retched. A small amount of vomit splashed onto the floor, and he lay back, groaning.

Thana knelt down and cleaned the floor.

When she had finished, she started to feed Titus, mouthful by mouthful. He looked up at her worn, anxious face and greyed hair. She had a freshly healed scar by her signum—Devin must have removed her implant too. 'We didn't send Isidora to rescue you, to then let you starve to death,' she said.

'Why?' he asked. 'Why did you save me?'

'Quiet,' she said firmly. 'Eat.'

He did not have the strength to refuse. Soon he drifted back off to sleep.

It was evening again when he woke next, but he was not sure if it was the evening of the next day, or the day after that. Thana sat in the corner of the room, watching him. He couldn't read her face. He knew that she hated him, she had said as much. This made no sense. He felt that some of his strength had returned; she had cared for him well. He sat up as far as he could, his back ached so much from the tiny cell.

'Why?' he asked again. 'Why are you caring for me? I am everything you hate.' He thought back to her words to him and Devin, as Devin had showed him the way back to Ceinwyn. Everything she had worried about had come true. He thought back to Ceinwyn's description of her, it made her sound like a vicious hyena. She had always been cold to Ceinwyn and hated Romans even more than Devin. He wondered for a moment whether the food might be poisoned.

'It doesn't matter now,' Thana replied bitterly.

'It does to me,' Titus replied. 'Why? I don't deserve anything except death.'

'You're right about that,' Thana said, her voice devoid of emotion. 'But you are the only thing that is left.' She got up and walked out, before Titus could ask anything else. He could hear her outside, as she slumped down on the other side of the door, crying. He tried to sit up properly, and slowly managed it. The soles of his feet burnt from his torture as they touched the carpeted floor. He inched his way over to the door and opened it a crack.

'Thana,' he said.

She looked up at him and tears welled up in his eyes too at the sight of her grief.

'I'm sorry Thana. You'd known her for a long time. Longer than me.'

'Since birth,' Thana replied, between sobs.

Titus sat down, that was not possible.

'You think that you've been through a lot Titus don't you?' Thana said accusingly now. 'Lost your wife, been beaten and tortured, on the wrong side of your own people?'

Titus shook his head. 'No...', he wasn't sure what to say. He had been through some terrible things, but he deserved all that had happened—he had been a fool.

'I heard you asking to die in your sleep,' Thana said harshly. 'It was very cowardly.'

Titus blushed, 'I just want to see her again,' he said, and the tears came once more.

'How could you bring yourself to see my daughter again without bringing her the head of the man who killed her?' Thana shouted.

'Your daughter?' Titus asked slowly. It did not make sense.

Thana took a deep breath. 'Your friend, Marcus Albus, who it seems you loved more than my daughter, was once a young boy of fourteen years old. Back then he was still indoctrinated, yes, just like you were. Slaves are animals, treat us like animals, dirty horrible creatures etcetera. But,' she said bitterly, 'a few teenage hormones are quite good at overruling dogma like that.

'He liked me,' she continued, 'and I can confess, perhaps I liked him too. Maybe I even invented scenarios in my head: how a young Slave of twenty could sleep with the son of her master. But I didn't enjoy it when it happened.' Her eyes glazed over as she spoke, and Titus could tell she was reliving the scene in her head. 'I hadn't realised how much he liked me, I should never have rushed to him when he hurt himself. I think he was embarrassed, to have cut himself with his father's gladius. He... hurt me, greatly.'

'I'm sorry,' Titus said, knowing his words meant nothing to her.

'If it wasn't for Devin, I would have died. He protected me, and he raised Ceinwyn as if she was his own.' She smiled, as if recalling a happy time.

'But then, when Ceinwyn was barely one year old, things changed.'

'What happened?' Titus asked, with a growing sense of dread as he started to put the situation together.

'The boy's father, Consul at the time. He found out. I think Albus still loved me, but he loved his father more. He loved his family more, and Rome. So he agreed with his father's plan.'

'To what?' Titus asked, with a horrible suspicion he already knew the answer.

'To kill anyone who might possibly be Ceinwyn. He didn't know the sex of the baby, but he did know she was born of a female Slave. So we changed our story, as did many of us of course who had a 'half-breed' as you would call her. I became the stepmother, and a story was made up about how Devin had been in love with a Roman woman who had died in childbirth. A story that Ceinwyn grew to love more than me.'

Titus saw the pain in her face, and suddenly understood what she had been through. Unable to love her own daughter openly in case the truth came out. Having to behave in a way that kept her distant, but yet loving her.

'It's the greatest love,' she said, her voice empty, 'to love someone so much, that you would deny loving them, just so that they can be safe. It's something I never expected a Roman like you could understand. But you,' she said with a whisper, leaning towards him, 'you put Hercna onto a ledge, in order that she could escape. You gave up your own chance of escape to save one of us. So you are not lost Titus, no matter what you think. You are better than I thought you were. You are better than you think you are.'

Anger rose up inside him in a great wave, and all desire for his life to end now so that he could be back with Ceinwyn, vanished. He needed to kill Albus first, whatever that took. Only then could he face his wife again. Thana was right—he should be ashamed for his weakness in the Mamertine.

Thana stared down at the floor, dejected. Titus suddenly remembered how Albus had behaved that night after winning the elections. 'Albus really loved you, you know? And I think he still does.'

'Then he is a fool,' Thana said bitterly, 'for I only wish death upon him, and one day I hope to deal it to him. But only after I let him know that, in his mad vengeance, he killed his own daughter—he killed the heir he's been trying for all these years. I want him to die knowing that.'

'Not if I get a chance first,' Titus said.

'You won't,' Thana said angrily. 'We are sending you as far from here as we can. It's what Ceinwyn would have wanted.'

'No!' Titus said, trying to get to his feet, but he was still weak and he fell back down.

'You're not ready,' Thana said coldly. 'You are weak, and this was never your fight.'

She carried his thin, weak body back to the bed and dropped him into it. He had never felt so useless.

'A volacurrus leaves tomorrow. We have bribed the crew to leave you in the Austrinalis. Go Titus,' she said. 'Leave and never return. I must preserve at least something of Ceinwyn, something she loved.'

The Austrinalis? Titus thought. That was the other side of the world. A place of desert and beaches, but almost no people. Another barren debated land like Northern Britannia. It would have once been exciting to him, but it was far from Albus, far from the vengeance he now craved.

At the door she turned and smiled, 'Titus don't worry about us, we destroyed the Void Levator. If we did that we can destroy Albus.'

Titus shook his head. 'Let me stay, help me grow strong. I will help you.'

Thana looked sad, 'I must care for you because my daughter loved you, but I can never fight beside Romans. Once you are on that volacurrus I never want to see you again.'

She turned and slammed the door, and once again Titus was alone.

L

Titus backed further into the recess and kept his breathing quiet and shallow. He had found the hiding place within minutes of boarding, but hadn't expected to use it yet. He hadn't expected the soldiers to board.

Devin and Thana had bribed one of the crew, and Titus had dressed in mechanics overalls and been hidden in the rear of the volacurrus, where the baggage was kept. The tail of the volacurrus rose back up and locked into place as the last of the baggage was loaded, and Titus was entombed for the remainder of the journey—safe from discovery by any of the passengers. It would take eight hours to reach The Austrinalis, and he had been told to sit tight and stay quiet.

The recess was perfect. He had planned to enter it as soon as they landed in The Austrinalis. The bribed crew member would hardly be able to enlist any help in looking for him, and he had suspected his hiding place would remain secure, allowing him to stow away for the return flight to Rome. He had no real plan; he just had an objective—kill Albus. Whatever Thana wanted, he was not going stay in the Austrinalis whilst Albus lived. The second objective was to kill Verres, the man who had betrayed him. They were both responsible for Ceinwyn's death.

But then, just as the volacurrus' engines began to warm up, the tail had opened again and Titus had had to run, scrabbling from the chair he had been sitting on, back to the recess. The door connecting the storeroom with the tail section itself, had swung open just as he dived into the recess. He had been lucky.

He sat in the recess and listened. He could hear men talking. They were clearly soldiers, and their mission was spelt out in a succession of overheard conversations. The volacurrus was being diverted to Asia Minor. They would be dropped off in a remote location near to Babil—the headquarters of the revolt. Their task was to simply cause as much damage as possible.

Once upon a time, Titus would have longed to join them, but all he wanted to do was remain hidden so that he could return to Rome.

One of the men was resting four feet from him, his back to the alcove. The inside of the volacurrus was dingy, and even if the soldier had turned around and peered into the darkness, Titus was confident he wouldn't see him. He just had to stay quiet. He closed his eyes and tried to sleep.

'Red light!'

He was woken by a bellow from the leader of the group. All around him, he heard the sounds of men pulling kit together and getting ready.

'Five minutes till the drop. Gather the equipment!'

Titus withdrew even further, until he was up against the far end of the recess. He would be safe here, and soon the men would be gone. His back pressed against canvas, not the metal he had expected.

'Where are the speculoscutums, Herrenius?' their leader called. Titus dug around in the canvas behind him with growing concern. His hand felt the soft, papery material underneath.

'They were stashed here last night by the boys from the fifth, along with our second ammo cache,' Herrenius replied, moving towards the alcove.

The bag Titus was leaning against was full of the camouflage used by special forces. Camouflage which bent light; it wasn't perfect, but if you stayed completely still and were already quite well hidden you could remain undetected. He thought for a moment of grabbing a set and pulling it over himself, but at close range like this it would not hide him, besides Herrenius would have to climb over him to get the other equipment out of the alcove.

There was no other way out of the recess, and Herrenius was coming right for him. He had to get out first. He dived forwards, hoping that the noise from the soldiers assembling their kit would cover his sound, and crawled out of the recess, keeping low behind supply crates. As he crawled away, he caught sight of Herrenius' boots. The soldier had reached the alcove and was climbing in. Somehow he had not been seen.

He kept crawling.

'Come on!' their leader called. 'Empty the crates. Eighty pounds each on your back men! You think you are Romans? You think you are men? Prove it!'

Titus heard the boots of several men moving his way. It was impossible that he wouldn't be discovered.

He spotted sonifi, in a pile, by a crate at the other side of the volacurrus. He looked left and right and reckoned that he had time to get there before he was spotted. He rose to a half crouch and ran, keeping low behind the crates.

'Stop!' a soldier shouted.

He froze, dropping to the floor, hidden still behind the crates.

'There's someone behind the crates,' the leader said quietly.

Titus stayed low. The door to the passenger section of the currus was so near but was clearly locked. There was no way out, except the tail section itself; perhaps a maintenance vent would lead from there into the body of the volacurrus? It was his only chance, the door was fifteen yards away—he could make it. The soldiers were still unarmed.

He rose up, and ignoring the pain in his legs, charged towards the open door.

'Get him!' he heard the leader call from his left.

He avoided a man who was trying to Harpasta tackle him, and leapt through the door. Turning around, he slammed his hand down on a switch, and the door swung shut in a split second. He heard it lock. He was safe for now. He wasn't sure exactly how many men were on the other side, or what equipment they had, for he had had no time to have a good look around—he had just run as fast as he could.

He started to look around for a vent that would take him from this dead end. The tail section was tiny and very dark except for the red light that flashed above him, warning that they were nearing the parachute drop zone. Besides the small ledge he stood on, the only other feature was the long ramp that made up the lower section of the tail. There were no vents. He was trapped. He heard the sound of hissing on the other side of the door, and a red glow began to form at one of the corners. They had cutting lights. He would not be safe for long.

He racked his brain, trying to think of options, but there were none. He was trapped in the tail of a volacurrus, and the only exit was lined with men with sonifi.

He looked back down at the ramp, and his heart started to beat faster.

He reached into the locker above and pulled out a parachute, it had been years...

He pulled the straps around himself and familiarised himself with the releases and chute tag; the sweat forming on his shaking hands slowed him. They were nearly through the door now—the cutting light had only a few more inches of metal to burn through.

His hand fumbled with another button on the wall, and the tail section started to split, the ramp folding downwards. Wind rushed in, buffeting Titus, sucking at him and unbalancing him. Far below, he could see the night's sky lit with white and yellow bursts, explosions that cast mushrooms of light onto the desert sands of Asia Minor, thousands of feet below. War was being waged down there, and it was the only possible route of escape, down into the abyss.

The hissing stopped. They had finished cutting. He walked to the edge of the ramp and took a deep breath. The wind billowed around him, cold against his bare arms, the first real thing he had felt in weeks. His heart quickened. He lifted his hands up to the parachute straps. On his sleeve, he noticed a single, long, copper coloured hair. He picked it off, wrapping it around his finger. He turned around and faced the door. He was ready.

The door fell forwards, and the soldiers stood there, sonifi outstretched.

Titus stepped backwards and fell into the darkness.

Epilogue

Akram rose early that day as he knew it would be a hot one. Allah had brought the hottest summer in living memory, and the Romans. They prayed daily, but could do nothing to shift the anger of the Lord.

He left his tent, his wife and children still sleeping, and pulled on his thobe. The well was nearby, that was why they had camped here. The journey to Babil had been difficult, but they were not far. Hakim Shariff had called all of the people to come to his side. They were to form as one and fight with him; all of the people loyal to him at least, and Akram was proud to count himself among them.

As he approached the well, a man appeared from the olive grove and approached him. Akram reached for his Janbiya, the short dagger that men of his country carried, but he kept it concealed beneath his thobe for this man might be a friend. He was sweating already, and the sun wasn't even up properly.

The man paused a few steps away from him. Akram approached the well and started to draw water and the man waited his turn. Akram drew water and then observed the man properly. His clothes were unusual, very dusty and worn, as if they were his only set, and his face was disconcerting: one half of it was sunken in. Here was a man who had been in too many fights. Akram turned to leave quickly.

'Which way is Rome?' the man asked suddenly.

Akram stopped. The man was tanned, but clearly not Arabic. He gripped the Janbiya tighter. 'You're a long way from home,' he said.

The man didn't seem to be armed. Perhaps he was a Roman spy. But if so, why ask for directions to Rome? It made no sense.

Akram pointed North West. 'That way,' he said quickly, 'if you head that way for a month you will reach the Roman Sea.' He looked down at the ground and began to draw a map with his finger. 'You would do well to overnight near Lake Hadithah; there is precious little water unless you follow the river all the way from there to Lake Al-Assad.'

He looked up to see if the man needed further directions, but he was already twenty paces away. Twenty paces closer to Rome.

Author's Note

When I wrote *Sacramentum*, I wrote it not knowing whether it would ever be published. As I'm sure is the case for any author writing their first book, this brought its own anxieties. Would anyone ever read the words I was writing? Was it any good? Should I change the storyline to make it more appealing to a publisher?

I was not expecting the level of interest that followed the publication of *Sacramentum*, and so I must apologise for being tardy in releasing the sequel. My only excuse is that I was trying to complete GP training at the same time.

Knowing that *Impietas* would definitely be published brought more joy to my writing, and I hope that this shows in the novel. Originally in 2007, I conceived this trilogy of books to be simply one book, a book that I intended to name, *'Decline and Fall'*. But, as I started writing, I quickly found that this book I had conceived would be far too long.

Sacramentum, therefore became a sort of 'prequel to the sequel', and is in many ways a microcosm of the main story I wished to tell—the first part of which is told here.

I do not mean to be hard on *Sacramentum*, but I am pleased that I was able to get the next part of the story into your hands, and hopefully the third and final part soon enough. *Sacramentum* was never meant to stand alone; it's the introduction to a much bigger story.

I envisioned *Impietas* as being a very different type of book to *Sacramentum*, and I think it is. As I have mentioned, whenever I've been interviewed, my main inspirations are Robert Harris (in particular the brilliant novel *Fatherland*), and Bernard Cornwell (especially his Arthur novels).

Although I clearly have a long way to go before I am writing anything even slightly approaching these fantastic books, I feel this darker tale flowed more easily from me. I was pleased that I didn't have to modify what I was writing to try to appeal to a publisher. I hope that you agree. I wanted to write a book that, as well as dealing with the main theme of a Roman world that never fell, also deals with important questions about life, about the masks we wear, about how we become the people we are.

Finally, I tried to avoid the trap of 'going political' with my second novel. I don't think I entirely succeeded here, but hopefully you will forgive me.

I have been very lucky to have received many kind reviews on Amazon, particularly from those who had advice for me regarding my writing. I have tried to take on your advice where I can, and I hope that this shows in my writing. As always I thank you for your comments, and am always very pleased to hear from readers, who can contact me easily on Twitter or Facebook.

Titus' adventures are far from over. His enemies are stronger than ever, and war is coming.

As always. Virtuna Fortuna Comes!

Dan Berkeley

@sirdanthethird
www.facebook.com/danielberkeleyauthor

5858720R00225

Printed in Great Britain
by Amazon.co.uk, Ltd.,
Marston Gate.